Praise

"James L. Rubart is on ... : *Chair* has the same depth and cu ... ossible for me to think of anything else until I finished it. I can't wait for his next book!"

—Terri Blackstock, author of *Intervention* and *Vicious Cycle*

"The genius behind *Rooms* has struck again, leaving his readers hanging on for an extreme ride that rushes to conclude with a surprise, but satisfying twist."

—Harry Kraus, MD, best-selling author of *The Six-Liter Club*

"*The Chair* is a compelling story that will draw the reader's attention immediately and hold onto it until the end. I've enjoyed all of James L. Rubart's books, but this may be my favorite."

—Tracie Peterson, best-selling author of the Striking
A Match series and *Song of Alaska*

"My kind of story: Thought provoking, filled with the truth of humanity and the compassion of Christ."

—Bill Myers, best-selling author of *Eli* and *The God Hater*

"James L. Rubart has taken an inanimate object—a chair—and built a page-turning story around it, interweaving romance, danger, mystery, betrayal . . . and most of all, a message of healing and restoration. Taking readers far beneath the surface, Rubart masterfully paints a picture of God's depth of love and longing for relationship with even those who are running away from Him as fast as they can. A tale of unimaginable sacrifice and unconditional love that will tug at your heart long after you've completed the last page."

—Kathi Macias, award-winning author of *Deliver Me from
Evil* and *A Christmas Journey Home*

The Chair

Other Novels by James L. Rubart

Rooms

Book of Days

JAMES L. RUBART

✝HE CHAIR

PUBLISHING GROUP
Nashville, Tennessee

978-1-4336-7152-4

Published by B&H Publishing Group
Nashville, Tennessee

Dewey Decimal Classification: F
Subject Heading: SPIRITUAL HEALING—FICTION
\ CHAIRS—FICTION \ SUSPENSE FICTION

1 2 3 4 5 6 7 8 • 15 14 13 12 11

For my Good Buddy, and for the gift of restoration

Hold a true friend with both your hands.

Nigerian Proverb

CHAPTER 1

On Tuesday afternoon at five thirty, an elderly lady strode into Corin's antiques store as if she owned it and said, "The next two months of your life will be either heaven or hell."

The corners of her mouth turned up a fraction. It was almost a smile.

"Excuse me?" Corin Roscoe stared at her over the mound of bills in front of him and stifled a laugh.

White hair, deep smile lines etched into her high cheekbones— she had to be at least mid-seventies. Maybe eighty, but she moved like she was in her forties. She wore a dark tan coat that bounced off her calves as she strolled toward Corin, ice blue eyes full of laughter. She didn't look crazy.

"I've brought you the chair, you see." She stared at him as if that statement would explain everything.

Corin brushed his dark hair off his forehead and slid off the stool behind his sales counter. "What chair?"

1

The woman looked around the store like a schoolteacher evaluating a new classroom of students. Her eyes seemed to settle on the pile of precisely stacked books from the 1700s. "I love books, you know."

Something about her was familiar. "Do I know you?" He took a step toward the woman.

"No." Her laugh had a tinge of music in it. "I hardly think so."

"You're sure?"

"Yes."

"You're a fortune-teller, right? And think a little heaven and a little hell is coming my way. Can't I just subscribe to your newsletter?"

She drew a circle in the air with her forefinger, cherry red nail polish flashing under the halogen lights of Corin's antiques store. "Probably an interweaving of the two realms. And I believe you'll discover the hope of restoration. The final outcome will, of course, be your choice."

Corin smiled. "You know, people think I'm a little crazy because of what I do for fun, but I don't think I have anything on you."

She didn't react; only stared at him, utter confidence in her eyes.

The lady had a sophisticated air about her in contrast with her odd proclamation. Since opening the store in his late twenties, Corin had entertained seven years of the occasional strange customer, but this lady was more than unusual. Her confidence and striking looks made her words almost believable.

"You need it."

"I think this is the moment you tell me who you are or I kindly ask you to leave."

The woman gazed out the windows toward Silva's Ski Shop across the street. "It is with regret that I cannot do that yet, but be assured eventually I will." The hint of a smile returned. "Now, I must be going, so if you could help me get the chair inside, I will extend you great appreciation." She motioned toward the front door of the store. "It isn't heavy, but we will want to be careful. It is priceless."

Just outside the door a tan sheet covered what must be the chair the lady referred to.

She stared at Corin, waiting, as if there were a contest going on to see who would drop their eyes first.

"I didn't order a chair." Corin opened his palms. "Sorry. And wouldn't you know it? I'm overstocked with them this month already." He smiled. "Thanks anyway."

"Listen to me." She intertwined her fingers, brought her thumbs up under her chin, and pointed her forefingers at him.

"Okay." Corin chuckled.

"This is a very special chair."

"I'm sure it is." Corin cocked his head and winked.

"Don't mock me." Her eyes locked on to his.

Corin took half a step back. If her eyes were lasers, smoke would already be curling skyward above his lifeless body. "My apologies. I'm sure your chair is exceptional, but my warehouse on the east edge of town is full of antique chairs that have collected dust for over six months. There isn't a big demand for chairs in my store right now."

Corin studied the lady. The lines carved into her light skin hinted of joy and pain, both in full measure. Her eyes, fire a moment ago, had softened and spoke of compassion and longing. Would it hurt to help her a bit?

"If you have any desks, I'll take a look at those. I could buy two or three, maybe more depending on their condition. And I can take the chair on consignment if you like. No charge whatsoever to display it."

She looked at Corin as if observing a small child. "You've misunderstood. I am not asking you to buy the chair. I am giving it to you."

"Why would you do that?"

"You are to have it." She motioned again toward the door.

"I am?" Corin slid his hands into his jeans and eased toward the woman. "Who made that decision?"

She stared at him and gave a faint smile but didn't answer.

"And what if I don't want this gift?"

"You do." She closed her eyes and bowed her head for a few seconds. What was she doing? Praying? "You will."

"You seem confident of that."

"Most certainly. It is a stunning piece." She looked down, laid a finger on the edge of a nineteenth-century French walnut side table to her right, and drew her finger slowly across the wood. "It was made by the most talented tekton craftsman the world has ever known."

"And who would that be?"

"You'll figure it out, Corin." She looked back up at him, the knowing smile back on her face. "I believe in you."

He didn't need to figure it out. He needed to get back to figuring out how he would keep the bank from saying, "Thank you very much. The few items from centuries past that you still have in your possession are now ours."

The lady continued to stare at him.

It was obvious she wouldn't leave till she got what she wanted. And what would it hurt? Free? The price was right. And if it was hideous, he could use it in the fire pit in his backyard. Or give it away as a white elephant Christmas gift in a little over two months.

"Okay, you win." Corin grinned. "How 'bout I take a look at it and tell you what I think?"

"Of course."

She stepped outside to get the chair, and a burst of cool autumn air swirled through the front door. Colorado Springs was normally in the low sixties this time of year, but it felt more like mid-fifties today.

Corin followed her out. "Here, let me get it." Thin twine ran up and over the sheet that covered the chair and around its sides holding it in place. He leaned over, grabbed the arms of the chair, and immediately felt a mild shock, like he'd shuffled his feet double-time on carpet, then touched something metal.

"Wow!" Corin stumbled back a step and rubbed his fingers.

"Are you all right?"

"Fine, just a little, uh, electric shock." He leaned over and picked up the chair.

"I see." She raised her right eyebrow.

The woman held open the store door for Corin as he carried it inside. She strode to a spot near his picture window that faced the street and motioned toward the floor with her hands in a big circle. "Here. It should go here."

Corin set the chair down and stepped back.

With a miniature pocketknife the woman cut the twine and let it tumble to the floor, then grabbed the middle of the sheet covering the chair. "Ready?"

"Sure." Corin held back a smile. He almost expected her to play a piece of classical music before pulling off the sheet. The lady glanced at him, then uncovered the chair as if she were revealing a glass-blown unicorn from seventeenth-century Venice.

Corin wasn't sure what he was expecting, but it wasn't this. Most talented craftsman the world has ever known? Certainly not for this piece. Describing it as plain would be generous. The only thing intriguing about the chair was the age. It looked older than any antique he'd ever seen. Made of olive wood, most likely. He strolled toward the chair, then circled it.

His first assessment was wrong. As he studied it longer, he realized its minimalism masked a complex beauty.

Interesting.

And its finish was . . . he didn't know. He'd never seen one like it before. Almost a translucent gold.

He stepped forward and rubbed his finger along its back. Again a tingling sensation ran through his fingers, lighter this time as if he'd stuck his finger in an electrical socket with a minimal current flowing through it. But the feeling wasn't painful. It was almost warm and tinged with energy. An instant later he felt . . . refreshed. As if he'd just taken a twenty-minute power nap.

He pulled his hand back and rubbed his thumb and fingers together. "Strange." He turned to the woman.

"Did you feel something when you touched the chair?"

"Yes."

"What?"

"Like electricity. And energy."

She nodded as if she expected his answer and wanted him to continue speaking.

"What did I feel?"

"It's a very special chair."

"Why is it special? Why did it do that to me?"

"I hope you find out, but that will, of course, be your choice." She eased over to it and placed both her hands on top of its back and slowly slid them down the sides as she knelt. The woman sighed and again bowed her head.

"Where did it come from? Who made it?"

She stood. "I told you. A craftsman."

"His name?"

She kept speaking as if she hadn't heard him. "Who lived long ago."

"What was his name?"

She looked up. "It's not important right now. In time it will be. So give this the time it needs."

She smiled, Julia Roberts wide, then turned and walked toward the front door of his store.

"You're leaving?"

"I'm sorry, Corin. I must."

"I'd like to ask you a few more questions about this chair."

"I would like that."

"Great." Corin pulled out his cell phone and punched up his calendar. "When can we set a time to—?"

"I am sorry; I have to go now." The lady put her hand on the doorknob.

Corin walked toward her. "Do you have a card?"

"No."

"And if I want to reach you?"

"Don't worry, my dear Corin. I will be in touch. I am very curious to see how this whole drama turns out."

"How do you know my name?"

"You are sharp, aren't you?" She laughed. "There isn't much you miss I imagine."

"You aren't going to tell me."

"No, not right now." She opened the door and stepped through it, then turned. "Oh, and Corin?"

"Yes?"

"Don't worry about sitting in the chair till you're ready." She strolled away and faded into the late-afternoon sun.

Corin closed his front door and stared at it till the bells on it went silent.

This one deserved a page in the manuscript of his book *Strange Antiques, Stranger Customers.* Maybe a whole chapter.

He shook his head and sighed. When he was her age, he hoped his eccentricity would be more self-contained than what he'd just witnessed.

Corin spun on his heel and eased back to the chair. Had he really felt something?

No question. And it wasn't a buildup of electricity on his carpet since his floors were made of ash hardwood.

He reached out, like he was sneaking up on a butterfly, and stopped with only centimeters between the tip of his forefinger and the chair.

After sucking in a deep breath and holding it for ten seconds, he let it out slowly as he leaned slightly forward and touched the chair.

Nothing.

He ran his fingers up and down the sides and along the edges of the seat.

This time there was no sensation. Did he imagine it? He'd been positive a moment ago.

Corin trudged back toward his six-by-six-foot office, past the sales counter, which had been sleepy for far too long, and slumped into one of the nineteenth-century black harvest stenciled Hitchcock chairs he'd restored four months back.

Two years ago the chair would have brought him a fifteen-hundred-dollar profit on a bad day. Now it seemed to be nothing more than a conversation piece for the curious window-shoppers who wanted to dream of older, better days when the world wasn't filled with chaos but who didn't feel a need to sacrifice any coin of the realm to acquire it for their homes.

Better days.

A distant memory professionally.

An ancient memory personally.

Corin opened his desk drawer and stared at the framed eight-by-ten picture resting on top of a thick stack of photos. Two men in their mid-twenties on street luges screamed around a corner at seventy miles an hour in matching black-and-red leather coats, inches from the ground, one thumb up and grins beneath their helmets. At least he thought Shasta had been smiling. Corin had been.

His brother had signed the shot, just like they signed all of their photos documenting their abundant adventures, and they'd added the caption, "To insanity and beyond!"

That had been their catchphrase, inspired by seeing *Toy Story* when they were teenagers. Buzz might go to infinity and beyond; their taste for extreme sports had taken them farther.

Too far.

Corin closed his eyes, tossed the photo back into the drawer, and slammed it shut.

Never again.

No more riding the thermals up to seventeen thousand feet on their hang gliders. No more flinging themselves thirty feet into the air on their dirt bikes. No more repelling into caves they might never climb out of.

All thanks to Corin Carter Roscoe.

His cell phone shattered the moment and he pushed the pain from his mind. Good. Time to get back to the present. "Hello?"

"Cor? It's Robin."

"Hey, how are you?" Corin shook his head. Speak of the devil and Shasta's strawberry blond wife ends up on the phone a few seconds later.

"Good. You?"

"Fine."

"Can I ask a favor, Cor?"

"Anything. You know that."

"I know, but only if it won't cut into any other plans you might have."

"What do you need?"

"I have buyers who have been looking at one of my listings who are willing to sign right now, and I don't want to lose this one. And I need someone to pick up—"

"My favorite nephew."

"Yes."

"That means I'd have to drop him off at your house." Corin opened the drawer and stared at the photo again.

"Yes." Robin sighed.

"Which means I would probably have to go inside to make sure—"

"Don't go inside. He's been working on a big case, and he's due in court next week and—"

"I know. You don't have to make excuses." Corin pushed the drawer with his pinky finger and watched it slide shut with a soft click. "It was only an idea."

"Not a good one."

When would it ever be good? Corin tried to swallow the regret, but it stuck in his throat. "I'll leave right now."

"Thanks." She took a long breath. "And Cor?"

"Yeah?"

"Have faith. This life isn't over yet. Shasta could still come around."

Corin hung up, glanced at his calendar, then his watch and swore. Tori's class would start in twenty minutes. There was no way he could pick up Sawyer from his Pee-Wee football practice, drop him off at his brother's house, and get to Tori's class on time.

This would be the third time this month he showed up after she'd started. Tori rarely complained about it, even though he often saw the frustration in her eyes. She always said don't worry about it, that she had her faults too, but he did worry about it. Women like her were as rare as the 1876 Winchester Deluxe rifle sitting inside the locked vault hidden at the back of his store.

After dropping off Sawyer and waiting till he stepped inside his brother's six-thousand-square-foot home, Corin glanced at his watch and mashed his gas pedal. No problem. He didn't have to be late for Tori's class. If he could average ninety-five mph across town, he'd make it just in time.

CHAPTER 2

Corin caught Tori's piercing eyes the moment he stepped inside the dojo. She didn't look mad. Not much. She glanced at her class, then back to him. Jet black hair. Almond-shaped eyes. Beautiful skin. There was something about Asian women that turned him into a moth, and Tori was Queen of the Flame.

"Hang on," she said to her students and jogged over to Corin. She cinched up the belt surrounding her gi and grinned. "You're late."

"Yes, I know."

"Don't worry about it." Tori stood on her toes and gave him a quick kiss on the cheek. "On the other hand, because of it I'm going to kick your hind quarters tonight."

"I am worried about it. It's my second time this month."

"Nah, I only kicked your caboose once in the past thirty days."

"I'm talking about being late."

"I know, and it's been four times so far this month."

"Really? I'm sorry."

"We've already started." Tori nodded, then jerked her head toward the mat filled with ten students ranging in age from mid-teens to mid-forties. "You better get changed."

"Right."

He'd agreed to take the class with Tori for three reasons: to learn self-defense. To be around Tori more. And to be around Tori more. He really didn't care about the first reason.

And not only because she was the polar opposite of his ex-wife in every way.

They'd met three months ago, but it was tough keeping his brain from imagining at least three decades together.

At five-three she was almost a foot shorter than him and weighed almost a hundred pounds less, but she'd proven the old adage about size not mattering when it came to martial arts. And she didn't think his obsession with BASE jumping, hang gliding, and other insane outdoor activities was, well, obsessive. She even joined him on many of his leaps into the rarefied air of courting Lady Death through extreme sports.

After fifteen minutes Tori had the class pair up to practice sparring.

"Faster!" she called out. "Strike then retreat with focus. With speed. All the time considering your next counterattack."

Corin's partner, an African American kid who couldn't be over fourteen, said, "Aren't you kind of old to be learning this stuff?"

"Thirty-four isn't old."

"Yeah it is."

Corin laughed. "Remind me in twenty years to ask if you still feel the same way."

After ten minutes Tori called the class together. "Are you ready to learn a new move?" She paced back and forth, her dark black ponytail bouncing in rhythm to her steps.

Most of the students nodded. Corin shook his head no. He knew what learning a new move meant. Pain. And humiliation.

"Do we have a volunteer? I need someone big and strong. An athlete. Someone who might have rowed on a crew team in college." She meandered her way back and forth till she stood directly in front of Corin. "Someone who's still in pretty decent shape. Someone who likes living on the edge."

Tori pretended to glance around the room before her eyes settled on Corin. She leaned forward, hands on hips, staring at him. "Anyone? Is there anyone here who fits that description? Come on, show me that hand."

"Sure," Corin said. "How 'bout me?"

"You?" Tori leaned back and frowned at him. "I didn't even see you there." The class laughed.

She led him to the front of the class and they squared off, their profiles to the students. "I want you to come at me. Hard. No holding back, okay?"

It still felt strange attacking a woman, especially one he was growing so fond of, but past experience told him he'd feel a greater degree of soreness the next day if he didn't and there was little danger of hurting her.

He lunged forward and launched his fist toward her stomach. *Wham!*

An instant later he stared up at her dark brown eyes, the back of his head pounding like a bass drum.

"You okay?" She winked at him.

"Super. This is better than bungee jumping any day."

AFTER A QUICK shower, Corin strolled out of the dojo with Tori and headed down the street to find a reward for their physical exertion.

"You need a haircut." She reached up and ruffled his dark brown hair.

Corin rubbed his head where she'd messed his hair. "A little long is okay. I'm a fashion pioneer. Longer hair will be coming back."

"At least you know how to shave your whole face."

He picked up a Gambel oak leaf from the sidewalk and held it up to her. "For you."

She took it and slid it under her Tech⁴0 sports watch. "I'll treasure it always."

Corin reached over and rubbed the back of her neck as they walked. "Are you thinking about stopping by Jamba Juice for a Blackberry Bliss, or does an Oreo cookie milkshake at Dairy Bar sound better?"

"Jamba. You need something healthy after a workout like that."

"Oreos are healthy."

"This ought to be good." Tori smirked.

"Emotionally healthy. They make me feel happy."

"And your gut big."

Corin patted his stomach. "What have you got against my one-pack?"

"Nothing. It's stunning."

"Hang on, I'll be right back." Corin glanced both ways before jogging across the street to Dairy Bar where he ordered a large Oreo cookie shake.

Tori poked her finger at him as he jogged back and joined her on the sidewalk. "You can't take that into Jamba Juice."

"Sure I can. Watch." He opened the door for her, and she scowled at him as she walked in.

Jamba Juice was empty except for one customer. Tori ordered a Caribbean Passion and they slid into a booth at the back of the store.

"It was a good class tonight, don't you think?"

"You kicked my butt. In front of everyone. Again." Corin sucked in a mouthful of her smoothie. "It's a little embarrassing getting handled like that in front of all your students."

"Why?" She grinned at him. "Because you outweigh me by at least one hundred pounds and are a foot taller?"

"Something like that."

"Karate isn't about size—"

"It's about technique, I know."

"Why were you late?"

"A slight emergency."

"Everything okay?"

"Yeah."

"Good to know." Tori stared at him over the top of her straw as she swirled it around her cup. Her eyes asked him to say more, but her mouth stayed silent.

Thank you for not pressing me.

"Anything fun happen in your store today?"

Corin downed a large gulp of milkshake as a teenager in a wheelchair inched past their table. He couldn't get away from it anywhere. Constant reminders of his idiocy. He rolled his eyes and shook his head. It happened, yes. But it was eons ago. And he couldn't go back in time to fix it.

So let it go.

Most of the time he could. Not most. Some.

"Are you all right?"

"Fine." Corin offered a smile that was only half forced. "And yes, as a matter of fact, something fun did happen. Peter Parker's aunt came by the store with a gift."

"Peter Parker?"

"You know, Spider-Man, Peter Parker. He has an Aunt May he lives with, or lived with, before he and Mary Jane got connected. This lady looked like her. Only prettier."

"I've never really gotten into comics."

"Didn't you see any of the movies?"

"Sorry." Tori shrugged. "I know they killed at the box office."

"We'll watch them sometime."

"I can't wait."

Corin laughed, reached for Tori's hands, and squeezed twice. She gave him two back.

"What was the gift?"

"A chair."

"I'll bet it was an antique."

"Lucky guess. She gives me all this cryptic mumbo jumbo about the chair, how special it is, how the greatest craftsman who ever lived made it, etcetera."

"She didn't say why it's so special?"

"She was a little strange. Wouldn't give me her name, number, nothing."

"Maybe she's playing hard to get."

"Ha."

"It's old?" Tori slurped up the last of her Caribbean Passion and tossed the cup at the nearby trash can. It hit the rim and tottered in.

"From what I can tell, really old. There's nothing special about it at first glance. The design is simple, but I'm going to give it a thorough exam this week. There's something about it that's different."

"How so?"

Corin hesitated. Should he tell her? No. Why not? Because he didn't want her thinking he was a whacko. He rubbed his fingers together where the tingling sensation had shot into his fingers and up his arm. He still couldn't decide if he'd imagined the feeling.

He hadn't known Tori long enough to predict how she'd react to his telling her an ancient chair provided by an enigmatic elderly lady was throwing off electric current.

"Maybe it was the way she looked at me. Or what she said. Might just be my imagination, but I think there's an energy around that chair. I'll probably have the thing dated to see exactly how old it is. I'm curious."

"Energy from the chair? Are you going New Age on me?"

Corin shook his head. "I just want to find out more about it."

"Is she trying to sell it on consignment?"

"No, it was clear she wanted me to keep it. She said I had been chosen to have the chair."

"*Doo doo doo doo—doo, doo doo doo.*"

"Is that supposed to be the theme music from the *Twilight Zone?*"

"I knew you'd recognize it." Tori thumped his forearm with the edge of her palm, fingers out. "Hey, changing gears, are you dead set on going this weekend?"

"I thought you weren't supposed to hold your fingers straight when you gave a karate chop."

"It's okay when it's a sign of affection." Tori smiled and reached for Corin's milkshake. "So you're set on going?"

"Yes, it'll be a killer adrenaline rush."

"Hmm."

"What's that mean?"

"Nothing." She looked at the table and chopped his arm again. "What time are we taking off on Friday?"

Corin waved his hand in the air as if to wipe away the question. "Who do you think is the greatest chair maker who ever lived?"

"I know what my slightly deranged parents would say."

"Really?" Corin leaned forward. "Who?"

Tori took a drink of Corin's milkshake, the chocolate staining her upper lip. "If we're talking about the absolute greatest, the answer is pretty obvious."

"And that would be?"

"Jesus." Tori shrugged.

"Son of God, Jesus?" Corin laughed. "Wasn't He more into the doing miracles thing and walking around from town to town with His band of merry men?"

"That's Robin Hood."

"Whatever."

"He did the carpenter thing until He was thirty. So who says He didn't make a bunch of tables and chairs?"

"So a chair is going to last for two thousand years?"

"I don't know. You're the expert on old furniture, Corin. You tell me. If it's treated right the wood isn't going to rot, is it? Plus He probably put some kind of spell or blessing or whatever on it."

"I suppose it's possible."

"They say with God all things are possible."

"I didn't know you were into Christianity."

"Are you kidding? I'm about as far away as you can get. But I grew up with my parents forcing me to go every Sunday. I gave it up the moment I headed off to college." She took a last drink of his Oreo shake and stood. "I'm still spiritual, but I bailed on the church long ago."

Corin creaked out of his seat, soreness already creeping into his quads. "Your reason?"

A darkness flashed over Tori's face almost too quick to notice.

She shrugged. "Too much religion. Too narrow minded. Everyone else except Christians are going to hell because they weren't born in the right country and weren't raised that way? Nah, I can't buy that. And I think Christians are way more excited to judge others for all their sins and tell them why they're wrong than love them. You know, the typical reasons."

She said the words with sincerity. But something about them rang false.

They stepped outside and eased back toward the dojo's parking lot where their cars were parked.

Tori spread her hands and gazed at the sky. "I don't think there's a singular God. I think God is in all of us, so collectively the good in people makes up something I call God." She gazed at him. "And you? Where are you at spiritually?"

"I definitely think there's something bigger than us. Maybe God. I think there's a force—"

Tori laughed. "*Da duh, da da da da duh, duh duh duh, duhhhhh.* Luke, I am your faaaather."

"Just because I like *Star Wars* doesn't mean I'm going all Lucas on you." He joined her laughter and slid his arm around her shoulders.

"I think it would be cool if you had a chair made by Jesus. You could start a cult. Pretend it gives people visions if they sit in it. Hey! Make them *pay* to sit in it to get their visions and make a few bucks. Or build duplicates, put them in the store and up on your Web site, and sell 'em."

"So you're still up for launching ourselves off that mountain this weekend?"

"Absolutely." She stared at him from under her eyebrows. "Kind of."

"Explain."

"Just promise me you won't go crazy on me again, okay?"

Was it that obvious? His penchant for buddying up to the Reaper? Probably. But he couldn't stop it. Maybe he didn't want to stop it. "I have no idea what you're talking about."

"That's what concerns me."

She was right to worry. But he'd never admit that to her. He barely admitted it to himself.

CHAPTER 3

At nine o'clock the next evening, the sound of thunder ripped through Corin's house, making him think once again they must have constructed his walls out of papier-mâché. The lamp on his workbench flickered. Welcome to late October in Colorado.

"No." Corin shut his eyes. "I don't need this. I want to get this piece finished."

A second peal of thunder reverberated through the room, and the lights went out for half a second, then back on.

Corin yanked open a drawer and pulled out a flashlight.

If the power went out, it meant another delay in finishing the table and getting it on his sales floor.

He ran his hands over the top of the Top Swan carved end table. It was turning out beautiful. Researching the type of stain that had originally been used had taken days. Finding the stain took longer. In the end he had the stain custom made. But there was no point in restoring the piece to its almost-original condition. Exact was the only acceptable standard.

He plugged in his sander and fired it up. In a few minutes he's have all the rough spots smoothed out on the final leg of the table. Corin glanced at the lights. Just give me power a little bit longer.

The lights flickered again.

Corin turned the sander on high and went to work on the leg. Three seconds later all the lights in his shop went out. Corin sighed, set his sander on his workbench, picked up the flashlight and turned to the door of his workshop. "What?" Dim light reached him from his kitchen. Oh no. The power hadn't gone out. He'd blown a fuse.

Corin swore, closed his eyes, and jammed his hands in his pockets to keep them from shaking.

Every time this happened he promised himself he'd cut a door from the outside of the garage so he could get to the fuse box without having to face the tunnel of fear that insisted on burrowing its way into his mind.

Sweat trickled down his forehead as he walked into his living room and stared at his couch. Maybe he'd sit in it for five or ten minutes—it'd give him time to work up his nerve.

Sure it would.

And at least three of the Fantastic Four were real and living in New York City.

Couldn't he even reset a fuse without morphing into a six-foot-two mass of fear?

What had the psychiatrist told him a few years back? Think open thoughts. Close his eyes if possible and think about meadows, the ocean, mountaintops with nothing but sky surrounding him. Yeah, right.

He took a deep breath. Something about holding his breath kept the claustrophobia at bay till he let the air out. Holding his breath meant he wasn't breathing in . . .

No. No point in going there. He relived it often enough in his nightmares.

Corin wiped the perspiration off his forehead again and shook his head.

Why couldn't he have a simpler fear like being scared of the dark?

The lead box for that kind of kryptonite was simple. Night-lights, flashlights, spotlights.

He roamed toward the garage door and reached for the knob hating himself for the slick coat of perspiration he left on it. As he stepped into the belly of the beast, he took another deep breath.

Corin eased toward the crawl space between the back of the garage and the wall that created an extra, hidden storage area. Shouldn't the home have been built with an easily accessed fuse box? Wasn't it important to get to these type of things? Or did the previous owner build this wall without getting permits?

I so appreciate what you constructed, pal. Thanks a bunch.

When he reached the spot where the wall started, he rubbed the Sheetrock with the palm of his hand and muttered for the 2 millionth time, "There's no logical reason to be afraid." And for the 2 millionth time it didn't help.

He clutched his knees to stop his legs from bouncing.

Why couldn't he shake this?

Closed spaces had nothing to do with water. He puffed out a quick breath. Yes, they did. It's why some people couldn't scuba dive or even snorkel. It felt like the water was closing in.

Corin shook the summer of 1987 out his mind, lied to himself, and pretended the two incidents weren't related.

He flashed his light at the opening. It was only fifteen feet to the fuse box. There was an abundance of air to breathe between here and there. And he could hold his breath long enough to get to the switch, flip it, and get back to the safety of the open garage.

He wouldn't allow himself to pit out another one of his *Crazy Shirts* just because he swallowed a few lungfuls of water when he was a kid. Big deal. Get over it. Be a superhero, face the fear, and get on with life. But he couldn't. Counseling, hypnosis, even acupuncture. Nothing had helped.

He sucked in a rapid breath and held it, closed his eyes, and imagined open fields. Why did his mind always flood the fields with water?

Go!

He turned sideways and shimmed in between the walls, almost hopping as he sidestepped toward the fuse box. In six seconds he reached it.

Flip the switch and get back.

Corin yanked the fuse down for his shop, then shoved it back up. It snapped into place.

Yes! Done.

Now to escape the confines of the crawl space before the air in his lungs forced its way out. As he reached the halfway point, his jeans caught on the head of a nail sticking out of a two-by-four. Its dull shape dug into the side of his shin sending a sliver of pain up his leg.

He swore and the air in his lungs burst out and panic rushed in.

His palms went clammy and the walls pushed in, crushing him, sucking the—*No. Stay calm.* The walls weren't moving. They weren't crushing him. If not for the nail, he would have made it in and out and been fine.

He jerked his leg forward, but the nail held and the tear in his jeans lengthened. He closed his eyes. *Open spaces. Think open spaces.* He opened his eyes, reached down, and yanked his jeans free of the nail, his legs shuddering. *Hang on. Just a few more feet.*

As he stumbled out of the crawl space, he lurched forward and fell across the hood of his car. Sweat covered the back of his shirt and his pulse must have been 140 plus.

A minute later he stood, pulled off his shirt, and trudged upstairs to the shower. When he reached the bathroom, he peeled off the rest of his clothes and turned on the water, waiting till thick steam filled the bathroom and shut out the haunted look he saw in the mirror. This shower would be long and hot. A reach for relaxation—and the smothering of his past.

After drying off and changing into sweats and a T-shirt, he sat on the front porch wishing he could talk some sense into himself.

He hated his claustrophobia. It didn't matter that as much as 7 percent of the world fought the dread of small spaces. It made him feel weak. Helpless. Vulnerable.

Corin went back inside and grabbed a drink. As he stumbled back onto his front porch, he pushed all thoughts from his mind except the jump that weekend. A jump that would make him forget all about his scrambled, neurotic brain.

Just before heading for bed, a meteor streaked through the earth's atmosphere.

> *When you wish upon objects in the sky,*
> *Not knowing if you'll live or die,*
> *Heal my heart and heal my head,*
> *And for once sweet dreams,*
> *When I crash in bed.*

Fat chance.

Corin stood and headed for his bedroom.

The amber plastic bottle that sat on his nightstand seemed to stare at him. His doctor had prescribed the pills to help him sleep, and more important, sleep with no dreams. Most nights it worked. Most.

Corin picked up the bottle and rattled the two pills left. He was only supposed to take two or three per week at the most. For the past month it'd been seven every week.

Because the dreams were getting worse.

Sleep covered him in minutes, but his pill once again decided to take the night off.

CHAPTER 4

Corin's eyes were slammed shut, but he didn't need them open to feel the cold water trying to thrust its way into his mouth.

An icy current surged against his face from the left, then another from straight on. Corin felt someone beside him and he forced his eyes open.

A blurry figure. A monster? Human?

Yes.

A hero.

His dad. Rescue. This time he'd be pulled to the surface, sputtering, but alive.

His dad grabbed the strap of Corin's life jacket, yanked him off the handlebars of the upside down bicycle, and pushed for the surface.

A few more feet, six, maybe seven. Then sweet air.

The light filtering through the water grew stronger. He saw the wavering forms of his mom and brother above the surface, kneeling on the pontoon boat, peering down at him.

Faster. Please.

Go faster, Dad!

Just a little more.

But an instant later the strap wasn't the strap of a life jacket any longer. As his dad pulled on it, it melted into a long strand of black licorice that snapped into pieces and floated down into the darkness of the lake.

Corin's life jacket turned to lead, and he sank like a boulder racing for the bottom of the lake.

The blackness reached up for him and accelerated his descent.

He spun deeper, holding his breath till the pressure of the deep water forced the air out of him and he gulped in lungfuls of murky, icy water.

Then darkness.

Then nothingness. Always the nothingness.

Then . . .

Corin woke drenched in sweat. Fear swallowed any rational thought of it only being a dream. Not a dream, a nightmare. He glanced at the digital clock on his nightstand: 4:15 a.m. He staggered out of bed, stumbled into his bathroom, and splashed cold water on his face.

Might as well try to wake up. Sleep was over for the night.

CHAPTER 5

Corin sat hunched over his desk doing a bill-juggling act and trying to ignore the article on the front page of the New England Journal of Medicine that kept screaming at him. He glanced at it for the eighty-ninth time that day, and for the eighty-ninth time felt a bowling ball take up residence in his gut.

New Surgery Working in High Percentage of Spinal-Cord Injury Cases.

It was wonderful news as long as you had three hundred thousand dollars fluttering down your chimney into your Christmas stocking.

But the insurance Grinch had stolen the stockings, and the only green flowing into Corin's life these days was his penchant for herbal green tea.

A moment later the bell on his front door announced the arrival of a shopper, thankfully interrupting the melancholy mood he'd let himself slip into. Corin stood and shook his arms. *Must wake up and be charming. Smiles, everyone, smiles.*

He walked out of his office in time to see a woman and a boy holding hands clump down the two steps inside his front door onto the main showroom floor. It was obvious the woman wanted to keep holding hands; the boy didn't. He tugged on her dilapidated purse with his other hand.

"Can I let go? I won't run, Mom, okay?"

She looked mid-thirties, reddish brown hair, jeans, and a faded T-shirt with a photo of three boys ironed onto it that said, "Sane Women Stop at Two."

"Do you promise?"

"Yes!" The boy bounced on his toes as he pulled on his mom's hand.

The woman released him and the boy stared up at her as if to show her he meant to keep his word. His blond hair was cut short and his brown eyes were full of energy.

"Hi, I'm Corin, welcome to Artifications. Have you been here before?"

"No, this is our first time."

"Can I answer any questions?"

The woman motioned toward the boy who wandered toward the back of the store. "He can't run because of his asthma." She gave a tiny shake of her head. "Not that he should be running in a store anyway, but there's something about the aisles of a store that make him want to race up and down them." A wave of sadness swept over her face and in that instant she looked fifty.

"I remember loving to do that as a kid."

"Me too." The woman shrugged and sighed.

"That has to be tough."

She gave a glum smile. "It's especially hard on him because his two older brothers are both basketball players and he'd love to be one too. He wants to follow in their sneakers, but with his asthma there's just no way." She sighed again and brushed back her hair. "He can't even play baseball, which is his favorite sport. So when there are game days or basketball practice like this afternoon, my husband goes with the two older ones and we look for places to go while his brothers play."

"I'm sorry."

"Us too. It's all he's wanted to do since he was little."

"What's his name?"

"Brittan. I'm Tracie."

"Nice to meet you." Corin stepped toward the small refrigerator next to his sales counter. "Would you like a bottled water?"

"No thanks."

He watched Brittan's head swivel from left to right as he strolled down aisle two gazing at the antiques. "How old?"

"I'm not sure you should be asking how old I am."

Corin smiled. "I meant . . ."

Tracie burst out laughing. "I know, I'm just being silly. He'll be seven in two months."

A joyful shriek came from the back of the store. "Hey, Mom! Look!"

They turned as Brittan streaked down the aisle with a Boston Red Sox game program from the 1950s wrapped up in thick plastic. "Look at this! Can we get it?"

"You can't run like that, Brittan!"

Seconds later the boy reached the end of the aisle and stumbled to his knees in front of them, wheezing in and out like a plugged-up vacuum cleaner. A moment later he crashed onto his side and gasped for air.

Corin staggered back and sucked in two quick breaths.

Out of air.

He was fine.

The kid is out of air.

Plenty of air to breathe all around him.

Relax.

Corin laced his fingers and squeezed but his hands still shook.

"Brittan!" His mom skittered over to him, fell to her knees, and jammed her hand into her purse. "Where is it?" She turned to Brittan. "Do you have your inhaler?"

She didn't wait for an answer. She continued to rummage through her purse obviously looking for one.

"Mom," Brittan wheezed, "I'm okay." The boy took an inhaler out of his pocket, placed it in his mouth, pumped it three times, then fell forward on his hands and continued his labored breathing.

His mom pulled him up and wrapped her arm around his shoulder. "Relax, you're going to be okay. Deep breaths if you can. Relax, Brittan." She turned to Corin. "I'm sorry about this."

Corin slowed his breathing and blinked. "What?"

"I'm sorry this happened in your store."

"No, it's fine. I'm fine."

But he wasn't fine. The anxiety waterfall rarely buried him except right after having the dream. He wasn't used to having it attack in public. He ran his hands over the top of his head and forced out a smile. "What can I do?"

She glanced around the room. "Can he sit someplace?"

"Sure, of course." Corin buried his fear and knelt next to the woman. "Does he need a soft—?"

"Anywhere is fine."

The closest piece was the chair the elderly lady had brought on Tuesday and Corin motioned toward it. "Let's sit him right here."

They settled him into the chair and Corin stood and took a step back. A moment later Brittan's breathing returned to normal and the boy smiled. "I feel good. I feel warm inside."

"You scare me when you do that, Brittan."

"I'm sorry for running, Mom. But look." Brittan coughed once and held up the program from an era when baseball players were true heroes, and if they did anything unheroic in their private lives it never made the papers.

"That's a good-looking program."

Brittan beamed, then looked at Corin.

"Do you like Ted Williams, mister?"

Corin stepped forward and knelt on one knee. "I do. I guess you do as well."

"Are you kidding? He's the last major leaguer to have a lifetime batting average over .400. He's a legend!"

"I'm impressed. A lot of kids your age wouldn't have any idea who he is."

Brittan smiled again, a big innocent smile only kids could deliver. "I know about Lou Gehrig and Joe DiMaggio and Roger Maris and Willie Mays is my favorite . . . and I'm only six years old. Almost seven."

Corin laughed. "How many home runs did Maris hit to set the record?"

"Sixty-one."

"And in how many games in a row did DiMaggio get a hit, something that no one has broken for over seventy years?"

"Fifty-six!"

"And how many teams did The Say Hey Kid play for during his major league career?"

"Mr. Willie Mays played for the New York Giants and the San Francisco Giants and the New York Mets."

"Folks, this kid is unstoppable." Corin glanced at Brittan's mom, who was all smiles.

"Okay, here's the bonus question for all the money and title of Grand Champion Baseball Trivia Quiz Master of the Entire

Universe." Corin started a drumroll on the edge of the chair. "Are you ready?"

"Yeah."

"Really ready?"

"Yeah!" Brittan clutched the seat of the chair and leaned forward.

"Here we go." Corin stopped drumming and spoke in his best announcer voice. "Who holds the all-time home-run record in the major leagues?"

"I've got this one easy." Brittan smiled and wagged his finger at Corin. "Hank Aaron."

"You sure?"

"I'm sure. I don't care how many home runs Barry Bonds hit, Mr. Aaron did it without putting funny stuff into his body to make it easier."

Corin shook his head and laughed. "You have an amazing kid there."

"Can we get it, Mom?" The boy held up the game program.

"Do Mommy a favor, Brittan, and rest for a minute, okay?"

"I don't need to; I feel really good."

"Brittan."

"Okay, Mom."

She rubbed her face. "I don't know what we'd do without that inhaler. It seems like we're always using it. Brittan can't keep from running when he gets excited and I can't blame him, you know? What boy doesn't want to run?"

Corin balled his hand into a fist and mock punched Brittan's forehead. "Glad you're feeling better."

"Me too, but I wish this would go away. I hate asthma."

"Did you know that almost everybody has stuff in their life they don't like dealing with? And stuff they're scared of?"

Brittan whipped his head up and stared at Corin. "Do you?"

"Sure."

"What?"

"I don't have asthma, but guess what I have to deal with?"

"What?"

Corin put his hands together like he was holding a ball and brought them up next to his face. "I don't like tight spaces."

"You have claustrophobia?"

"Wow, you know that word?"

"I'm almost seven. I know lots of big words."

"I'm impressed. Most kids twice your age wouldn't know what that word means."

"Are you afraid of anything else?"

"I'm not too fond of water."

"Really? Why not?"

Corin grimaced. "That's a long story we probably don't have time for today."

"Okay." Brittan leaned against the back of the chair so his feet stuck out and he closed his eyes. "I feel a little sleepy." A peaceful look settled on his face.

"Even though I've been through it hundreds of times, it still scares me when an asthma attack hits." Tracie leaned over and brushed Brittan's head. "I think this is the fastest he's ever recovered."

"He'll be okay now?"

"Fine. Until the next time he runs." She smiled her sad smile again, then spun to her right and looked down aisle two. "Now, I'd love to see if you have any other baseball treasures from the 1950s and 60s."

"I might have a few things." Corin motioned with his hand down the aisle. "After you."

Ten minutes later they returned to Brittan with a *LIFE* magazine with Ted Williams on the cover and a signed Joe DiMaggio auto card.

Brittan's eyes were still closed and his breathing was deep and rhythmic.

"I think he might have fallen asleep."

"Brittan?"

The boy's eyes fluttered open and widened as he stared at the magazine. "Wow, where did you get that?"

"I don't have a lot of baseball things, but this is definitely a classic. It's the issue from September 1941 and even has pictures inside of Ted's famous swing." Corin opened the magazine and held it out for the boy. "Take a look."

"Is that his signature?" The boy glanced back and forth between Corin and his mom.

"The genuine article."

"What's an our tickle?"

Corin laughed again. "You're a great kid, Brittan."

"Thanks, I think you're a great mister."

Tracie said, "Thanks for your kindness toward Brittan. Most people don't know what to say when he has one of his attacks."

"My pleasure. I hope he grows out of it someday."

"Me too."

Tracie turned back to Brittan and gazed at her son. So did Corin. Innocent, full of wonder and anticipation. How did you protect a kid like Brittan, or any kid, from the ravages life would pitch at them?

"He looks good in that chair and it's beautiful. I don't see a price tag on it. Is it for sale?"

"It should be soon. I think." He hadn't decided whether he would sell it or not. But he needed the cash. The elderly lady's statement floated back to him about the chair being for him, but he batted the thought away. "I just got the piece in and need to determine how much it's worth."

"Well, I doubt we'd be able to afford it, but we can at least dream, right? It would look good in Brittan's room. When do you think you'll be ready to put the chair up for sale?"

"It should be ready for purchase in two or three days at the most."

"There's something special about it, don't you think?" She ran her fingers down the back of the chair.

"I don't know. Maybe."

Tracie gathered up the baseball antiques, walked over to Corin's sales counter, and set them down.

Corin glanced at Brittan, then strolled behind his sales counter and rang up the items. "Four hundred thirty-seven dollars and eighty-two cents."

"Oh yes." Tracie's face flushed and she stared at her purse. "I should have asked. We can't—"

Brittan's face pinched together but he didn't say anything.

"Wait, I forgot to tell you about our discount." Corin smiled. "You didn't realize this, but anyone who becomes Grand Champion Baseball Trivia Quiz Master of the Entire Universe gets a 70 percent discount on anything in the store."

"What?" Brittan said from across the room. "So I helped with my mom's finances?"

"You did, champ. Nice work."

"No." Tracie looked up and whispered, "You don't have to do that. I know these things are valuable and you're in business to make money." She fumbled in her purse, her fingers bumping against what looked like a VISA card. "They have to be—"

"Seventy percent off." Corin motioned toward his office. "I can show you the official company policy if you like."

"I . . . we . . . I'm not sure what to say. Thank you."

"You and Brittan are entirely welcome." Corin placed the items into a large plastic bag and handed them to Tracie. "Just make sure you keep loving on Brittan his whole life."

Tracie closed her eyes and smiled. "Thank you again. You don't know how much this means to me."

"Are we going now?" Brittan slid out of the chair and skipped toward his mom.

"Brittan!"

"Sorry, going fast is my favorite thing."

"Can you say thank you to Mr. . . . ?"

"Roscoe."

"Thanks, Mr. Roscoe. Maybe I can come back sometime and we can talk more baseball together."

"I'd like that, Brittan. And if it's okay with your mom, you can call me Mr. Corin."

Brittan glanced at his mom and she nodded. "See you soon, Mr. Corin."

Corin gave him a two-finger salute as Brittan and his mom eased out the front door. If God was still alive in the twenty-first century, Brittan would get Corin's vote for being healed.

CHAPTER 6

That evening Corin picked up the November 1963 issue of The Amazing Spider-Man, brought it over to his couch, and escaped into its pages. Spidey versus The Lizard. Their first battle. Why did he still read these things? The counselor he saw for the first year after his divorce would say the explanation was easy. Corin still felt like Peter Parker inside, the skinny scared kid who finally became something more. Who overcame his fears and became a hero. Became more than he ever expected himself to be. And Corin longed to be those things.

Longed to have special powers that would free him from the mundane place the world had become. A power that would crush his fear of tight spaces and the lake.

A power that would give him ability to slay The Dream and keep it from ever torturing his nights ever again.

The power to heal a kid like Brittan and let him run with abandon every day of summer.

The power to heal his brother and make things go back to the way they'd been before.

Or maybe he still read comics because he simply liked being a kid again, pretending there were such things as superheroes. Maybe it was because it made him feel like doing things only superheroes could do. That wasn't a maybe. It was a definite. One reason his marriage fell apart.

She never could understand his obsession with extreme sports. Every time he went skydiving she shouted, "You'll never fly like the Human Torch." She thought he'd "grow out of it." It didn't happen. In their final months together, he tried to explain why he did it, but how could he get her to understand the reasons when even he didn't know what they were?

Of course, her choice of extracurricular activities didn't exactly solidify the marriage either.

He closed the comic and looked at the cover again. Spidey was in fine form, web shooting out from his wrist, hanging forty stories above Manhattan.

He pushed the self-analysis from his mind and decided on option number two. He loved comics simply because he longed to go back to being ten again.

The way he was before the day he had died.

When it happened there was no white light. No soloing angels with voices of silver. No gates welcoming him to a garden of utter bliss.

There had been only nothing.

He wanted to return to the innocence before he'd sputtered back to life, hacking up brackish lake water and having his world turned inside out.

Corin's thoughts drifted to the chair sitting in his store. What if Jesus really had made the chair? Would it be full of power? Tori had been joking, but what if she was right? The lady had talked about him sitting in the chair when he was ready. Maybe it could give him visions about the future.

Sure, and maybe there was hidden gamma radiation trapped inside the chair that would turn him into the Incredible Hulk.

At the very least he'd give it a close examination in the morning. Corin rubbed his thumb and fingers together—to see if the tingling feeling returned.

CHAPTER 7

How did she ever get this old? It was criminal.

Nicole gazed into the bathroom mirror and stared at the old woman looking back at her. Inside she was still twenty-eight. Maybe not twenty-eight, but thirty-eight at the most.

Certainly not the eighty-eight years the calendar claimed.

At least she didn't try to wear clothes made for women in their fifties. Not a chance. She stuck with the clothes styled for women in their forties. Because she could pull it off.

Nicole walked out into the hallway then into the kitchen where she eased into the oak chair next to the table in her breakfast nook and picked at a spot of strawberry jelly she'd missed the day before.

Had she given the chair to Corin too soon?

Maybe.

But when would the time have been right? If not now, when?

She had prayed for days, seeking confirmation this was the time, but the only answer was a hollow silence in her soul.

And why give it to Corin when Shasta was the logical choice, the one who seemed to need the chair more?

But while doubts skittered around the edges of her heart, deep down she knew what God had told her and she believed it. Corin was the one. He was older.

She shook her shoulders as if to throw off any last vestiges of doubt that might try to imbed their claws in her faith and rip it away. Of course he was old enough.

She was much younger than him when she'd been given the chair. And more foolish. She laughed. Certainly more foolish. But God had seen her through it. And He would see Corin through his leg of this never-ending journey. She would finish the race strong and then trust that Corin would continue on.

The clock on her wall above the table chimed eleven o'clock. Not much time before the day was done. How much time did she have left on this earth? Years? Days? It didn't matter. His will would be accomplished.

She reached for the picture of Corin that sat in the middle of her breakfast table and turned the photo over. *Summer 1996.* His hair was longer and there were no lines in his face yet. But he didn't look much different now fifteen years later. There was strength behind his eyes. And fear. The fear she had watched him struggle with most of his life. The fear she would ask him about when the time was right.

Soon she'd reveal herself to him. Not all, but enough. As much as he needed.

Was he strong enough to face the trial coming his way? Was his fear too great for him to break through to the other side?

She stood a moment later and pulled the worn leather-bound journal off the bookshelf lining the walls of the nook, sat again, and started to write.

Half an hour later she shelved the journal and patted it twice before turning and walking out of the kitchen.

The journal would be his someday. Lord willing.

CHAPTER 8

On Friday morning Corin walked into his store and stopped just inside the front door and looked toward the chair. He'd covered it with the tan blanket after Brittan and his mom left; he wasn't sure why. It just felt right. Maybe because if there was something more to it than just an ancient hunk of wood, he didn't want every shopper through his door pawing at it.

More than just an ancient chair.

Right.

He needed to stop his comic-book imagination from flying into the realm of the ludicrous.

Corin glanced at his watch. Nine o'clock. An hour before opening. Plenty of time to give the chair a meticulous examination.

After dropping his keys and wallet on his sales counter, he flipped on the radio to 88.7 KCME FM. Classical seemed the appropriate music to set the mood.

He eased over to the chair, drew back the blanket, and started with a visual inspection. Like before, the coloring captured him. It was surprisingly even for a chair this old that there were no cracks in the finish.

Beautiful. Looking at it stirred images of standing on Pikes Peak as dawn broke into the eastern sky.

Time to touch the chair. See if the tingling in his fingers was imagined.

Corin walked around to the back of the chair and held his fingers just above it. Then he lowered them to the chair as if he were touching a newborn's cheek.

He waited.

Nothing.

He slid his fingers back and forth over the surface. Still nothing.

Must have been his imagination. Had to be. At least that's what he told himself.

He circled around to the front, then placed both palms on the sides of the seat and slid them back and forth.

Still nothing.

After twenty or thirty more seconds he shrugged, leaned in close, and ran his forefinger along the seams where the legs met the seat of the chair.

Then where the seat met the back.

Marvelous.

It was so precise it looked and felt machine created. No gaps anywhere; no bumps where the pieces came together; no cracking in the wood, which meant previous owners over the years had either taken great care with it or the wood had been cured in such a way that the changes in climate and ravages of time hadn't adversely affected the chair in even the slightest degree.

He pulled out a small tape measure and studied the chair's dimensions.

Amazing.

The dimensions were perfect. Absolutely even distance along every centimeter between the edges of the seat. The legs were the exact same length. Exact.

After another ten minutes of examination, he stood back, gazed at the chair, and smiled. He needed to do research before he could set a price, but his instinct told him he had a piece worth thousands on his hands. Maybe hundreds of thousands.

God's chair? Maybe not, but it still might be manna from heaven.

Could he sit in it? Was it sturdy enough? The woman had said he shouldn't sit in it till he was ready, but what did that mean?

Brittan sat in it, why couldn't he? He couldn't be more than 120 pounds heavier than the kid.

Corin grabbed the back of the chair with one hand, the seat with the other, and gave it a gentle twist. Solid. He set it down and leaned into it with most of his weight. No movement. No creaking. It was as if the chair was carved out of a solid block of wood.

He squatted in front of it and rapped the seat with his knuckles. It could take his weight easily. Corin stood ready to sit but something stopped him. The feeling was like the time in high school where he'd been part of a trip to the state capitol and had been invited to sit in the governor's chair. The same nervousness he'd felt twenty-one years ago filled his mind.

Corin sniffed out a laugh at his foreboding and sat.

It was comfortable and fit his body well.

Another few seconds and he'd need to get up and open the front door. But he didn't want to. He wanted to wait for . . . what?

Don't be an idiot.

What was he expecting? A spiritual massage? A vision from heaven? It was just a chair.

Old, yes, maybe very old, but just wood.

It felt like a thousand other chairs he'd sat in over the years. Hard seat. Constructed well. End of story.

But still, the lady was right; whoever crafted it had considerable skill. And to make the sales copy more interesting when he started advertising it, it would be nice to know who built it.

After grabbing his camera and taking thirty or thirty-five shots of the chair from all angles, and then ten more with his cell phone, he threw the cloth back over the chair and clipped toward his front door to welcome the hoards of customers who would fling cash his way today.

Early next week he'd spend some time on the Internet and maybe head for the library to dig up any info on the chair.

If he lived through the weekend.

CHAPTER 9

The sun crept over a small tree behind their camp at 5:45 a.m. and splashed its light on Corin's face, reminding him where he was. Seven thousand nine hundred and forty-one feet above sea level. But not for long. He stretched and breathed out a hard yawn. Too early for most Saturday mornings, but this wasn't most Saturdays.

He was already awake—thinking about the jump—and the sunlight peppering his eyelids convinced him to get up. A hint of blue spruce filled his nostrils and the deep cold of the morning almost felt like splashing water on his face.

He glanced at the others. Still sleeping but he'd need to wake them as soon as he made coffee. Instant java yes, but it was still coffee. The forecast said no wind, but he didn't want to take chances. This would be the lowest jump he'd done in two years, and he didn't want any uninvited breezes to crash the party.

The lower the jump, the higher the adrenaline factor. He smiled and rubbed his hands together.

By the time the water boiled like a minicauldron, Tori had crawled out of her sleeping bag and sat on a boulder next to the Soto OD-1R Micro cooking stove.

"Morning," Corin said.

"Barely." Tori frowned at him. "Ugh."

"I love you too."

"Remind me." Tori pulled off her stocking cap and ran her fingers through her tangled hair. "Why did we hike for three hours yesterday to get up here?"

"Are you kidding? Look at this view." Corin motioned to the stunning display of the Rockies in the distance. "Plus no one has ever BASE jumped from this spot."

"I'm feeling better already." Tori extended her coffee cup and Corin filled it halfway.

"No, I paid for a full cup. I need it to the brim."

He laughed and complied.

"This coffee looks thin." She stared into her cup.

"Jittery and jumping only should get close to each other in the dictionary."

"Coffee doesn't make me jittery. Jumping does." She took a sip and grimaced. "Should I get the others up?"

Corin rubbed his head and squinted at her through the sun filling their small campsite. "The other night, when we were talking about that chair I got the other day, you said your parents would say it was made by Jesus."

"So?"

"Do you think it's possible?"

"That He made the chair the lady brought you?"

"Yeah."

"I don't know; why does it matter?"

"I took a good look at the thing yesterday. She was right. Whoever made it had considerable skill. It's a fascinating piece. The quality is a little mind-blowing."

Tori stood, drained the last of her coffee, and dropped her cup at Corin's feet. "You're making my head hurt. Too early for comic-book talk, okay?"

"Agreed." Corin laughed and picked up her cup. "But not too early for jumping off a cliff. Let's get the others up."

Twenty minutes later Corin, Tori, and six others stood in a circle, arms and hands locked onto each other's shoulders.

Corin glanced around at their bright eyes staring back at him. "Ready?"

In unison they chanted, "Some people snort for it, some people eat mushrooms for it, some people mainline java. All we gotta do to get that wonderful wired feeling is jump, baby, jump!"

The group broke up to put on their parachutes, and the only sound for the next five minutes was the cinching of harnesses and the deep breathing of people scared enough to feel like they had to pee, even if they'd gone two minutes earlier.

"All good?" Corin asked.

After hearing agreement from the other seven, he led them to the edge of the cliff, then put his arm around Tori. "You want to go first?"

"Be my guest." Tori motioned to the edge and Corin laughed.

Tori looked over the drop-off. "This never fails to get my heart beating five hundred times faster than it should be."

"Heart rate up without exerting yourself. It's the noncardio, cardio workout," offered another of the jumpers.

Corin looked over the edge and his heart pounded like an Olympic sprinter after running the hundred meters. No matter how many times he'd flung himself over the edge of a cliff, his hands still went damp the moment he looked down.

And every time an image of himself lying broken on the rocks below seared itself into his mind. And every time he pushed the image from his head and refused to give in to its morbid portent.

It was all part of the game. A game he had to play.

A game he had to win.

The canyon floor was only 465 feet below the cliff, which meant they needed to release their chutes almost immediately after jumping.

Which meant they had to leap out at least twenty feet away from the cliff to avoid having their chutes catch on anything sticking out from the cliff wall. Branches, rock outcroppings, everything.

Which meant there was no room for even tracing paper-thin errors.

It heightened the terror factor considerably more than most of them were comfortable with.

But it also shoved their brains into the higher reaches of the thrill-zone.

Krystal's eyes ping-ponged back and forth between all three of them. "This is good? We're going to be all right? We're going to survive?"

"No doubt. It's just like taking a stroll through Riverside Park," Peter said.

"Twenty feet out," Corin said. "That's our target distance. Which means you sprint as hard as you can toward the cliff's edge and push off with your foot like a trampoline when you jump and you've got two seconds *max* before releasing your chute. There shouldn't be any wind in the canyon, but if there is, it will be updrafts that will help us, not hinder."

Corin looked around at his friends. Rush time. "Anyone want to say a prayer?" Wow, this chair business was frying his brain.

They all laughed except for Krystal. "I think that's a pretty good idea."

Corin looked at her. "Are you serious?"

"You weren't?"

"Not really."

"I'm scared." Krystal hugged herself. "This is the craziest thing we've ever done. Jumping from this low is . . . crazy."

"We're just upping the rush a little." Corin smiled. "Nothing to be scared of."

"Just death."

"I'm not scared of dying." He looked toward the edge. "Not at all." He ignored the increase in his heart rate that seemed to beat inside his head instead of his chest. "The only thing I'm scared of is not living while I'm still alive."

The instant Corin said he wasn't scared of dying, a shadow seemed to drown out the sun and his mind felt like it was wrapped in lead pulling his head to the ground. Where was this coming from? He wasn't scared of dying. It's what allowed him to dance on the razor's edge without slicing his feet open. It's what freed him each time he jumped or rode or luged or glided or took part in any of his insane adventures.

He shook his head and swallowed. Time to roll before his mind told him another lie. "Let's do it."

Corin strode back twenty steps, spun on his heel, and without hesitating sprinted toward the edge of the canyon, every step pumping another nitro-shot of adrenaline into his veins. Launch codes were locked and loaded. Ten feet. Three. None.

Go!

An instant later he was airborne, wind racing past him like a hurricane, the river and the shore below rushing up to meet him like a giant silver snake ready to strike.

One thousand one.

On thousand two.

He should pull.

No, half a second longer.

Pull! His mind screamed.

A little longer.

What are you doing!

Corin stared at the ground streaking toward him at warp speed, a surge of panic ripping through his body and he released his chute. Too close. He'd waited too long. Why wasn't his chute opening?

C'mon!

A second later his chute opened with a familiar *thwap,* sounding like a muffled shotgun blast arresting his free fall.

Twenty feet till impact. He would hit the ground hard. Fifteen. He gritted his teeth and pulled hard on his side cords to give himself as much lift as possible.

"Uhhh!"

He landed hard in a tiny grass clearing fifty yards from the edge of the river and rolled to lessen the impact.

It didn't help much.

That hurt.

He rolled to his left like a slug and stared at a row of rocks three feet to his left. That would have hurt even more. A lot more.

He stood, stepped out of his chute, and squinted up at the others floating down.

"Whooooohooooooo!" Tori's scream echoed off the canyon walls. Then Krystal's, then the rest of them.

Corin grinned. Another good time enjoyed by the crazies he called friends.

TORI'S FOLDED ARMS and scowl complemented her silence nicely, but after half an hour of it Corin was through. "I'm tired of getting a blast of freezing air from your left shoulder. Do you mind turning up the heat?"

"Very clever."

"Are you going to tell me what you're ticked off about?"

Tori pulled her feet off the dashboard of Corin's truck and turned in her seat, keeping her arms locked to her chest. "I know we've only been dating for three months, but I've grown to like you a lot in that time."

"Me too. What's your point?"

"You almost killed yourself today."

"No I didn't."

"Do you want me to call the other six witnesses to the stand who let out a collective gasp as they watched you this morning?"

"They actually gasped?" Corin grinned. "Cool."

"It's not funny, Corin."

"I think you're overreacting." He flicked on his headlights for safety and pulled on his right ear. "I was fine."

"What is it with you?" Tori turned back and stared out the passenger window. "You want to kill yourself? Do you have some death wish you haven't told me about?"

"No."

"Then what were you doing out there?"

What could he tell her? There was always the truth. Might as well.

"I honestly don't know." He gripped the steering wheel hard.

But I need to find out.

CHAPTER 10

Corin pulled up the Internet early on Monday morning to get his local news fix as he chowed on a sausage-egg-and-cheese English-muffin sandwich. The weather would be decent for the next few days. Nice. And the Broncos won again. Amazing. The temperature in hell must be dropping.

He was about to click to a new page when a headline made his finger freeze.

Boy Cured of Asthma. Family Says Miracle.

That's what his new pal Brittan could use. Corin clicked on the story, took a sip of his chai green tea, and started reading.

Colorado Springs—A young boy in our city has lived with severe asthma every day for nearly seven years. No more. His parents say something extraordinary happened to him four days ago. They claim it is nothing less than divine intervention. Last Thursday evening,

when they went to give their son his daily asthma medicine, young
Brittan Gibson . . .

"What?" Corin lurched forward splashing green tea on his
table and his English muffin. He snatched a napkin and dabbed at
the spill and kept reading.

. . . said he didn't need it, that his asthma was gone. At first they
didn't believe him, but after he insisted he show them what he meant,
they gave in and allowed him to give a convincing demonstration.

The story was cut in two by a still of a video. Corin clicked on
the Play button, and a few seconds later he was watching video of
the front yard of a middle-class home with a freshly cut lawn and a
white minivan in the driveway.

The next shot was of a young boy.

Corin leaned in and stared at his computer screen. No question.
It was the kid from his store.

"Just like he did for our cameras, Brittan Gibson ran the length of his
yard back and forth for his parents. He was winded, yes, but noth-
ing more than what any healthy young boy would experience after
sprinting around his front yard."

Corin rested the side of his face in the palm of his hand and
glanced at a picture of the chair he'd tacked to the bulletin board
in his kitchen.

The reporter said, "His doctor confirms Brittan did indeed have
severe asthma and is at a loss to explain how or why the asthma
vanished."

The video cut to the doctor.

"Sometimes asthma will slowly leave children in their late teens
or early twenties. I've never seen a case like this, but I suppose it's
possible for it to leave this rapidly. There's always a first time. The

Gibsons aren't calling it outgrowing the disease; they're calling it a miracle."

The video cut to Brittan's mom and a reporter.

"Did you do anything unusual earlier that day?"

"We went shopping. Brittan had an attack inside an antiques store. He took a short nap sitting in a chair inside the store while I bought him some baseball memorabilia, and we went home. That's it. Four hours later his asthma was gone."

Corin slumped back in his seat and gazed at the photo of the chair again, arms folded.

The kid sits in the chair. Boom, a few hours later he's healed.

It was beyond odd. It was fascinating. An amazing coincidence. But somehow he knew it was more than chance.

CHAPTER 11

Pastor Mark Jefferies tossed his black leather jacket onto the back of one the two tan leather chairs in front of his cherry wood desk and checked his black hair in the mirror to the left of his office door. Not bad. Spike it up a little more. He massaged it with his fingers till it looked perfectly disheveled. Nice. He spun and strode to his desk.

Thirty-seven wasn't too old to go for the emo look. Besides, not only did he pull it off, YouTube hits had rocketed up 17 percent per week after he adopted the new style. Plus people said it made him look thirty. Had to carry the image to carry the crowd.

And the church crowd in La Jolla loved him. Along with the five satellite churches spread through the rest of the greater San Diego area.

Rent a building, give 'em lightning in a Bible every Sunday morning and Sunday evening, and church growth was inevitable.

After he plopped into the chair in front of his desk, picked up his Bible, and kissed it, he pulled up his Facebook fan page. Sweet. Three hundred and seventy-two more followers since yesterday. Probably time to put up another post on how he loved taking his wife out on dates.

Always got strong responses to those types of posts. Then follow up with a post about boys becoming men, men becoming leaders, leaders becoming kings, kings expanding their kingdoms.

Talk about strong men, men who knew where they were going and why. It was true. They needed that kind of inspiration. Don't tickle their ears, drown them in a Super Bowl Gatorade bucket of truth.

It wasn't like he didn't believe in what he served up for worldwide consumption. He did enjoy taking his wife out. And he believed what he preached. It was right and it was true. But all the better if it endeared him to his legion of fans. All the better if it ticked some people off, especially those far-left whackos who wanted to turn the world over to the democrats and love gurus. Because that gave him press and press gave him attention. People wanted a figurehead to rally around. And he was the figurehead who would lead them back to God. Maybe America was going to hell in a handbasket of intolerant tolerance, but that didn't mean he couldn't try to reweave the thing on the way down.

He shook his head. It was only six years ago when he had been preaching in his living room to his wife and three other couples. And now thousands and thousands hung on every word, every YouTube video.

Did a part of him long for those early days when the pressure of being an icon wasn't squeezing him like when he did his scuba diving thing at 120 feet below the Pacific? Absolutely.

Had he been ready for the church to explode as fast as it had? Probably not.

But someone had to be the point of the wedge.

And if he had to become a star to accomplish what needed to be done, so be it. The end most assuredly justified the means.

A rap on his door frame startled him and his head snapped back. "What?" He looked up to see Ben Raney standing in his doorway, a stack of papers in his hands.

"Are you ready to meet?"

"It's time already?" Mark glanced at his watch and scowled. Time was always sprinting too fast and too far ahead of him, and lately it seemed time had lengthened its lead.

"Yep." Ben tapped his watch with his pinky finger.

Why did the kid do that? Made him look so metro.

"Three p.m. on the button."

"Give me ten minutes."

Ben turned to go.

"Wait, why are you smiling?"

"I'll tell you when we meet. You're going to love it."

"Tell me now." Mark slid out of his chair, sauntered around the end of his desk, and leaned back against it.

"It can wait. I'll be back in ten."

"I'm ready now."

Ben smirked, so slightly Mark almost missed it.

"Have you studied the local news feeds from around the country yet?" Ben pushed his dark red hair off his forehead, which flopped back down a moment later.

"No, I pay you to look at it for me." Mark folded his arms.

"Ah yes, that's right. I'll be back in three minutes. I might have missed a story or two."

Passive-aggressive little snot. He hated passive-aggressive behavior. Straight aggressive worked faster and kept people in their places more effectively. When he shot people, at least he had the courage to shoot them in the chest.

"Ben, what do you think you're doing? Do you think God condones that attitude?"

"What attitude?"

"Cut it. We both know you're pitching me nonsense and it won't fly. If you want to be sitting where I am someday, you have to submit to my authority. Got it? Not just your actions—your attitude. Are we clear, or do you need to start looking for another job right now?"

"I'm sorry, Mark. You're right. I totally get it. Forgive me."

Grace. He needed it himself. So he needed to give it. Even when his emotions screamed to do the opposite. *Breathe deep. Offer grace, c'mon.*

"Done. It's over, forgiven, forgotten." Mark clasped his hands behind his head. "Now talk. Tell me about this story."

Ben set a printout of a news story onto Mark's desk. It featured a picture of a young blond boy with what must be his parents on either side. The headline read, *Boy Cured of Asthma. Family Says Miracle.*

"So what?" Mark pushed the paper back at Ben. "God still heals people these days."

"I believe He does as well. But when the healing comes from involvement with a certain type of inanimate object I believe you have an absorbing fascination with, it makes the whole scenario much more interesting."

Mark's pulse spiked. "If you're grinding my gears—"

"I'm not." Ben shook his head and tapped the paper. "I'm betting the chair that kid sat in before he got healed was a chair you're extremely familiar with."

"You're serious."

"Yes." Ben tapped the article again. "It was an antiques store."

Mark leaned forward and read the entire article, raked his fingers through his hair, and said more to himself than Ben,

"So this mom and her son wander into an antiques store, the boy had an asthma attack, the kid sits in a chair, and four hours later he's healed."

"That's what it looks like."

"Where is the store?"

"The article didn't give the name of the store."

"Yes, I know." Mark smacked the article with the back of his hand. "I can read. But the article is out of Colorado Springs, right?"

"So you want me to—?"

"Get on a plane tonight. Fly out there and find the store. Then charm the owner and find out everything you can about this chair."

"And you'd like me to do it yesterday."

"Precisely."

Ben turned to go. "Anything else?"

"Nope." Mark rubbed his mouth. "Wait." He went to his desk and slid open the top drawer. "I'm booked tomorrow night, so I can't use these." He handed Ben two tickets to the OneRepublic concert.

"Are you serious?" Ben's face spread into a grin. "I love these guys."

"I know." Mark patted him on the shoulder. "Enjoy."

Mark stood at his office window and stared at the unsightly souls trudging up and down the sidewalk in front of his building. Most of them had no awareness of the eternal. No realization that immortality was all around them. That certain inanimate objects could set them free.

If it really was *the* chair, he'd need to move fast.

Yes, the legend was obscure. The odds of the store owner knowing what he had, if it truly was the chair, had to be close to zero. But might be others fascinated enough to watch the tabloids and the news and would be ready to move almost as fast as he was.

He smiled. With any luck, Ben should be able to grab the thing for a few hundred bucks and have the chair sitting in his office by tomorrow afternoon.

This could be it. With the chair he could finally slay the beast forever.

CHAPTER 12

Corin drove toward Tori's house trying to decide whether to tell her about the chair healing Brittan. Maybe he should, maybe he shouldn't. And not because she was down on Christianity. But because part of him deep down wanted to believe the chair could heal, and talking about it made the belief grow. Then when an inevitable rational explanation for Brittan's healing surfaced, he'd be left with another crystal hope for his brother dashed into tiny fragments.

He pulled onto the freeway, shifted into fourth gear, and glanced at his watch. Why did she have to live so far outside of town? Why did he have to be such a bad judge of time?

Corin rang Tori's doorbell at 6:10. Ten minutes, only ten minutes.

She flung the door open and frowned. "Are you okay?"

"Why?"

"Only twelve minutes late, something has to be wrong."

64

"Ten."

"Twelve." Tori tapped her watch. "But twelve signals improvement. Won't you come in?"

Corin offered her what he hoped was a plastic smile and trudged over the threshold into her entryway.

Tori brushed past him into the kitchen. "Would you like some wine?"

"No thanks."

"Really?"

"If I'm going to figure out what's going on, I gotta keep my head clear."

"Ah, one of those days. In one word how would you describe it?" She called out from the kitchen.

Should he tell her? "Disturbing."

"That sounds interesting. Would you like to talk about it?" Tori walked back in with a glass of dark red, the rest of the corked bottle under her arm. "You don't mind if I have a glass without you, do you?"

Corin shook his head and tried to decide if he wanted to talk. Did he? Yes. Besides, since he knew little about Christianity and Tori did, she might be able to spill some rays of sunshine on what had happened to young Brittan Gibson.

They stepped outside onto Tori's covered porch and settled into the two Adirondack chairs nestled in the far right corner.

Corin stared at Cheyenne Mountain in the distance and let the tranquil image of the setting sun sink into his shoulders. "It's peaceful out here."

"So it's worth the long drive to get here?"

Corin smiled and nodded. He leaned over and gave her a quick kiss.

She toasted him, then flicked the edge of her glass with her fingernail. The ching filled the cool early evening air. "So are you ready to give me your definition of disturbing?" Tori crossed both her legs, took a sip of her wine, and leaned forward.

Corin continued to stare at the jagged peaks to the west. "If Jesus made an object during the years He was doing the carpenter thing, would it be possible for it to have healing powers?"

"What?"

"You heard me."

"Are we talking Indiana Jones here or real life?"

"Real life."

"How would I know?"

"You told me you did the church thing all the way through high school. I thought you would know if religious artifacts had healing powers."

"Sure!" She laughed. "Ask me anything you want to know. And don't forget, I know all about UFOs too."

"I'm serious."

"That kind of stuff is for guys making movies, not kids traipsing in and out of Sunday school. Can we move on to other subjects?"

"Why?"

"I don't want to talk religion."

"Why?"

"I told you already, religion was my parents' thing, not mine. When I left for college I left it too. I'm not into talking about church or God's love or Jesus or any of that stuff."

"I'm not talking about church or God; I'm talking about whether religious objects somehow have some kind of super powers."

"Real life isn't like those comic books you love so much."

"I realize that. It's why I'm trying to have a conversation with you about it so I can learn something."

"Fine." Tori flopped back in her seat. "Let's talk about the chair that old lady dumped in your store a few days ago."

"She's not old."

"I thought you said she was in her seventies."

"She's elderly, not old."

Tori laughed. "Sorry. The chair the *elderly* lady said was made by Jesus."

"She didn't say it was made by Jesus. She implied it. You're the one who—"

"Whatever."

Talking about God turned Tori into the ice queen. Why? "So if Jesus did make this chair, could it heal a little boy?"

Tori leaned forward again, a frown etched into her forehead. "Did someone get healed?"

Corin pulled the Internet article on Brittan out of his back pocket. "Did you see that story about the kid who was cured of asthma?"

"No."

Corin handed her the article.

She uncrossed her legs and took small sips of wine as she read the paper. When she finished the story, she set it on the armrest of her chair and smoothed it out with her palm. "What a joke."

"What?"

"Are you saying you actually believe your chair healed this kid?" Tori leaned back again and folded her arms.

Corin waggled his head back and forth. "I'm saying it might be possible."

"You're serious."

"Maybe."

"Maybe?"

"A few hours before the supposed miracle hit, he was in my store. He fell asleep in it. So maybe it healed him."

"So you're saying catching a few winks in that chair helped get rid of his asthma?"

"I don't know; I'm just exploring the idea."

"Do you think if I fell asleep in it thinking about my feet, I wouldn't get any more ingrown toenails?"

"I'm serious, Tori. I think the chair has something to do with his getting cured."

"Okay."

"Answer me, from what you know, do religions believe artifacts like this chair have healing powers?"

Tori took another sip and stayed silent. The scowl that had taken up residence since they started talking about the chair shifted into sadness.

"You all right?"

"I'm good."

"So do they?"

Tori stared into her glass, her lips pressed together.

Corin stood and walked to the end of Tori's porch, tapping his fingers on the railing as he moved. "Okay, I get it. No talk. Listen, don't worry about it. I can start Googling this stuff. I just figured you might know something about it since you grew up in the church."

Tori ran her fingers through her black hair and tugged on the ends. "Yes, there's a bunch of people who think religious objects have miracle powers."

"Like?"

"Haven't you seen those pieces of toast where Mary shows up in them? Or Jesus appears in a piece of avocado?"

"Are we going to talk about this or not?"

"I'm serious. People think that."

"I was hoping for something a little more substantial than food."

Tori pulled her dark hair back into a ponytail. "Yes, there are serious stories about healings being tied into religious artifacts."

"Like?"

"In ancient days up through the Middle Ages, most Christians believed amulets or blessed objects had healing powers. At times Christians used the Bible like a talisman in desperate situations, like when someone was dying. They'd put it under the bed, thinking it would heal the person."

"Anything else?"

"The Shroud of Turin. People claimed just looking at it had cured them." Tori stood and pointed at his stomach. "Do you have any room in there for some Brie and crackers?"

"Sure, love it."

Tori kissed Corin's cheek and scuttled into the house.

Hot . . . cold. Doesn't want to talk about it, then willing to talk about it. Then prickle city again. What did she have against religion? Those kind of prickles didn't come from nowhere. The more someone railed against something, the greater the odds that the something burned them at one time. What scars of religion did Tori carry under her usually perky personality?

She returned with the cheese and crackers. "I have a question about your healing chair." The sadness had been replaced by a curiosity, a longing in her eyes for something.

"Okay."

"Have you sat in it yet?"

"Yes."

"Did it heal you?" Her eyes made him imagine her as a little girl in a pretty dress, traipsing off to Sunday school.

"The only injuries I've ever gotten are minor bumps and bruises, and I've never had a chronic illness, so I'm not sure what it would heal me of."

"What were you thinking you wanted to be healed of when you sat in it?"

"You should do that?"

"I'll bet if you ask that Brittan kid, he'd say he was wishing he could be healed of his asthma when he was sitting in your chair."

Tori brushed her hair back from her face. "That's what happened in the Bible. I remember there were these guys who begged Jesus to stop as He walked down the road, and He turned to them and said, 'What do you want?' and they said, 'We want to see.' So it makes sense that you should know what you want to be healed off when you sit in the chair. You need to believe it's going to happen."

He smiled. "It almost makes me wish I had something to be healed so I could test the chair that way on myself."

Tori arched an eyebrow but said nothing.

"Do you want to elaborate?"

She shrugged. "No."

"Please elaborate."

"Well, who's to say the chair can't work on mental conditions as well as physical?"

He smirked at her. "You're saying I'm mental?"

"Yes."

"Thanks."

Tori took his hands. "If I'm setting my feet on Fantasy Island for a moment, yes, I would love to think your sitting in a chair or lying on a bed or swinging from a rope would help rid you of some of those fears swirling around in your conscious and subconscious mind. Wouldn't you?"

"I told you about those?"

"Yep."

Corin popped a piece of Brie into his mouth and watched a Flicker dart back and forth between two limber pine trees.

Yes. He would like to be healed. More than she could imagine.

But Brittan's healing was physical, not emotional.

Tomorrow he'd call a few local churches. See if they knew anything. Also, do a little Internet research on the healing powers of religious artifacts as well as what the Bible said about healing.

And maybe he'd take another ride in the chair.

CHAPTER 13

A rap on the door of Mark Jefferies's den made him jerk.

"Hey, honey, dinner is almost ready." Mark's wife stood in the doorway smiling, her black hair cascading over her shoulders.

"How soon is soon? Can you give it to me in minutes, please?"

Irritation flitted across her features. Mark thought about pointing it out, then decided to ignore it. Give her grace. Grace was always a good choice.

"Ten or fifteen minutes."

"Which one?" Mark turned back to his computer. "Ten or fifteen?"

"Fifteen."

"Perfect. Thanks." He looked up and winked at her. "You're awesome."

She smiled and turned to go.

"Hey, I almost forgot." Mark leaned back, hands cocked behind his head. "*Sports Illustrated*'s swimsuit issue should be hitting our mailbox in the next few days. I don't need that garbage filling my brain."

"True."

"So I need you to make sure you pick up the mail for the rest of this week, and when it gets here, burn it or toss it, whatever."

"A lot of men would take that mag—"

"I'm not a lot of men." Mark picked up his remote, turned on the TV, flipped to ESPN, and smiled.

"I'm grateful." She walked over to Mark and kissed him on the cheek. "I'll keep an eye out for it."

"And burn it."

"Don't worry; you'll never see it."

"Thanks, gal pal."

AT MIDNIGHT, MARK woke, slipped out of bed, and wandered into his study. He glanced at the shelves packed with books from the past five centuries, then wandered over to his black leather chair, sat, and flicked on the lamp sitting on the end table next to the chair. The warm light fell on the small book sitting next to the lamp illuminating its worn brown leather cover. Mark picked it up and ran his finger along its surface.

If this Corin Roscoe truly had The Chair, Mark's prayers had finally been answered. All the clues he'd collected in the small journal would prove true.

He tried to rein in his hope but after a few minutes let his emotions run.

If it was real and if it truly had the power to heal? His life would never be the same.

Tomorrow. Ben would find Corin's store tomorrow and start digging. And depending on what he found, Mark would make Corin Roscoe his new best friend.

He stood, went to his desk, woke his MacBook Pro from hibernation, and started surfing. Facebook was quiet. So was Twitter.

He pulled up *Sports Illustrated.com* and pretended he was interested in the predictions for that weekend's games, pretended he didn't care about the banner ad promoting the latest issue of the magazine about to arrive in millions of homes, pretended his mouse clicked on the ad by itself.

Mark glanced at the door to his office and beyond it. No lights. His wife and kids were long asleep.

Just a peek. Just a quick look; that's all he needed. It was okay; it would be forgiven. He was only doing it to see what the men in his church would be fighting against for the next month or three. He needed to know the enemy so he could battle against it.

Instantly photos of stunningly beautiful women splashed onto his screen adorned in little more than inches of fabric, staring at him with eyes so provocative his pulse spiked.

He clicked through the pictures like popcorn popping. Just a glance. Nothing more. No harm, no foul, no guilt.

It wasn't wrong. It was just like going to any beach in the world and stopping for a moment to admire what God had created. Just a slice of the Creator's beauty on display to be admired.

Stop.

The thought rose from his heart into his mind like lightning.

Why?

It was nothing he wouldn't see on any of the exotic trips he and his wife would take in the next year. Nothing thousands, millions of men weren't looking at right now on computer screens across the globe.

What if that were your daughter? Would you want men slobbering over her like you're slobbering over these women?

He wasn't slobbering.

What if they were daughters of the men you supposedly lead?

The thought ripped through his mind and stabbed at his heart.

But they weren't his daughter. He thanked God he had sons.

After fifteen minutes he stopped fooling himself, slammed his laptop closed, swore, and slumped back in his chair. It was the last time he'd do it. Never again. Never. But he didn't believe the lie.

Mark rubbed his face with both hands and rested his elbows on his desk and let out a soft moan. When he sat up again, his wife stood in the door of his den and his heart shifted into double-time. How long had she been there?

"Are you all right?"

Did she know? She couldn't. There was no reflection for her to see what he'd been looking at, but maybe his face had already betrayed him. "Wow, you startled me."

"Sorry, I woke up and you weren't in bed. Are you okay?"

"Fine, just trying to figure out what I'm preaching on this Sunday." Mark stretched his neck to the right and then the left. "And I'm a little tense."

"What's on your heart?"

"What?"

"On your heart, what are you hearing from God?"

Hearing? That he hated himself for not being stronger; hated himself for failing his kids, his wife, his church; hated the image of who people thought he was.

"Lots."

"Then preach on that."

Right. And lose his church. "Okay. I'll be back to bed soon, sweetie."

His wife shuffled away, undoubtably with an angelic smile on her face.

She was pure, a good heart, believed in him, even though he didn't believe in himself.

He needed healing. Deep. They said admitting it was the first step.

And the chair might be the second.

CHAPTER 14

As the sun crested a ridge to the east, Corin stood with A. C. Avena at the top of a long winding road, adrenaline pumping through his body. This would be a rush of nitro proportions. A great way to start a Tuesday morning.

"Are you sure about this run?" A. C. looked at him with the crooked smile that drove girls nuts when they were in high school.

"Shasta would have done this with me in half a nanosecond."

"Only after you talked him into it." A. C. pulled on his leather luging gloves and stared at Corin. "I heard you got a little crazy up near Pikes Peak last weekend."

Corin grinned. "Wish you could have been there and done the jump with us. It was cool."

"I heard you almost got yourself killed."

"Not true."

"Uh-huh."

They'd driven the length of the road—two and a half miles—three times, studying the curves and the slope.

"Perfect hill." Corin rubbed his hands on his thick leather pants. "Let's shoot it from the top with a no-brakes pact." He held out his forefinger toward A. C. and bent it in.

"Are you crazy?" A. C. took a step back.

"Yes."

"No brakes, no do."

"Why not? I thought we wanted to get a serious adrenaline rush."

"There's no way you can hold the corner on that final turn."

"How do you know that?"

"Because I read about this road. Five guys have tried it and each one has ended up with an asphalt beard." A. C. frowned and grinned at the same time. "We both read the same pieces on this run. I'm not telling you anything you don't already know."

"So the sixth time should be the charm, right?"

"You think you're Superman, don't you? Nothing can touch you; nothing can take you out."

Corin frowned. "No I don't."

"Someday kryptonite is going to spring out of nowhere and kill you."

"I can make it."

"You don't want to do this without braking."

"Yeah I do." Corin locked his fingers together and squeezed till his hands hurt. "I have to."

"Why do you always push the envelope so far it tears?"

He cocked his head. "I might have stretched it a few times, but it's never torn."

"Not yet." A. C. picked up his street luge and spun the wheels. "This shoot has paper shredder written all over it. Sometimes I wonder if you've got some kind of weird desire to hurt yourself."

"I don't care if I get hurt." Corin stared at the shoot. "It would be good for me."

"I'm not tracking with you here, Cor. How does getting hurt do anyone any good?"

Corin didn't answer. He set his board on the ground and sat on it, then snugged up the strap on his helmet and flipped his visor down. "You coming?"

AS CORIN TORE through the final corner, the one A. C. said would make him Mr. Hamburger Face, Corin reached for the brake, his fingers trembling. No. Can't do it. He didn't deserve the chance to be safe.

He leaned to the left, the centrifugal force of rocketing down the road at seventy miles an hour trying to fling him off the edge of the road to his right.

C'mon, stay with it! Lean in!

His wheels skidded across the pavement as he leaned harder to left. Too close. The edge of the road just feet away a moment ago was now just inches.

Rolling over the edge at seventy miles an hour. Not good. Not healthy.

Three more seconds. *Hang on. No brakes, no brakes.*

An instant later he was through the turn and streaked straight down the road, relief flooding his mind and body.

Two minutes later A. C. skidded to a stop beside him.

Corin whipped off his helmet and grinned at his friend.

"You did it, didn't you?"

He nodded, still grinning like a kid at his first pro baseball game.

"You're insane, you know that?"

Corin nodded a second time. "It's my calling."

"What are you going to do when a call comes that you can't answer?"

Corin swung his helmet up to his shoulder, bent to grab his sled, and admitted a small piece deep in his heart hoped that call would arrive soon.

CHAPTER 15

On Wednesday morning Corin made coffee and plopped onto his couch ready to play artifact detective. He pulled up Google and punched in "chair of Christ" and in .24 seconds got nothing. Nothing on Bing or AltaVista either. "Chair made by Jesus" didn't bring any hits either. Jesus made furniture, didn't He? Tables, plows, benches, chairs. Isn't that what carpenters back then did? He had no idea.

Then he stumbled across an article talking about a saint named Justin Martyr who lived in Galilee during the second century. Martyr said it was still common during his lifetime to see farmers using "plows made by the carpenter Jesus of Nazareth" into the second century.

Good. This was promising.

If a plow being battered daily by dirt and weather could last one hundred-plus years, why couldn't a well-cared for chair last till today?

When he typed in "religious artifacts" things got even more interesting.

He clicked on a link that said *Sudarium of Oviedo* and started reading.

Fascinating.

The Sudarium was a blood-stained cloth thirty-two-by-twenty inches that Jesus's head was supposedly wrapped in after He died. And tests on blood from the cloth confirmed a common blood type among Middle Eastern people but rare among medieval Europeans.

Pollen residue showed strong evidence the cloth was at one point in the Palestine area.

Corin read further. Nothing about the Sudarium healing anyone.

Next was a link to the *Image of Edessa,* a picture of Christ allegedly sent by Jesus Himself to King Abgar V of Edessa to cure him of leprosy, with a letter declining an invitation to visit the king.

Now he was getting somewhere.

But as he read on, it was clear rampant speculation far outweighed the facts.

Corin kept clicking.

According to legend The Veil of Veronica was used to wipe the sweat from Jesus's brow as He carried the cross and rests in Saint Peter's Basilica.

He skimmed the research.

Nothing about it having healing powers.

He clicked past the *Holy Grail.* Indiana and Henry Jones had taught him all about that one. But at least that legend supported the idea Christ objects could have healing powers. No, actually, it didn't. That was a movie and as he read further, it confirmed his feeling. There was less evidence for the existence of a real chalice than for the Sudarium, Image of Edessa, or the Veil.

He skimmed over articles on pieces of the cross, nails from the cross, the Coat of Christ, and the Crown of Thorns.

Again nothing about those objects healing anyone.

Corin sighed and stretched. The best he'd come up with in three hours of research was maybe something Jesus made could have lasted until today.

Time to see what the Bible said about healing.

His fingers flew over his laptop keyboard and he watched Google splash multiple Bible verses onto his screen.

Twenty minutes later he smiled.

He copied three verses into a Word document, saved it, then printed the page and read through over it, his smile growing into a grin. At least according to the Bible, the idea of a chair with healing powers was very, very possible.

> *Acts 19:11–12: "God did extraordinary miracles through Paul, so that even handkerchiefs and aprons that had touched him were taken to the sick, and their illnesses were cured and the evil spirits left them."*

> *Matthew 14:35–36: "People brought all their sick to him and begged him to let the sick just touch the edge of his cloak, and all who touched it were healed."*

> *Mark 5:27–29: "When she heard about Jesus, she came up behind him in the crowd and touched his cloak, because she thought, 'If I just touch his clothes, I will be healed.' Immediately her bleeding stopped and she felt in her body that she was freed from her suffering."*

Corin leaned back and smiled. Handkerchiefs, aprons, and clothes. Why not chairs? Especially one constructed by Christ.

And it sat in his store smack-dab in the middle of the picture window.

Not good.

When he got to the store he would move it to the hidden vault at the back of his store.

What next? He needed to talk to someone who knew more than Tori. But who? Corin strolled into his kitchen, stuck two pieces of eight-grain bread into the toaster, and brainstormed. Before the toast popped up he had an answer.

After slathering both pieces with a robust amount of strawberry jam and pouring himself a glass of nonfat milk, he settled back onto his couch, Googled churches, and dialed the first one listed.

"Hello, Cold Canyon Community Church." A woman with voice two ticks beyond perky answered.

"My name is Corin Roscoe and I'd like to talk to someone about . . ."—what should he say, 'I found a magical chair that might be healing people?'—"a possible religious relic."

"What is it?" The perkiness dialed down four pegs.

"A chair. Very old."

"Have you talked to an antiques dealer?"

Corin sighed. "I am an antiques dealer."

"So why are you calling a church?"

"I think it might be tied into Christianity."

"I see." All perkiness was gone. "And how is that?"

"The person who gave it to me said it was made by Christ."

The receptionist sniffed out a laugh. "That must be a very old chair."

"It is."

"She told you it was made by Jesus?"

"She didn't right out and say it. But she strongly implied it."

"I see."

The woman didn't offer anything else.

Corin rubbed his eyes. "Would I be able to talk to someone about it?"

"What would you like to know?"

"If there's . . ." Corin hesitated. What did he want to know? If it was real? If it had really healed Brittan? "Did you see the story in the paper the other day about the kid who was healed of his asthma?"

"Yes."

"The chair he sat in was mine."

"I see." The woman again offered nothing more.

Corin shifted the phone to his other ear. "I was hoping to talk to someone who knows about religious artifacts . . . someone who might be able to explain if this whole sitting-in-the-chair thing and him getting healed is a coincidence or if some kind of miracle really happened."

The line buzzed for ten seconds.

"I'll tell you what," she finally said. "If you'd like to give me your name and number, I'll find out who the best person is to talk to and have him give you a call back. Will that work?"

"Fine." Corin gave her the information, hung up, and stared at his cell phone. No one would be calling back.

He dialed two more churches and had the same conversation.

Corin didn't blame them. It sounded like something out of *The Amazing Spider-Man*. Who was he kidding? He should probably just stick it on the floor with a hefty price tag, write up copy offering up the idea it was made by Christ, and make some coin.

Who could he talk to about it if not someone from a church? Tori he'd already dismissed, he didn't have any friends who were religious, and the lady who gave it to him hadn't followed up on her promise to stay in touch.

A moment later Corin laughed. He knew exactly who to talk to about it. Maybe not someone who knew about ancient healing chairs, but definitely someone he could probably talk into experimenting on: A. C.

A. C. rode with him on all his extreme adventures. Why wouldn't he go on this one? When A. C. dropped off that rolltop desk this afternoon, Corin would get his friend to go for a little ride in the chair.

CHAPTER 16

A. C. stepped through the back door of Corin's store that after-noon at three thirty, lugging a rolltop desk as if it were made of balsa wood. "Hey, Cor, got your rolltop; where do you want it?"

Corin jogged toward the shipping entrance. "Need a hand with that?"

"Nah, only weighs about three hundred pounds." A. C. grinned and carried it over to the door outside the prep room. "Can I set it here?"

"Perfect."

Forty-one years old and still built like an NFL middle linebacker. Slightly damp strands of his blond, still-teenage-thick hair fell across his forehead, the only indication he was straining at all to carry the desk, his taut biceps pressing into the sleeves of his *Where the Wild Things Are* T-shirt.

If Ultimate Fighting had been as big ten years ago, before A. C. had kids, he would be dancing around a caged ring and ripping his competitors apart like they were made of cardboard. In fact a large part of A. C. was still considering getting into the ring.

A. C.: The Aqua Cowboy. The nickname their mutual friend Jeff Stucky had given him because of the way he rode a tube called the Extreme anywhere there was a body of water big enough for a ski boat. The tube was the bronco and A. C. was the bronco buster. Most tubers gave the kill sign at twenty-five knots. For A. C. that was warm-up speed. Same thing on a water ski. Barefoot as fast as the boat could go was his comfort zone.

Ironic that his best friend would be named for going extreme in an arena Corin would never enter again.

"Thanks for dropping it off."

"No problem. You're right on the way to the job I've got going."

"What are you working on these days?"

"Nothing fancy. Pouring sidewalks and driveways for a new housing development up north."

"One of the few I'm guessing."

"Work's been a little lean, but not bad." A. C. rubbed his hands on his jeans. "How about you?"

"Still the same. Skeletor lean."

"Sorry."

"No worries. People will start buying again."

"Do you believe that?"

"No."

They both laughed.

"How was the weekend hanging out at Disneyland?"

"Fun. Sticky, but fun. Kids loved it. Dineen loved it. I loved it." A. C. ambled over to the coffee pot, grabbed an oversized cup, and filled it to the rim with black tar.

"That coffee's six hours old."

"Perfect." A. C. glanced at his watch. "I should hit the pavement. I want to avoid afternoon rush hour if possible."

"Before you go, let me ask you something."

"Sure."

"Are you scared of anything?"

"What?" A. C. gave Corin his trademark crooked grin. "Did you pick up a copy of *Psychology Today* recently? How to examine your friends for cracks in their psyches?"

"No, I have a reason for asking."

A. C. threw back a big swig of his coffee. "How long have you known me? Twenty years? You ever seen me scared of anything in all that time?" He smirked. "How about you? Is there anything that keeps you up nights?"

Corin's face instantly felt scorched. He'd never told A. C. about the drowning or even about his fear of tight spaces, but if A. C. noticed he didn't say anything.

"Nothing? Public speaking? Heights? Clowns? Death?"

"That's it, clowns." A. C. nodded. "You got me."

But Corin had seen the fear in A. C.'s eyes when he'd said "public speaking."

"Talk to me, buddy. I have real reason for asking."

"What did you smoke today?"

"I want you to try something for me." Corin rubbed his knees and leaned toward A. C. "Something that might get rid of that fear."

"You picked up a hypnosis course on the back of a matchbook, right?" A. C. folded his arms and laughed. "And I'm your first patient."

Corin took his keys out of his pocket and walked toward the vault at the back of the store where the chair now rested. When he reached it he inserted a key as A. C. strolled up behind him.

Corin spun the combination on the vault door and swung it open.

"What've you got in the inner sanctum these days?" A. C. said.

Corin motioned with his eyes for A. C. to follow and stepped inside the room.

"Nice chair." He joined Corin inside the vault.

The chair sat in the center, nothing else within ten feet of it.

"I want you to sit in it."

"Oooooo." A. C. grasped at the air with his hands. "Let me guess. After I sit you'll say the magic words and instantly I'll be over whatever fear you think I have."

"Precisely." Corin smiled. "So tell me the fear and we'll get started."

"Nah, I don't think so." A. C. shook his head.

"What?"

A. C. rarely held anything back. Even the uncomfortable things. *My Life Is an Open Book* should be a bumper sticker on his car.

"I'm not sure I want to admit that fear to anyone."

Corin studied his friend. There was no one more loyal than A. C. As well as wise, heroic, and larger than life. No wonder the kids on his son's football team called him Mr. Incredible. He even looked like the Pixar creation. Corin wouldn't ever try to push him into something he didn't want to do. As if he could push A. C. into anything.

"No worries. You can tell me about it another time or never. This was just a stupid experiment."

A. C. didn't move. "You've brought up a memory I rarely think about." He rubbed his face and frowned. "In fact, if I didn't like you, I'm not sure I could resist the temptation to break your face for making me think of it." The frown turned into a smile.

"Face-breaking day is tomorrow, isn't it? So let's—"

"But maybe I should talk about it." A. C. folded his arms and suddenly grew an intense interest in his tennis shoes.

"Nah, later."

"I'm okay, Cor. Really."

"You sure?"

"Yeah." A. C. gritted his teeth, shook his head, and after another ten seconds began speaking. "When I was in sixth grade we did a unit on speaking. I liked doing it. Three speeches to the class, and I nailed every one of them, but then we gave our fourth talk in front of the whole school. The kids in my class were cool, they liked me, but . . ."

A. C. glanced up at Corin. "I had a pretty bad lisp back then. The rest of the year, every time I stepped on the playground for recess kids said things like, 'Howth it going lithpee?' I beat a few of them up which felt good, but it landed me in the principal's office every other day. I stopped hitting kids but they didn't stop saying things."

A. C. unfolded his arms and locked his hands behind his head. "That summer I worked on getting rid of the lisp and by fall it was gone, but so was any ability or desire to get up in front of a crowd. Scared for life." A. C. tried to laugh but it died on his tongue. "So even thinking about speaking in front of a group makes me want to mainline Prozac."

"Sorry."

"Forget it." A. C. straightened up and rubbed his shoulder. "I'm over it."

"Uh-huh."

"Fine, I'm not. But since no one is demanding I go on the motivational-speaking circuit, I'm not too worried about it."

Corin eased up to his friend. "Do you want to get rid of the fear?"

"You're serious."

"Yes."

"What, I sit in your chair here and suddenly I'm booking a show at Madison Square Garden and making like Demosthenes?"

"Exactly."

A. C. looked at him, his crooked smiled mixed with a frown that said, "Do you need a white jacket with thick leather straps?"

"Are you reading the local news these days?"

"No."

"Let me show you something." Corin handed him the story on Brittan.

A. C. studied the article, then stared at Corin, a quizzical look on the big man's face. "You're saying your chair healed this kid?"

"I'm not saying it; I'm just wondering. And I am saying it's a pretty interesting coincidence, and why not try it with someone else?"

A. C. stared at him for twenty seconds before answering. "You are serious."

"Yep."

"And I'm your guinea pig?"

"Yep."

"Have you sat in it?"

"Yeah."

"And what happened?"

"Nothing, and that might be what happens with you."

"Right." A. C. looked back at the story and tapped twice. "You don't really believe this, do you?"

"Most of me, no I don't, but again, what would it hurt to try?"

A. C. ran his fingers along the back of the chair then moved to the front and stared at it for a good thirty seconds. "What the heck, let's do it." He turned and eased onto the chair. "Where'd you get it?"

"It was donated to me last week from some lady. Totally out of the blue."

A. C. gazed up at him. "What was her name?"

"She wouldn't say."

"Was she cute?"

"She's probably in her seventies, maybe eighties." Corin thought back to her eyes that had no age. "But yes, beautiful."

A. C. grinned up at him. "You're not going to chant anything, are you?"

"Maybe I'll sing you 'The Pickle Song.' The extended concert version. If you're lucky."

"My eardrums can't afford that kind of pain."

Corin folded his arms and leaned back against the workbench along the back wall of the vault.

"What am I supposed to do?"

"I really have no idea, but I'm going to suggest thinking about what you want healed. That's what I think the kid did when he got healed, and from studying the Bible that's what people who got healed by Jesus did."

"You're studying the Bible?"

"I'm almost a scholar, baby. I'm now up to fourteen verses in my entire life."

"Okay, here we go." A. C. leaned his head back slightly, took in a deep breath, and let it out slowly. A second later an emotion flitted over his face. Surprise? Peace? Corin couldn't tell.

"Not bad. This is more comfortable than I thought it would be. It's a perfect fit." A. C. patted the sides of the chair and breathed deep again.

"Nice to know."

As Corin watched, his friend's countenance slowly changed, as if a layer of worry was melting off of him, revealing the little boy A. C. had once been, before the concerns of life had etched themselves into the lines on his face.

"Wow, I like this."

"Like what?"

"I just . . ." The transformation continued. A. C. looked more relaxed than he'd seen his friend in years. A look of contentment was smeared all over his face. "It feels like I'm sitting on a beach in Costa Rica with nothing to think about but how my tan is developing."

It was the same type of reaction Brittan Gibson seemed to have had. So why hadn't Corin had the same sensations when he'd sat in the chair?

"Anything else?"

"Not at the moment. Other than I think I could sit here forever." A. C. let out a contented sigh. "What happens now?"

"I go back into the store and wait for a customer to come in and drop ten grand on a chair and desk set from the mid-1700s and you hang out in here as long as you want."

"That's it?" A. C. frowned. "Don't I have to recite some prayer or something? Something to make the magic work?"

Corin smiled. "Whatever you feel like doing." He walked out of the vault. Yeah, why didn't it heal him? It healed the kid.

If his theory was right, it couldn't heal him unless he thought of what he wanted to be healed from while he sat in the chair. And when Corin had set in it, he didn't know.

After helping a customer buy a pair of cuff links from the early 1920s, he wandered back into the vault to check on A. C.

His friend's eyes were closed, the peaceful look still on his face. As soon as Corin cleared his throat, A. C. looked up, his face groggy as if he'd been asleep.

"Anything?"

"This is a great chair. Don't sell it. I could sit in it for hours."

"Did it do anything?"

A. C. laughed. "Other than make me relax for the first time in forever? Yeah, absolutely. I have a sudden urge to talk to the UFC about being a ringside announcer."

"I guess it worked then."

"Sorry." A. C. stood slowly. "But I liked sitting in it."

"Thanks for trying it."

"No worries."

SIX HOURS LATER as Corin drove home he called A. C. "Anything now?"

"You mean did I get healed?"

"Yeah. It took four-plus hours for the chair to work on the kid."

"Listen, Corin. We've been friends forever, so let me shoot straight. With the financial problems you've got screaming in your ear, this isn't the time to get distracted with ideas of chairs that heal people. Like I said, nice chair. It really did feel comfortable, but I'd leave the *X-Files* and *Fringe* fake-healing stuff for the movies and the televangelists, okay? It's a good-looking chair. People will like it. Sell the thing and make a little cash or a lot of cash if you can. You need it."

Corin sighed and hung up. A. C. was right. He'd put it on the floor tomorrow.

It would take a neon sign to convince him otherwise.

CHAPTER 17

Corin pulled the covers over his chest and sank into the dream almost immediately. He stood in his store staring at the chair, a short man, slightly hunched over, stood beside him.

"*That chair is valuable. Worth a great deal of money. And we both know you need money. I believe you could sell and wipe out a good portion of the debt you currently swim in. That's the wise decision.*"

"How much is it worth?" Corin said. *The figure of the man wavered like Corin was looking at him through water. "How much could I sell it for?*"

"*Tell people the chair was made by Christ and let the religious fanatics bid its price up into the hundreds of thousands.*" *The man shrugged. "Or I could take it off your hands for you. In fact, I'll confess, that is most assuredly the best plan.*"

Corin turned to face the man, but in the next instant he sat in the back corner of his store, a cup of coffee in his hands, the lady sitting directly across from him.

"*We should go from here,*" *she said, and in the next moment they stood side by side on a cliff overlooking a stretch of ocean, wind whipping through his hair.*

The water seemed to pull at him as if it wanted to seize him and wrench him over the edge. Pull him to the bottom and hold him in dark arms.

"*You must protect the chair with everything in you. You must guard it with all your heart. Do you understand?*"

"*Why?*"

"*You must. Do not let it go. Ever.*"

"*Why did you give it to me?*"

"*You are the one.*"

"*I don't understand.*"

"*I know. I am sorry I cannot say more.*"

"*Who are you?*"

"*Someone who has waited long to know you.*"

Was it the woman? The one who gave him the chair?

An icy wave crashed onto the beach in front of them . . . or was it—?

He woke to a strong, cold wind pouring through his open window, the blinds smacking into his sill like waves.

Corin sat up, rubbed his eyes, and sucked in a deep lungful of air.

Great, now the chair was invading his dreams.

He pushed the dream out of his mind, turned over, and started counting chairs. No help. After ten minutes of doing the alligator roll, he threw off his covers and staggered into his kitchen. The green numbers on his microwave read 1:55 a.m.

He tapped his laptop to bring it out of hibernation and glanced at the e-mails that had stuffed his in-box since he last checked it.

Junk.

Junk.

Junk.

Corin carried his laptop over to his tan couch where he settled down and stared out the window at the wind whipping through the cottonwood trees.

Why couldn't he get that stupid chair out of his head? Or his dreams? It was just a chair. Just a chair no one else would be interested in.

But he knew that wasn't true.

Not even close.

CHAPTER 18

Corin had just finished restoring a mahogany bookcase from the early 1900s when a man walked into the store with a light brown leather notebook under his arm, a venti-sized drink full of something of a raspberry color in his other hand, and a furtive look on his face.

"Hello, may I speak with the owner?" He set his drink and notebook on a Victorian burr walnut round dining table, shoved his hands in his pockets, and rocked back and forth on his heels.

"Speaking." Corin wiped the stain off his hands and looked at the man. Five eight or nine, white polo shirt, pressed khaki pants, pointy Italian shoes that looked uncomfortable, and dark red preppy-boy eighties-styled hair. The hair didn't fit. "What are you selling today?"

"Selling? Nothing." The man glanced around the store as if looking for something specific, then frowned.

"Most people don't come in here looking as polished as you do carrying a notebook unless they're selling something."

The man shook his head. "Like I said, I'm not selling."

"Then can I help you find something?"

"I'm not buying either." The man strolled forward, grinned, and stuck out his hand. Corin didn't shake it.

"I see. So what can I do for you?"

"You're the owner?" The man brushed his hand on the side of his pants as if pretending he hadn't been dissed.

"Yes." Hadn't he just told the guy that?

"You're Corin Roscoe?"

"Who are you?"

"I represent the senior pastor of a church in southern California who would like your cooperation, and in turn we would like to assist you."

"Assist me with what?"

"Whatever you might need."

Interesting. Maybe this was fortuitous. Maybe this guy would be able to fill in the considerable blanks in his "Does This Chair Heal?" dissertation. But something about the guy bothered Corin. Phony? Yes, but it was more than that. Something used-car salesman about him seeped through the GQ clothes and looks.

"Whatever I need? Uh-huh." Corin tossed the rag he'd used to clean his hands into a bright orange plastic bucket. "And why did this pastor send you? He didn't want to be seen in public with me?"

"Whatever you say to me will stay in strict confidence. I will not repeat a word of it. You have my honor on that count."

"I'm thrilled to know that." Corin walked behind his sales counter and leaned forward, his hands spread wide on the counter.

"I'm not someone who abides sarcasm well."

"And I don't abide well someone who comes into my store and insinuates I have to accept his counsel when I've never met him before." Corin stared at the man.

"That's valid."

"Do you have a name?"

"You can call me Ben."

"What do you want, Ben?"

"A few short questions and I'll be on my way. Okay?"

Corin opened his palms.

"Thank you. We understand you came into possession of a unique chair recently."

"How do you know that?"

Ben held up the news article from the Internet.

"I see."

"Is it true? Did sitting in your chair heal Brittan Gibson?"

"I have no idea if he's healed. I know he and his parents claim he's healed."

Ben opened his notebook and scribbled on the white lined paper. "Where did you get the chair?"

Corin strolled over to a collection of wood radios from the 1930s. Beautiful pieces. None of which worked when he'd brought them into the store. Now they all did, reception as clear as on the day they were made. He even replaced the tubes with the originals. Those had taken ages to track down. He turned the knob on one of the radios to 103.9 FM, even though the radio wasn't plugged in.

"Explain something to me, Ben."

"I'll try."

"Why is any of this any of your business?"

Ben smoothed his hair back and tried to smile. "It isn't."

"Exactly right. Glad we agree on that." Corin offered a thin-lipped smile. "Tell me the truth about something else. You're here to talk to me about the chair instead of your pastor because he doesn't want his reputation soiled by being seen talking to a guy about a subject straight out of Science Fiction Theatre."

"Something like that." Ben shifted his weight from one foot to the other. "Our pastor leads over ten thousand followers every weekend, and he would never do anything that would make one of his flock stumble. And for a rumor to start that implicated him as seeking something as outlandish as a chair that heals people when they sit in it, well, that wouldn't be a wise choice."

"I never said the chair heals people."

"Doesn't it?"

"I already told you once, I have no idea. Why aren't you talking to the mom of the kid who was supposedly healed?"

"I might do that." Ben picked up his notebook and drink. "Before I go, would it be possible for me to look at the chair?"

"I'm guessing you already know the answer to that question."

"True." Ben smiled, a genuine one this time. "I know how it must look, me barging into your store asking all these questions. But truly, our intent is to help, not to hinder."

Something about the way Ben said this rang true. He didn't trust Ben, didn't like him, but Corin was curious about the offer.

"If I did decide to accept your help, what do you think you'd be able to assist me with?"

"I don't think you know what you're dealing with."

"And you do?"

"No." Ben shook his head. "I don't think we do either. If the Holy Grail showed up in the crypt of a European cathedral, we wouldn't know what to do with it. If pieces of Noah's ark were discovered in Turkey, we would be extremely presumptuous to say we knew what we were dealing with." Ben lifted his raspberry concoction to his mouth and looked over the top of it. "But I will say we likely know more about what to do with supernatural relics than you."

"Probably true."

"And we know more about the supernatural aspects of Christianity."

"I'll give you that as well."

"And we could examine the chair, give you our thoughts, and store it in a safe place for you."

"You want me to give you the chair?"

"Not give, just protect."

Before the dream and Brittan's healing, Corin would have walked the guy right into the vault and showed him the chair. Probably would've offered to let Ben borrow the thing and report back in a few days or a week what he found out.

But maybe God spoke to people in dreams. Hadn't he seen that in a movie once? So for the moment he'd take the dream as a warning and err on the side of the lady's advice. Because he couldn't get the idea out of his brain that his benefactor and the lady in the dream were the same person.

Corin strolled toward his front door. "Thanks for stopping by, Ben. I appreciate it. And if I have any questions I'll know who to talk to."

"Right." Ben frowned and handed Corin his card. "Thanks for your time." He pushed open the front door, stepped through, then turned back to Corin. "My pastor is a powerful man. Influential. And driven to get what he wants."

"Thanks for the warning."

"It wasn't a warning; it's an invitation to accept his help."

Corin turned and walked back toward his sales counter. "Thanks for the warning, Ben. If I need to, I'll be in touch."

When he drove home that night, the bed of his truck held a tightly wrapped and very secure artifact from ages past.

CHAPTER 19

Corin picked up his cell phone on the way home and dialed his brother's house to see if the gift he'd sent had arrived. It was a way to be a part of Shasta's family, even if it was only looking through darkened windows. Plus his nephew was an amazing kid. Robin answered on the first ring.

"Hey, Cor. Sawyer once again thinks you're the coolest uncle ever."

"I had to send it. It's his birthday. Every ten-year-old boy needs *Race Town III* on his birthday." And every ten-year-old boy should somehow be protected from what Corin went through at that age.

She laughed. "I think his hands are going to fuse into the shape needed to hold the controller."

"But you'll limit his playtime to three hours a day, right?"

"Less than that. I'm not sure I want him to grow up to be a thrill junkie like you."

Corin hesitated. "Maybe someday soon I'll be able to play the game with him."

Robin didn't answer.

"Sorry, had to say it."

A short sigh floated through the phone in concert with his own.

Should he ask the follow-up question? He knew the answer, so why did he always ask? "Will you and Shasta and the kid be coming to my house for dinner next weekend?"

"I think you know the answer to that one."

"Yeah. What did he say this time?"

"That he's busy."

"You'd think he'd have a better excuse by now." Corin kneaded the steering wheel. "Does he miss Mom and Dad? The anniversary of their passing was six weeks ago."

"I know." Robin coughed. "He misses them a great deal."

"But that same emotion isn't extended my direction." It was a statement, not a question.

"Hang on a second."

Corin heard a door shut through the phone, and when Robin spoke again it was in a whisper. "He still cares about you. And I'll never stop talking to God about it."

"Right."

"Deep down he does. I see it in his eyes when your name comes up."

"All I saw in his eyes during my last impromptu visit was apathy. A healthy dose of it. It's not that he hates me; it's that he's devoid of any type of emotion toward me."

"He cares."

"If I died tomorrow, he wouldn't cheer, he wouldn't break down. He wouldn't do anything."

Five seconds passed.

"Do you know what he had restored to pristine condition and keeps out in the garage?"

"No idea."

"His Honda CRF 230."

A memory flooded Corin's mind as he considered the implications of Shasta keeping the Honda. His brother had almost killed himself on that bike on that August morning in 1994.

"You always have to push me a little farther than I want to go, don't you?" Shasta tried to pretend he was frustrated, but Corin knew underneath his helmet his brother was laughing.

They sat on their dirt bikes, revving their engines, staring at an eastern Colorado gorge with a seventy-foot drop to a thundering river.

"Not a little, a lot farther." Corin shifted into first gear, revved his engine, and let out the clutch. The wheel of his Honda CR 500 popped into the air and the bike screamed forward, the rush of acceleration making him laugh. The jump wasn't long, but being short wasn't an option. He let the whine of first gear get to ear piercing, then shifted into second, then third. He needed to be going at least forty-five when he hit the ramp, fifty would be better.

The wind whipped against his chest and he leaned forward in the seat.

Thirty feet to the ramp. Twenty. Five more feet. Launch!

The ground vanished and he flew thirty feet into the sky.

Corin's landing was perfect and he skidded to a stop forty yards on the other side of the gorge.

He threw his bike into first gear and raced back up to the edge of the cliff and shouted across the gorge. "You coming, little brother?" Corin shouted.

Shasta revved his engine in response. Corin imagined he could see Shasta rolling his eyes under his helmet.

"Just don't be slow, little bro."

Shasta hit the ramp dead center but Corin's heart clenched. The bike didn't have enough speed.

C'mon! Be enough.

Time slowed as Shasta arced across the ravine, body and bike in perfect form.

Be enough.

An instant later the back tire of Shasta's Honda smacked down high on the ramp sending a mini dirt shower into the air. Shasta threw his hands up in victory.

He yanked off his helmet, long dark brown hair swirling in the wind, and grinned at Corin after skidding to a halt twenty yards away. "Yeah, baby!"

"I don't need a heart attack, bro. What were you thinking?"

"What are you talking about?"

Corin jogged up the ramp to see where Shasta's tire had landed. He coughed out a frightened laugh when he reached the edge. A foot and a half, maybe two. He stared at Shasta.

"More speed next time."

"Hey, I wanted to make it interesting for you."

"Too interesting." Corin jogged back down the ramp over to his brother and slapped his hands down on Shasta's shoulders. "That kind of interesting I can do without."

"I was just curious how riled up I could make you."

"This cat doesn't want to get killed."

"But I was satisfied."

"Get serious, did you do that on purpose?"

Shasta took off his gloves and stuck them in his back pocket. "True serious?"

"Yes."

"I blew it back there. Thought I had enough speed. I'm sorry, bro; didn't mean to scare you. That one even made me nervous."

"Don't do that to me. Losing you would not be good for my mental health, get it?"

"Got it."

"Cor? You there?"

Robin's voice sliced through the memory and brought him back to the present.

"Yeah, I'm here."

The image in his mind of the dirt bike jump faded into a picture of the ski slope. "I made him do it."

"It was his choice."

"I forced him into it."

"You pushed him down the hill? Forced him up that ramp?"

Corin massaged the knots in the back of his neck. "Nice try. I appreciate it."

"I'm not trying to placate you. Yes, you were probably persuasive, but in the end it was his choice. He chose to launch himself into the air; you didn't choose it for him."

"Life would be different if I hadn't talked him into it."

"Promise me something," Robin said.

"Anything."

"You'll never stop trying."

"Never." Corin looked at himself in the rearview mirror and studied his haunted eyes. "I'll die first."

CORIN STRODE THROUGH the doors of Tori's dojo early Friday evening determined to talk to her about the chair. She wasn't warm to the subject, but things were getting too weird and she was the only one who he could trust.

Hey!" She bounced up to him in a bright blue top and black gym shorts and planted a kiss on his lips. "Ready for a slash-and-dash workout?"

"Slash and dash?"

"Slash through this thing and still dash out with plenty of time to enjoy that dinner you promised me at your place plus get to the theater in time to catch a late flick together." She glanced at the clock on her wall over the mirrors that ran the length of the dojo, then trotted over to the gray workout bags hanging from the ceiling.

As Corin peeled off his sweats he said, "I need to talk to you about something."

Thwack! Tori gave her bag a roundhouse kick. "Talk."

He jogged over to the bag next to Tori and struck it like a boxer.

"This isn't boxing, bub; it's mixed martial arts."

"Right."

"What do you want to talk about?"

"The chair."

"Again?"

"A guy from some megachurch came in today wanting to, 'Give me expertise in what I'm dealing with.'"

"What are you dealing with? Is the thing going to explode?"

"Then he insinuated I would be wise to let him study it and keep it for me."

Thwack! Thwack! Thwack! Tori kicked the bag three times in rapid succession, then finished with a shot from her fist. "Just sell the thing. Or give it to this guy."

"Don't you think there might be something a little weird going on here with this chair? The healing of that kid, now a sudden interest from this church?"

"Definitely something weird." *Thud, thud, thud!* Tori pummeled the bag with her feet.

"I need to know if this chair can heal people." Corin gave his bag a swift kick and followed it up with a forearm blow even Tori would be proud of. "Could it really have been made by Christ? Where should I take it? I have to talk to somebody who knows something about this. Figure out what to do with it."

"Shut up, Corin." Tori grabbed her bag with both hands and stared at him.

"What?"

"You heard me."

"What's your problem?"

"The weird thing I'm talking about is you. Just because a kid gets healed, you're suddenly wanting to be Pastor Joe-Bob and start preaching to the world."

"Hello?" Corin knocked on his skull. "Anyone home? What's wrong with you? I'm not wanting anything but to know what this thing is and what I should do. Doesn't it freak you out at all that I might have a miracle chair sitting in my basement? Wouldn't you want to find out more about it?"

Tori let loose with a double shot to the bag with her fists. "Sorry, I'm just getting tired of all this God talk."

"It's not God talk." Corin popped the bag so hard his fist stung. "It's chair talk. Why are you stonewalling me on this?"

"I'm not stonewalling; I'm just not into talking about religion. I told you that."

"This isn't religion. It's a chair. That might be doing bizarre things. I'd like some answers."

"Call James Randi."

"Who?"

"Founder of J.R.E.F. The James Randi Educational Foundation. He has a standing offer of a million bucks to anyone who can demonstrate any psychic, supernatural, or paranormal ability of any kind. I bet he'd be able to prove your chair isn't anything more than a nice-looking piece of wood."

"I'm not calling some celebrity."

"Fine." She gave her bag three sharp kicks. "But can we be done talking about it now?"

They stopped talking and Corin pounded away, hoping to take out his frustration on the bag. She'd locked him out. But it didn't mean he couldn't keep trying to pick the lock.

"I don't want to talk about the chair anymore."

"Good." Tori pounded her bag.

"I want to talk about who made it."

"C'mon, Corin." Another three kicks.

"It's one question."

She whirled to face him. "One? Only one?"

"Yes."

"After this can we be done talking about your chair?"

Corin delivered three kicks of his own. "I don't understand why this is such a sore spot for you."

"It's not; it's just boring talking about it all the time."

"Last question."

"Why don't I believe you?"

"Because I'll probably have one more question after this one." He grinned. "But at least not today. I promise. Guaranteed no more religious questions until at least twenty-five hours have passed."

Tori rolled her eyes and put her hands on her hips. "What?"

"Is it possible Jesus was who He said He was? That He really was the Son of God?"

"He never said that. He didn't ever say He was the Son of God."

"What?"

"He said he was the Son of Man, that 'I AM,' that 'I and the Father are One,' but He never said I am the Son of God."

"What's your point?"

"That maybe He was just a man who got really close to God, so people started saying He was God." Tori snatched her sweat towel off the top of her workout bag and turned toward the back of the dojo. "Are we done?"

"That wasn't all of the question. There's a second part."

"Sorry, that's the only one you get today."

"But—"

"Fine!" Tori tossed her towel to the ground.

"What burned you so deeply about Christianity?"

"That's off-limits."

"That bad, huh?"

"Drop it, Corin. I'm serious."

"So am I. The preachers who rail against gay people the hardest are the ones who are meeting other guys behind locked closet doors. The ones always talking about staying away from porn are the guys racking up hefty Internet bills."

"What's your point?"

"I think you see my point."

"I'm going to take a shower." Tori kicked her towel into the air and grabbed it as she strode toward the locker room. "See you at your place in thirty-five."

CORIN'S DOORBELL RANG thirty-four minutes after he'd left Tori's dojo and he smiled. She was always on time.

"Come in, Queen of Precision." He opened the door.

"Are we okay?" Tori hugged him. "Sorry I got so riled up."

"We're good."

Tori gave him a quick kiss, then strolled through the door and into his living room and stopped in front of his brick fireplace. "This mantel is stunning." She touched it with her fingers and leaned in to take a closer look. "Really beautiful."

"I put it up yesterday."

"Where did you get this piece?"

Corin smiled and ran his fingers over surface of the mantel. "You've seen it before."

"No." Tori gave a tiny shake of her head and eased over closer to him. "This I would remember."

Corin laughed. "Let me show you something." He turned and clipped toward his den, snatching a manila folder off his desk when he reached it, then turned and strode back to Tori. "Take a look." He handed her an eight-and-a-half-by-eleven piece of paper with two photos on it and folded his arms.

She glanced back and forth between the two pictures. "Same mantel," she said, more to herself than to Corin. "Amazing. You'd never know. It looks like junk in the before picture."

"Yep." He tried to keep from smiling.

Tori tilted her head and stared at him. "You didn't tell me your talents including restoring old furniture. I thought you only sold the stuff."

"The dream starting out wasn't to sell the pieces; it was to make them."

"What happened?"

"Not enough profit margin in selling new pieces. When someone sees something old they think it's worth more than something new." Corin rubbed the mantel. "I'll give them that. The history, imagining who might have stood or sat or eaten at a piece hundreds of years before gives it a value you can't hang a price tag on, but I've never thought it was ten times the value of a new piece. I think some things are better when new, then you can grow old with them."

Tori slid her arms around Corin's neck and kissed him. "Like relationships?"

"In some cases yes."

"Any specific piece you'd like to restore that you haven't been able to yet?"

Corin gazed at a picture on his wall of his brother and him skydiving over the badlands in North Dakota. Their photographer on that jump caught them with the sun lit up behind them like a trillion-watt spotlight. Two-man star formation, rocketing toward the earth at a million miles an hour.

"Some pieces can't ever be restored."

"We're not talking about furniture anymore, are we?"

Corin snatched his car keys off the mantel. "Let's get out of here; we don't want to miss the previews."

He squeezed his keys so hard they bit into his fingers and sent shoots of pain slinging up his arms. Why did he have to be reminded of his brother in every moment? Between thinking about Shasta during the day and fighting The Dream at night, he was ready to crack.

And no amount of wood glue could fix him.

CHAPTER 20

"No!" On Saturday morning Corin lurched up and out of bed and moved toward his door, dragging damp sheets with him, then crumpled to his bedroom floor as his legs were caught in the blankets.

"Oh, wow. Hold on, hold on." The words puffed out of him like blasts of steam from an old train. Corin tried to slow his breathing and raked his hands through his hair, as if he could tear the images out of his mind—of a torrent of water cascading into his lungs till they burst, the terror of it suffocating him, burying him in darkness.

The Dream hadn't been this bad for three years. Maybe more. He rose to his knees and held his head.

Just a dream, just a dream, just a dream.

"Whew."

C'mon, get a grip, Cor.

After a few more deep breaths he glanced at the blue numbers on his digital clock: 3 a.m. Later than normal.

He sunk back against the side of his bed and waited for his pulse to settle.

The darkness rocketing out of the bottom of the lake had been thicker than he'd ever felt. Deeper, and the nothingness more consuming. He shook his head.

Corin went to his bathroom, splashed water on his face, examined his puffy eyes, and cursed the face in the mirror.

He'd slept long enough that he'd have to count a million sheep to get back to sleep, but he hadn't gotten even close to enough rest to be up for the day.

Besides, he wasn't ready to submerge himself back into dreamland with the emotions of the drowning still churning through his gut.

He stumbled into his living room and grabbed *Demon: A Memoir* off the coffee table, a novel he'd picked up at Barnes & Noble earlier that afternoon. He'd asked one of the clerks about the supernatural being real and she recommended that book along with *The Screwtape Letters*.

After three chapters he set the book down and considered the implications. Demons and angels flitting around the world, taking on human form? Right. And little green Martians would be visiting his store tomorrow to pick up some European antiques for their home planet.

And more chairs made by God would show up on his doorstep.

His laptop pinged. He got up and ambled over to his kitchen table, reached over, and tapped the space bar to wake up the screen and see who was e-mailing him at three in the morning.

From: NicolerIIV@gmail.com
Subject: Good fortune
To: CorinR@artifications.com

Translation: Another Nigerian trolling for suckers who had been living under a rock for the past ten years and might still believe a fifty-eight-year-old Chinese woman dying of cancer wanted to share her vast fortune.

He turned, trundled back toward the couch, and picked up his book. He'd plow through another couple of chapters and then try to get back to sleep. With no dreams.

Another ping.

He spun on his heel. Maybe it was the Tooth Fairy this time.

Same name.

Different subject: *One more thing.*

He slumped into the chair in front of the table and wiggled the mouse. Why not?

He set his book down and opened the first e-mail.

> *Hello Corin,*
>
> *I hope you are well, although I would guess you are going through a number of strange mental machinations at the moment.*
>
> *Do not worry; there is purpose in what you're experiencing. It is good fortune and favor on you that has drawn you into this journey. Believe this. And keep asking. Keep seeking. Answers will come.*
>
> *Keep pressing forward, will you now?*
> *Your friend,*
> *Nicole*

Corin rubbed his jaw. It had to be her. He opened the next e-mail.

Corin,

One more thing: I'm sure you know this, but trust is to be earned and not given lightly with regard to everything and anyone having to do with the chair.

Exercise caution in all you do, will you? With everyone you interact with, yes? In both the natural realm and the realm of the spirit.

Your friend,

Nicole

Friend? She wasn't his friend.

He pulled up Google and plugged in her e-mail address to see if he could trace her e-mail address to a phone number or address.

Corin didn't think she'd be that careless. She seemed savvy enough to block his efforts to try to track her down. But it was worth a shot. Fifteen minutes later he gave up and typed a response back to her e-mail.

Nicole,

You're right; strange things are happening and I don't know where to go for answers.

When can we meet?

Can I at least call you?

Corin

A moment after sending the e-mail a noise from his basement startled him. It sounded like a stuck door being forced open, the latch scraping against the doorjamb.

He stared at the door that led downstairs. A dim light came from under it. He didn't remember leaving a light on down there. Corin set his laptop to the side and slowly rose without taking his eyes off the light under the door.

His pulse spiked. The light along the bottom wasn't steady. It ebbed softer and brighter with the rhythm of a slowly beating heart.

A moment later the light vanished and didn't come back on.

Corin glanced furtively around his living room, then stood and eased over to the basement door. He placed his hand on the knob and listened. Nothing.

A fly buzzed past his head as he opened the door and flicked on the light at the top of the stairs.

He swatted at the fly and descended the fourteen steps like each one was a thin layer of ice he was scared of breaking through.

An electrical problem? The house creaking as it settled into the fall season? Maybe. An older house like his had quirks.

When he reached the basement he flicked on the light and glanced around the main room. Nothing was out of place. But he let his imagination roam anyway. Could it have been the chair? Throwing off some kind of supernatural glow? Mocking him, teasing him about its secrets?

No. Knock it off. The dream and the novel had scrambled his brain.

He looked toward the padlocked door at the back of the room where he'd put the chair yesterday. It was open a few inches. Hadn't he shut and locked it? Corin wasn't sure. No light came from within.

A moment later the room grew brighter, then immediately dimmed. Corin whirled toward the source of the light.

The incandescent lamp in the far corner of the room flickered to life, then sputtered off, then back on again. It buzzed and started through its routine of off-on, off-on again.

Corin sighed. Of course. If you turned the knob too far the lamp would come on and off, sputtering and humming as the current to the bulb ebbed and flowed.

He sat on the lowest stair and rubbed the back of his neck. Maybe he'd move the chair to his storage facility east of town. That way his overactive comic book mind wouldn't create bizzaro scenarios out of nothing and play ping-pong with his emotions.

He turned his focus to the door behind which the chair sat. Corin wandered over to it, pushed it open wider, and flicked on the light just inside the door. The chair rested in the same spot he'd left it in the day before.

Resting? Same spot? Did he except it to jump up and dance the rumba? It was an inanimate object! He sighed. But if the Son of God had made the chair, wouldn't it be more than a chair? It would be alive in a sense. If His hands had touched it, crafted it, maybe even blessed it, it could hold a spark of His divine power.

He stepped farther into the room and eased up to the chair. "Are you real?" Corin pulled up a small stool, sat in front of the chair, and stared at it. At the perfect lines. The intricate patterns in the ancient wood.

"Where have you been over the centuries? And if you are a chair formed by a Jewish carpenter, how did you end up here? Talk to me."

Corin laughed at himself, but soon the moment of levity vanished replaced by a sense of foreboding. If it wasn't the chair of Christ, he should sell it for as much as he could and be done with this strange adventure. But if it was formed by the Son of God . . . he needed to know more about it, needed to know what to do next.

An ocean of questions was forming and Corin was drowning in them. He needed someone with skills to navigate the uncharted waters he now swam. He needed a boat.

But where could he find one?

A name popped into his mind.

Yes. Why hadn't he thought of Travis days ago?

He trudged back up the basement stairs, across the living room to his laptop. After three minutes he hit Send, slinging off an e-mail to Travis. If anyone could provide a few answers it would be him. Not religious speculation but rock-hard, scientific answers.

Which meant tomorrow he would reluctantly do a bit of necessary surgery on the chair.

PASTOR MARK JEFFERIES jammed his finger into his cell phone's End button. He didn't like hanging up on people, but when they pushed the right buttons his reaction was automatic. And having women in his church challenge his authority was the hottest button in his brain.

He stood and paced in front of his corner windows, gazing out on the trees littered with gold and red leaves about to fall and clutter the street with their failure to stay on the tree.

A few minutes later he picked up the phone and hit redial.

"Hello?"

Mark clenched the phone. "Eric, it's Mark again. Listen, I lost my temper. It shouldn't have happened." He sucked in a quick breath. "But you need to keep your wife in line. It isn't her place to challenge me." Mark paused. "Or any man in the church."

"All she was doing was expressing her opinion. She wasn't saying you were wrong, just saying how she felt."

"That's fine. Everyone is entitled to his or her feelings. But it has to be done in the right context. And a woman expressing her feelings to the senior pastor of the church during a small-group gathering with almost seventy people in attendance is not the place or the time. Are we clear on that?"

The phone went silent.

"Are we clear on that, Eric?"

"Listen, Mark. You're a man of God and you've helped both of us a tremendous amount, but we're done. Best to you."

Mark rubbed his forehead and with his other hand mashed his Bluetooth deeper into his left ear. "You're leaving the church? Over this?"

"A lot of things, but this straw probably weighs the most."

"What other things?"

"Good-bye, Mark. Thanks for all you've done."

Click.

Mark waited a moment, then yanked his Bluetooth out of his ear. People leaving the church: his second hottest button. He should have kicked them out before they could quit.

He lurched back his windows, clenched his arms across his chest, and seethed, staring at nothing.

A knock on his door broke him out of his daze. "What!"

The door opened a few inches and Ben poked his head into Mark's office. Mark motioned him in with his head.

"Bad time?"

"No. Perfect." Mark didn't speak again for over a minute. "You know, Ben. I hate it when I'm the quintessential example of Balaam's donkey."

"You've been prophesying?"

"No, I was referring to the species as representative of my behavior."

"Excuse me? I'm still not tracking."

"Forget it. Sit. Just in a bad mood today, which makes me do things I regret soon after. Happens to everyone, right?"

"Everyone."

"Coffee?" Mark motioned toward his espresso maker, which sat on the counter that lined the wall to his left.

"No, thank you."

Mark strolled toward the counter and stuck his half full vanilla latte in the microwave next to the coffee machine and punched in forty-five seconds. "Talk to me. What did you find out about this antiques store owner?"

"He's not stupid."

"What does that mean?"

"He's not begging for our assistance."

"Pity." Mark paced in front of the microwave. "Is he a Christian?"

"I highly doubt it."

"Does he believe in God?"

"I don't know."

"We need to know." Mark drilled Ben with his eyes. "You should have asked."

"I'll find out." Ben shuffled his feet. "Sorry."

The microwave dinged and Mark marched back to snag his drink. "Does he know what he has?"

"If he does he's not letting on."

"Do you think the chair is genuine?" Mark settled back in his leather chair and took a sip of his coffee.

"You mean do I think the chair sitting in an antiques store eight hundred miles away is the one you've been searching for most of your adult life?"

"Yes."

"I don't know. He didn't let me see it."

Mark downed another slug of his coffee and wiped his mouth. "I want you to keep a watch on this guy. You know what I mean, right?"

"Yes."

"What's his name?"

"Corin Roscoe."

"I want to know where Corin goes, who he hangs out with, who he talks to, everything. Understand?"

"It's done." Ben cocked his head. "Do you mind me asking what you're going to do with his chair if it does turn out to be the one?"

"Yes."

"I'm sorry, I didn't mean to pry."

"Yes, you did." Mark took another drink of his coffee. "But it's okay. I admire your ambition. I'd want to know the same thing if I were in your shoes. Well done."

Mark opened the top right-hand drawer of his desk, pulled out a full-sized notepad, and began jotting down what he'd learned from Ben. After few moments he glanced up at Ben. "Yes? Is there something else?"

"No, I, uh." Ben shifted his notebook from one hand to the other. "I thought you were going to tell me why the chair was so important to you."

"You thought incorrectly." Mark leaned back in his chair and glared at him.

Ben narrowed his eyes. "If you want me to help you with this little side project, don't you think I should know a mite more than you're telling me?"

"Excellent. Well done, well done." Mark stood and clapped. "That is assertion and courage in the face of opposition. The kingdom of heaven is violent and violent men take it by force."

"Thank you." Ben gave Mark a thin-lipped smile. "So are you going to tell me?"

Part of him longed to tell someone. About the darkness inside that stabbed at him with daggers made from anger and ego that melted into mist when he tried to destroy them. The longing that welled up in him to know he was truly forgiven for his sins and accepted no matter what. The craving to be the man he pretended to be. About the hope of what the chair could do.

But he couldn't tell this kid. He couldn't tell anyone.

As soon as Ben left, Mark spun in his chair and slid back a bookcase behind which sat a safe. He spun the combination and opened the door a crack, spun to make sure the door shut completely behind Ben, then opened the safe door the rest of the way.

He pulled out a notebook and flipped toward the middle and turned pages back and forth till he found the page he wanted. If the true chair had surfaced, then the lady had to be close by.

He needed to meet her.

And he needed to meet Corin Roscoe and use considerable powers of persuasion to get the guy to give him the chair. After a few minutes of contemplation, Mark smiled. He knew the perfect instrument of influence to use on Corin.

CHAPTER 21

The next morning before heading to the store, Corin descended into his basement and twirled the combination padlock on the door at the back of the room, his hands shaking. Why? Because of what he was about to do? Or because he felt like he was sliding into quicksand and this would only speed up his descent?

The door squealed open and he stood at the entrance and stared at the chair.

Move. He needed to do this. It was one of the best ways to know if he was dealing with a legend come to life or a hoax out of this Nicole woman's fertile imagination.

He strode up to the chair and circled it counterclockwise, hands on his hips. "I somewhat loathe to do this, but I have to find out more about you. Starting with your age."

He stopped, turned, and continued circling, now clockwise. "Which means I'll need to take a small sample to send to the lab.

A friend of mine will discover myriad facts about you through the process. I hope you can understand."

What was wrong with him? He was talking to the chair like it was alive, like it was a golden retriever he was about to do a biopsy on. It was a hunk of wood. Maybe old. Maybe beautiful. But probably nothing more than finely turned pieces of wood from centuries ago.

Or maybe only decades ago.

Or maybe it was the greatest archaeological find of the century.

He stopped walking, pulled a small blade from his pocket, and knelt in front of the chair. As he touched the inner left leg—where taking a sample from would be the most hidden—the air in the room seemed to grow warm, then back to its normal temperature a moment later.

Mind games. He wouldn't let his brain start playing tricks on him again.

With wood this old he needed to be careful. If the blade bit too deep, he'd end up taking off more than he wanted to. Corin ran his finger over the section he was about to cut into.

The wood was hard; he'd have to apply more than the usual pressure to remove a piece.

He pressed the edge of his knife into the tip of his left forefinger. Sharp. Should he sharpen it more just to make sure? No. It was an excuse to keep him from marring the chair. But he didn't really have a choice.

He set the blade into the wood at a twenty-degree angle. All he needed was a sliver. To his amazement the blade slipped under the surface of the wood like he was carving on a cube of butter. No resistance. After a quarter of an inch, he pulled up on the blade and watched a thin slice tumble into his palm.

He stared at the spot on the chair where he'd taken the sample and pressed the edge of his blade gently into the cut. It was rigid.

He pressed harder. Where before the wood had been softer than Play-Doh, now it was like pressing into stainless steel.

Corin fell back on his heels and focused on the chair.

Weird was getting weirder.

Was there a faint glow around it now, or was the light playing tricks? He got to his feet and shut off the lights to see if the glow remained.

Nothing. Complete darkness.

He pulled a glass vial from his pocket, slid the sliver in and capped it. After shutting and padlocking the door, climbing the stairs, and locking the door to the basement with a keyed dead bolt, he poured himself his eighth cup of black coffee and picked up his cell phone.

"Hello?"

"Travis, it's Corin. Did you get my e-mail last night?"

"I got it."

"I just took a sample. Can I drop it off this afternoon even though it's Sunday?"

"Of course."

Corin stared at the door to his basement. He eased over to it and checked the dead bolt again. Still locked. He laughed at himself, wandered back past his espresso maker, and grabbed his car keys off the kitchen table. "How soon can you have the results back?"

"Soon."

"How soon?" Corin shut his front door and strode toward his car.

"Do you want the full workup or just its age?"

"For now just how old." Corin fired up his truck and started down the road in front of his house toward I-25.

"You think you have a fake antique on your hands?"

"Something like that."

"What year is it supposedly from?"

"Can't tell you yet."

"Me?" Travis laughed. "You can't or you won't?"

"Both."

"Now I'm really curious."

"I will, just not yet." Corin veered to the left on Mesa Road to pass a slow-moving yellow Slug Bug.

"At least tell me what the piece is from."

Corin paused. He'd known Travis for six years. They weren't friends, but he'd easily have a beer with the guy if they bumped into each other on the street. And he was trustworthy.

"It's from a chair someone gave me the other day. Probably Middle Eastern. If I'm right, it's old. Very old. And it has me curious enough to want to get some details about it."

"Disappointing. I was hoping it was something from King Arthur's armor."

"Now that would be worth keeping secret." Corin pulled up to a stoplight and glanced at the wannabe cowboy in the Nissan truck next to him. Had the guy just been looking at him? Corin put on his sunglasses.

"You're bringing it in now?"

"I have a few stops first, so I should be there in about an hour."

Ten minutes later he pulled into Hardline Hardware to pick up a few home-surveillance cameras for the store and for his house. He'd been meaning to do it for a while, and now that Ben Raney and Nicole had heightened his senses regarding people potentially after the chair, it was time to get cameras installed.

Corin shut off his engine but didn't get out of his Toyota Highlander. Six rows over sat the same truck he'd been next to at the stoplight. A few seconds later the cowboy got out of the truck and ambled toward the hardware store. He didn't glance at Corin, but Corin couldn't shake the feeling the cowboy purposely didn't look his direction.

As Corin drove away to drop off the sliver of wood with Travis, he tried to relax.

Whew. He needed to get a handle on his emotions. When had the seeds of suspicion grown into a fully grown redwood of paranoia?

But his gut told him someone was planting an entire forest.

CHAPTER 22

As the sun hit the top of the sky, Corin grabbed his in-line skates and set off on Sundance trail in the Cheyenne Mountain State Park thinking he'd get away from everyone. Nice plan for a Sunday afternoon.

An hour and a half later—after tackling six more of the park's trails—he slumped to a bench and let his heart rate return to normal. The workout cleared his head, and during the time on the trails, he didn't think about the chair more than once.

Those were the type of moments he needed to steal more of.

A few minutes later two men in black leather jackets strode over the grassy rise directly across the path from Corin and marched in his direction. The man on the left looked like a wannabe emo-version of Bono, the guy on the right looked like a genuine wiseguy.

When they were twenty-five yards away, the Mafia man peeled off and stopped to lean against the trunk of a quaking aspen.

The other man continued on, staring straight at Corin, a

knowing smile on his face, intensity in his eyes. Corin was about to turn and look behind him to see if the man was walking toward someone else when the man lifted his hand, pointed his finger like a gun, and pulled the imaginary trigger.

When the man reached Corin, he looked down at him and said, "Hello, Corin."

His hair was jet black, his eyes a placid green. He was just over average height, five ten maybe five eleven, with one of those lanky builds that hid extra girth under a layer of clothes. At first glance he looked mid-thirties, on second Corin guessed early forties trying to look mid-thirties.

"Who are you?"

"Mark Jefferies." He stuck out his hand. Corin didn't take it.

"How do you know my name?"

"An associate of mine met you the other day." Mark motioned to the bench. "Do you mind if I sit?" He didn't wait for an answer and sat beside Corin.

"Ben."

"Yes."

Corin slid a few feet away from Mark. "So the pastor comes out of hiding to meet the keeper of the chair face to face. Then again, this isn't exactly Times Square."

Mark turned toward Corin, slid his arm onto the back of the bench. "My talking to you in private is as much to protect you as it is me."

"From who?"

"The others who might come after the chair."

"Why would people come after the chair?" Corin knew the answer. But he was curious how Jefferies would answer the question.

"You don't think a kid getting healed by your chair has brought or will bring a few whackos out of the woodwork?"

"Like you?"

Mark glanced at his Mafia-looking pal, then back to Corin. "No one talks like that to me."

"I just did."

Anger flared through Mark's eyes but settled a moment later.

"Are you going have your pal over there shoot me now?"

"You have a decent sense of humor, Corin." Mark crossed his legs and reached into his inner coat pocket as if he was going to pull out a pack of cigarettes. Almost. It was a tin of Kodiak chew. "Like I already said, we want to help you, protect you. So we're keeping our eyes open. Watching to see if anyone is tailing you."

"So the cowboy I noticed yesterday—?"

"You noticed him following you?" Mark stuck a wad of the chew into his cheek. "I'm not surprised. He's not too discreet."

"What is a pastor doing with the kind of people who know how to track others?"

"When you get to my level of fame, you have a target on your back. A lot of people love me and a lot of people hate me. So I protect myself with people in every city I visit across the country who have skills I don't."

"So that guy over there, he's your bodyguard?"

"Yes."

"Looks like he has a rap sheet."

"He does." Mark spit. "I think all people have things in their past they need forgiveness for. In their present as well. And they need to be extended grace for what they regret."

They sat in silence for a minute except for Mark's occasional spitting.

"So if I wait long enough, I suppose you'll tell me why you're here. But since we probably both have a few more places to go today, why don't I ask?"

Mark smiled and drummed his fingers on the back of the

bench. "I'll say it a third time, I'm here to help you." He opened his palms and looked out from under his eyebrows.

"What kind of help?"

"If this chair truly healed that boy, then you're dealing with powers you don't understand. You need someone who understands the power behind the chair, how to contain that power, and how to keep it and yourself safe while you have it."

"*How to Handle God's Chair for Dummies*, huh?"

"You could have in your possession one of the most powerful artifacts ever to come out of the church age. A chair I've been hoping to see my entire life. A chair that can do miraculous things. You could help a lot of people with that chair, Corin."

"You don't think this is something I can handle on my own, hmm?"

Mark pulled a small, worn Bible from his back pocket. "First, I'm going to guess I know more about this chair than you do. Hmm? And more about this book."

Corin nodded but didn't say anything.

"Second I would guess I've studied the legend of the chair more than most." Mark chuckled. "My wife would say I've obsessed over the chair more than most." He paused. "Which is probably true."

"What legend?"

"You just proved my point."

Corin leaned forward. "What's the legend?"

"I'm not surprised you haven't heard of it." Mark stared at him as if he were reading Corin's mind. "You probably haven't heard that some people believe the Apostle John is still alive, or that the true Ark of the Covenant is hidden beneath the Temple Mount accessible through a series of secret underground passages."

"People believe those things?"

"Passionately." Mark nodded. "And they have extensive evidence to back it up. The only reason you've heard of the Holy Grail or the Ark of the Covenant is because of Monty Python and Steven Spielberg decided to turn those legends into entertainment."

"So if I trusted you, which I don't, what would you want to do?"

"Educate you on the legend. Coach you on what you should and shouldn't do with the chair. Introduce you to the Person who created the chair."

"And come see it."

"Eventually, yes."

"Examine it."

"I've spent the past twenty years scouring the earth for stories and clues about where this chair might be. I've interviewed hundreds of people, most who knew nothing that could help me. I've poured my life into this mystery." Mark's eyes bored into Corin's. "So yes, I would like to examine it."

"And take it with you. To test your theories."

"No. The chair would remain with you. It is not mine to take unless you want to sell it or give it away. If God has chosen you to have it, it should stay with you till you choose to turn it over to someone else."

"How do you know it's the chair you've been searching for?"

"I don't. Maybe it's not the genuine chair. If it isn't, then I'll stop wasting your time and mine."

"And if I ever did let you see it, how will you know if it's authentic or not?"

"I'll know. And so will you." Mark leaned toward Corin. "Maybe you already do."

Corin pawed the ground with one of his skates, sending the wheels spinning. Jefferies wasn't a guy he could ever trust, but something about the pastor was magnetic. He could see why thousands of southern Californians worshiped Mark Jefferies on Sunday mornings and thousands more on the Internet.

But Corin wouldn't be one of the faithful. Jefferies should have *Loose Cannon* tattooed on his forehead. The man was dangerous.

"Let me ask you, did the lady who gave you the chair tell you her name?"

"No," Corin lied, "she didn't."

A satisfied look passed through Jefferies eyes and his mouth formed into a thin smile. "I see."

Jefferies stood and offered his hand again. This time Corin shook it. "Think about it. I'm on your side." After jotting down a number with a Montblanc pen, Mark handed him a business card. "You can reach me at anytime at that number. Any time."

Jefferies turned and strode down the path leading out the park. He didn't stop at the tree his bodyguard leaned against or even look at the man.

There was no meandering. No stopping to smell the dandelions. No pretense to form an impression before a conversation. Mark had found out what he had come to discover. If only Corin knew what it was.

No one but Tori and A.C. knew how he'd gotten the chair. And Corin had just told him about the lady.

Jefferies had gone fishing and Corin had taken the bait.

CHAPTER 23

Corin weaved through traffic on the way home, changing lanes like Speed Racer looking in his rearview mirror every five or ten seconds and glancing at every car that passed him.

Was Mark's Colorado contingent of Mafia pretenders still following him? Probably.

Corin smiled at the woman looking at him from her car sitting next to him at the stoplight. She was adorned in a pink stocking cap that looked like it was knitted in the 1970s. He didn't think she was one of Mark's minions. What kind of self-respecting tracker would wear something like that? Of course that would be the perfect reason to wear something like that.

For the hundredth time since Nicole had appeared outside his store, he told himself he had to find someone he could spill the whole story to that knew Christianity and knew history.

And knew something about this legend Jefferies referred to.

Corin felt like he was an Egyptian standing at the bottom of the Red Sea after the Jews had passed through. He needed to ask questions of someone he could trust, get answers from someone who would know what they were talking about. But who? Trustworthy genius historians weren't hanging out on street corners offering insight and the unraveling of ancient mysteries for food. And he wouldn't be calling Mark Jefferies.

Wait.

A moment later he threw back his head and laughed. Of course. If anyone could help it would be Tesser—if the guy was still alive.

Corin pulled up his contacts on his cell phone and typed in his old professor's name. Corin rubbed his face and sighed. Not in there. Maybe the university would have his last known phone number, even if it had been eighteen years since he taught there.

Or he could simply take a shot and call Information.

Two minutes later he dialed Tesser's number. It rang seven times before his old friend's voice came on the line. *Yes.* He was still among the living.

"Tesser, Tesser, I'm a professor. Are you? Well, I used to be. But maybe you aren't what you were anymore either." *Beep.*

"Tesser, it's Corin Roscoe." He paused. "It's been a few years." Sure ten was more than a few, but why point that out? Corin hesitated. How much should he reveal on voice mail?

"I've stumbled onto something that's soaring way over my head and I need to come see you about it. Soon. Any time that works for you will work for me." Corin gave his cell phone number and hung up.

He couldn't think of anyone better than Tesser who had expertise in archaeology, history, and anthropology. If anyone knew about a legendary chair from the time of Christ, it would be his old professor. He could be a human Google, if Corin was able to keep Tesser on point.

TWO HOURS LATER Corin's phone vibrated. He glanced at the caller ID. Tesser. Sweet. "Hello?"

"Corin Roscoe?"

"Yeah, it's me, Professor."

"Oh my, a delight to hear from you. It hasn't been a few years, you know; it's been ten. Ten, my dear Corin. That's too many. You never call me. Never. But now that you need something, I'm suddenly on your speed dial."

"Did you break *your* fingers?"

Tesser laughed his staccato-chuckle bringing back memories of him filling the streets of Greece with it as they wandered though its glories a lifetime ago. "Touché, yes, I could have called you. Point taken. So let's forgive each other, extend grace, and be grateful we're talking while I still have a modicum of my brain left and we can enjoy each other's company again after too many years. Hmm?"

"Fine." Corin laughed.

"Splendid." Tesser cleared his throat. "Now let's see, when to meet. How urgent is this?"

"Very."

"All right then. Let's say six tomorrow morning. At my house. It's the same one as last time we saw each other. I think. Let's see, I haven't moved for forty-three years and I last saw you . . . yes, same house. I'll persuade you to tell me all about what kind of waters you've muddied your feet in, and I'll tell you about the trouble I've led skirmishes into for the past decade."

Corin inwardly groaned. He'd forgotten Tesser's penchant for early morning meetings. Night Owl meets Crack of Dawn Man. But the price was small. If anyone could pull back the layers on the chair it was the professor.

CHAPTER 24

That night Corin served Tori a spaghetti dinner with three different sauces and tried to ignore the anxiety pressing out on all sides of his chest like an overinflated soccer ball. Would Tesser have any answers? He needed them.

By the time they polished off their bowls of Cookies and Cream ice cream, he'd successfully shoved his worry to the back of his brain but it refused to vanish completely.

"Great dinner, we need to get a picture of it," Tori said.

"But the meal is over. We should have taken a shot before all the bowls were empty." He motioned toward the red-stained bowls and plates sitting on his seventeenth-century seven-foot Jacobean oak table.

"Nah, now is the best time; it shows we enjoyed it."

Corin smiled. "Okay, I'm with you." He laid his camera on his built-in bookshelf and set the timer for ten seconds, then scuttled back to Tori, put his arm around her waist, and smiled.

Ten seconds later the camera flashed and Tori pranced over to the camera and pulled up the shot. "Nice!"

"Let me see."

Where they'd stood obscured most of the dishes, but years from now—if they were still together—they'd be able to remember it was spaghetti.

Tori studied his camera. "You have 238 pictures on here as far back as three months ago. Don't you ever download your photos?"

"I should, but I never seem to get around to it."

"I'll do it for you right now if you want."

"Sure, you get that going and I'll clean up the table and get the dishes taken care of."

A few minutes later Corin stood at his sink hand washing the dishes from their meal. It's not that he didn't appreciate his dishwasher. There was something about washing dishes by hand that was therapeutic, as if he could wash away the regrets of the past and photos he wanted to wipe out of his memory forever.

He glanced through the kitchen door at Tori sitting in front of his laptop. Would they be together in two months? Two years? Two decades? Did he want to be with her that long? Maybe. He didn't know and suspected she didn't know either. Three months together wasn't long enough to know. Actually it was, but he still needed time to . . . He stopped, plate in one hand, a light blue scrubber in the other.

He needed time to fix things that never could be fixed.

He shook the thoughts from his mind and turned off the water.

"Hey!" Tori called from the living room, "I got 'em all downloaded."

"Great. Thanks." Corin wiped his hands on a dish towel and joined her.

"Is this where you keep all your photos?" Tori sat on the couch, studying his laptop, her legs crossed on the coffee table in front of her.

"What?"

"On your laptop, is that where you keep all your pictures?"

"Yeah." Corin sat beside her and propped up his legs next to hers.

"And where do you keep your backups?"

"Backups?"

Tori flicked him on the shoulder with her forefinger. "You are not going to tell me you don't back up your photos."

"No, I would never tell you that. I'll let you come to that conclusion on your own."

"Tell me you're kidding." Tori clicked on a folder opening up some year; he couldn't tell which one unless he squinted and he didn't feel like squinting.

"I'm not exactly a technowizard when it comes to computers."

"I understand. It's quite a challenge to stick a blank DVD into your computer, drag your photos over into a file, and hit Burn."

"Ha."

"I'll do it for you if you like." She opened another folder and spun through a set of photos. It looked like his backpacking trip to the top of Castle Peak.

"You would?"

"Sure. And you should back them up into the Cloud too."

"The Cloud?"

"You have to know what the Cloud is."

"Storing it on someone else's server where people can steal your images." He closed his eyes and leaned his head back into the softness of his leather couch.

"We're talking pictures here, Corin. Do you really have such valuable pictures that people would try to steal them?"

"Probably not."

"Wow." Tori bumped him with her elbow. "I didn't know you skied."

"I don't." Not for the past ten years.

"This isn't you in this picture?"

Corin opened his eyes and looked at the computer screen. His heart rate accelerated and his face grew hot. How did she find that? "What?"

"Right here." Tori pointed to the picture filling his laptop's monitor. "Looks like a wicked jump. You have to be twenty-five feet in the air. Nice. Who's that with you? It is you, right?"

Heat continued pouring into Corin's face. "Where did you find that? Why did you dig that up?"

"What's your problem? It wasn't hidden; it was right there in that folder with a bunch of other pictures from long ago and far away. Are you one of those people who puts dead-end signs on memory lane?"

"Delete it." Corin reached over and slammed his laptop shut. "I . . ." He got up, strode to the front door, yanked it open, and spilled down his steps into the front yard.

Not cool. Not right for that photo to pop up out of the past and grab him around the throat. Especially with Tori there. He spit on the ground. Why did she pull that thing up?

He grabbed the aspen tree at the end of his walkway and squeezed. He needed to get a hold of himself. It wasn't her fault. He should have deleted the picture a long time ago, but he'd buried that part of his life and hadn't remembered the photo was still on his computer. It must have been transferred over when he did the dump from his old desktop.

Corin turned and stared through his living room window, the warm glow of the lamps on either side of his couch bathing Tori in a soft light. He would have to tell her something, but what? How the day that photo was taken was the darkest of his life? How he'd unsuccessfully wiped its existence from his memory? How a few minutes ago his heart had once again been ripped from his chest and doused in forty thousand gallons of guilt and regret and she'd just lit the match?

As he hiked across his lawn, up his front porch stairs, he decided to tell her as little as possible.

She looked up as the front door creaked open. "Are you okay?"

"No."

"Do you want to talk about it?" She gestured toward the laptop.

"No."

"You should."

"I know."

"Talk to me."

Corin stumbled over to the couch and slumped down beside her. "Did you delete it?"

"I get the feeling it's not mine to delete."

"I suppose not." Corin leaned his head back again and clicked his teeth together as if he could bite the emotions coursing through his soul in two and make them die.

"You need to let some light into whatever dark closest you're hanging out in at the moment."

"You can't image how dark."

In the next moment the entire memory flooded his mind as if it had happened yesterday.

"That's a double black diamond just begging to be conquered," Shasta said after he skidded to a stop at the top of a narrow chute barely ten yards wide and sidestepped over to Corin.

"You think it's enough of a challenge for us?"

"Hardly. But for the next week I can't do anything pegging on the far side of mildly challenging."

"No worries; I'm not taking you down it. We have other plans."

"And you're going to tell me about them when?"

"When we get there." Corin motioned with his ski pole toward the lift that would dump them at the top of Heaven's Gate. "Let's go."

A minute later they settled onto the lift and lurched up the mountain at a forty-five degree angle, the sun creating a blazing white carpet dotted with cliffs and bristlecone pine trees.

"How are your feet?"

"Toasty." Shasta laughed. "I'm so ready to marry Robin."

"Good. Then coming up here wasn't a waste of time." Corin swung his boots and skis to keep the circulation in his legs moving.

"The place we're going isn't packed with our usual insanity, right?"

"Nope. We're going someplace special."

"Why doesn't that bring me any comfort?"

Corin smiled. "If after we're done, if you don't agree it was the absolute right call to do this, I'll eat one of my gloves." He shook one of his blue-black gloves in the air and shouted, "Chow time."

"I'm going to hold you to that."

Four minutes later they skidded to a stop at the top of the lift and gazed out over the miles of slopes below them. A pin-thin road slalomed through the white miles to their right, to their left were bright red signs proclaiming DANGER.

"Right or left?" Shasta asked.

Corin grinned. "Left."

"Why did I know you were going to say that?"

"Because I'm your brother."

"Nothing crazy."

"Nope, nothing crazy." Corin raised his dark brown sunglasses and winked. "Trust me."

After tightening his boot buckles, Corin shoved off and traversed over the edge of a small cliff just past the danger sign, and the sound of the lift vanished. They'd have to take it slow for the first fifty yards, but after that the slope was more than manageable for skiers of their ability.

He led them down a narrow, tree-lined path that stayed high on the ridge. Six hundred or so yards later, they emerged into an open bowl offering another panoramic view of the resort two thousand feet below them.

Corin threw his arms wide and gazed from side to side at the snow-shrouded mountains. "Nice scenery, huh?"

"Gorgeous."

Cars crept along the winding highway just beyond the resort. Tiny specs, dark against the pristine slopes, were skiers and snowboarders carving up the snow, looking for a slice of fun on the frozen water.

Corin smiled to himself as he squinted toward the spot he'd picked out last week a half mile away. This day was perfect. No snow, only sun creating the perfect setting. Shasta would love it.

"Ready?"

Shasta nodded and Corin shoved off across the face of the bowl of virgin powder. Five minutes later they reached a long chute with a moderate slope.

"We're here."

"You ready to reveal your grand plan?"

Corin pointed to a rise at the bottom of the slope and Shasta studied the area below them.

"You've found a jump." Shasta took off his sunglasses and squinted against the glare ricocheting off the snow. "A big one."

"That I have."

"I can't do it, bro, you know that." Shasta put his sunglasses back on. "How would I look walking down the aisle with crutches?"

"Stylish." Corin grinned. "C'mon, you want to do this. Last jump before you're locked in forever."

"Locked in?"

"In a good way."

"Why do you always do this to me?" Shasta sighed. "For the last few years you've been making us skate on paper-thin ice."

"What's that mean?"

"It means we're getting older and you're like a junkie always having to find a higher high."

"You're not saying you're getting scared in your old age are you?"

Shasta stared at him. "I'm saying there's an edge over which adventure turns into leaving any kind of control too far back in the rearview mirror."

"It's one jump."

"Besides, Robin will kill me if I'm sitting in Jamaica with my leg wrapped in a thirty-pound cast."

"They don't do casts like that anymore; it would be four pounds max."

Shasta glared at him.

"You really want to bag out on this?" Corin spread his arms, palms up. "Last jump as single brothers?"

Shasta dug his ski into the snow. "How big?"

"Twenty-five, thirty feet high. Sloped landing, forty degrees. Perfect. I was here last weekend to check it out and did the jump three times."

"That's the jump?" Shasta asked as he gazed down the slope.

"Yeah, you're looking at the right one. Straight down the chute, just to the left of the jagged rock about two thirds of the way down."

"I shouldn't do this, Corin." Shasta zipped up his coat to his neck. "I'm not doing it."

"You have to."

"Why? We've jumped off millions of these things. Why is this one so important? Why can't my wedding take priority?"

Corin pointed down the slope. "See anyone moving down there?"

Shasta moved his head to the left, then to the right as he peered down the slope. "Yeah, I see someone. You know him?"

"It's Tony Budiseski. I asked him to come."

"Why?"

"It's your wedding present from me to you, bro." Corin smiled. "When we launch ourselves into the air, Tony is going to snap a thousand high-speed shots. We pick the best one, blow it up into a poster, and you put it on the wall of your garage so you can remember us when you're all domesticated. 'Cause after we do this, life will never be the same."

"You're a piece of work."

"I sure hope so." Corin waved to Tony, who waved back. "Hey, before we do this, look behind you."

Behind them sat a wall of snow and trees so faultless it was like a painting. The sun lit up the snow so brilliantly it was blinding, and gray-black rocks poked out of the snow in a chaotic, beautiful pattern.

"That's the background I want for this picture."

"How long did it take you to find this spot?"

"Only three weekends."

"I love you, bro," Shasta said. "Even though you revel in making me dance on tightropes I don't even want to put a toe on."

Corin adjusted his sunglasses. "Ready?"

"Let's do it."

Side by side, four feet apart, they sliced through the snow carving almost identical turns. Fifty feet from the jump they glanced at each other and turned straight downhill. Four seconds to launch.

Corin glanced at Shasta as the jump surged toward them. Only seconds before they'd be captured on film for eternity. Three, two, one . . . then the snow disappeared and he and Shasta were eagles, soaring together forever.

Corin let out a whoop, arms and legs splayed out like he could stay in the air for ages. Seconds later his skis whapped onto the steep slope and he slid into a hockey stop, skidding to a halt twenty yards down the chute.

He let out a victory shout and spun to find Tony. "Did you get it?"

Tony didn't answer. He stared over Corin's shoulder, face pale, eyes wide.

Corin whipped around searching for Shasta.

His brother lay face to the snow, fifteen yards down the slope, skis still on his feet, one arm on top of his back, the other splayed out to his side.

"Shasta, you all right?" No answer. No movement. Corin tore off his skis and tried to run through the snow but kept falling as he struggled to keep his feet from sinking into the soft powder. "Shasta!"

The only answer was a soft wind that pushed up the sheet.

A minute later he reached his brother and fell to his knees next to him. "Talk to me, brohan." Corin ripped off his gloves and placed two fingers on Shasta's neck. He had a pulse. Weak, but it was steady.

He turned to Tony. "We need to get him out of here fast!"

"There's no one out here and with no SAT phone—"

"Ski down; you'll have to get the ski patrol!"

"I'll be back as soon as I can. Don't move him."

Corin nodded and turned back to Shasta. His breathing was shallow but rhythmic.

"I'm here, bro. Wake up. Please." Corin sat back on his heels as heat washed over him. This couldn't be happening.

Corin checked his pulse again, keeping the sun from his face, trying to keep the panic rising in his chest from boiling over.

What have I done?

"Hey," Tori said. "Where'd you go?" She rubbed his shoulder and tilted her head.

"Sorry." Corin shifted forward on the couch and scratched his face. "That photo brought it all back."

"Brought all what back?"

Corin stood and stared at the front door. "I gotta go. I mean, I need to be alone with this."

"You're sure?"

He nodded, walked to the front door, and held it open. "Sorry, it's not something I can talk about right now."

Fifteen minutes later he lay in bed, willing sleep to take him, but when Z-land came, it was worse than the memory of Shasta's accident.

CHAPTER 25

Corin stood on the edge of the bicycle raft trying to step away, but his legs and feet felt wrapped in saltwater taffy. "Move!" he screamed into the air, but no sound came out of his mouth and his mom and dad and Shasta just smiled at him.

"Let's switch so I'll be with Shasta and you can be with Mom . . ."

"No, Dad, it will tip!" Corin shouted as loud as he could, but the words dropped to the surface of the water and disappeared.

"Here, let me help you, Corin." His dad cradled Corin's elbow in his palm and pulled.

Corin yanked his elbow away.

"What's wrong?" His dad frowned.

"It's going to tip and I'll be caught underwater and I'll drown. We need to stay where we are!"

An instant later Corin stood on the other pontoon with the rest of his family. No! His mom and Shasta started to step off onto the other pontoon, smiles on their faces.

"No! Don't!" But it was too late. Corin tried to jump into the water, but his feet were superglued to the pontoon.

Time shifted into slow motion as the pontoon flipped. His stomach churned and he tried to suck in a breath before the water swallowed him, but his mouth was locked shut and a moment later he was under. The chill of the water threw its tentacles around him.

Sound vanished as he sank into the lake.

The dark water spun, like a whirlpool sucking him ten feet deeper in a blink. Then twenty, thirty. Corin forced his gaze upward. The light filtering down through the green water grew hazy, then vanished as the lake pulled him farther into the dark.

"No!" He tried to shout out but water surged into his mouth and lungs choking his cry. Then darkness. And nothingness. Always the nothingness. Thicker this time as if it had fingers pulling him down and pulling the life out of him.

Pulling his soul out of him.

CHAPTER 26

Corin pulled up to Professor Tesser Lange's home at 5:55 a.m., excited to see his old friend and glad he'd made it a few minutes early. The professor didn't like people to be late. Especially on the first day of the week. Or he didn't use to. Had it really been ten years since he'd seen the old man?

He'd meant to come by more often, but there was always something urgent pounding at him, keeping him from dropping by. Growing the business. Taking care of the business. Trips overseas to find exotic treasures people would pay thousands for, which translated into bread on his table and a car in his driveway. Going through his divorce. The tyranny of the urgent subduing the important and memorable.

Corin trod the walkway leading to Tesser's house and smiled. The home still needed painting. The dark brown paint was peeling in a thousand places. The lawn needed mowing. Strike that. The lawn needed a machete taken to it. His roof could probably be sold in Corin's store for a hefty price it looked so ancient.

Professor Ted C. Lange. Tesser hated the name Ted and had told his students on the first day of class to call him Tesser or nothing. He and Corin had struck up a friendship that grew from frequent visits in the professor's office at the university into dinners at his home that lasted late into the night into three trips together to Italy, Greece, and Spain.

Corin saluted as he climbed the cracked steps leading to Tesser's front door. It was good to be back.

Corin pushed the doorbell right at the same moment he noticed a tiny sticky note in the middle of the door.

Come in, Corin; it's always unlocked, you know that.

He did. They'd argued countless times about Tesser leaving his door unlocked even when he went on trips. Corin tried to convince him that with the valuable volumes on his shelves and priceless artifacts stored in glass cases throughout his home, it was like giving a standing invitation to people with no interest in respecting other people's property.

But the professor said if people wanted the books and antiques that bad, they could have them.

The door squealed as Corin pushed it open, but not as loudly as he expected it to. Maybe Tesser had discovered WD-40 in his old age. "Professor?"

No answer.

He glanced around the large entryway to a dark wooden staircase curving up to the four bedrooms no one slept in to the hallway to the left leading to a vast kitchen that probably hadn't seen a meal cooked in it for over five years.

And the hallway to the right, leading to Tesser's massive library and study, where high odds said he'd find the old professor bent over an even older book.

Corin tiptoed—he wasn't sure why—down the corridor and peeked in each room on his right and left as he passed. Nothing had changed. The smell of musty books floated through the air and he breathed in memories of pouring over hundreds of those tomes with Tesser during his college days.

"Tesser? Are you here?"

All was dark wood, and though a number of lights were on, the house still felt like it was lit with forty-watt bulbs when it should have one hundred watters in the sockets.

He was almost to the study and still no answer. "Professor?"

"Coming!" A voice finally called out from the study.

Tesser was at least ninety years old. He wore white slippers, yellowed with age, that were at least two sizes too big for his feet, which made him shuffle when he walked. The public never saw him without his tattered baseball hat with *Find It!* stenciled across the front, wispy white hair sticking out from underneath it in all directions.

Behind his back they called him eccentric.

To his face they called him brilliant.

Tesser was both.

No one meeting him for the first time would guess Googling his name would pull up 10,543 entries and an extensive Wikipedia entry.

When Tesser and he used to frequent coffee stands together, the old professor often brought a stack of newspapers to sell to tourists in town for a smile and a memory. He'd pepper the people with jokes, tell them he was famous and to look him up on the Internet.

Corin tried to imagine the looks on the faces of those who did do a Google search. What did they say when they discovered the person they thought was a homeless man peddling newspapers to survive was really a renowned professor revered in academic circles?

Gold wire-rimmed glasses—more silver than gold where the color had worn off—sat halfway down his miniature hawkish nose. As soon as Tesser spotted Corin he stopped and cocked his head. "You're on time."

"I'm trying to form a new habit."

"Excellent. I'm working on a few right now myself." He ran his palms down the sides of his cheeks. "You'll notice I shaved today. That's twice this week alone."

"Congratulations."

He shuffled over to Corin, reached up, and patted him on the shoulder. "You look sprightly."

"That was going to be my line."

Tesser laughed. "No, I look old."

It wasn't true. At least no older than when Corin had last seen him. It seemed some people hit a certain age, and as the ravages of time passed, it didn't cause them to look older.

"Look, look, look." Tesser pointed to a series of photos lining the wall to Corin's left.

"What?"

"That one in the middle."

Corin squinted. Tesser and he were toasting each other with glasses of red wine.

"Was that Italy?"

"Yes, good memory." Tesser grabbed his elbow and led him back the way he'd come. "A fine trip that was, yes? Pompeii was a highlight. As was Capri. Although I didn't get to the Blue Grotto with you. I should have gone."

"It was the trip of a lifetime." Corin glanced at the other photos on the wall. "What's this one?" He pointed to a grainy picture on the far right.

"Munich 1972."

Corin stared closer at the picture. "Is this from the hostage crisis?"

"Yes, yes, what a fiasco that turned out to be."

"I'd describe it as more than a fiasco."

"Horrible mess." Tesser rubbed his forehead and looked at the ground.

After ten minutes of catching up, the professor clasped his hands. "We'll do more chitchat later, but I think it's time to talk serious."

"About?"

Tesser rolled his eyes. "Your mystery!"

"Right."

Corin pulled the photos of the chair he'd taken the day before out of his briefcase and handed them to his old friend.

Tesser stared at them for over a minute in silence. "Whew." He squinted up at Corin from under his glasses for a moment, then turned back to the photos. "You've got something here all right."

"What?"

"Amazing. When did you take these?"

"Just last night. With my cell phone."

"These were taken with your cell phone?" Tesser stared at him with suspicion. The old professor poked at them with a vintage Waterman pen, then pulled a magnifying glass out of his oak desk and studied each picture again.

"Well?" Corin said.

"Fascinating." He set down the photos with a look of amazement on his face. "Utterly fascinating."

"Tell me." Corin's heart pounded. Finally it seemed he'd get answers about the chair. "What?"

"It's truly incredible what I'm seeing here."

"I got that part. Talk to me." Corin leaned in. "What's incredible?"

"That these photos could be taken with a phone." Tesser tapped one of the photos again. "The detail is astounding."

Corin let his head fall back and he groaned. "Tesser, I need to get your thoughts about the *chair*. Where it came from, who could have made it, how old it is."

Tesser laughed. "You used to enjoy my playful side."

"I still do, but can we get to the subject of the pictures?"

"Of course." Tesser picked up the photos and lined them up next to each other in a row. "This is an unusual chair."

"I figured that part out on my own."

"Where did you get it?" Tesser stroked the sparse clumps of hair coming out of his chin he called a goatee.

"An elderly lady showed up one day and dropped it off at my shop with no explanation."

"A lady?"

"Yes."

Tesser scratched the tip of his nose and was silent for a long time. "She said nothing?"

"Not really."

"Tell me what she said when she gave you the chair." He pulled his glasses off his face—the first time Corin had ever seen him do it—and rubbed his ninety-two-year-old eyes. "Her exact words."

As Corin told Tesser what the lady had said, he gave slight nods and motioned with his hand toward his head as if to invite every word into his mind. When he'd finished Tesser stood and paced in front of the fireplace rubbing his hands and muttering to himself.

After a few minutes of pacing he stopped and drilled Corin with his eyes. "Did she say why she was giving it to *you*?"

"Something about I was the one who should have it."

"Fascinating." A muted chuckle floated out of Tesser's mouth. "Anything else?"

Corin considered telling Tesser about the strange tingling sensation he'd felt when he touched the chair but decided against it.

"Did she say during what age the craftsman lived?"

"No, just that it was a long time ago."

Tesser picked at his lower lip for a few seconds, then spun and gazed at Corin. "What did she look like?"

"Did you see the Spider-Man movies?"

"No. Should I?"

Corin shook his head and described the woman. As he did, Tesser's eyes went wide then narrowed then back to wide.

"Hang on." Tesser grabbed a pencil and an artist's sketch pad. "Tell me again, with as much detail as you can remember."

As Corin described the lady again, Tesser's pencil dashed over the pad like a water skimmer in heat. When Tesser finished he held up the sketch to Corin. "Does this resemble her?"

Now Corin's eyes widened. The drawing depicted his elderly visitor with such precision, he was shocked at how fast Tesser had drawn her image.

Tesser tossed the sketch pad onto his desk and whistled. "I never thought this day would come." He pointed his forefinger in the air and smiled. "But I wanted it to."

"What day?"

Tesser pointed at the notebook. "I know her."

"What?"

"I mean, I don't know her." He coughed. "I didn't give in much to my hope they still existed—most think the last one died one hundred years ago—but I've always believed she was out there somewhere, waiting to reveal herself at the right time." Tesser patted his stomach in a quick rhythm. "Your friend bears a striking resemblance to the ladies in the book."

"What book?"

Tesser ignored his question. "I'd like to meet her."

"What is she?"

"She's a spiritual being . . ." Tesser seemed to consider his words carefully "She's the holder of a spiritual legacy."

"You're saying she's an angel?"

"No, no." Tesser waved his hands high in the air and shook his head. "Not like an angel. She's as human as you and I. But she's been chosen by God. This lady friend of yours could be the one. She certainly could be."

Tesser shuffled off at twice his normal gait toward a large stack of books in the far corner of his office next to the door. "When I show you this book, it'll feel like two tectonic plates have snapped into place inside your mind." When he reached the stack he took a hard right and trundled out the door and into the hallway.

"Where are you going?" Corin leaned to his left to see if Tesser was going to stop. "Am I supposed to follow you?"

"Bathroom first, solving the mystery second. Not solving it. I've already done that. Explaining it, showing you what I know about that chair of yours. That's what I meant."

Corin looked at the ceiling and shook his head. Tesser was on an intellectual level with Hawking but on a social level with Mr. Magoo.

Tesser trudged back in rubbing his head through his baseball hat. "Ah, I feel better. Do you?"

"I didn't go to the bathroom."

"Right, of course." Tesser winked at him and pulled a small wooden step up against the middle of the shelves along the back wall. He strained to reach the highest shelf, balancing on one foot, and teetered like he was seconds from falling.

"I can help you get that if you want," Corin said.

"Now where is that smiggily tome?" He yanked two thick books off the shelf and let them tumble to the hardwood.

Wham! Wham!

They sounded like gunshots as they hit the floor.

For a man who revered books, Tesser didn't show much respect for those that filled his library.

As if reading Corin's mind Tesser said, "Those books are now rubbish. Disproven three times over. But at the time they were published, people, me included, revered them." He drew his fingers along the books one shelf down. "Makes one wonder what books we bow down to today will be thrown on the fire tomorrow, doesn't it?"

"Sure."

A few seconds later Tesser pulled a thick volume off the shelf and stroked the cover. "Ah yes. Here it is. Please don't drop it." He held it up for Corin to see, then tossed it toward him like a Frisbee.

Corin stuttered forward and caught the book just before it struck the floor. The title of the book was written in faded jade calligraphy. Underneath was a subtitle. "What is this?"

"It might help us. You, I mean. Understand what your chair is all about. I've already read it."

Corin pointed to the cover. "It would help if *I* could read it. What's the translation?"

"It's Latin and roughly translated says, '*Ladies of the Christ Chair: Order of the Ones Who Are Known 1785–1969.*' There are other volumes of course." Tesser creaked down from the step onto the floor. "But that's the only one I can easily get to. The others are locked away."

Corin's body tingled as if his skin was being peppered with mild electric shocks. Unbelievable. The chair legend was real. "I Googled everything I could think of having to do with a chair Christ made and didn't find—"

"Pshaw." Tesser waved at Corin and scowled. "Everyone thinks typing a few words into Google and hitting return is research. No one looks in books or libraries anymore. It would take too much time. Wikipedia is the teacher of the world, without the credentials to back it up." Tesser stared at Corin. "Hmm?"

Corin ignored the comment. "So there really is a fully formed legend about the chair."

"Yes, absolutely of course, of course, as you can see from the book in your hand. The Holy Grail gets all the press, but there are other legends of other artifacts surrounding Christ that have been passed down through the ages—things He touched, or used during His time on earth—along with one about a certain chair." Tesser held out his hand. "Let me see that."

Corin handed him the book and the professor thumbed through its pages, stopping on some for a few seconds, flipping through others with only a short glance. When he got about halfway through he set the book down and pointed to a line drawing. Corin blinked. It was Nicole.

"Unbelievable. That's the lady who gave me the chair."

"Uh-huh, uh-huh, yep, that's right." Tesser rubbed his chin and nodded in double-time. "You've found her or she's found you. Can you get to her?"

"No. She e-mailed me and I wrote back asking to meet, but so far she hasn't written back."

"Let's hope she does." Tesser picked up the book again. "Guess what the legend says about the chair?"

"Tell me."

"It isn't just a chair that Christ made." Tesser's face sobered. "It is supposedly a chair Christ sat in after He rose from the dead and appeared to the Twelve. The same meeting where Thomas had said he wouldn't believe till he saw the scars in Christ's hands. And the legend says it's a chair that contains all His power." Tesser got a distant look in his eyes.

"You're kidding." Heat washed through Corin as he thought of Brittan. Shasta. Was it possible?

"According to the legend He gave the chair to Peter before the Ascension. When Peter was crucified upside down, the chair was passed to John, who took it with him when he was banished to the island of Patmos."

"Do you think it could heal people?"

Tesser ran his fingers over the open pages and kept talking as if he didn't hear Corin. "Think about that. If only it were more than a legend. Christ's power placed in that chair." Tesser snapped his fingers and stared at Corin, bouncing slightly on his toes.

"Think about the army you could have if the legend were true!" Tesser swiped his hand through the air as if it held a sword. "No nation could stop that kind of power."

"So what supposedly happened to the chair after they tried to kill John by boiling him in oil?"

"I'm impressed. You do know a bit of church history."

"A very little bit." Corin held up his thumb and forefinger with a small space in between them. "I learned that in one of your classes."

"So you did listen off and on." Tesser thumbed through more of the book. "Just checking to see if my memory is accurate. Ah yes, here we go." He tapped a page three times. "Apparently after John miraculously survived the boiling incident, he and the chair went to Patmos, and after he died it stayed there, tucked away for over three hundred years till it slowly slipped from consciousness. It wasn't till early AD 400 when a small band of Christian women discovered the chair and bought it from the owner of the building in which it sat who didn't realize what he had. They formed a sect or an organization and called it *Custodis of Chair*, which in English means 'Keepers of the Chair.'"

Tesser turned another page. "Their goal was simple. Protect the chair. Keep its location secret. Use it only in times of great need."

"Use it?"

"Didn't you hear what I said about it containing Christ's healing power? They believed the chair had special powers. That is a key component of the legend. It was proof the chair was made by Christ."

"Such as?"

"The usual. Healings. Deep insights into the human condition. Visions given to people who sit in the chair. Seeing Christ appear as they sat in it, those sorts of things."

"And these things were written down?"

"Right here." Tesser picked up the book and waved it in the air.

"So where did the chair end up?"

Tesser spread his hands and chortled. "You have it."

"Seriously."

"I'm not kidding. Kind of not kidding. I mean, okay, I am kidding. I think. But who knows? Maybe you really have it sitting in your . . . ?"

"Someplace safe."

"Where is safe?"

"I appreciate the concern." Corin patted Tesser on the arm. "But don't worry; it's safe."

"Let's find out what supposedly happened to it before it was given to you." Tesser pawed through more of the book. "It might give us a clue as to whether your chair is one and the same." For a few minutes the only sound in the huge library was of Tesser turning pages. "Okay, here we go."

Corin stared at the seconds ticking off the Seth Thomas Queen Anne clock on Tesser's wall as the professor scoured centuries of legend.

"Here we be, yes indeed." Tesser repeatedly tapped the upper half of the page with his forefinger. "After the women found it on Patmos, they held it there, one generation passing it to the next.

Then around AD 820 the Catholic church heard of the legend and came after the chair. But the women were warned and took the chair to France.

"Throughout the subsequent generations, they claimed the chair had been passed down from mother to daughter along with the secrets of the chair and an oath to protect it above all else."

"And the lady who popped up on my doorstep is supposed to be a descendant of these ladies?"

"Apparently."

"Why come to America with the chair?" Corin meandered over to Tesser's fireplace and held his hands out to be warmed by the flames leaping off a large pile of cracking logs. "Wouldn't they want the chair close to the Holy Land? Why risk taking it across the ocean?"

"I'm sure it was a matter of debate among the ladies, but America makes sense." Tesser waved his hand over a map of the world that hung on the wall behind his maple desk. "I would guess the chair was brought over in the late 1850s. By that time the country was well established. Laws were in place to protect people's property. And if you were going to hide something from prying eyes, would you rather hide it in a country so vast it would take eons to search every nook and cranny?"

It made sense. Corin turned and let the flames from the fire warm his back. "Here there'd be fewer unscrupulous treasure hunters. The Holy Land is rife with them. And America was a place where fewer people had ever heard of the legend."

"Exactly. Then as the eastern seaboard filled up with people, they decided to take the chair to a place farther west."

"Why Colorado? Why not Seattle? Or Los Angeles?"

"It's just a guess, but with visions of gold swirling around every claim and every curve of the creek bed, why would someone bother to get excited about some old chair?" Tesser sat back and folded his hands across his chest. "And the chair continued to pass from mother to daughter."

"But now, the chain is broken with me."

"Maybe she doesn't have a daughter."

"But why me? I'm not ready to be a guardian of some miracle chair—"

"It's a legend, Corin!" Tesser laughed. "It would make a good movie, but it's fiction. You're not starting to take the healing part seriously, are you?"

Corin sighed as he stood and strolled back over to Tesser and sat next to his old friend. "No, of course not."

But he had. For a moment, as he thought about the lady's eyes and the intensity in them, he believed she could be the keeper of the genuine chair of Christ. That her ancestors formed an order that had passed a chair from one generation to the next for over sixteen hundred years. If a chair built by Jesus still existed, Corin would vote her as curator. And when he read the story about Brittan being healed, he'd believed for more than a moment.

Tesser patted Corin's knee. "For this next part, take a deep breath, all right?"

"Why?"

"You'll see."

Tesser turned to the middle of the book and spread the pages with both palms but didn't lift them for Corin to see. "Ready?"

"For?"

Tesser lifted his hands slowly as if he were a conductor raising his baton to start a symphony.

Corin leaned forward and looked at the four sketches on the pages. "Oh, wow." He fell back in his chair as heat instantly raced to every corner of his body. The drawings—drawn from four angles— were exact representations of the chair locked in his basement.

"That's my chair."

"Yes, I know." Tesser held up the photos Corin had given him earlier and gazed at them. "See why I'm saying your chair could be the one in the legend?"

"Whew." Corin rubbed his forehead and let out a long breath. He stared at the drawings. There were two possibilities, maybe three. His was the chair of legend, it was a duplicate made from these drawings—he couldn't think of a third option.

"You wanted a little excitement in your life, right?"

"I didn't say that."

"Oh sure you do. Everyone needs a little excitement now and again." Tesser rubbed his hands together as his head bobbed.

"Do you?"

"Yes, and you've just given it to me. One more adventure to go on."

"And if the chair turns out to be the real thing?"

"Why I'll sit in it and live forever." Tesser smiled.

"You think it can cure death? That the power in the chair means—?"

"No, Corin." Tesser patted Corin's hands again. "Fiction, remember? But humor an old man, eh? I won't believe in the chair's healing power till I see it with my own eyes, but I'm certainly fascinated by the legend. And even if your chair is only a duplicate made from these drawings . . ."—he laid his palm on the book—"we'll have fun tracking down this mysterious lady. Find out if she's real or a fake. And figure out why she gave the chair to you."

"Is there anything else I need to know about the legend?"

"Yes, I think so." Tesser closed the book and waddled over to his old maple desk, set it down, and patted it once. Then he sat and picked up a stack of mail.

"Well? Are you going to tell me?"

Tesser glanced up as if seeing Corin for the first time that day. "Let's save something for next time, hmm? I think you have enough to digest for one day. But we should get together again soon." He glanced at the book. "I'll read through it again during the coming week and see if the other things I remember being between its covers are indeed still recorded there."

Corin was tempted to tell Tesser to read through it in the coming *day*, but he stayed silent and left without comment.

CORIN DROVE AWAY from the professor's house with conflicting emotions bouncing through his mind. Could this really be happening? Could such things as a chair containing Christ's power really exist? Ridiculous. But hadn't Brittan been healed?

He got to his store just in time to open but got little accomplished all day. He couldn't stop thinking about the chair sitting in his basement.

By the time he locked the store's front door and climbed into his Highlander, it was close to eight thirty. Time to head home and crash.

As Corin pulled out of the parking lot, he glanced at his cell phone. Whoops. He'd left it in the car all day. He picked it up and pushed the bottom to pull it out of hibernation. Wow. Five voice mails had come in while he was at the store. He pushed the recorded messages icon and stared at the little red dots seeming to scream for attention. All five calls were from Travis DeMiglio. That could only mean one thing.

The results of the carbon dating had shocked him.

CHAPTER 27

Corin played the first message: "It's Travis; I have your results. Very strange. Call me ASAP."

He deleted the call and played Travis's next message.

"It's Travis again. Call me about what I found out about your piece as soon as you get this. I've never seen anything like it."

Delete.

"Corin, sorry to bug you, but we have to talk about this chair of yours. It's weird."

Corin pulled into traffic and cued up the next message.

"Travis again. Listen, I ran the tests again and they came back even weirder. Let's talk as soon as you can."

He played the last message.

"Corin? Travis. I want to see that chair. Call me."

He glanced at his watch: 8:35. Travis had probably left the lab at least two hours ago, but what could it hurt to try? He could at least leave a message. He tapped Call Back on his phone and waited for his Bluetooth to kick in. A moment later Travis answered.

"Hello?"

"Hey, you're still there—"

"Tell me all about this chair, Corin. Where you got it, how long you've had it, where it's from, what it's made of—forget that last part I know what it's made of—but I want to know everything else."

It almost sounded like Travis was panting through the phone. "Are you all right?"

"Yes." Travis's pen or pencil was tapping on a hard surface sounding like a woodpecker through the phone. "Not exactly."

"You're all worked up over some lab results?" Corin heard papers shuffling in the background and then something crash to the floor. It wasn't like Travis. He was organized to a fault. "You okay?"

"Fine, just dropped some papers. And my briefcase."

"You're not drunk, are you?"

"Hah."

"Whatever you found really has you flummoxed."

"You could say that. More excited than anything else."

"About the results from testing my chair."

"Yes." Travis sighed through the phone and stopped talking.

"Are you going to tell me?"

"I'm just trying to figure out where to begin." For ten seconds the only sound was the hum of the phone. "How important is this chair to you?"

"Important."

"Something you want to keep?"

Corin considered the question. Before he'd met with Tesser? He might have sold it if he could get some serious money. But now? No way. He wasn't letting go.

"Definitely want to keep it." Corin swerved around a slow-moving dark blue Infiniti G35. Those cars were fast. What was the guy doing going forty in a forty mph zone? "So tell me."

"No actually, I'm not going to tell you."

"What?"

"Not over the phone I mean. We need to do this face-to-face, all right?"

"What, you think your phone is bugged?"

"In person."

"Fine. When?"

"Now."

"You're forty-five minutes away from me and it's eight forty-five. You sure?" Corin hoped Travis would say yes. He didn't want to wait to find out what Travis had discovered.

"If you meet me halfway, it will only be twenty-two minutes and thirty seconds for each of us."

"Where?"

"Palmer Park. West end."

"A park? Why a park? Why not a restaurant where we can get a drink and catch up?"

"You're not getting it, are you? There's some weird stuff going on around the piece you gave me." Travis paused. "Very weird."

"Okay, see you in twenty minutes."

Travis was a scientist. Logical. Not easily blown by the winds of emotion. But something about the chair was pounding gale force winds at his friend's sails.

The saga of the chair was growing stranger by the hour.

CORIN PARKED HIS car and walked toward the west end of the park. Before he'd walked thirty yards he spotted Travis standing under the going golden leaves of an aspen tree, glancing furtively around the park and up at the trees, as if the squirrels were about to start firing missiles his direction.

Corin sauntered up behind Travis and tapped him on the shoulder.

"Whaaaaa!" Travis spun and popped Corin on his shoulders with the palms of both hands. "Don't do that!"

Corin laughed and shoved his hands into his 501s. "Sorry, all this cloak-and-dagger stuff brings out the practical joker in me."

Actually it didn't bring out the joker, it brought out the formidable Stress Man, able to double Corin's heart rate in a single bound. Sneaking up on Travis, keeping the moment light, should keep his foe subdued, but something told him the carbon dating info he was about to learn would wake Stress Man back up again.

"This isn't a joke."

"What isn't?"

"Your chair."

"Yeah, I get that part. Something has you a little spooked. So why don't you let me get behind the curtain with you and maybe I'll join you in your paranoia."

"I'm not spooked and I'm not paranoid. I just want to make sure our conversation stays between the two of us."

Corin pulled a small piece of bark off the tree. He wouldn't be telling anyone. Maybe Tesser. "I'm guessing my chair is older than this aspen?"

"I'm not sure."

"What does that mean?"

"It's the strangest thing I've ever seen." Travis rubbed the sides of his nose and tried to smile. "I'm not even 10 percent sure."

"What does that mean?" Corin repeated.

"We ran the test eighteen times and got eighteen different results."

"Is that possible?"

"No." Travis dug in his ear so hard Corin thought his friend would lose his finger.

"You're saying you got eighteen different ages?"

Travis nodded.

"From the same piece of wood?"

"Yes."

"What was the oldest date?"

"Over thirty thousand." Travis said it more as a question than a statement.

"Years old?"

"Yes."

"You're joking." Corin leaned forward to be able to see Travis's eyes.

"No."

"And the youngest?"

"Today."

"What?"

Travis rocked his head back and forth as if he were a bobble-head doll. "The tests came back saying the wood from the chair came from wood harvested sometime in the past year."

"That's insane."

"Now do you see why I called you incessantly?" Travis held his fist up to his ear as if it were a phone.

"And the dating ages in between?"

"Five thousand five hundred years, three hundred and seventy-five years, thirty years . . . like I said, each time the results were different."

"How can that happen?"

"It can't."

"Never?" Corin paced. Three steps to the right, then three back to the left.

"And one of the tests came back 50K plus."

"Meaning?" Corin rubbed the bark on his chin, just hard enough to register an unpleasant sensation.

"Our dating can project back forty five to fifty thousand years. Anything older we classify as greater than 50K." Travis opened his hands and tilted his head.

"You're saying the reading came back saying this piece is older than your instruments can date it?"

"Exactly."

Corin stopped pacing. "Explain."

"There's nothing to explain. The reading says this piece of wood is fifty thousand years old or maybe a million years old."

"What does that mean?"

"It means everyone around here is begging to have whatever that piece came from brought in here."

"You weren't supposed to tell anyone you were testing this. I thought my e-mail made that clear." Corin broke the strip of bark into pieces and tossed them to the ground.

"I couldn't help it. We typically run three nine minute tests and average the three to determine the age of the object. They're usually within a few years of each other. So when your readings started bouncing all over the universe, well, people noticed."

"I don't need anyone else noticing." Corin kicked at a small pile of leaves on the ground.

"Where did you get that chair?"

"It was given to me."

"By who?"

"Some lady named Nicole."

"Have you talked to her since then?"

"Not really. She sent me an e-mail. That's it."

"Do you have a way to get a hold of her?"

"No."

The implications of Travis's findings swirled through Corin's head. Of course a chair imbued with the essence of God would have no age and every age. If Christ had made the chair and Tesser was right—that Jesus's power flowed throughout it—wouldn't the chair somehow be outside of time?

"What would the age of the chair be if you took an average?"

"There's no point in doing—."

"But if you did."

"Well . . ." Travis's gaze moved up and to the right. Corin almost expected smoke to come streaming out of the man's head. He was a human computer. He had all the results packed into his brain and his mental hard drive was accessing the data and crunching numbers.

"The average would be two thousand years old."

Corin let out a puff of a laugh. "That makes perfect sense. If the chair was built by a certain carpenter."

"What?"

"This Nicole lady who gave me the chair called him a carpenter."

"Who was a carpenter?"

"The guy who made the chair. Two thousand years ago."

"Two thousand years ago? That's good." Travis laughed. "Next you're going to tell me Jesus Christ was the carpenter in question and part of the family business was making tables and chairs and you're the proud owner of one of His dining room creations." Nervous laughter sputtered out of Travis.

Corin stared at his friend.

"No, you're joking."

Corin shook his head.

"Seriously?"

Corin shook his head again. "I'm beginning to believe."

"No wonder you wanted me to keep it quiet."

Corin peeled another piece of bark from the tree. "You didn't tell them what the sliver was from?"

"I told you I wouldn't."

"*Danka.*"

"What?"

"It means 'thank you' in German. I got in the habit of saying it back in high school when I learned the language and sometimes it still slips out."

"Sorry to hear that." Travis grinned and scrubbed his thinning brown hair with his fingers. "But I should tell you, toward the end of the day I overheard a phone call that sure sounded like the person on the other end was asking about your chair."

"What?"

"Yeah."

Corin popped the tree like it was one of Tori's workout bags. Great. Another chair stalker. "Tell me who called."

"I only heard one end of the conversation."

"What did you hear?"

"My boss was saying we test a variety of things, but if the person wanted to call back in a few days, he'd let them know the items that have been tested during the past week. It seemed like he knew the caller."

"Is your boss religious?"

"Yeah, how'd you know that?"

"Lucky guess." Corin jammed his hands in his pocket and bit his lower lip. His cell's ring tone sliced through the night air. He glanced at caller ID. It was A. C. He let it go.

"There's a pastor from Southern California who is overly interested in this chair." Corin glanced around the park. "And you know that story the other day about the kid being healed of his asthma?"

"No."

Corin rolled his eyes. "Doesn't anyone read the news anymore?"

"I don't have time."

Corin gave Travis the *Reader's Digest* version.

"So even if the chair wasn't the thing that healed him—"

"If the dating of the chair thing gets out, combined with the insinuation that it healed the kid, it'll have the religious nutcases storming my store like it's the Bastille."

"I hope it's no longer in your store."

"It isn't."

"I gotta get going." Travis pointed over Corin's shoulder at the parking lot and they walked toward it. "If it's genuine it could also be worth a lot of money."

"If it's real it's priceless."

"How is your store doing these days?"

"I could use the money." Use? Had to have was more accurate. For the store. For Shasta. For any hope of a future.

"So why not sell it for everything you can?"

"It's a serious consideration."

"You should."

"Why?"

"A lot of potential money mixed with religious zealots often means people winding up dead."

"I've thought of that too." Corin glanced around the parking lot, not sure what he was looking for.

"And if the chair really does have power to heal people—you're in over your head."

"So far it's just an idea. No proof." Unless you counted the kid, which Corin was willing to do, but coincidences were a part of life, maybe even more than miracles.

"For your sake I hope it stays just a legend."

Corin's cell phone vibrated. Text message. From A. C.

WE NEED TO TALK. I'M FINE, JUST A LITTLE
WEIRDED OUT. CALL ME IF YOU'RE STILL
AWAKE.

A wave of heat passed through Corin's body. He turned to Travis. "I'm sure that's all it'll end up being."

They reached their cars.

"Then how do you explain the results I got at the lab?"

"I have no idea."

"Keep me posted on this thing, Corin."

"Absolutely."

Corin drove out of the parking lot and hit one of the new favorite numbers on his cell phone.

"Hello there, Tesser, everyone's favorite professor."

"You need to get a new line. That one's wearing so thin it's translucent."

"The better to see me with, my dear." Tesser coughed. "How are you, Corin? How is the quest going?"

"Getting weirder."

"That's good."

"Good?"

"When you're ninety-two you'll hope for weird things to make life interesting just like I do. What's the latest?"

"The age of the chair."

"You want to know how old it is?"

"Since you know all about this chair, how old do you think it is?"

"If it's genuine, we know how old it is. At least within a few years."

"So you're saying my having it carbon dated was a waste of time?"

"No, you didn't take a piece off the chair. Tell me you didn't. Not smart. Not wise. Foolish to the fifth! To the ninth. To the googolplex."

"It was a small piece, Tesser."

"How small?"

"It's just wood."

"If it's the real McCoy, you've just desecrated a chair made by the Son of God. What idiot told you to have it carbon dated?"

"Me."

"Fffffffffhhh." The sound coming through the phone sounded like the air had been let out of a tractor tire. "Aren't you far enough down this path to realize it could very likely be much more than just a chunk-a-hunk of wood?"

"No. One minute I think it's real, the next moment I'm not sure."

"Oh, for crying in my ice cream Sunday with a gallon of Hershey's syrup on top. Yes, you are."

Corin sighed. "Do you want to know what the carbon dating says?"

"I don't need to."

"Why, because if Jesus made the chair the carbon dating will show that it's two thousand years old?"

"Precisely."

"The year Jesus was born."

"Most competent historians place the birth of Christ around 4 or 5 BC, not the year AD 1. When the church decided to assimilate one of the pagan holidays, they moved—"

"Tesser, I love your history lessons, but can we focus on the chair?"

"Yes, yes, of course."

"So does this mean it's real?"

"The evidence is building. I'm not saying it has healing powers, but I'm certainly saying you might have a genuine religious artifact that was made by the historical figure known as Jesus Christ."

Corin's cell phone buzzed again. He glanced down. A. C. again.

GOING TO BED. WILL BE AT YOUR STORE
FIRST THING IN THE MORNING. I HAVE TO
TALK TO YOU. PLEASE BE THERE.

"Tesser, I gotta go, I'll call you tomorrow."

Corin hung up and called A. C. No answer. Must have turned his ringer off as soon as he sent the text.

A. C. wasn't easily bothered, but he was bothered about something now.

And Corin would be there first thing to find out what it was.

CHAPTER 28

Y ou all right? Your face is acting like a split personality," Corin said as he approached his store.

A. C. stood at the front door, the expression on his face shifting from bewilderment to joy back to confusion every few seconds.

"Fine. I'm good." A. C. shifted his weight from one leg to the other and rubbed his shoulder.

"Then why'd you say you were freaked yesterday and why do you want to talk first thing this morning?" Corin opened the front door and they walked inside.

"Something has happened."

"To you?"

"Yeah." The alternating emotions on A. C.'s face morphed into an all-out grin.

"And the cause of your apparent happiness?" Corin flicked the switch on the coffee maker behind his sales counter.

"You," A. C.'s eyes fixed on Corin, "and the chair."

Corin sucked in a quick breath. "Talk to me. What happened?"

"It worked."

A chill played rugby up and down Corin's back as he studied A. C.'s eyes. Was his friend trying to be funny? Hardly, it wasn't A. C.'s style. It wasn't a joke; A. C. was serious.

"You're saying you're healed."

"Yep."

"You're no longer scared of public speaking?"

"Yes." A. C. rubbed his left ear, his eyes full of laughter.

"Yes what? You're still scared? Or you're not scared?"

"I'm still not a fan of getting up in front of a crowd of more than one person."

Corin's heart rate settled back to normal. "I'm not following you. I thought you said the chair healed you and you're ready to go out on the speaking circuit."

"Not exactly." A. C. ambled to the vault at the back of the store and glanced inside. "Where is the chair?"

"I took it home and locked it up."

"Good idea."

"Why do you say that?"

"You need to keep it in a safe place." A. C. walked back to Corin and settled into a Hepplewhite dining chair from the early 1900s. "I've never been a religious person, but if God were to come down out of the sky and fill me up with Himself, sitting in that chair is what I think it would feel like."

"What are you saying?"

"As soon as you left me alone the other day, the chair started giving off this electrical charge or something—I felt like I was wrapped up in this ocean of warmth and peace. Wow, it felt good. Then this light sweeps around the room—yeah, I know light doesn't sweep a room like that; I'm just telling you what I saw."

A. C. closed his eyes "It was like a merry-go-round made of light, and I was in the middle slowly spinning as the outside of the ride whipped by like cars at the Indianapolis 500."

"Why didn't you tell me about this?"

"Because I didn't know if I'd imagined it or not." He laughed. "And I didn't want you to ask what kind of mushrooms I had on my omelet that morning."

Corin poured himself a cup of coffee into his Thor coffee cup and offered A. C. some as well.

A. C. shifted in his chair. "You know why I didn't end up playing pro ball, right?"

"You blew out something, your knee if I remember correctly."

"Shoulder." A. C. squeezed his left shoulder and stared at Corin. "It never healed right and I couldn't hit like I used to. Cortisone shots, physical therapy, three operations. Nothing helped. I couldn't get used to the pain shooting through my shoulder every time I crunched a running back. I missed my window." He pushed on his shoulder with his fingers and gave tiny shakes of his head.

Where was A. C. going with this? That's why A. C. was freaked out? Because he got some spiritual buzz? Because his brain played a few tricks on him while he sat in the chair? Corin opened the blinds and let the October sun stream in and light up the dust particles swirling through air. "I need to change the air filter again."

"Listen to me, Cor."

He turned toward A. C., then back to the blinds. "I'm listening."

"No, look at me."

Corin faced him and gazed into eyes more intense than he'd ever seen in A. C.

"In all the years I've worked concrete or helped you haul furniture back and forth, I've never lifted anything without a dull ache reminding me of that shoulder injury."

Corin sat and took a drink of his coffee as he realized what his friend was about to tell him. Tesser's words reverberated in his mind: *"Healing power."*

A. C. stood and grabbed a Sheraton Revival mahogany coffee table with his left hand and hoisted it over his head. "No ache."

Corin stared at his friend.

A. C. set the table down and grasped his shoulder again. "I went to the gym this morning and benched 350 pounds. No pain, not even a shadow."

"You're telling me—"

"It's healed."

"You're serious."

"You've got something in your house," A. C. jerked his thumb to the north, "that's out of control."

Heat surged through Corin's body. It worked; it had healed again.

And this time it wasn't some kid he didn't know.

He needed to find Nicole. He needed answers. And he needed them now.

CHAPTER 29

C orin sent Nicole three e-mail messages before he closed the store and another just before leaving to meet Tori for dinner at Dale Street Bistro Café.

No response to the first three. Probably not to the fourth either. On the way he called Tesser.

"It healed your friend?" Tesser's breathing quickened through the phone. "Are you sure?"

"If A. C. says his shoulder is healed, it's healed."

Tesser let out a long, low whistle. "You need to get that chair in a safe spot." Tesser coughed. "You should bring it to my house."

"Don't worry, it's safe.

"Good, good."

"What do I do now?"

Corin could hear Tesser clicking his pen like a metronome set on high speed. "You should contact the lady."

"I'm working on it."

"I'm headed out of town for a few days, but we need to meet again as soon as I'm back."

"Agreed."

"And, Corin?"

"Yeah."

"Trust no one. I mean that."

Corin hung up and weaved through traffic as the image of his brother kept pounding through his brain. A chair of healing. Since it had healed A. C., it could heal Shasta. Couldn't it? But the chair didn't heal A. C. of public speaking; it chose to heal something else. The thing seemed to have written its own agenda. It wasn't a comforting thought because that agenda might contain items he would want sent to the paper shredder.

TORI WAS ALREADY seated at a table when he arrived. "Don't worry, you're not late. I was early."

Corin sat and pulled his napkin off the table. "How were your classes today?"

"Same as always."

"You're bored?"

"A little. The gold is wearing off this adventure a little bit."

"Then come join mine. It's getting more intense every day."

"No thanks." Her eyes told him she knew exactly what adventure he was talking about and she didn't want any part of it.

After their waitress came and took their order, Corin said, "I think there's something to this chair thing, Tori."

"What makes you say that?" She slumped back in her seat.

"A. C."

"What, he got healed or something?"

Corin nodded.

"Come on, you're not serious." She shoved her knife toward him and scowled.

"He walked into the store this morning and laid the whole thing out. He sits in the chair, starts feeling all warm and fuzzy. A few hours later the pain in his shoulder from an old football injury? Claims it's gone."

"And you believe him?"

"He lifted a hundred pound coffee table over his head with his bad shoulder, no pain."

"And you believe he did it without hurting?"

"He's lying to me?"

"No, I think he's convinced himself the pain doesn't exist." Tori tore off a piece of sourdough bread from the loaf in the middle of the table and dipped it in a mixture of oil and balsamic vinegar. "What was it you told me about A. C.'s wife? That she was dead set against him doing UFC because of his old shoulder injury?"

"So?"

"So? So?" Tori smirked. "Haven't you heard of cortisone? He tells his wife about his best friend's magical chair, then a few days later gets a cortisone shot in his shoulder, then goes home and shows his wife how he's been healed so now he can fight."

"Why would he lie to me?"

"A secret is kept by one."

"A. C. wouldn't lie to me."

"Uh-huh."

"What about Tesser and his verification of a legendary chair being passed down since the time of Christ?"

"Who is Tesser?"

Right. He hadn't told her. Corin explained who Tesser was and what he'd revealed about the chair. "There's enough evidence piling up here that I have to be open to it being real. First the kid with the asthma, now A. C. I'm supposed to ignore that?"

The waitress brought their order and they ate in silence. Tori would fight him all the way on this thing and he still didn't know why. Sure, she decided to leave the church because she was tired of Christians being hypocrites. But there had to be more to it than that. She wasn't indifferent. Under the surface she was hostile. What happened to her?

He stabbed a baby red potato with the tip of his steak knife. "If this chair contains genuine healing power, then it's hard not to conclude God is real."

Tori averted her eyes and sliced off another piece of her halibut. "Can we for once talk about something other than that chair of yours?" She dropped her fork and it clanged against her plate. "I have to use the restroom. When I get back I'm sure we're going to talk about something else."

So be it. It wasn't his goal to tear off whatever scab covered her abhorrence of God, but at some point the time would be right. If he was going to have a future with Tori, he needed to know what it was.

After Tori returned, her usual brightness had reemerged, and she smiled at him, any hint of animosity had vanished. "Let's talk about this professor of yours. You've never told me about him."

"I haven't seen him for eons."

"He had a major impact on you."

"Why do you say that?"

"I can see it here when you talk about him." Tori reached across the table and wiggled her finger in front of his eyes. "Admiration. Respect. Fondness."

"Yeah, I liked the guy. Still like him."

"I think it's deeper than that."

"What do you mean?"

"I mean I'm using my college degree at the moment."

"Psychology."

"You had dad issues, didn't you?" She winked at him.

"What?"

"You know, dad issues. He wasn't there or was there and was always drunk or didn't pay attention to you or beat you up verbally or physically."

Corin shook his head.

"Every man has dad issues." Tori took a long drink of her water.

"I didn't have a father for very long. He died when I was twelve." Corin offered a weak grin. "So no issues here."

"Classic!" Tori smacked the table with both hands. "You have the ol' didn't-have-a-dad-as-a-teenager-on-up syndrome so you looked for father figures most of your life, and none of them could measure up to your romanticized fueled-by-the-movies image of what a father would be . . . until you met Tesser. And since you were mature enough by that point to realize no man could be the perfect father, Tesser became the dad you always wanted even with his faults, and you and he lived happily ever after."

"Do you enjoy psychoanalyzing people?"

"Thoroughly."

"Fun hobby." Corin finished his steak and pushed his plate back.

"Am I right? Did you look for father figures?"

She was dead right. Tesser was the closest thing he'd had to a dad, and he'd be loyal to the old professor forever because of it.

"We only spent five or six years really hanging out, but yeah, it was good."

"During and after college?"

Corin nodded.

"Why'd it stop? What happened?"

"Nothing happened. We saw each other three or four times a year after I graduated, but then I stopped calling as much or he did, and we gradually wound up just talking on the phone every few years. Then it sort of trailed off."

"You don't resent him for fading out of your life?"

"Resent him? No. Do I regret not being with him more? Do I regret not picking up the phone or dropping by to see him more often? Sure. But that's my fault, not his."

"Your fault?"

Corin shook his head. "He's been a great friend. There for me whether I called or not."

"He could have called you. Dads are supposed to pursue sons, not the other way around."

"He did. And I got busy with life and marriage and would forget to return the call, or I'd put it on my to-do list and never get to it." Corin slipped his credit card to the edge of the table. "Like I said, my fault."

"Have you ever told him how you feel? What he meant to you, what he probably still means to you?"

"No." Corin folded his arms. It might be fun for her—pitching him all these probing questions—but it felt like he was the baseball and Tori was the bat. "Don't you think it's about time to tell him?"

"No."

"Why not?"

It was the obvious question. Without an obvious answer. The real reason? Because he was making excuses for Tesser and had just lied to Tori. Tesser hadn't called after college. Corin had. And Tesser was the one who was poor at returning phone calls. Finally Corin got tired of being the one who picked up the phone and he stopped. He figured Tesser would eventually call, but after a year crawled by, Corin realized he never would. So he stuffed the father figure into the back closet of his heart and hadn't opened the door again till he'd been inside Tesser's home yesterday.

But it was okay. Truly. It didn't matter if Tesser had called him or not. Corin still loved the guy. And he could tell Tesser's affection for him had never changed. Being with him yesterday had confirmed it.

Corin smiled. "Tesser knows, and so do I."

After paying their bill, they strolled out of the restaurant and Tori said, "You're hitting the skies tomorrow with A. C., right?"

"Yep."

"Who's watching the store while you're flying like an eagle?"

"Hailey, as always."

"Are you looking forward to it?"

Corin drew his hand through the air as if it was a wing cruising on the wind. "Can't wait. It's been too long. I'm just hoping A. C. doesn't talk about anything too deep. I just want to have a nice simple adrenaline rush."

"What makes you think he'll—?"

Corin smiled. "Because A. C. said he needed to talk to me about something deep."

CHAPTER 30

"Should be a stellar day for soaring across the sky."

Corin and A. C. tore along the dirt road in Pikes National Forest toward the top of Badger Mountain, flinging up a dust curtain behind them. Corin rolled down his window and stuck his arm out. Warm for this time of year. The thermals should be strong which would keep them in the air for hours.

A. C. hit a pothole that sent Corin toward the ceiling of A. C.'s Jeep. "Hey, think you could keep it under fifty going up this road?"

A. C. laughed. "No problem, we're only going forty-eight right now. I won't speed up."

"Most people crawl up this thing at twenty."

"We're not most people." A. C. threw his head back and let out a whoop.

Sometimes Corin thought A. C. was even crazier than himself. He patted his pants pocket and sighed. "I think I left my cell phone in my truck."

"So? We'll touch down at our landing site in an hour. I'm sure your truck and cell phone will be waiting for us down below with big smiles."

Four trucks and a van came into view to their right as they crested the final rise and pulled into the dusty open space one hundred yards to the right of the mountain's peak. Three hang gliders looked ready to launch. Another two were doing final testing and checks. Good sign. Other gliders meant the air was handing out thrill-ride thermals for the taking. And Corin was ready to take.

When he was streaking through the air with no sound but the ripple of the wind buffeting his glider and nothing but sky for thousands of feet below him, he never thought of the dream, never thought of Shasta, never thought of his business going bankrupt.

Before A. C.'s Jeep came to a stop, Corin threw the door open, ready to step out into his favorite recipe for freedom.

Twenty minutes later he stood next to A. C. ready to launch, their hang gliders resting side by side, only waiting for the two of them to hoist them up, strap in, and go.

"You have your oxygen?" Corin said.

"Why, you think we're climbing to fifteen thousand feet or higher?"

"Absolutely." Corin stared at the sky. "You ready?"

"Did I tell you I went to the doctor?" A. C. patted his left shoulder.

"What for?"

"To have him take a thorough look at my shoulder."

"I thought it was healed."

"It is." Contemplation filled A. C.'s eyes.

"So why'd you go?"

"I wanted the doctor to get in there and look at every muscle, every fiber. To see if it really had been restored. To see if this chair of yours did more than mental gymnastics on me."

"And?"

"He's never seen anything like it. He called in three other doctors to see me." A. C. rubbed his shoulder with a red-gloved hand. "He even pulled up the old X-rays and shot new ones so he could study them side by side."

"What did he say?"

"He wouldn't call it a miracle, but he kept saying, 'This shouldn't be, this shouldn't be,' as he pointed to one X-ray, then the other." A. C. laughed. "It made me think of that old *Sesame Street* song: 'One of these things is not like the others, one of these things just doesn't belong.'" He shook his head, then cocked it to the side and pulled his goggles off his face. "Do you know why I'm telling you this?"

"Yeah, because it's unbelievable."

"Because I don't want you to have any doubt I've been 100 percent healed."

"Okay."

"Because when it really sank in that I've been restored, I couldn't help thinking of something." A. C. stared at Corin, eyes intense.

"What?"

"It's made me think of some*one*." A. C. glanced at the slope in front of them and out toward the shimmering lakes ten miles into the distance, then back at Corin, his eyes still throwing off light like a Fourth of July sparkler.

"Do I want to hear this?"

"No."

"Then don't say it." Corin knew the path his friend was about to jump on and try to go down. But it was so overgrown, the sharpest machete in the world couldn't cut through the underbrush choking the trail.

"You know I have to."

"If you're a friend you won't even think about suggesting it."

"If I'm a friend I'll make you think about it."

"I'm not going there, A. C."

"When's the last time you talked to him?"

"Are we going to catch these thermals before the wind dies?"

"When?"

"I'm not having this discussion."

"Yeah, you are. If I die on this flight and you don't, I'll at least know I talked to you about this and you'll have to wrestle with making the right decision."

"That's a road that has Dead-End signs packed in so thick, a Hummer couldn't plow through them."

"When?"

"You don't think I try? Every week I find an excuse to call his house." Corin took off his gloves and spiked them onto the ground. "Every week I send an e-mail. I pick up his kid. I send gifts. He's never. Going. To. Respond."

"He's your brother. And he was your best friend."

"What's your point?"

"Friendships are worth going through hades for. They're worth fighting for."

"I am fighting. And I've been through the deepest part of the darkness so many times I could draw you a map."

"How hard are you fighting?" A. C. cinched up his harness and looked at his glider.

"Hard." Corin kicked a clump of dead grass at his feet. "It rips me up inside."

"When is the last time you showed up at Shasta's front door and refused to leave until he talked to you?"

Corin didn't answer. He stared at the launch path they would run down in a few minutes that would send them into the sky. His escape route.

"When?" A. C. repeated.

"This isn't any of your business." Corin picked up his gloves and put them on again.

"When I see my best friend being shredded emotionally and see a possible way to make it stop, yeah, it's my business."

Corin walked to his glider and hoisted it up.

"And when sitting in some weird chair heals me, I can't help but think if you don't use any and every way possible to get your brother in it, you're crazy."

"Can we get into the air?"

"Don't tell me you haven't thought about it during these past three days. That you haven't gone to sleep thinking about it. And woken up thinking about it. And thought about it twenty times a day."

"Of course I do." Corin stared at A. C. "I know you're trying to help, but what happens if I ask him and it doesn't work?"

He turned to the launch path and started down it without looking back. Twenty seconds later the earth fell away and the only sound was the swish of the wind against his glider—and the echo of A. C.'s words in his mind.

Sure, he could stand on his brother's front porch and wait for eternity before Shasta would come out. Or he could break the front door down and stand in his brother's den staring at the back of his head and his electric wheelchair wishing he could go back in time and change what he'd done.

And Shasta would never settle his chin on his wheelchair control and turn to face him. Corin could speak of a fantastical chair that healed his friend and a little kid, and Shasta would laugh at him and reel off all the mystical and magical cures he'd tried—mostly at Corin's urging—during the year after the accident.

And it would shut his brother down even further—if that was possible.

Once again Corin would be reminded of how utterly he'd destroyed their friendship for the rest of their lives.

No thank you.

If God really wanted to help him, He'd have two hundred and fifty thousand dollars show up on the seat of the chair. The surgery was something Corin would fight for. At least that had proven science behind it, and it had worked two-thirds of the time. Sit in the chair? Shasta would laugh at the idea no matter how many people were healed.

But a small part of him knew A. C. was right. A part that was growing. A part that said he had to find a way for Shasta to be healed. And that meant thinking of the chair as one option.

Corin shook his head. This was where he was supposed to be free. For the next hour he was. He pushed consideration of Shasta and the chair from his thoughts and let his mind soar along with his glider on the thermals.

A. C. was to the left and slightly ahead him. Corin radioed him on his walkie-talkie to confirm their landing spot was about three miles ahead. After another fifteen minutes he focused on Badger Flats where A. C. and he would land. It looked good. Wait. What was that?

A figure stood in the meadow near Corin's truck. Odd. It was the first time anyone had been waiting to greet them after one of their flights.

Whoever it was, he hadn't been invited to the party.

Corin radioed A. C. "Are you seeing what I'm seeing?"

"If that's a scarecrow he's come to life."

"Any idea who our welcoming committee might be?"

A. C. laughed. "You're going to get followers, buddy. Probably some groupie from the chair fan club."

"Let's hope not. Some of them are more stable than others." Corin leaned to his left and started a long, sweeping turn that would bring him around to see the figure from the front.

Thirty seconds later and three hundred feet lower, he got a good look at the person. A. C. was right. But it wasn't just a member of the fan club. It was their president.

Corin's radio squawked and A. C.'s voice poured out of it. "Can you see who it is?"

He saw. And it made him wish his hang glider was equipped with a cloaking device. Or lasers. At least one of the Green Goblin's exploding pumpkins. Why was the guy so relentless? Corin was grateful he hadn't taken this sky spin solo. "It's my number one fan."

"Mark Jefferies?"

"Bull's-eye."

Mark stood with feet a bit more than shoulder width apart, arms folded, black sunglasses matching his black leather jacket. He stared into the sky, his gaze shifting back and forth between Corin and A. C.

Corin finished his turn, straightened, then banked again. He considered landing as far away from Mark as possible—make the pastor trudge across the lumpy field in his European shoes—but what was the point? The pastor of Stalkerville wouldn't leave without cornering Corin so he might as well get it over with.

He landed fifty feet from Mark, his back to the pastor. The crunch of Mark's shoes grew closer, then stopped—maybe fifteen feet behind him. "How was your flight?"

"Good, how was yours?"

"Fine."

"Too warm for you in La Jolla?"

"No."

"How did you know we were going to land here?" Corin slid off his harness, his back still to Mark.

A. C. glided in on his left and landed fifty yards away. Corin motioned him closer. If Mark ever got physical, Corin was confident he could handle himself, but having A. C. next to him would be a nice backup, both physically and verbally.

"There are only a few places around here to land," Mark said. "This is one. I have friends at the other in case you landed there instead."

"You're still tracking me."

"Yes."

"What do you want, Jefferies?"

"As I've said before, to help you."

"We've been over this. If I need your help, I'll ask."

"This is a different kind of help. A kind I haven't given yet and I don't offer lightly."

A. C. trundled up and set his glider down next to Corin's. "Are we having a party?"

Mark ignored him. "You want this kind of help, Corin."

"A. C., meet Mark; Mark meet A. C."

Both men stared at each other, neither spoke. A. C. finally nodded in Mark's direction and the pastor nodded back. "How's your shoulder?"

A. C. frowned. "What about it?"

"The left one. Better than usual?"

"They're both fine."

"I'll bet." Mark laughed. "Look, I'm not one for games, so let me be blunt. I have a lot of friends in this town in high places. So when a miracle happens to someone's shoulders or carbon-dating samples come back with bizarre results, I'm going to hear about it. Clear? So don't play the coy card, all right?"

"Unless you want to infuse my business with a large influx of cash, I'm not interested," Corin said.

"It is cash." Mark folded his arms and raised his chin. "As you say, a large influx."

"What, you're going to give me five hundred thousand dollars for the chair?"

"Eight."

"What?" Corin stared at Mark, then glanced at A. C., who looked back with raised eyebrows.

"Eight hundred thousand dollars. I give you the money; you give me the chair." Mark took off his sunglasses and hooked them on the front of his midnight blue T-shirt.

Corin blinked and studied Mark's face. The man was serious. "Why?"

"Because as you know, the chair is an obsession for me and I've come to believe in its authenticity. Because I want the deal done now and that kind of cash shows you how serious I am. And because this will help your current circumstances considerably." Mark motioned as if handing out dollar bills. "I know you need the money."

This guy wasn't just the pastor of Stalkerville. He owned the place. Corin folded his arms and narrowed his eyes. "You better explain how you know that."

"I need to know what's going on in your life, Corin."

"In other words you've had your personal Mafia delving into everything about me."

"Precisely."

"But none of them are here now." Corin held his palms up. "I'm guessing you don't want anyone else to witness this suggestion of what do with the church's money."

Mark walked up to within a foot of Corin. "This kind of money could dig you out of the debt your store is in." He leaned in, his face now only six inches from Corin's. "But that's only secondary to the primary thought bouncing around your brain right now." Mark glanced at A. C. and lowered his voice. "You're thinking this money could pay for an operation that insurance companies won't touch because of its experimental nature. An operation that has worked for 60 percent of the patients who have gone under the knife. An operation that might put someone's life back together."

Corin's body temperature notched up two degrees as two thoughts flashed through his mind. First, how did this guy know so much about him, and second, how absolutely correct he was. Eight hundred thousand would take care of the store and provide the funds for Shasta to have the surgery. If his brother would try it. It was a Mount-Everest-sized if. But getting him to sit in the chair would be a trip to Jupiter.

"Talk to me, A. C. What do you think?"

A. C. strode slowly behind Mark, who kept his eyes fixed on Corin. "I don't trust the guy. More importantly, you don't trust the guy."

"How do you know that?"

"Let's see, I've only known you for twenty years."

Corin studied his friend. "In other words, you'd want to see the money in the bank before you turned over the chair."

"I wouldn't turn over that chair for eight hundred million dollars."

Jefferies spun toward A. C. "But you're not the one whose brother sits in a prison every waking hour of the day knowing you were the cause of it, are you? And you're not the one who is about to lose his business."

Jefferies was right. A. C. wasn't drowning in debt and didn't have a seven-course meal of guilt every morning. "How soon could you have the money?"

"I could have it in your account before nightfall."

"I'll think about it." Corin carried his gliding gear to his truck.

"I want an answer by nine tomorrow night."

"I'll give you an answer in a week."

"Two days."

"Three."

"Fine." Mark whirled and strode toward his car. "Three days. Not four. Not three and a half. At the stroke of midnight on the third day, the offer turns back into a pumpkin and your glass slipper will shatter on the ground."

Corin didn't answer. He stared at the back of Mark's silver Cadillac DTS till it faded from sight behind a cluster of golden aspen trees. Churches must be paying well for him to rent a car like that.

As they drove back up to the butte to retrieve A. C.'s Jeep, their entire conversation consisted of three lines.

"Will you sell it to him, Cor?"

"It would solve a lot of problems."

"What's the biggest problem it would solve?"

Corin didn't answer.

Three days to decide.

Tomorrow he would drive out to the lake—he hadn't been there in over a month—and make himself face his demons.

CHAPTER 31

Early the next evening, after closing the store, Corin drove out Sky View Drive toward Woodmoor Lake—as he normally did every two or three weeks—to go another three rounds in the ring with his old buddy Terror.

He would keep wrestling the fear till it crashed to the mat, he choked it to death, and he was free of the memory. "Face your fears," that's what his counselor had said.

And now he had a new psychological opponent in the ring. To sell the chair or keep it.

Woodmoor Lake was nearly the same size as Lake Vereor, maybe a few acres bigger. Woodmoor Lake served as an excellent substitute for what had happened at Vereor when he was ten. He closed his eyes and bit his upper lip. A trip there wouldn't be happening anytime soon.

He shuddered.

Lake Vereor.

The lake he'd drowned in.

Died in.

Where his heart had stopped and he hadn't filled his lungs with anything but water for over five minutes.

When he arrived at Woodmoor Lake, he parked his car in his usual spot, then sat in his car for ten minutes. *Get out and face the fear. Wrestle with the dream demons and crush them under your heel.*

After throwing on a raincoat and scrunching an old Rockies baseball hat onto his head, he got out and meandered up the small grassy rise shielding the lake from the parking lot. When he reached the top, Corin jammed his hands in his pockets and squeezed his fingers into fists.

The sun briefly poked through gray clouds as it slithered its way down into the night and Corin blinked against the intermittent moments of brightness.

His breaths shortened as he stared at the lake and he forced himself to breathe slower.

No fear.

Nothing to fear.

Nothing he couldn't conquer.

If only it were true.

NICOLE WATCHED CORIN settle onto the bench overlooking the lake as she'd done for the past nine years. How many hours had she prayed for him as he sat there? Probably hundreds if they were added up. Finally time to see if those years of prayer would bring healing or hell.

So much good surrounded the chair. So much evil drawn to it because of its power. Impossible to have one without the other.

Had he discovered the chair's healing power yet? Most likely yes. Corin had to realize the boy with asthma was healed because of the chair. She walked toward him, determined not to reveal too much of who she was, even though she desperately wanted to.

Nicole asked once more for wisdom before she would enter Corin Roscoe's life and stay in it no matter what happened.

CORIN LET THE memory of the drowning flood his mind, let the fear wash through his heart, and tried to fight the terror that seemed to claw at his brain.

No, it's over; you lived. You have nothing to fear. Nothing to fear. Nothing to fear.

But it didn't help. It never helped. The dream would still come.

Why couldn't he shake it? Why couldn't he accept the fact he didn't die in the lake that day; accept the fact he'd lived and get over the fear? He'd been to counselors who kept asking him, "How do you feeeel? How do you feeeel?" without ever giving him concrete steps to eradicate the incident from his mind.

The sky shifted, a set of dark clouds cobbled across the sky, and a few minutes later a fine rain drizzled onto Corin's Patagonia jacket, the bench he sat on, and the grass that surrounded him. A minute later the rain thickened. He was about to get up when the sound of drops dancing on an umbrella made him spin to the left.

Nicole.

She stood ten feet to his side, a smile shining under her intense eyes. Eyes that seemed to drill into his soul. Eyes that seemed to know him beyond what they should.

She stepped toward him and stopped in front of him.

"Do you mind?" She motioned toward the bench.

"Please."

Nicole sat, her umbrella covering both their heads. She wore a black raincoat, which contrasted sharply with the sun-bleached bench. Black gloves covered her hands.

"How is your life progressing these days, Corin?"

He studied her face. Joyful. Serious. At the same time. One moment she looked thirty-five, the next she was ninety.

"I e-mailed you back. I've been dying to talk to you." Corin rammed his hands deeper into the pockets of his coat. "Is this the point in the script where you tell me exactly why you showed up at my store two weeks ago and gave me the chair? And if the chair was really made by Christ? And if you're one of the legendary Keepers of the Chair, some kind of spiritual being?"

She laughed—a kaleidoscope laugh that made him think of a rainbow. "I am no angel. Of that you can be certain."

"Why did you give me the chair?"

"That is something I am anxious to tell you, but not before the time is right." She removed her gloves and reached over and patted his shoulder. "We don't want to move too quickly, I don't think."

"Maybe you don't. I'm ready to slide behind the wheel of a Ferrari and mash the accelerator to the floor."

"The faster you go, the higher the chance of an accident."

"I'm willing to take the chance."

Nicole turned her gaze to the lake. "Why do you come to the water?"

"Is the legend true? Has this chair been passed from mother to daughter for centuries?"

Nicole nodded.

The rain pinged the surface of the lake as it grew darker. "And does it truly contain the healing power of Christ?"

"At this point it doesn't matter what I tell you; it matters what you believe." Nicole adjusted the umbrella so it covered Corin's legs. "Has it healed anyone?"

"Yes."

"You're sure?"

Corin hesitated. "Yes."

"I see."

They sat in silence, as the clouds continued their trek north across the sky and the rain returned to a drizzle, then stopped.

"Why do you come to the water?" Nicole repeated her question.

"I think you already know."

She smiled. "I don't know everything about you."

"How do you know so much?"

"Enough."

Corin stared at the dark undulations in the water's surface, mocking him, laughing at him, daring him to enter the lake.

"Do you know what happened to me when I was younger?"

Nicole shook her head. "Only that you almost drowned. I know none of the details."

Corin leaned back and pulled his baseball hat farther down his head. Tell her? Why not?

"When I was ten my family took a camping trip to Lake Vereor. The third day of the trip we rented these pontoons with bikes welded on top of them side by side. They looked like they were made by someone in their garage who took a shot of whiskey with every weld. You pedaled the bikes and they moved underwater paddles that propelled us around the lake. I was with my dad; my brother was with my mom."

Corin rubbed his face. "We all had life jackets, being safe you know. After we tooled around for fifteen or twenty minutes, we decided to switch. I'd join my mom, my brother, Shasta, would push the pedals with my dad."

Corin closed his eyes as the memory pressed into his mind as if the Incredible Hulk was squeezing his brain into pulp.

"You step here next to me, Corin," his mom said.

Corin hesitated, then stepped on the back of the pontoon next to his mom and brother.

"That might be too much weight . . ." His dad stared at them.

Corin glanced at the pontoon as it sank into the dark green water, then back at his father. "Dad?"

"Get off!"

Too late.

"Jump! Before it flips and hits you—"

His dad's words were smothered as the combined weight of his mom and him flipped the craft over and Corin was pulled underwater.

Something thumped him on the head and he started to go dark. No, he had to get to the surface. He kicked hard but didn't move. Corin opened his eyes and looked up. The pontoon was upside down, and he was next to one of the bicycles. Next to the handlebars. He kicked again.

Nothing.

Then he saw why. One of the straps of his life jacket was wrapped around a handlebar of the bike.

He yanked on the strap. It was like a steel cable.

Suddenly, movement beside him. He whirled to see his mom next to him. She grabbed the strap and yanked on it. It didn't budge. She pulled again. Nothing.

She wrapped the strap around her hand and wrenched on it a third time. Slight movement. Too slight.

He was running out of air. *Please, Mom! Get me to the surface!*

Twenty more seconds. He could hold his breath twenty more seconds.

She motioned with her hands as if to tell him to stay calm and then swam for the surface.

No! What are you doing? Don't leave me!

Fifteen more seconds before his air was gone.

An instant later his dad was next to him, grabbing the strap with his iron hands and yanking it so hard the handlebars bent.

Ten seconds.

He was still tied to the bike. He clawed at his dad, tearing into his skin, not caring, only knowing he had to breathe.

Seven seconds.

Another heave with all the strength his dad possessed. Corin kicked his legs as hard as he could, knowing it wouldn't help but unable to stop himself.

Three seconds.

Another pull by his father. Corin grabbed the handlebar as if he could break it in two. His eyes went wide, his mouth opened to scream.

One second.

A moment later Corin let out his air and sucked in the coldness of the lake.

His dad was still pulling on the strap when the darkness took him.

Corin laid his shaking hands on his jeans and tried to smile. Although he'd relived the memory thousands of times, when awake and in his dreams, it was the first time he'd told the story out loud.

"You didn't almost drown that day."

He shook his head.

"You died."

Corin nodded at Nicole and sucked in a quick breath. "Clinically dead for five minutes. Revived and the doctors said there was no damage to my mind."

"Except for your fear of the water."

Corin took off his hat and massaged the Rockies logo with his thumb. "If there is a God behind this chair of yours, He certainly has a sense of humor."

Nicole tilted her head and glanced at him. "How so?"

Corin let out a bitter laugh. "Did you know that Olympic-caliber coaches can spot an athlete with innate natural talent as young as three?"

"No, I didn't."

"I was picked out of a crowd of four-year-old boys as having exceptional talent, and I exercised that talent for the next six years."

"What was the sport at which you showed such aptitude?" She asked the question as if she already knew the answer.

Corin stared at the water for a few seconds before turning and looking at Nicole. "Swimming, of course."

"I'm sorry." Nicole sighed and gave a tiny shake of her head. "Do you ever miss it?"

"Never."

It wasn't true. Swimming wasn't an extreme sport, didn't give him the rush that hang gliding or BASE jumping or street luging did. But in the water he'd always felt free, alone with the surge of the water as he pulled himself to another record-breaking time for eight-year-olds, then nine, then ten-year-old boys. While the water terrified him now, an atom-sized part of him missed the water, missed what it used to be to him.

"Did your mom carry guilt for what happened?"

"She had giant backpacks stuffed with guilt and she carried them everywhere she went till the day she died." Corin picked up a handful of gravel and started tossing the pieces at the water. "I never stopped trying to convince her to let the guilt go, but she couldn't ever watch Olympic swimming after that. She blamed herself for my not wearing gold around my neck. Never could accept that the accident wasn't her fault."

"Then whose fault was it?"

"Everyone has some kind of kryptonite in his or her life. I suppose that's one of mine."

"So you need a lead box in which to mute its power?"

Corin rubbed his collarbone. A lead box? Sure. If only the solution for his life could be as simple as it was in his comic books. "Are you offering?"

"In a way, yes."

"How so?"

"The chair."

"It can heal me, huh?"

"It is a way to healing."

"What does that mean?"

Nicole patted his hand. "I'm sorry; I can't tell you that part."

"I have to figure that out on my own."

She nodded. "A man who is told learns with his head; a man who experiences the lesson learns with his heart."

"Who said that?"

"I did."

Maybe it was time for him to sit in the chair again. He wasn't sure what had kept him from trying it a second time. Maybe he was scared it wouldn't work. Maybe he didn't know exactly what to believe for when he sat in it. Maybe it was because it might peel back a fear so deep he'd never faced it.

Then again, maybe it was time to sell it. "There's this pastor of a megachurch who wants to buy the chair."

"I see." Nicole glanced at the sky and folded up her umbrella. "Do you think you should, or is there something or Someone orchestrating a symphony here greater than you know? Can't you feel it?"

Corin hesitated. The obvious answer was to say yes. But was there? Emotions were not reality, and even though he'd felt an affinity toward Nicole, felt hope after A. C. was healed, felt a sense of wonder after little Brittan was supposedly healed by the chair, it didn't mean some Higher Power was directing the whole thing.

And what if God *was* behind all of it? Maybe Mark's offer was God's way of sending him a boat to rescue him from the encroaching waters. A path of hope he could offer Shasta that might lead to a healing that seemed insane to hope for two weeks earlier. "I don't know if something greater is going on here."

"When does this pastor want his answer?"

Corin smiled at her. "You know who the pastor is. I think you're tracking me."

"I'm watching out for you."

"It seems a common hobby for people these days."

"Quite."

Corin tried to stir up a feeling of mistrust toward Nicole. Impossible. Tesser had said to trust no one, and the counsel was wise, but with Nicole he couldn't help it. "I have three days to decide. And one of them has already passed."

"Why would you sell it?"

"I need the money to keep my store from going under."

"Anything else?"

Corin shrugged. "A friend of mine has to have an operation."

"Has to?"

Corin hesitated. "Yes."

"And this money could pay for it."

"Yep."

"Why not have your friend sit in the chair?"

"Because from what I've seen, the chair decides what it wants to heal and what it doesn't want to heal, and I can't risk this friend sitting in the chair and getting nothing."

"Why is that?"

Corin stood and stepped toward the lake. Sorry, no one got that story. After two or three minutes he sat again.

"Have you sat in the chair, Corin?"

"Yes."

"And?"

"It didn't heal me of anything."

"Did you believe it would heal you?"

Corin didn't answer.

"Maybe you should sit in it again."

"I don't have anything wrong with me except a stiff knee."

"That's all the healing you need?"

"It's rarely stiff."

"Healing is healing. Western culture makes the distinction, but God does not. What good is an arm or leg that is healed when the mind is still broken?" Nicole paused till Corin looked at her. "Also, you might consider your sitting in the chair might not be only about your healing, but about someone else's."

"Can you explain that with fewer cryptic drapes covering up the meaning?"

"I think we've had enough time together for the moment." Nicole stood. "We'll talk again soon, Corin, I promise."

On the way home, he gripped and regripped his steering wheel as if he could strangle it into giving him an answer as to what Nicole meant. But he didn't need it to speak. He already knew.

It wouldn't surprise him if Nicole knew all about Shasta. Why did she want Corin to push his brother into sitting in the chair? Did she truly believe it would heal him? And why would his sitting in the chair help his brother?

It didn't matter. He wouldn't be dragging Shasta to the table inside the restaurant of Hope-U-Get-Healed. If God wanted that done, He would have to do it Himself.

But maybe Corin would sit in the chair again.

Maybe tonight.

CHAPTER 32

Corin strode through his front door, tossed his keys onto his couch, and stared at the door to his basement.

Should he? Shouldn't he? An old football injury stiffened up his knee a few times year. The forefinger on his left hand ached sometimes due to breaking it when he was in the sixth grade. That was it. Sit in the chair for those things? No. And certainly not for his fears.

Healing for those? *Sorry, Nicole, I'll get through my mental torments on my own.* He'd learned to live with his kryptonite.

No you haven't. You need to sit again.

The thought flashed through him with such clarity, Corin's head snapped back and he blinked.

No, he didn't need to.

He needed to sell the chair to Mark and use the money to get Shasta that operation.

He didn't need healing.

He didn't.

But the lie kept sticking halfway down his throat and refused to be swallowed.

He paced in his living room, trying to decide whether to face the truth or build himself a web of self-deception. After three minutes he admitted the real reason he didn't want to sit in the chair. He was just like his brother.

For twenty-four years Corin had tried to get healed of his claustrophobia and fear of water. Through hypnosis, acupuncture, counseling . . . And just like Shasta, he wasn't willing to release even a sliver of hope that would once again only be obliterated.

Come sit.

The impression was stronger this time.

Great. Now he was hearing voices.

Come.

Corin strode over to the basement door and yanked it open.

Fine. He would sit in the chair. And he would believe. And prove to himself the chair wouldn't heal anything inside him.

When he reached the bottom of the stairs, he went to turn on the lights, hesitated, then left them off. He could use the light from his cell phone to unlock the padlock on the door.

Corin slid his cell phone into his pocket as he eased the door open and stepped inside. He could almost feel the chair ten feet in front of him. One more step. Then another.

What was he thinking? He was sneaking up on an inanimate object. But the next moment he smiled as a faint light emanated from the middle of the room.

No question. The chair was glowing. The faintest of lines ringed its outside edges and the light seemed to be creeping counterclockwise.

After two more steps the glow faded and vanished.

Darkness enveloped him as he stepped forward and felt for the chair. There. He had it. Its surface wasn't hot. Wasn't cool. It felt normal.

He slid into the chair without hesitation, closed his eyes, and waited for . . . what? Corin didn't know. What had Avena said? A. C. had seen a light show, a feeling of warmth and peace.

After a minute Corin still felt nothing.

Two minutes. Still nothing.

"God? Did Your Son make this chair?"

Silence.

"Did He?"

Then a tingling in the chair, so soft he couldn't tell if it was real or imagined, but at the moment he decided it was real, it vanished, and again he wasn't sure if it happened only in his mind.

Five minutes later he still felt nothing.

Maybe he needed to concentrate on what needed healing. Isn't that what Tori and he had talked about? As Corin let the emotions of the lake rise around him, he swallowed and his breathing grew shallow.

"Take me," he whispered the words, then louder, "take me!"

He clenched the seat of the chair till his fingers ached, as if he could squeeze a reaction out of the ancient artifact. "Heal me. Please."

Cynicism gave over to hope and he tried to imagine a heat coming from the chair or a great peace. A comfort. Anything.

"Do something!"

The only alteration was the seat growing slightly cooler.

He closed his eyes again and tried to relax.

Corin glanced at his watch. Fifteen minutes had passed. How long had Brittan sat in the chair? A. C.? He couldn't remember—as if it would matter.

"Change me." The words were almost inaudible.

Again, an impression filled his mind.

Call him. Offer healing. Not through the surgery of men.

Corin gave a slight shake of his head.

Impossible. Shasta wouldn't come.

Call him.

The thought lit up his mind like lightning; there for an instant then gone, and afterward his mind felt darker than before the idea had come.

Twenty more minutes of sitting in the chair didn't bring any light and something told him the next day wouldn't get any brighter.

THE NEXT MORNING, Corin grabbed a cup of straight-drip java at Jade Shot Coffee, made sure the lid was on tight, and half jogged toward his store. He was already late.

Sixty seconds later his progress was thwarted by three men who looked like the NFL's version of the Hells Angels. Each of the four men towered over Corin by at least five inches. In the middle, with his arms folded, black sunglasses on, stood Mark Jefferies.

"Good morning, Corin."

Corin took a sip of his coffee as his eyes bounced from one end of the line to the other. Mark motioned the man on the end with a flick of his head, and the four linebackers eased around Corin till they encircled him. Great. He would be even later thanks to this religious whacko.

"What a pleasure to bump into you, Mark. With you up here so much lately, who's preaching back home?"

Mark motioned with his head again. The mountain men moved two steps closer.

"I see you flew in some of your congregation." Corin took another sip of his coffee. "What do you want?"

"To talk. To see if you've made a decision on my offer." Mark glanced at his watch. "It expires in a little over thirty-nine hours."

"I'd love to chat, but I'm late."

"This will only take a moment."

Corin glanced around the circle. "It looks to me like you're getting ready to threaten me. Or something maybe a little bit grander than that."

"Not at all. I only want to know if I'm going to write you a check or not." Mark pulled a set of papers out of his back pocket. "We could sign everything right now if you like. Since we haven't talked in the past two days and you haven't responded to my e-mails and phone calls, I simply thought it would be good to have a little chat."

Corin motioned toward the men who surrounded him. "Do they chat?"

"Sure. But do they need to? Or do you understand their body language?" He glanced up and down the street. If any of the pedestrians thought their gathering looked odd, they didn't express it.

"I suppose this is the part where you tell me if I don't accept your offer, you still want the chair, won't take no for an answer, and your buddies here will use their body language on me in a way that is universally understood."

"Once again you've misunderstood me."

"I keep doing that." Corin offered his finest plastic smile and gave a quick nod. "No idea why."

A condescending smile rose on Mark's face and quickly faded.

"The chair is yours to do with as you want. And always will be. This isn't a TV show. I simply want you to understand how serious I am about my beliefs and about giving you the money." Mark cracked his knuckles. "We want to understand; we want to help you. And if you don't accept my offer, I will still continue to help you in any and every way I can."

He suspected accepting assistance from Mark would be like living in that old Eagles song "Hotel California." He'd be able to check out any time he liked, but he'd never be able to leave Jefferies's clutches. "And if I don't want help?"

Mark smiled his half smile, part of this teeth showing, most covered by his Elvis-sneerlike mouth. "You need my help."

"To protect me."

"Yes."

"From . . . ?"

"Everyone." Mark held his palms up to the brilliant October sun and spun a slow 360 on his heel.

"And why would you extend your generosity to me even if I don't agree to your helping my bank account grow?"

"I'm not." Mark zipped open his black leather jacket. "I'm doing it because I want to see the chair remain safe."

"In other words, you're not losing sleep over me."

Mark nodded with his whole body. "I still care about you. Just not as much as the chair."

"I appreciate your honesty." Corin looked at his watch. "I have to go."

"Tell me about the lady who gave you the chair." Mark paced, two slow steps right, then two back to the left.

It made Corin feel like he was in a courtroom cross-examination during a high-profile trial. He wasn't the lawyer. "Why?"

"Because I suspect she can tell me much about it."

The guy wouldn't take a hint even if it was grand piano-sized and landed on his head. Corin stepped to the side of Jefferies and up to one of his bodyguards. "I have to get to my shop. Now."

"Are you going to allow me to give you the money that can help your store and your brother?"

"I'll let you know by the end of the deadline. But I should tell you, the answer is probably going to be no."

The mountain man shifted back a step and Corin slid through the opening and strode down the sidewalk.

"That'd be a mistake," Jefferies said.

"I'm so grateful for that penetrating spiritual insight, Pastor Mark. I'll be sure to meditate on it all day." Corin considered the wisdom of making the comment. It would undoubtedly tick the pastor off. Corin smiled. Exactly.

THAT NIGHT AS Corin slumped at his desk and attempted to balance the books, his gaze kept falling on the papers describing the results of the experimental spinal-cord surgery. Sixty percent success rate. Sixty. It was far higher than the success rate from the two delusional doctors from Mexico Shasta had gone to in the first year after the accident. The ones promising immediate healing.

Two hundred and fifty thousand dollars. And Mark was offering him eight hundred thousand.

The decision was simple, wasn't it? He'd be able to offer Shasta the surgery and have enough left over to save the store, pay off his house, and still have enough to take that trip to the Swiss Alps he'd been promising himself forever.

So why did he hesitate to make the call?

No idea.

Corin picked up his phone and tapped in Mark's cell phone number.

He stared at Mark's card taped to his computer monitor and flicked it with his finger. He wouldn't give him the chair till the money was in his account.

As the phone rang a second time, the sound of shattering glass pierced through Corin's thoughts. "What the—?" He lurched to his feet and staggered out his office door and onto his showroom floor.

Broken glass was strewn across the desks, tables, and chairs at the front of the store, the fluorescent light making them sparkle like diamonds. A cold wind meandered through the spot where his storefront's picture window had been.

Corin glanced around the room. Had someone shot the window?

On his second visual sweep of the floor, he spotted a rock just smaller than a baseball resting next to the leg of a burr walnut wine table from the late 1800s. He stared at it as if he expected the rock to move. Finally he strode over to it and picked up the almost perfectly round stone.

On one side were three words: *We want it.* On the other it said: *The old Tahmahoe barn. Leave it just inside the door. Tonight after midnight. No heroes. No hurt. We both live happily ever after.*

Twenty-three minutes later the police pulled up in front of Corin's store.

The cop nodded hello, then studied the window. "When did it happen?"

"About thirty minutes ago."

"Was anything stolen?"

"No. I was in my office and came out right after it came through the window."

"Any idea who played John Elway with the rock?"

Corin plucked the stone off the table he'd set it on and handed it to the cop.

"I grabbed it without thinking about fingerprints."

"Don't sweat it; rocks like this wouldn't take a print anyway." The cop stared at him. "Any idea?"

"No." Corin lied. He wasn't sure what Jefferies was capable of, but he suspected his linebacking cabal had a certain proficiency for these type of projects.

The policeman turned the rock over and looked at the words. "What's 'it'? What do they want you to leave in the barn?"

Corin lied again. "I don't know."

"You're sure?"

"Positive."

"I see." The cop held Corin's gaze long enough it was clear he didn't believe him, then jotted a note on his pad. "There's not much I can do other than file a report and make a few more passes through this neighborhood each week."

"I appreciate it."

"Do you have any enemies you know of?"

"No." This time he didn't have to lie.

"You're sure?"

"I'm sure."

"Well, you do now. This doesn't look like the work of a couple of kids. Which means whoever it is will probably be back."

The cops stayed another few minutes, doing a quick sweep of the store, and then turned to Corin. "You get any ideas who did this, let us know, okay?"

After boarding up the broken window, Corin e-mailed Nicole and asked her to meet him as soon as possible. Then he called Tesser, got his voice mail, and asked the professor the same thing.

No way would he be dropping the chair off in some old abandoned barn.

But he needed answers. The water was closing in and he needed a life jacket.

No, he needed a speedboat.

CHAPTER 33

The next morning at eleven thirty, Corin met Nicole at Rob's Ruby Rocket Diner, just off Highway 24 and fifty miles east of the city, focused on one thing: getting answers.

The door squealed like a pig in labor as he opened it, and he glanced around the restaurant. There were ten or eleven tables, all of them empty except for the one farthest from the front door where Nicole sat staring at him.

He eased toward her, studying her eyes, which were serious and seemed full of concern. When Corin reached the table, he slid into a red vinyl chair straight out of the sixties, folded his hands, and rested them on the table next to the salt and pepper shakers that were even older than the chairs. He brushed the remnants of a French fry off the table and interlaced his fingers again.

"Thanks for meeting me on such short notice."

She didn't answer, just nodded.

"Is there a reason you wanted to meet at a restaurant an

hour from town in a dive that probably hasn't seen a mop since Washington was president?"

Corin had been so focused on Nicole, he hadn't noticed a plump blond woman in a uniform two sizes too small standing at their table, pen and pad in hand.

Whoops.

She slapped two glasses of water onto the table. "We've only been in business since the Lincoln administration. And we did a remodel when Roosevelt came into office."

"Which one?"

"Teddy." She smiled and asked what they wanted.

"You have a great sense of humor."

The waitress nodded and winked at him.

Corin ordered iced tea and a hamburger and Nicole ordered black coffee and French onion soup.

"Why here?" Nicole said. "Because he probably wouldn't follow you out this far and wouldn't think of you coming into a place like this if he did."

"Who is 'he'?"

"The person who is after the chair and would possibly even kill to relieve you of it."

The scene with Mark's linebackers flashed into Corin's mind. "Jefferies, right?"

"I'm not going to tell you who it is."

"You're kidding."

"No."

For the first time Corin wondered about Nicole's mental stability. She had never been anything but fully self-assured. She appeared that way now. But this was the first time she'd said something crazy.

Actually that wasn't true. From the start her ideas had been dancing on the edge of the universe.

"Why not?"

"It's part of your growing up. You need to learn who to trust and who not to trust rather than be told."

"My growing up? I'm thirty-four years old." Corin bent his cardboard coaster two ways so he could spin it like a top on the grease-stained table.

"Some people die still as children."

"What does that mean?"

"I think you know, Corin."

He did know. He'd heard a single traumatic incident in a person's life could freeze his emotional age at the moment the event happened. So intellectually he might be thirty-four but emotionally he was, what? Ten? "So I'm ten years old?" The coaster slowed to a stop.

"It's time to face your fear. You're in the midst of doing that, which I applaud you for."

"What does facing my fear have to do with telling me I'm still ten years old?"

"I didn't say that, you did."

"I'm scared of drowning. So what? I'm sure a lot of people are." He dropped a penny in his water glass and watched it sink to the bottom. "And I am trying to face it."

"How?"

"I sat in the chair again."

"And?"

"Nothing."

"Nothing? That surprises me." She stared at him till he dropped his eyes.

The waitress arrived with their food. A welcome distraction. It gave him time to think. Should he tell her? The revelation he'd received probably wouldn't surprise her. Nicole had almost predicted it.

"When I sat in the chair I got the impression I should call my brother."

"I see." Nicole sipped her coffee and studied him over the top of her cup. "Are you going to?"

"I doubt it." Corin devoted the next five minutes to devouring his burger and slurping down his iced tea. Nicole stayed silent but continued to laser him with her piercing blue eyes.

"Why me?" Corin slid his water glass back and forth in front of him, the penny sitting in the center of the glass, looking bigger, feeling bigger than it was. Just like his fear. "Why did you give the chair to me?"

"You were the one I was supposed to give it to."

"And how did you determine that?"

For the next two or three minutes Nicole only looked at him as she took small spoonfuls of her soup. It was unnerving. He was about to ask again when she finally spoke.

"I've been watching you and the other possibility for many years now. It became clear early on you were the most likely candidate, but I couldn't give it to you till the time was right."

"You've been watching me for years?" Corin leaned back in his chair and scowled. "That creeps me out."

"Does it surprise you?"

No. It didn't. Based on what he knew about her, it didn't shock Corin at all. The confidence with which she'd given him the chair and their interactions since made it seem like she'd known him all her life.

He pushed his plate to the side of the table. "Why me? Why not the other one? I'm no one special."

Nicole smoothed her pants as a lilting laugh escaped her lips. "That is so far from true."

"It is true. I've done nothing."

"You can do a dance step around your destiny for a time, but you can't escape it forever."

"What destiny? What are you talking about?"

"Your destiny. To have the chair."

"It doesn't make sense. I'm not female for one thing. Plus I'm full of doubt, full of fears. I've made—"

"Mistakes you regret with everything inside." Nicole smiled. "Welcome to the human race. Let me read you something a friend gave me many years ago." She pulled out a yellowed envelope and from it drew out a small gray note card.

> *"You are no one and you are everyone.*
> *You are glorious and you are nothing.*
> *You are mountains and valleys,*
> *You are glory and sin,*
> *And even when in the heart of your glory you can't comprehend*
>   *how deep His passion for you runs,*
> *Take hold of who you are.*
> *Know it in your soul.*
> *Run before the wind of the destiny He has created for you,*
> *And seek Him in every moment."*

Nicole slid the card back into her purse and wove her fingers together. "Do you understand?"

Corin reached to his left and grabbed a French fry off his plate. "You're saying God chose me."

"Yes. But be careful. Death has always surrounded the chair. As has healing. Dark and light. Evil and goodness. Joy and sorrow."

"And His purpose in my having the chair is what?"

Nicole smoothed her coat. "That is the one part of this whole drama I have no doubt I know the answer to."

"What's the answer?"

She slid her chair back, stood, leaned over him, and patted his shoulder. "We'll talk again soon, Corin. Stay strong and believe."

Nicole snatched a twentydollar bill from her purse and dropped it on the table. "He is for you."

The click of her heels on the old linoleum floor seemed muted as she walked away. Or maybe it was because his brain was spinning too loudly for him to hear well.

He popped the French fry in his mouth. It was cold and he spit it into his napkin which he crumpled and tossed onto his plate. Corin stood and glanced at his watch.

The guy fixing his store window wouldn't be done for another two or three hours. Tesser hadn't returned his call so this was a perfect time to get in a workout. Time to go for a long inline skate. Time to get his mind off the chair and his brother and his own nagging neuroses.

But as he left the restaurant, something in the jangling of the bells on the front door gave him the feeling he wasn't going to get it.

CHAPTER 34

On the way to G. Peterson Park, Corin considered putting a gun to Shasta's head. It would be the only way he'd get his brother to sit in the chair. Or maybe he should sell it to Mark and try to forget it ever existed. Or give Tesser the chair and let him figure out if the thing was real.

Or move to Mexico with Tori and live on a thousand dollars a year.

He pulled his truck into the parking lot in front of the skate path and threw his gearshift into Park. The perfect spot to get away from everything and everyone. Few people would be here this time of the year with the temperature only in the mid-fifties.

After jamming his in-line skates onto his feet, he pushed off onto the path that wove through clusters of narrow-leaf cottonwood trees, scattered red and gold leaves mixed with their brothers and sisters who still held the green of summer in their hue.

Stop thinking about the chair for an hour. He could do it. Give himself just sixty minutes with nothing on the brain except working up a good sweat.

It wasn't going to be possible.

Five minutes into his skate a scream sliced through his mind from over the hill to his right.

"Please, help me!"

Corin pulled off his skates on the edge of the grass and jogged toward the voice. A woman by the sound of it. As he crested the hill he spotted a heavyset lady who took tiny staggering steps back and forth in front of a large drain pipe.

She turned as Corin ran up to her. "Can you help me? Will you, please?"

A muffled yapping drifted out from deep inside the pipe.

"What's—?"

"My puppy . . . she's . . . I'm too . . ."—she brushed her hips—"big to get in there . . . I need . . . can you crawl in? Get her, please?" The woman's baby blue mascara was smeared with tears and her hands trembled.

Corin squatted and glanced at the pipe. Forget it. Someone else would need to be Superman today. He could fit into the pipe but not comfortably and his brain wouldn't fit at all.

"I'm sorry, tight spaces and I don't get along. I can't—"

"Please? There's no one else out here. She's already been in there for ten minutes." The lady blinked and rubbed her stomach with both hands.

"Don't worry. I can go get help, send someone down here to get your—"

"She's my only family. She's a cockapoo, so sweet, you know?" The woman knelt next to the pipe and sobbed. "If I lose her . . ."

"How far in?" Corin gritted his teeth. Why did he ask? He couldn't do it even if the dog was only twenty feet in.

"I don't know. Scoundrel sniffed inside the pipe and then started to go in . . ." More tears. "She yanked at the leash—I should have bought a new one, I know—and it snapped and . . . maybe she saw a rabbit . . . And I've called and called and she won't come out . . . and I don't know if she's stuck or hurt or—"

"Listen, I'll run and get some help, get someone back here in five minutes, ten at the most."

"Fine." All emotion drained out of her face. "That's fine. It's fine. I'll be okay."

"Are you sure?"

"No." The woman shook her head and started crying again. "I don't know if I can last that long. She's probably not very far in."

This was all too cliché. Woman's dog gets stuck in drainpipe. Man happens along who is paralyzed by small spaces. Woman cries. Man gives in and crawls in pipe hating the woman, hating the dog, hating his fear. Why couldn't it be a cat seventy feet up in a tree?

Corin peered into the pipe. Ten feet at the most before the darkness swallowed up the light. He could hold his breath for two and a half minutes. It was a trick he'd learned to give himself a shield of seconds against the panic onslaught. For some reason while holding his breath, the fear flitted at the edges of his mind and didn't enter until he'd released the air. If only it worked for more than just the first lungful. "I'll try, but I doubt I'll do any good."

"Thank you," the woman whispered.

Corin closed his eyes, put his ear next to the pipe, and listened for the dog's whimper. Nothing. How deep had the mutt gone?

Arrooo.

Faint.

Wonderful. The thing was probably three hundred yards in. Concrete could magnify the sound making the dog's cry seem closer than it was. Maybe she was six hundred yards in by now.

"What's the dog's name again?"

"Scoundrel."

Corin squinted up at her. "You don't happen to have a treat she'd be interested in?"

The woman shook her head.

Of course not.

"Like I said, I'm not fond of tight spaces so I'm going to give this a shot, but I won't be able to last in there very long, understand? A couple of minutes at the most."

The woman nodded.

"You don't happen to have a flashlight, do you?"

She nodded again, reached inside her purse, and pulled out a small pink flashlight.

"I was kidding. I didn't think—"

"Always be prepared I say."

Except for having a new leash. Or a treat.

Corin took the light and flicked it on. It would help. Not much, but he'd take it. At times seeing how tight a space was helped. Most of the time it made things worse.

He studied the pipe again. He'd have three or four inches on each side, but it wouldn't be easy to turn around once—if—he found the dog. Backing out if he couldn't turn around? Lots of fun. And twice as long to do that as going forward.

"Once the panic button in my brain starts buzzing, I'll have to come out and I'll go get some help."

The woman nodded again, wiped her eyes, and pointed. "Now? Please?"

"Okay." Corin grabbed the sides of the pipe and pulled, as if he could expand the opening to three times its size, and took three long breaths. *Here we go.*

He sucked in hard, filling his lungs to capacity, then slung himself into the dark tube. Corin dragged himself forward by his elbows, pushing with his feet. This situation was a good thing. Fate was training him, pushing him to overcome the fear. He tried to believe it.

Aroooooo.

Close. The dog sounded close.

Think logically. The tube won't collapse—wrong! Not the right kind of talk. Wrong word. *The tube is strong. There's plenty of air. This will be over soon. Stay strong.*

There was no sensation of panic; he felt calm. But as soon as he needed another breath the feeling would vanish, replaced by a tingling sensation what would quickly morph into full-blown terror.

The pressure in his lungs built, pressing to get out. *No. Think. You have plenty of air in your body. Ignore the pain.* He didn't need to breathe yet. He'd only been in the tube thirty, maybe forty seconds and was thirty-five, maybe forty yards inside the tube.

Two minutes thirty seconds.

He could hold his breath at least that long.

Steady. Plenty of time left.

Another whimper. Closer.

Time to turn on the flashlight. He pulled it from his hip pocket, flicked it on, and shone it down the pipe. Nothing.

Wait.

The light flashed against something metallic. Ten yards away. He had about twenty more seconds before he had to turn around.

"Scoundrel, come on, girl." Corin puffed out, letting some of his precious air escape.

Another whimper, but no closer.

He pushed farther in and shone the light toward the sound. It reflected off Scoundrel's eyes and he smiled. Corin was wrong. He'd misjudged. Scoundrel whimpered at him only five yards away.

They were going to make it.

Five seconds later Corin reached Scoundrel.

What the—?

The cockapoo wasn't stuck. It strained against a thin rope that ran from its collar to a small piece of rebar that stuck out of the concrete pipe. Scoundrel wasn't snagged; she was tied. Tight.

Corin ignored the sick feeling growing in his gut and dug into the rope. Too long, it was taking too long.

Finally he got it untied and yanked the cord through Scoundrel's collar. The dog sprinted past Corin toward the light fifty yards behind them, claws rapping against the dry floor of the pipe.

Corin mashed himself into a ball and turned around, the walls of the pipe scraping against his arms and legs, then he glanced at his watch. Fifteen seconds to get back to the opening.

Not enough time.

Come on, Superman, move!

With twenty yards to go his lungs refused to hold the air any longer and it whooshed out of him like a geyser. He gasped and sucked in air like he was hanging on to a rubber raft in the middle of a class 4 rapid.

"You're fine, you're fine, you're fine," he puffed out as he waited for the fabricated wall of control to be demolished and the familiar waves of panic to rip through his mind. Let the battle begin.

But panic didn't fill the empty space in his mind.

It would. He had only seconds now.

Think about being in Belize sipping a drink with an ugly little yellow umbrella. But he knew it wouldn't help.

As he pulled in his second breath, he steadied himself for the onslaught of panic and continued to crawl toward the opening. But the fear didn't come. Ten more seconds passed. Twenty. Thirty. Still nothing but calm sweeping through his mind.

He pictured the walls crushing in on him. Nothing. No fear. No panic. Just a peace that seemed to swirl from his feet to the top of his head, then it reversed itself and completed the circuit through his body again.

It made no sense.

An image of the chair filled his mind.

Yes, it did.

Unbelievable.

It was real.

Thirty seconds later he looked up toward the opening, a silhouette of the woman filling the opening of the pipe, sunlight streaming past the outline of her curly hair.

"Are you all right?" she called out to him.

"I'm good. Scoundrel is okay?"

"She's fine." The woman's voice seemed different. The emotion gone from it. "You seem like a kind man."

"Thanks, you seem kind too." Another fifteen yards and he'd be outside.

"Which makes me feel really bad." She kicked the inside of the pipe.

"What do you mean?"

"I'm so sorry for this. I don't want to, but they told me I had to help and if I didn't they'd . . . Well, I don't want to talk about that, so just forgive me, okay?" Her arm disappeared as she reached up above the pipe. A moment later the iron grating slammed in front of the pipe and echoed in Corin's ears.

She wouldn't.

No.

"What are you doing?" Corin crawled like a wild man, tiny specs of gravel digging into his elbows and knees. Five yards.

The woman wrapped a padlock around the grate and slammed its latch shut. "I'm so sorry; I am." She bent down, the crossed iron bars of the grate framing her large face. "I'm supposed to say you should have dropped it off like they asked you to, whatever that means."

"Don't lock me in here."

"I'm so sorry."

The woman lumbered away, Scoundrel's bark fading as Corin slumped back and rubbed his face with dirt-covered hands.

He'd jumped right into their web and cuddled up next to the spider.

If he hadn't been . . . he didn't know what to call it . . . cured? healed? of his claustrophobia, his brain might have short-circuited.

Exactly what they'd wanted.

And when they came again for the chair, he would have melted in front of them and told them whatever they wanted to know. Maybe they'd be by in a hour, or two, or three and make him a simple deal: tell them where the chair was in exchange for setting him free.

Who had set him up?

At the moment it didn't matter. All he wanted was to escape the pipe.

Corin spun and crawled back into the blackness till he reached a *T* in the pipe. He flashed on the light on his watch. He'd crawled for fifteen minutes. Right or left?

Left. It just felt right. He tried to laugh at his lame joke, but his brain gyrated with too many other questions.

Why had the chair healed him? He hadn't felt anything when he sat in it.

Was it Jefferies? He was the obvious choice, but Corin couldn't convince himself the pastor would go this far.

Would this lead to a way out, or was the pipe closed off at both ends of the *T*?

Seven minutes later he had his answer as he pushed up out of a storm-drain grate on a side street. Ten minutes after that he was back at his car, firing up the engine, knowing three things with absolute certainty.

First, he wouldn't be selling Jefferies the chair.

Second, he had to tell Tesser and Nicole about his healing.

Third, he had to find a safer place to hide the chair.

CHAPTER 35

Y ou'd better be there, old friend.

Corin had reached Tesser the night of the tunnel episode and arranged to meet out at Seven Falls on Sunday morning before Corin opened his store.

When he arrived, the old professor was already there, sitting on a bench perfectly centered in front of the 181-foot thundering waterfall, sipping a cup of coffee.

"Why do we have to meet here?" Tesser swatted at a mosquito on his wrist, then picked up his coffee and poured a splash on his forearm to wash it off. "I hate bugs."

Corin had asked Tesser to meet him at the base of the falls for three reasons. First, it would be private this time of year. Back in August the tourists would swarm like the mosquitoes attacking Tesser. In late October people were stacking wood and starting to think cozy.

Second, he was paranoid. Whoever had tried to scramble his brain by locking him inside that pipe would likely be watching him closer than ever now. Technology certainly made it possible for the people after the chair to bug his home, Tesser's home, and his car, and the thunder of the falls would keep their conversation private.

Third, he didn't want Tesser distracted by all his books and the Internet.

"They wanted me to crack open like an egg, so they could spread it in their pan and figure out where I've hidden the chair," Corin said as he sat beside Tesser.

"That would be a sterling example of stating the obvious." Tesser shifted on the thick, planked bench and stared at the falls towering above them. "Now what is this startling news you need to tell me but couldn't and wouldn't tell me about on the phone?"

"I'm getting paranoid in my old age."

Tesser patted his leg. "Old age doesn't kick in till you're eighty."

Corin cleared his throat. "There's no doubt about the chair: It is healing people."

"Has there been an addition to the pantheon of healings you've told me about?"

"Yes."

Tesser tugged on his right ear, then in apparent innocence rubbed his forehead with his middle finger. "You actually think the chair is truly 100 percent grown in America, healing people?"

"Yes. Ninety-nine percent of me believes it. And there's still the one percent that doesn't know what to believe any longer."

"But you seem more convinced of its healing power now than when your friend was cured. Your skepticism has waned."

"That's why I'm talking to you."

Tesser leaned back and rubbed both ears this time. "You want to know what the book says about it. If multiple healings would break out like this. If this is part of the legend."

"That and I want to know if you think it's possible."

"Who was the latest person healed?"

Corin stared up at the wall of white cascading down in front of him. "Me." He turned to watch Tesser's reaction.

If his face could have gone whiter than it already was, it probably would have.

"No, is this true?" Tesser rubbed his hand together. "It truly healed you?"

Corin told him the story of the pipe. When he finished Tesser said, "Fascinating. Utterly fascinating."

Tesser picked up his coffee and poked at the outside of the cup with a twig for a long time before answering. "I've always liked you so much, Corin." He turned and smiled. "You were my best student ever. And my friend. I'm sorry."

A burst of autumn wind rained leaves down around them like giant gold snowflakes.

"For what?"

"That you have to get mixed up in all this." Tesser dug into his kneecap with his fingers.

"What are you talking about?"

Tesser sighed. "No, I think I'll leave it at that." He stood and ambled over to the bridge that crossed over the stream that flowed out from the pool under the falls and stared down at the water.

"Uh, I don't think so." Corin stood and joined Tesser on the bridge, waiting till his old professor looked up. "Talk to me. What are you worried about?"

The old man puffed out his cheeks till he looked like a giant squirrel with a mouth stuffed full of marshmallows. "Think about it. Any time you get an object or an idea that purports to have powers beyond our understanding, you start attracting others like . . . like . . ." He swatted at another mosquito that landed on his arm. "See what I mean?"

"Bloodsuckers out for my chair."

"Well, someone convinced that woman to lock you in that pipe." Tesser rubbed the blood from the dead mosquito on his arm. "But they want more than blood, more than the chair. They want its power. They'll be coming out of the woodwork soon. And they'll be willing to do anything to get it."

"I think I know who is behind all this. This religious whacko has been after me to see the chair, telling me he can protect me from its powers."

"Oh? Who?"

"Does it matter?"

"No, I suppose not, but still." Tesser shuffled his feet on the concrete as if he was doing an impromptu dance. "Maybe it matters. Maybe not." His feet kept moving. "If the Mob was after it, that would be different than if it was a lady running a local day-care center."

"Hey, some of those day-care ladies are pretty tough."

"Tiz true."

"It's a guy named Mark Jefferies. Pastor of a huge church down around La Jolla."

A startled look flitted across Tesser's face and vanished a moment later.

"You know him?"

Tesser looked away. "No, but I've heard of him."

"How?"

The professor waved his hands above his head. "Doesn't matter, but it proves my point."

"That people are coming after it."

"Yes. Exactly. Which means it must be hidden well." Tesser waved his hands again. "You must hide it. I want no part of that piece of this chaotic equation."

Corin tapped his knuckles on the railing and watched the

curtain of mist float across the pond at the base of the falls that hid the surrounding foliage.

Tesser shuffled over the end of the bridge and back, grabbing the scraggly tufts of gray sprouting out of his chin and yanking on them like he was starting a leaf blower. "Where is the chair now?"

"It's in my vault in the store." Corin lied. He was done trusting anyone 100 percent, including Tesser. Including Nicole.

"Not good. Not safe. Need to have it someplace safe."

"No one is breaking into that thing."

Tesser stopped pulling on his goatee and glared at Corin. "The right people can break into anything."

His friend was right. His basement wasn't secure enough. The incident in the pipe convinced him he needed to move the chair to the secret bunker he'd built years ago in the woods behind his house. He would move it soon.

"Any thoughts on where I should hide it?"

Tesser paced past Corin and back three times before answering. "Maybe to my house."

"What?"

Tesser stopped and stared. "You must move it to my house. Soon. Tonight."

"Why yours? I thought you said you didn't want to get wrapped up in this problem."

"Equation. I said equation, not problem."

The surge of a car engine startled Corin. He turned to see a Honda Accord with tinted windows pull into the parking lot.

"I thought you said no one would be coming out here today but us."

The car crunched over the gravel parking lot straight toward them.

"Let's take a little walk," Corin said.

"You are paranoid."

"Thank you." Corin strode down the path on the other side of the bridge, glancing back to make sure Tesser kept up with him. "C'mon, let's move."

The old professor shuffled along somewhere between a slow jog and a fast walk.

"A little faster, Prof., yeah? I don't think we want to be meeting any new friends at the moment."

"I haven't moved like this in decades, maybe centuries."

They turned left down a path that would provide a screen of trees in another thirty yards.

"You with me?" Corin asked as he looked over his shoulder.

"Can't we wait to see if it's Guido before I give myself a coronary?"

Corin turned and grabbed Tesser's elbow to support him but kept walking, backward now, and stared at the car. It stopped at the edge of the parking lot closest to them. Why did the car have to be black? Somehow sky blue would make him feel better.

A few seconds passed and the passenger door opened. A moment later the driver's door opened. Two women got out. Young, probably mid-twenties. Camera bags were slung around their necks.

He breathed deep. Paranoid for nothing. What was wrong with him? Corin glanced at Tesser. "If we get shot, it will only be digitally."

Tesser sucked in and pumped out little puffs of air like he was blowing out a row of birthday candles one at a time.

"You going to survive?" Corin tried to repress a smile.

"I see that . . . whew . . . smile!" Tesser put his hands on his knees. "Believe me, when you hit 92 and I'm 150, I'll be in better shape than you are." His friend coughed.

"That I'd like to see." Corin put his hand on Tesser's back. "Really now, you okay?" Seeing Tesser have a heart attack because of his paranoia wasn't his idea of the ideal outing.

The women walked to the halfway point of the bridge and set their camera bags down. Picture time. Of the falls.

"Can you walk?"

"Of course I can walk." Tesser scowled.

They ambled down the path for a few minutes before Corin reverted back to their earlier conversation. "You think I should bring the chair to your house to hide it." Maybe that was the better idea. Corin's house was a target. Tesser's wasn't.

"Yep, yep, yep." Tesser's head moved up and down like a bobble-head doll.

"Why?"

"For your protection. I don't want you to be hurt."

Corin slung his arm around Tesser's shoulder. "I feel the same."

"Until recently, we haven't seen each other in years. There's no connection for anyone who comes after you to make between you and me. And you need someone you can trust." Tesser yanked up on his pants and tightened his belt. "Plus it will give me more opportunity to study that fascinating work of craftsmanship, so my offer isn't entirely altruistic."

"Do you have a secure room?"

Tesser waggled his fingers in front of him like he was playing air piano. "I have a basement that no one has been in for years."

"In other words, no."

"Pshaw. No one will look there."

"I don't know, Tesser." Corin turned and guided them back toward the parking lot. "I want some place with a lock on it. A big lock."

A tinge of frustration passed over Tesser's face. Corin sighed. He knew his old friend only wanted to help. But until he figured out what this thing was, Corin wanted it in a spot he could get to anytime he wanted, and he didn't want anyone else knowing the spot. It would protect them as much as it protected him.

"It'll be okay in the safe. Trust me."

"Okay, okay; it's just if anything happened to you, I'll never forgive myself and all that . . ."

"You're not getting mushy on me are you, Tess."

"You call me Tess again and I'll deck you."

Corin laughed.

They walked in silence, the coolness of the air trying to find crevasses in his clothes where it could streak in and send a chill into his marrow.

"Now that I've been healed, are you convinced the chair was made by Christ Himself and truly has powers to heal?" Corin asked.

"Almost. It could be psychosomatic."

"What?"

"Psychosomatic healing. The mind convinces the body it's healed, and for a time the symptoms are overridden and things seem to be different. But in a majority of cases the symptoms come back."

"In other words, the healing was in their minds? In my mind? I believed it strongly enough for it to become real?"

"Something like that."

"You're kidding." Corin reached out and caught a gold aspen leaf as it fluttered toward the ground. "If this leaf believes strongly enough that it's green, will it turn green for a few hours?"

Tesser tapped the side of his head and spoke in a Scottish accent. "Ye cranium is a powerful beasty if ye allow it to be."

"Doesn't make sense." Corin let the leaf fall from his open palm and settle to the ground. "The kid, Brittan, wasn't believing he was healed of his asthma. He was just sitting in the chair resting. I wasn't believing I was cured of my claustrophobia. I was just trying to save a dog."

"Yes, but your mind has been stirring and boiling and baking the idea of a chair with healing powers for almost two weeks now. At night while you sleep, during the hours you're awake, your subconscious could have convinced you your mind was healed."

"A. C. felt a warmth and a supernatural peace. He saw these lights and he lifted a three-hundred-pound desk over his head without any pain."

Tesser kicked at a pile of leaves alongside the path, shooting a good portion of them into the air, and watched them twist back to the ground. "Don't go all logical and mystical on me at the same time. That's the kind of cocktail that stings the throat going down."

"Seriously, do you think it's all in our minds?"

Tesser smiled. "I've lived through enough moons to be honest enough to say I don't know everything. I've also lived long enough to see something supernatural, if there is such a thing in the world, and I haven't seen conclusive proof of that. So truly, I wouldn't go around convincing myself I've got a chair of power when in all likelihood you don't. But on the other hand, given the fact you've been healed—someone I know and trust—I could almost be persuaded you have in your possession the genuine healing chair of Christ."

They reached their cars and Corin took Tesser by both shoulders. "Thanks for the wisdom, Prof."

"Anytime." Tesser opened the door of his Lexus. "And please know that my hiding the chair for you is a standing and sitting and lying-down offer."

"I know." Corin squeezed Tesser's shoulders, then released his grip. "I appreciate the concern, old friend."

"Of course." Tesser shrugged. "Now, given the new light that has been spilled on this adventure, I think we need to get on a plane to Patmos, don't you?"

"Where John the apostle lived?"

"Precisely." Tesser rubbed his hands together. "We'll talk to the locals. This is the kind of legend that never leaves the land in which it was birthed."

"Tesser—"

"Then we'll fly from there to Greece where the author of *Ladies of the Christ Chair* used to live and talk to his children—if they're still alive which they're probably not—and his grandchildren if need be."

"Tesser—"

"See if there's anything else we need to know that he didn't put in the book."

"Tesser!"

The old professor stared at Corin with an irritated look on his face.

"I've got a store to run. I can't jump on and off of planes for weeks at a time. Not to mention I'm broke."

"No, you can't worry about those things. You have an adventure to take hold of."

"I can't just drop everything and leave for a month."

"Why?"

Corin sighed. "I have to make money. At least try to make money."

"I took adventures when I was your age."

"You didn't drop your classes and jump on a jet whenever the wild goose squawked your direction."

"Sure I did. You forget, I went on numerous adventures while you were one of my students and I was working full time at the university. You even complained about how many guest lecturers I always had." Tesser pulled off his baseball hat and rubbed the stained brim. "How did I do it?"

"You cheated. You had tenure by that time, and you pretended you were in countries on the university's behalf that you never put one footprint on." Corin tapped on the roof of Tesser's Lexus. "You told them you were bringing back artifacts from overseas that would enhance the university's reputation, when in reality you were buying those pieces from some of your less-than-reputable contacts while you played in exotic ports of grandeur."

"I didn't ever do anything immoral."

"Are you forgetting I joined you on a few of those adventures?"

"I didn't cheat. Those pieces did enhance the university's reputation."

Corin laughed and shook his head. "Someday I'm going to write a book on the adventures we had together and will reveal all your little secrets."

"I'm an open book. I have no secrets." Tesser closed his eyes and patted his chest.

Corin smiled. How could he keep from loving the guy? Predictable. Unpredictable. Funny, smart, caring, indifferent. The quintessential contradictive personality. The networks should have made a TV sitcom about his life. It would have been a number-one show.

"Can I bring up something from your past that's a little painful?"

"I'm too old to carry any pain from the past."

"Your brother."

"I see." Tesser pulled on his chin hairs. "I told you about me and him, huh?"

"Not much, just that you had a falling out and didn't make it right before he died."

Tesser closed his eyes and sighed.

"We don't have to talk about it."

"Pshaw." Tesser batted his hand toward Corin. "Of course we're going to talk about it. What do you want to know?"

Corin told his friend the story of Shasta and him and as he did, the old man's eyes watered off and on. When he finished, Tesser took Corin's hands in his and squeezed for a long time without speaking.

Finally he patted Corin's arms and rubbed his eyes with the back of his palm. "It is my greatest regret. I didn't try with my brother. There was always tomorrow. Always one more day I could put it off." Tesser stood up straight and took Corin by the shoulders. "But you have today. And probably tomorrow. But how many more days, only God can tell. And I don't think He's telling." Tesser let go of Corin's shoulders and leaned against his Lexus looking five years older. "No regrets, Corin. You know what must be done. Maybe there is healing in the chair."

Corin nodded and blinked back his own tears.

The thought of calling Shasta and telling him about the chair just took another shift from the realm of insanity into the arena of definite possibility.

SHASTA ROSCOE SAT in his wheelchair staring at a photo of Corin and him at the top of Breckenridge Ski Resort. Big smiles splashed on their faces. Arms raised in victory.

The sound of feet behind him on the hardwood floor of his den interrupted his thoughts.

"Why do you keep that photo up?" Robin asked.

"To remind me of what he did."

She came around to his side and knelt beside his chair. "You can't hate him forever."

"I don't hate him." He swiveled his head toward her. "I don't feel anything toward him."

"I don't believe that."

Shasta turned back to the photo, then closed his eyes.

It seemed like centuries ago he'd opened his eyes after the accident, then shut them immediately to block out the harsh glare of the sun. But it hadn't been the sun.

He reached up to see if his sunglasses were on his face, but his hand didn't move.

"Mr. Roscoe, I think he's awake."

Shasta turned his head to the source of the voice, or tried to. Why wouldn't his head turn?

The sound of shuffling feet scurried toward him. "Hey, bro. I'm here."

Corin's face appeared over him.

"What's going on?"

"It's going to be okay."

"What's going to be okay? Where am I?" He wasn't sure why he'd asked the question. He knew exactly where he was. He'd worked two years as a volunteer in high school at a hospital near his house. The smells of a hospital were as familiar to him as his own home.

"You're in Memorial Hospital."

"Why?"

"You had an accident." Corin glanced toward the end of his bed. "When we jumped, you didn't land right."

The jump off the ramp flashed into his mind, then the sickening crack he'd felt when he landed. Then blackness. The truth swept over him.

"I'm paralyzed."

Corin wiped his mouth with the base of his palm and looked away.

"I am, aren't I?"

"They haven't finished running all the tests they need to, that they want to. They wanted you to be awake before—"

"Tell me the truth."

For a long moment Corin looked like he did when they were kids and their Scottish terrier, Max, passed away.

His brother sucked in a breath and held it so long Shasta almost expected him to faint. After finally releasing it Corin said, "They think so."

"How bad is it? My neck, is it broken?"

Corin paced next to the steel bed rails that held Shasta like he was in a cage. "It's not good."

"I'm paralyzed." Shasta said it again out loud, even though he was speaking to himself. "From the neck down."

Tears formed in Corin's eyes as he told Shasta how sorry he was. Over and over and over, but his voice faded as the words he'd spoken echoed through Shasta's mind. *"After this, life will never be the same."*

"You made me jump." He stared at Corin's pale face. "Why did you do it?"

"I know, Shasta. I know. I wish—"

"Wish what? You could take it back?"

"Yes. With everything in me. I only did it for—"

"For who, Corin? For me? Or for you to prove what a cool brother you are? So you could have another picture of us doing something crazy to show everyone? Or because you have to have someone with you when you dance with insanity?"

Corin wiped the sweat off his forehead and started to speak. "I—"

"You need to go, Corin."

"I won't leave you, I—"

"Leave me? You won't leave me?" Shasta spit over the railing of his hospital bed, the spittle seeming to hang in the air before it splattered on the floor next to Corin's shoe. "That's exactly what you need to do."

"Shasta . . ."

He closed his eyes and didn't open them till Corin's footsteps faded far down the hospital hallway.

At 2 a.m. Shasta woke with an itch just above his left eyebrow, the kind of itch that demanded immediate attention, the type that felt like a soft needle was winding its way into your skin.

He willed his arms, his hands, his fingers to move but they ignored him and lay like discarded driftwood washed up next to his body.

He forced himself to think of anything else but the itch, but it was impossible.

"Hey!" he called. No response. Louder. "Help!" Nothing. And no answer the second time, third time, fourth time. He ranted into the dark hallways of the hospital and eventually the itch faded.

But the rage inside him didn't. Rage toward himself. Rage toward the gods who would allow this to happen. Rage toward Corin who had altered his life for the rest of his days.

But whose fault was it? Shasta's for agreeing? Corin's for pushing him to go off the jump? Maybe both. Maybe neither.

It didn't matter.

He vowed to block Corin out of his life forever.

"Shasta, are you with me?"

He opened his eyes to find Robin standing in front of him, eyes questioning.

"I'm here." He blinked as if that would throw off the emotions the memory had stirred.

"Corin loves you deeply."

"I don't care."

"Yes, you do." She kissed him gently on the forehead. "And you'll never convince me otherwise."

Robin's footsteps faded just as Corin's had all those years ago, and Shasta let his head fall back against the headrest of his chair.

No, he would never let Corin back into his life.

He couldn't.

CHAPTER 36

After Corin wrapped up another day of almost nonexistent business at his store, he drove to Tori's dojo and picked her up, ready to talk about a subject he knew she wanted to bury. They were headed to see Tori's nephew perform in a junior high rendition of *Guys and Dolls*. The play a little mature for a crew of sixth, seventh, and eighth graders, but apparently the drama teacher was a frustrated Broadway wannabe.

As they pulled out of Tori's parking lot Corin said, "I'm giving serious consideration to calling Shasta, to see if he'll come sit in the chair."

Two night earlier he'd told Tori about Shasta's accident, about the experimental operation, and about Jefferies' offer.

"You're going to what?" Tori squinted at him as if she had chugged two shots of straight lemon juice.

"You heard me."

"Great idea. Brilliant." She flipped on the radio and Coldplay blared out of his speakers.

"I'm hearing a sliver of sarcasm in your voice." He turned the radio down.

"Really?"

As they pulled up to a red light, Corin turned to Tori. "I have to try."

"Just sell the chair to the pastor and run."

"I have to try this first."

"You're still thinking this comic-book-healing-people story of yours really has come to life, aren't you?"

"Yes." Corin turned and stared at the stoplight until it turned green. Green equals go. And the impression he'd gotten from sitting in the chair was a brilliant emerald shade. So was talking to Tesser. So was talking to Nicole. How many more lights did he need? But what if it didn't work?

"What if Shasta doesn't get healed? What will that do to your relationship?"

What? Did she read minds now? "It has to."

"Do you really want to ruin any chance of having a relationship with him if it doesn't work?"

Corin ground his fingers into the back of his neck in a vain attempt to loosen the gathering knots under his skin. "I don't have a relationship with Shasta now. What difference would it make?"

"It would make a difference, believe me." Tori slumped back in her seat and huffed. "At least now there's hope. Didn't you tell me he's slowly thawing? That his wife said there were signs of hope?"

"Yeah, the glaciers in Alaska are thawing too."

"Don't cause another Ice Age."

"I haven't told you what happened." Corin switched off the radio. "The chair healed someone else."

"Who?"

He took in a deep breath and let it out slowly. "Me."

After telling her his story, Corin waited for Tori to respond. She didn't.

"Did you hear me? *I* was healed, Tori. Me. This isn't a legend or a fairy tale any longer. If A. C. and Brittan and I can be healed, so can Shasta."

"How do you know it wasn't your mind finally letting go of your fear?"

"It wasn't. I would know."

Tori shrugged. "I'm not buying. Brittan outgrows his asthma around the time he sits in the chair, A. C. gets a cortisone shot or breaks up some painful scar tissue after he sits in the chair, and you finally get control of an emotional—not physical, mind you—issue and you're convinced this chair contains the healing power of God."

"Why are you so against the idea of this chair being able to bring people healing? Does it have to start curing cancer for you to believe?"

"No reason." Tori cranked her arms tight across her chest.

"Your body language doth scream in protest that this be a statement devoid of truth."

"Nice work, Agatha."

"Ms. Christie wrote about the detectives; she wasn't one herself." Corin stepped on the gas to get through an intersection before the light shifted from yellow to red. "Are you going to tell me?"

Tori turned toward the window of Corin's Toyota Highlander.

"Wow. I wasn't trying to get in the ring with you on this. If you don't want to talk about it, let's not talk about it. No big deal." Corin glanced at her. All he saw was the back of her head.

They drove in silence for five minutes. Probably his move to chip at the wall of ice that had formed between them. "Any of your students impressing you these days?"

"My uncle."

"Your uncle is taking karate from you?"

"My uncle is the reason I think you should keep your brother away from the chair."

"What does your uncle have to do with Shasta?"

She didn't answer for so long Corin thought she wouldn't say any more. But she shifted toward him in her seat—arms still folded—and stared out the windshield.

"Growing up he was my favorite uncle. When I was fifteen he was diagnosed with an aggressive form of MS. In four months he went from running marathons to spending all his waking hours sitting in an old wheelchair.

"Except for Sunday mornings and Wednesday nights." She wriggled her hands in the air. "Twice a week we piled in the car and drove—sometimes for hours—in order to endure a three- or five- or eight-hour healing service that never healed my uncle. Those quacks claimed to be men of God, to be able to channel His miiiiiiighty healing power, but for some funny reason, they couldn't see my uncle where he sat ten feet in front of them.

"For some reason God told them to bring other people up on stage who 'the spirit of God had fallen on' and lo and behold, they were healed!

"My uncle started to resist going, but my dad kept pushing. He was always convinced the *next* healing service would be the one that would restore my uncle to full health. Finally my uncle said no more and refused to go. But my dad got out the crowbar and my uncle went a few more times." Tori went silent again, the only sound her accelerated breathing.

"Finally my uncle shouted enough and stopped talking to my dad, my mom, even me." Tori blinked but the tears still came. "When my uncle died I said enough as well. I was done with God."

Corin gripped the wheel tighter and tried to find the right words, but none came.

As they rode in silence, Tori dabbed at her eyes with a tissue.

"They chased a dream made of broken wings that never flew." She blew her nose and brushed back her hair. "All I'm saying is, you need to get out some seriously sensitive scales and decide if this is worth your relationship with Shasta. Maybe I'm wrong. Maybe the three of you were healed supernaturally. But if you weren't, and Shasta sits in that chair and nothing happens, my prediction is any hope of having a relationship with him will be lost forever."

They pulled into the parking lot of the junior high, found a spot, and Corin shut off the engine. But they didn't get out.

"One more thing, Corin."

"Yeah?"

"If you go down that path, I'm not going with you."

"What path?"

"I see the look in your eyes. You're thinking if the chair is real, then God must be real. You're thinking God really could be intervening in the lives of men and if that's true you need to look into Him more."

"So?"

"I'm not going there."

"What does that mean?"

"If you're going to get into God, it's okay by me—I still love my parents and I have lots of friends who are Christians—I just want to be clear I don't want to be part of it."

"But we can still be together."

"I don't know. You get converted and things would get weird."

"I'm not getting converted. But I can't ignore what is happening to me."

Corin got out of the car, went around the passenger side, and opened Tori's door. She stared at him for five seconds before getting out. "Just think about what I said, okay?"

He would and did. The play might have been good. Corin didn't know. He spent the hour and a half inside the cramped junior high theater trying to make a final decision.

When Corin got home that night, he e-mailed Nicole and did something he'd never asked anyone to do for him.

> Dear Nicole,
>
> Part of me is determined to call Shasta in the morning. Another part says it would ruin any chance of seeing our relationship healed. I could use wisdom. Could you talk to God about this for me? I'm making my decision one way or another in the morning.

He stopped typing and once again played through the scenarios Tori and Tesser had planted in his mind. The image of Tesser's eyes filling with tears won out and Corin turned back to his keyboard.

> Actually, I just made the decision. I promise you tomorrow morning I'll pick up the phone and call him.
> Corin.

He hesitated, then depressed the key on his laptop and sent his e-mail down the cyber corridors into Nicole's in-box.

Now he was committed.

CHAPTER 37

Corin stared at his cell phone and played mind games with himself. Ten o'clock. Still two hours of morning left. He'd committed to himself and Nicole he'd call Shata in the morning. He could wait another hour and fifty-nine minutes before calling. Sixty seconds before noon was still morning, right?

No, he had to call soon. The store needed to be open by noon and he didn't want to race through town to get there on time. He'd been so certain last night. And now resistance had risen like the Green Goblin to fight what he knew needed to be done.

He set his cell phone down, eased over to his basement door, and slowly opened it. The stairs popped with creaks and moans as he descended into the basement. He opened the locked room that contained the chair, inched over to it, squatted down, and tapped the wood as if he were a concert pianist warming up.

"Will you heal him?"

There was no answer. No warmth, no glow to give him courage.

It didn't matter. Corin turned and clomped back up the stairs, sat at his kitchen table, and spun his phone in a circle. "God, I could use some help with this call."

Make the call.

The idea filled his mind along with a sliver of peace. He could do this.

How long had it been since he'd actually spoken to Shasta? Three years? Or was it four?

Corin spun his cell phone again on his oak table and dug his fingers into the knot at the base of his neck. How would he start the conversation? "Hey, it's me, the person you hate most in the entire world."

Corin picked up his cell phone and walked back to the door to the basement.

As he eased back down the stairs into the basement, he changed the settings on his phone to block his caller ID. If Shasta didn't know who was calling, maybe he would take it. But if he knew it was Corin, there was even less chance. Shasta would let it go to voice mail and Robin would call the store or Corin's phone and express her regret once again.

Corin entered the vault, sat cross-legged next to the chair, and sucked in a breath, then held it as long as he could before letting it out in a rush.

It was time.

He punched in his brother's number and waited for voice mail to kick in.

"Hello?"

Corin puffed out a surprised cough.

"Hello?"

"Shasta. It's Corin." His heart hammered like the bass drum at a rock concert.

For fifteen seconds the only sound was Shasta's labored breathing.

"Why did you call me?"

"I need to talk to you."

"I'd rather not. I'm not ready to talk yet."

"It's been ten years, Shasta."

Another thirty seconds of breathing.

"You shouldn't have called. I appreciate what you do for Sawyer; you've been a good uncle to him. But there's no point in our talking about anything till I'm ready. Today is not that day."

"This is important. We have to talk now. Two minutes, Shasta, two."

"No, we don't have to talk. Good-bye—"

"Do you want to be healed?" Corin blurted out before thinking. It was the worst thing he could say. And the best.

Again, only breathing.

"Why are you doing this to me?"

Corin didn't know. Maybe he was insane. Maybe the chair wouldn't work on Shasta. Maybe? Likely. Maybe Tori was right and nothing but pain would come of this. Maybe all he was doing was resurrecting the horror of that day that changed both their lives when it should stay locked away in the basement of both their hearts forever.

"Because I have to." Corin stood and glanced at a picture he'd brought down a few days earlier and propped up at the back of the room. He and Shasta on their dirt bikes, arms raised in victory.

C'mon, God, I need some kind of victory right now.

"I have to go." Shasta took two long breaths. "I wish I could pretend the past doesn't exist. But I can't. I don't need to dwell on it and neither do you. So don't call me again. It's the best for both of us, don't you think?"

He had time to say one more thing. And since Corin was

already over the edge, he might as well see if the parachute would open. He ran his finger along the back of the chair and a current of warmth ran up his arm.

"I think I've found a way for you to be healed."

"Don't do this to me."

"It's something you need to try."

"Have you wiped the days after you did this to me out of your memory? I've tried everything. Even drinking special concoctions of foul-tasting herbs four times a day for a month." Shasta let out a disgusted laugh. "Everything."

"A few weeks ago I was given a—"

"I don't want to hear it."

"Do you remember Avena? A. C.? He was healed. He sat in this ancient chair I was given and two day later an old shoulder injury that's bothered him for years vanished."

Corin could still hear Shasta's breathing so he plowed ahead.

"And this kid who came into my store and almost keeled over from an asthma attack sat in this chair, and the next day he's completely cured."

Shasta stayed silent, sighed through the phone, and then finally spoke. "I don't care what worked for A. C. I don't care if this kid thinks the chair healed him. I don't need you stirring up hope where there is none and never can be. I don't need you pretending you can fix my life like you've been trying to do for the past ten years through gifts and e-mails saying you're thinking of me and expressing an interest in my son. You already changed my life once. That's not enough for you?"

"When this woman showed up in my store three weeks ago with the chair and told me the next month of my life would be heaven or hell and that I would be given hope for restoration, I thought she was loco. But I've seen a slice of heaven and, yeah, these healings have given me hope."

"So I sit in this magical chair and suddenly I can move something below my neck?"

"I don't know." Corin gripped the leg of the chair. "I hope that will happen."

The electrical whirl of Shasta's chair echoed through the phone. Probably his brother turning to look out the picture window in his den, staring at a playground he hadn't stepped into in ten years.

"Have you sat in it?"

Corin hesitated. "Yes."

"Were you healed?"

"Yes."

Shasta took in a deep breath. "What part of you was healed?"

"My claustrophobia."

"I see." Shasta paused again. "And your feelings about being underwater?"

Corin stared at the chair. He knew where his brother was going and didn't know how to respond. If he lied and said his deepest fear was healed, his brother would see through it like a window. If he told the truth—that his fear of the water was as deep as ever—he'd be handing his brother a verbal baseball bat.

"No, not that." Corin wiped the moisture from his forehead.

"What about your right knee? Still stiff in the mornings?"

"Yes."

"So nothing physical was healed, and not your major malady, just a small neurosis in your mind."

"Shasta, you—"

Shasta laughed sarcastically. "But you're sure this chair will work for me, why? Because I'm a cripple and am more worthy to be healed?"

"If I hadn't seen the healings with my own eyes, I wouldn't have called. If it hadn't healed me. There's power in this chair. Isn't it worth trying?"

"No, it's not. Hope is better left dead. Each time it's resurrected, its subsequent death is a little harder to take. So I've killed it for good. Or I've tried. But you and I know, and the whole human race knows, you can't kill hope entirely because there's always one little bubble willing to rise with the slightest encouragement. And that would happen if I let you put me in that chair. I would hope once more, I would let it sweep me into your little shop, and I would sit in your ancient artifact and nothing would happen."

Corin let go of the chair. "I had to ask, Shasta."

"No, you didn't."

"Yeah, I did." Corin climbed the stairs up from the basement one at a time, resting for a second or two on each step. "Do you remember when Dad taught us to fly those stunt kites the summer of 1985? And we started having dogfights in the sky? Do you remember what he called us? Snoopy and the Red Baron. You were Snoopy; I was always the Red Baron. I was the bad guy." Corin walked across his living room and stared out at the same gray sky his brother was probably looking at.

"No, Corin. You weren't the bad guy then and you aren't now. I know you didn't mean to shoot my plane down."

What? He slumped onto his couch. Was Shasta saying he didn't hold what Corin had done against him? "If . . . then why won't—?"

"Because when the night goes silent and I fall asleep and enter the world of dreams, I do fly, and I dream of the adventures you and I used to have, and I can't live with those memories filling my mind." His brother's voice trembled and he stopped talking for thirty seconds.

"And every morning when my eyes flutter open, I remember I will never get in the cockpit again. And do you know who I see sitting in the seat behind the cockpit?"

"No."

Shasta sniffed. "I see my son. I see Robin. I see other friends who I will never be able to take into the sky. I see the longing on their faces to watch me do more than sit in a chair, a longing they try so hard to conceal from me but can't entirely. They pretend it's okay that I can't throw a baseball or stake a tent or take a stroll through gold and red leaves scattered in the park.

"I sit on that tarmac in my wheelchair almost every night and fight through the despair almost every morning." Shasta coughed, from emotion or something caught in his throat, Corin couldn't tell. "And do you know who I miss sitting in the cockpit with most of all?"

Shasta sucked in three heaving breaths. "Do you know who I dream about at night the most often?"

Corin knew.

"We were free together. We were free." Shasta didn't try to hide his emotion any longer, and the sound of his tears filled Corin's phone. "I have to fight the dreams every night, brother. I can't do it in real life as well."

Corin glanced around the room as if he could find something that would tell him how to react, what to say next, but there was nothing to save him. "Shasta, I—"

"Good-bye, Corin. Don't call me again."

Corin watched the display on his cell phone hibernate into darkness.

He slipped his phone into his jeans, then picked up the chair and moved it to the hidden bunker he'd constructed, which sat in the woods behind his home. Corin spent the rest of the day at his store trying to push his way through the haze of disappointment and trying to figure out what to do next.

He drove home that evening wanting only one thing. A night without having to think about anything other than if *The Avengers* movie next summer would be any good. But a nagging voice inside said he was about to be given a lot more to consider.

CHAPTER 38

Corin pulled into his driveway that night at seven thirty wanting to escape the pain of Shasta's reaction but refusing to give in. He thought his brother hated him all these years. But it wasn't hate. It was regret and longing mixed into an emotional Molotov cocktail Shasta refused to drink.

He sighed as he slid his satchel onto the kitchen counter and stared at *Outside* magazine sitting next to his espresso maker. It sat further forward than he remembered leaving it. The mind was already going and he was still six years away from forty.

Given the stress he'd been under lately, he was surprised he remembered anything.

He stopped in the bathroom, doused his face with cold water, slicked his hair back, and walked back to the kitchen. After grabbing two hard-boiled eggs out of the refrigerator, he trudged toward his dark living room, flopped onto his couch, grabbed the remote, and flicked on the TV.

Wait.

Movement. His heart pounded.

Something in the corner of the room had moved. Heat filled his body as he stared at the outline of a figure sitting in the chair in the far corner of the room to his right. A second later the lamp next to the chair snapped on and bathed Mark Jefferies in a soft gold light.

"Hello, Corin."

"What are you doing in my house!" He leaped up and backed up toward his kitchen.

"Trying to get your attention." Mark smiled, his ultrawhite teeth shouting confidence along with a dash of desperation at the same time. "I think it worked."

"What do you want?"

"Just to talk."

Corin waited for his heart rate to ease back toward normal. "Looks like you're flying solo tonight." Corin glanced around the room. "Where are your thugs?"

"They don't like being called thugs. I don't either. Don't do it again."

"But isn't that what they are?"

Mark drilled Corin with his green eyes. "You want to die on this hill?"

"No worries about guilt by association?"

"I only have one person I'm worried about appearances for."

"And that would be?"

"Christ."

Unbelievable. If this guy was a representative of Jesus to the world, then the future of Christianity was in ocean-deep trouble. "I see."

"No, I don't think you do see." Mark waved his hand around Corin's living room. "I'm not interested in houses or cars or boats or vacation homes or fame. I'm interested in the truth. And speaking the truth makes some people mad."

"And that's why you have your, uh, bodyguards?"

Mark and stretched his neck. "When I talk about the gay agenda and rights for the unborn, death threats fly at me like a hive of mad hornets. So I make the target on my back as hard to hit as possible." Mark crossed his leg and beat out a rhythm on it with his hands.

"What do you want?"

"Like I've said from the start, I want to help you. You need someone on your side."

"No thanks."

"Why?"

"I didn't sign up for this mission. If I could make the chair disappear tomorrow I would. The only reason I've hidden it is because of people like you."

"Really?" Mark uncrossed his leg and leaned forward. "You would walk away? I don't think so. If that were true, you would have jumped at my offer to buy the chair. I think you want answers."

"Not interested."

"I believe I have something that will persuade you to think differently."

Corin strode to his front door and held it open. "Time to go, Jefferies."

"No problem." Mark raised his hands, then stood and lumbered toward the front door. Just before he got to Corin, he took a small dark book out of his coat and smacked Corin's shoulder with it. "I came by because I thought you might want to take a look at this." Mark held the book with his fingers on the edge as if displaying a framed photo. "Definitely interesting reading. It might enlighten you considerably."

The cover read, *The Chair of Christ: The Reality Among the Legends.*

Adrenaline surged through Corin.

"I take it from the look on your face you haven't read this."

"Can I see it?" Why hadn't Tesser talked about this book? Maybe he didn't know about it. Or maybe he had the entire text memorized, but it wasn't worth bringing up because Tesser considered it—in his words—"bunkum."

Or was it a fake?

"Of course. But I'd want something in exchange." As he passed Corin he held the book out just beyond reach. "Why don't we plan on talking about this more tomorrow morning? Let's say ten o'clock at Forest Lawn Park? I'll bring a football and we'll toss a few while we talk, all right?"

Football? This guy was swimming in the deep end without a paddle. "I need to think about that."

"You need someone on your side, Corin. And you need to see this book."

"I have plenty of people on my side."

"Who? Your mysterious lady friend? Tesser?"

"Yes."

"They're not on your side."

"Why do you say that?" Corin leaned against his front door and stopped a few feet from Jefferies.

"What do you really know about Tesser? You took some classes from him? You went on some trips together? And what do you know about Nicole?"

"I know enough."

Mark waved his hand. "Yes, of course, you know her name. Her first name. What else? I haven't been able to find anything on her." Mark squinted. "We're coming up blank. Which means unless she's

spilled her life story to you, you don't know any more than I do."
Mark cocked his head. "Am I right?"

Heat rose to Corin's face. Mark was right. Tesser he knew.
But Nicole? He knew nothing about her. Only what she'd told
him. And why had he taken that as truth? True, his gut told him
he could trust her. An extraordinary lady. Wise. Caring. But he'd
believed his ex-wife was telling the truth the whole time she was
having an affair with his cousin. Ex-cousin if that was possible.

"How do I know you're worthy of my trust? That you're telling
the truth?"

"You don't."

"But you're still asking me to trust you, just like Nicole."

"Yes."

"I let you see the chair, you let me see your book."

"Exactly." Mark licked his lips. "Plus I want to meet Nicole."

"I don't think that's going to happen."

"You can at least ask her."

Corin looked at the book and at Mark. Then he dropped his
arm and took a step back. "I'll think about it." Corin motioned for
Jefferies to leave. "I'll let you know in twenty-four hours."

Mark stared at him for ten seconds before turning and walking
out the door.

Corin settled onto his couch, flicked on the TV, pulled up *Iron
Man* on Netflix, and watched it for an hour. An hour in which he
wrestled with the possibility of Nicole having fooled his gut into
trusting her when her trust wasn't warranted.

As his clock struck midnight, he still hadn't reached a
conclusion.

Time to go wrestle his dreams.

Just like Shasta. Like brother, like brother.

Mark had planted a seed of doubt, and Corin wasn't sure if that seed was a flower to be watered, or if he should take weed killer to the idea and scorch the life out of it.

Tomorrow after he closed the store, he'd try to get an answer straight from the gardener.

CHAPTER 39

Corin watched Nicole sit as if carved in stone on a park bench too close to the waters of Woodmoor Lake. Only ten yards between her and the lapping waves. Had she sat that close to the lake with intent?

The sun lit her hair and turned its white shades whiter in spots and made her profile stand out in stark contrast to the gold and red shades of a November afternoon behind her. It looked like her eyes were closed.

As he stared at her all doubts Mark Jefferies had stirred the night before were swept away by the breeze meandering off the lake.

He was still staring at her three minutes later when she turned and spied him. She smiled, blinked, then closed her eyes again and resumed her imitation of Lady Liberty.

As Corin approached Nicole, he studied the undulations in his nemesis and for the millionth time tried to make peace. *You survived. You were a kid. Let the fear go!* But the roar of his heart said never.

"We have to stop meeting like this. People will start to talk," Corin said when he reached Nicole and sat beside her.

"Let them." Nicole turned and rested her elbow on the back of the bench. "How have you been, Corin?"

"The chair continues to make life interesting."

"That I don't doubt." She smiled. "Did you keep your commitment? Did you call your brother?"

"Yes."

"And?"

"We had the longest conversation we've had since the accident."

"Did he give an answer to your invitation?"

"Yes." Corin leaned forward, elbows on his knees, fingers intertwined. "He will never sit in the chair. And probably will never speak to me again. I took my shot."

"So what do you do now?"

"You don't have that answer for me?" Corin tried to smile, sat back, and folded his arms. The sun spread diamonds across the surface of the lake, which made him squint against their power. But their power was nothing compared to the hold the water held over him. It squeezed him in the middle of the night when the nightmares came and he drowned again and again. It pummeled his mind as if he were in a washing machine.

Why hadn't the chair healed him of that fear?

"And what about you, Corin. Did you sit in the chair again?"

"Yes."

"And?"

"It healed me."

"Of what?"

"My claustrophobia."

"I'm glad." Nicole nodded as if she had been expecting him to tell her that. "Do you believe now?"

"It's crazy to say this, but I'm still not sure, even after being healed. Maybe Tori is right and all the healings came from our minds." Corin kicked at the stones at his feet. "Do you really believe this chair was made by the Son of God?"

"I'm not sure it matters what I believe as much as what you believe."

"I believe there's some type of power attached to it."

"Then you have your answer."

"But it's not the way you would answer the question."

Nicole shook her head. "No."

"Then what type of power do you think is in the chair?"

"Not yet."

"Not yet, what?"

"It's not time to answer." Nicole reached in her pocket, took out a handful of seeds, and tossed them toward a sparrow that flitted on the grass on the other side of the path.

"Why not?" Corin gritted his teeth. All she ever seemed to give was nonanswers or cryptic replies that only led to more questions.

She smiled at Corin but didn't answer.

"Tell me!" He leaned toward her. "If I'd convinced Shasta to sit in the chair, would it have healed him?"

She patted his hand in the same way Tesser often did. "I do not know. I am not God." She threw more seeds for another sparrow that had joined the first. "I listen to His voice. I follow where He leads me. I hope I am listening with ears to hear."

"What does that mean?"

"That's it's not yet time to tell you what I believe to be true about the chair."

"When will it be time?"

"When it's time."

Corin let his gaze follow the shoreline from the far left of the lake to the far right. There was beauty in the water. Part of him could reach back to a time where he loved the water, when he longed for summer afternoons full of cascading down a river in inner tubes too big for him or any of his friends, of finding tree branches over the water strong enough to handle a rope and a swinging boy. And of racing through the water in swim meets, pinning another blue ribbon to the wall of his room.

"The chair didn't heal me of my fear of the water."

"No." Nicole clasped and unclasped her hands.

"Why not?"

"I don't know." She glanced at him with her piercing blue eyes. "He knows."

The look in her eyes unnerved him. So confident. So knowing. So . . . "Who are you?"

"A friend."

"You're more than that."

"Do you think Tesser believes the chair holds the power of God?"

"How do you know I've been talking to Tesser? Have you been spying on me?"

"Most assuredly. We've already talked about this." She laughed like liquid light. "That chair is too much of a lightning rod not to keep tabs on the person it's been given to."

"What about the chair itself? Aren't you worried about it?"

"Not as much. It doesn't match my concern for you."

Corin turned to her with a question she might not answer, but he'd be able to learn something from how she responded. "Are you a descendant of the order that swore to protect the chair?"

Nicole smiled and slid her eyeteeth over her lower lip. "It sounds like your studies with the professor have enlightened you."

"True."

"And have you enjoyed what you've learned?"

"You're not avoiding the question, are you?"

"Most assuredly."

"But if you were to answer the question, how would you respond?"

Nicole smoothed the nonexistent wrinkles in her pleated slacks. "I would tell you if the fantastical legends purported in Tesser's book were true, that yes, I would likely fit the profile."

"Mark Jefferies wants to meet the legend."

"He does, hmm?"

"Badly."

"That's interesting."

"Why?"

Nicole didn't answer.

Two boys, eight, maybe nine years old, stumbled past them, one with an old NFL Junior Football grasped in his arms, the other tugging on it with his arms and the full weight of his body.

"Give it up!" The boy without yanked hard on the ball.

"Make me!" the other said, twisting to pull away.

"I will!"

Corin grimaced as the war raged between the two boys. Had he and Shasta fought the same war thousands of times as they'd grown up? Or was it ten thousand? He smiled. Their fights always ended in them making up and building a jump for their bicycles or climbing the tallest tree in the woods across the street from their house.

But their war ended ten years ago, after he'd made his brother ski off a ledge into a world where one side had retreated beyond the battlefield to a realm Corin couldn't reach.

The pain of yesterday's conversation continued to echo in his mind as loud as summer thunder. Corin gave a quick shake of his head, as if to purge his mind, and then turned to Nicole. "*Are* you the lady from the legend?"

"Corin, you don't need to ask me that question again. You know who I am. You need to choose to believe or not believe. In me. In the chair. In yourself."

"Me?"

"Yes. Choose to believe you are the one the chair is to go to. That you will write the next chapter in the legend, because I think deep inside, you believe fully in the chair and are coming to believe in its Maker."

She was right; he had taken the idea of the chair deep into his heart. Strongly. It gave him a purpose. Something of lore, of legend. Not a comic book, but real life.

"But you were supposed to give the book to a daughter, a direct descendant, not some stranger." Corin hesitated and rubbed the bench with the palms of his hands. "Did you never marry? Didn't you have a daughter to pass the chair to?"

"Yes, I married." Nicole pursed her lips and stared at the lake.

"And?"

"And yes, I had a daughter."

Corin wasn't sure how to ask the next question so he simply stated it. "And is she alive?"

"She is not."

"I'm sorry."

"As am I." She patted his hand then. "Thank you, Corin."

For the first time, Nicole's eyes clouded and moisture filled them. She tried to laugh as she wiped her cheek with the back of her fingers. "It was a long time ago."

"What was?"

"Nothing." Nicole blinked back more tears.

"I didn't mean to pry."

She smoothed back her hair and didn't speak till at least a minute had passed. "I didn't get to say good-bye."

"I'm sorry."

"She wouldn't let me. She thought my belief in the chair was crazy." Nicole massaged the top of her hand with the other. "She didn't want me talking to her children about it and made me swear I would never contact them."

"Did you keep your promise?"

She turned and offered Corin a sad smile. "No, I did not."

"Do you regret breaking that promise?"

"No."

"Why—?"

"Have you decided if you'll follow the One who made the chair?"

"No, I haven't."

"When you've made your decision, I think it will be time to tell you why I gave the chair to you." Nicole stood and held her hands out to Corin and he took them. "This was a delight, but I must go. Those clouds look like rain and I want to get home before the skies open up." She squeezed his hands twice, then turned to go. "Don't worry," she called out over her shoulder as she clipped away, "we'll chat again soon."

"When?"

"Sooner or later."

Corin puffed out a long sigh and decided to head for the cemetery. He needed to talk to his parents.

CHAPTER 40

Corin drove away from his meeting with Nicole hoping the rain would hold off till he reached the cemetery and was finished with his time there. It didn't. A light mist filtered down out of the darkening sky and blanketed his windshield as he pulled into the parking lot.

It was empty except for his car. It didn't surprise him. Who else came to graveyards in the evening unless it was October 31 or prank night for high school kids looking for a rush? Corin did it to be alone.

After he slid out of his car and locked the doors, he shuffled down the familiar path that would take him to his parents' matching headstones. Two minutes later he slipped to his knees in front of their graves, the dampness of the lawn seeping through his jeans, chilling his knees. He didn't care. The loamy smell of the soil filled his head and he breathed it in deeply.

"Watching us grow up, did you ever think Shasta and I would arrive at this spot? Two kids who did everything together, who made you wear grooves in the road taking us to the emergency room after one of our adventures."

Like the time they were six and four and jumped off the roof and discovered that Superman and Batman capes didn't automatically make them fly.

"All you wanted for us was to be friends—and you got your dream. And left us thinking we'd be best friends forever. But if you've watched lately, the dream crashed and burned." He glanced from his mom's headstone to his dad's. "And now it looks like the final chance for restoration has vanished. Just thought you should know."

He jammed his hands into his coat pocket. "What did you think of my final try? Did you think Shasta could sit in my magical chair and it would heal him and we'd be jumping dirt bikes over canyons again? Did we ever tell you about the time Shasta came six inches from landing his bike three hundred feet down in the Metus River and almost beat you to this cemetery?"

The lamppost to his right flickered and then went out as if on cue, smothering him in the darkening twilight. "I'm sorry, Mom. I'm sorry, Dad. So sorry."

Corin closed his eyes and instantly images flooded his mind. First the accident, the numbness in Shasta's eyes as he lay on the slope waiting for the ski patrol, soft flakes of snow landing on his face and Corin realizing in a flash why his brother didn't brush them off.

An instant later that scene was replaced by the rippling surface of Lake Vereor. He wasn't sleeping, but the pictures in his head were just as vivid as if he were buried deep in the dream. A shake of his head did nothing to rid him of the terror. He tried to stand but instead tumbled onto his side and his eyes closed and he entered the world between dreaming and waking.

This time no light filtered through the surface of the water five feet over his head. There was only darkness as his dad yanked on his life jacket.

Water flowed around his body, pressing in on him as if he was hundreds of feet down, pressing into his eardrums like ice picks.

His dad dove a second time. A third. A fourth.

But it no longer mattered. All the air had been purged from his lungs and now they were full of water.

There was no panic this time, no determination to reach the surface, no life in his fingers to scrawl his desire to live into his dad's forearms. Only acceptance that all hope was gone.

And the fear. Deeper this time than it had ever been.

Corin shrank inside himself till he was smaller than an atom, but still the fear came and found him, mocked him, and a moment later devoured him.

He woke to the kiss of soft rain on his face, the lamp to his left flickering off and on, and the smell of damp soil.

The vision or dream—he couldn't tell which it had been—faded quickly but left him with a thought that lingered like a chilling fog.

Death would win, had won, had always held him in the palm of its hand, and would never let him slip through its fingers.

CHAPTER 41

When Corin arrived at his store on Wednesday morning, A. C. stood leaning against the front door with two oversized chocolate muffins and two large cups of what he assumed was industrial-strength coffee and a big grin on his face; an I-want-something grin.

"What are you doing here?"

"I thought I'd bribe you into letting me take another ride in your chair."

Corin laughed. "What now? Broken toenail?" He opened the door and held it for A. C.

"Nah, I just want to sit in it. Find that peace again." A. C. lumbered in and set the muffins and coffee on Corin's sales counter.

"You're going all spiritual on me?"

"Haven't you thought about it? About God since all this started happening?"

He had. More than once. More than twice. The idea had been

pinging around his brain long before Nicole had brought it up the day before. "Yeah." Corin flicked on the store lights. "I have." He turned but A. C. must have already ambled back to the vault.

Corin was halfway back when A. C. pounded toward him, face white, eyes intense.

"You all right?"

"It's gone!"

"What's gone?"

"What do you mean what, the chair!" A. C. paced the lamp aisle like he was getting ready to punch something. "Did you hide it?"

"No."

"Don't rock me, are you serious?"

Corin pushed past him and walked to the vault.

It was empty. Corin's face flushed.

"That chair healed me." A. C. slammed his palm on the vault door. "It could have helped a lot of people. It could have helped your brother."

"It's okay, A. C."

The big man turned to Corin. "What's wrong with you?"

"What?"

"You don't seem that upset."

"It's okay; I'm not thrilled about this, but it's okay."

"The chair is gone, Corin. It's not okay. We lost it!"

"No, we didn't." Corin offered his friend a slight smile.

"You're kidding me."

"Nope."

"You built a duplicate."

Corin nodded. "Just in case." He waved his hands. "Reconstructing the chair was intense. The thing mesmerized me. So simple, so complex. It took me seven tries before I got it right, and even then I wasn't even close."

"But close enough. You fooled them."

"Apparently."

"You are brilliant, Roscoe." A. C. smiled, but a moment later his mood darkened. "But we still have the issue of someone breaking into your store and stealing what they think is the chair."

"Exactly. We're not talking vandalism anymore; we're talking a full-out crime. No signs of forced entry, which means they're pros. Probably thought they'd have a few days before I found the 'chair' was missing. And yes, I fooled them for a while. But once they figure out it isn't the real chair, they'll come after it again."

Corin paced in front of vault. "I built the duplicate just in case something like this happened, but I wanted to believe it wouldn't." He crossed his hands on top of his head. "Wrong."

"Who? Who took it?"

"Jefferies. I suppose it could have been someone else I haven't bumped into, but that's where I'd place my bet."

"So where is the real one?"

"Safe."

A. C. laughed. "Where is it?"

"Safe."

"You're not going to tell me." His friend cocked his head. "Thanks for the trust."

"I trust you. I don't trust them. If you don't know, you don't have to lie. Something you're not good at."

"Where do you go from here?"

"Get in touch with my new pals down at the police department, explain what happened, watch them serve me up with platitudes, and walk off with nothing but a 'we'll try to locate your old piece of wood and track down the people who took it.'"

"Don't you think you're in a little over your head?"

Corin glared at him.

"Sorry, wrong metaphor."

"No worries."

"I'm just saying this is beyond you at this point. You need to get someone else involved. To protect you."

"Who?"

A. C. threw his arms wide. "Me."

Corin shut the vault and spun the combination. "I don't need protection. I have a feeling this thing is going to be over soon, one way or another."

"What does that mean?"

"I wish I knew."

As Corin drove home that night, he tried Tesser but there was no answer. Next he tried Nicole. Something she'd said made him realize who she was. And who he was to her. Waiting till she could confirm what he suspected wouldn't be easy.

CHAPTER 42

I've been praying for you, Corin."

"It's making things worse." He yawned and stretched his legs.

"Tell me about that."

Nicole and he sat at the lake, both covered in heavy coats against the cold of an early November night.

Corin gazed at the lake and told Nicole about the replica of the chair being stolen and the dream and what had happened at the cemetery.

"It seems Someone is trying to get your attention."

"God."

"Only you can answer that." She rubbed her shoulders and pulled her wool hat farther down her head. "And how are you feeling about Shasta?"

"I'm burying the hope our relationship will ever be restored."

"Oh, don't do that."

"Why not?"

"Because you don't want to. As painful as it is, the deepest part of you wants to hang on to that hope. To deny that hope is to deny one of the most significant parts of yourself."

She was right of course. He would never be able to snuff out the pilot light that burned for Shasta. But after his talk with his brother the other day, any hope of the fire blazing again had vanished.

"I will hold on, always. He's my only family." Corin glanced at Nicole. "At least I thought he was my only family."

An enigmatic smiled played at the corners of her mouth. "Why do you say that?"

"What is your last name?"

"I think you've already guessed, have you not?"

"The same as my mom's maiden name."

"Of course." Nicole smiled. "How long have you suspected?"

"In my subconscious, probably from the day we met."

"Good, I'd be disappointed if you didn't feel a strong connection. I certainly feel it with you." Nicole patted Corin's hand. "How did you figure it out?"

"The final puzzle piece snapped into place yesterday when you told me you hadn't kept your promise to your daughter."

"To not talk to her children about the chair."

Corin nodded. "Plus all the other pieces fit. The legend says the keeper has always passed it down to a daughter. That isn't an option for you since you don't have a daughter, so the next option is a granddaughter who will agree to the vows. But you don't have one of those either.

"The final option is to give it to a next of kin who will agree to the vows and who is a follower of God. I didn't agree and I'm not a follower of God, yet you gave it to me anyway."

Nicole smiled and patted his knee. "It is sometimes necessary to follow the spirit of the law rather than the letter. I knew you wouldn't believe me if I'd just showed up one day and tried to make you understand who I was."

"And my mom?"

"Like we talked about already, your mom never wanted to believe the chair was real and didn't want to be a part of it, didn't want you or Shasta to be a part of it. Which meant she didn't want you to be a part of me."

Corin sighed. He'd been cheated out of so much. It wasn't right. It wasn't his mom's choice to make, but she'd made it for him anyway.

"The only time she spoke of you was about how you were gone a lot."

"Yes, my duties surrounding the chair kept me busy. There was too much travel. It's what drove your grandfather away too." Nicole smiled a sad little smile. "And I'm not sure what I accomplished. Your mom turned away from Christianity primarily due to my being gone so much, and you weren't raised in the faith."

"Why did you devote your life to it?"

"I didn't feel I had a choice."

"Did you?"

"Yes." Nicole rubbed her forearms and stared at the water. "In my defense I can't remember if I knew I had a choice at the time my mother passed the chair to me."

"And do I have a choice?"

Nicole laughed and tilted her head. "Of course."

Corin shifted on the bench. "What about Tori?"

"What about her?"

"She's not a fan of the chair. She's been so burned by religion."

"Maybe she needs to sit in it."

"I think that would take a miracle."

Nicole looked at him with eyes wide open and eyebrows stretched to their limits.

Corin laughed. "I get it. Yes, I've seen a few lately. I suppose God could pull off one more."

"Indeed He could." Nicole stood. "I need to go. There's someone I have to see. He needs to hear the truth. He needs to see the light."

NICOLE DROVE TOWARD the Garden of the Gods praying for the right words. Words that would penetrate past the polished veneer, into the heart of Mark Jefferies.

As the mile markers flashed by, she let the sorrow of the time she'd missed with Corin and Shasta seep out of her heart into her soul. So much that was gone forever. Time with her daughter she'd never been allowed.

Nicole's thoughts turned to the last time she'd seen Rachel. It was the last day she'd seen Corin and Shasta as well. She sat with Rachel at her breakfast table, having the same argument they'd had for the past three years.

"They need their grandma."

"No, they don't, Mother. I don't need your strange ideas and obsessions filling their heads."

"I need them."

"You should have thought of that ages ago when that chair became the most important thing in your life."

Rachel was right. The chair had consumed her. She'd lost her daughter because of it, and now she was in danger of losing her grandsons as well. "I'm sorry, Rachel, you're right, I—"

"Fine. Nice. Good." She brushed her dark blond hair back from her forehead. "Apology accepted. But it doesn't change anything."

"I've changed. I know—"

"Too late, Mother." She glanced over Nicole's shoulder.

Nicole turned toward the sound of shuffling feet to her right.

"You're our grandma?"

Corin and Shasta stood staring up at her, eyes full of questions and a tinge of fear. Three and five. Full of innocent wonder.

"Yes."

"How comes we don't see you ever?" Corin said.

"I hope to see more of you in the future."

"When?" Shasta said.

"I'm hoping this summer we can—"

"That's enough, Mother." Rachel turned and shooed the boys away. "Mommy needs to finish a conversation, so go find something to do."

"Can we slide?" Corin said.

Rachel rolled her eyes. "Yes, fine. Just give us a few minutes here."

Corin and Shasta scrambled to the top of the stairs and moments later sat on a lumpy mattress at the top, goofy grins plastered on their faces. In unison they cried, "One! Two! Three! Launch!"

They lurched forward and the mattress spilled over the edge of the top stair. Corin and Shasta rode the mattress like an out-of-control toboggan, their eyes flashing joy only possible in the very young. They reached the bottom, skidded over the floor, and slammed into the wall across from the stairs.

"Again! Again!" Corin said.

If she were twenty years younger, Nicole would have joined them.

"I don't like them doing it, but it's the only way I can get them out of my hair for a few minutes," Rachel said.

Her grandsons climbed back to the top of the stairs, lugging the mattress behind them.

"They're so young. If you rid your life of me now, they might not remember me."

"I don't want them to remember you."

Nicole forced her tears to stay inside as she stood and nodded to her daughter. "I see." She turned and walked to the door, waiting for, praying for Rachel to call her back. But her daughter's voice was silent.

Nicole blinked and the memory faded. She'd wondered what she would tell Mark when they met. Now she knew; she'd tell him what she'd learned too late in life. That an obsession with the chair was a path of despair unless it led to an obsession with the One who made it.

CORIN SWUNG OPEN the door to Tori's dojo at 8:20 that night, enough time for any straggling students from her last class to have left. Kings of Leon blared from the four Bose speakers in each corner of the room. She stood at the counter with her back to him, tapping away at her computer, probably recording comments on each student's performance that night or answering e-mails from aspiring black belts trying to get into her perpetually full class schedule.

He held the yellow roses he'd picked up on the way behind his back and eased toward her, his shoes silent on the sparring mat.

She laughed and said without turning, "True masters can see without seeing and hear when there is no sound."

"How do you do that?"

"Quite well, thank you." Tori turned and smiled.

"This is for you." He handed her the flowers and she took the roses and rubbed them across her cheek. "Thank you. I accept your peace offering."

"So gracious of you to receive it." Corin gave a mock bow and returned her smile. "Can we sit?"

"Sure." Tori came out from behind her counter and they walked toward the double row of white plastic chairs used for parents, grandparents, siblings, and friends who came once a month to see the students spar in a tournament.

They sat and Corin took both her hands in his, stared at her fingers, and rubbed them in his.

"So, you have something to tell me, or did you come down here just to give me a hand massage?"

He looked up into her eyes. "I want you to try sitting in the chair."

Tori pulled her hands away and leaned back. "You are a stained and polished platinum piece of work."

"What would it hurt to sit in it?"

"Why should I?" Tori tapped her feet on the floor almost fast enough to double as a drumroll.

"Because it might free you from your past."

"What in my past do I need to be free of?" Tori folded her arms. "I got free when I left home."

"Free of your resentment?"

"I'm not holding on to any resentment."

"Right."

Tori stood. "Listen to me closely. I'm done talking about the chair forever. Got it?"

"Got it."

"And if we want to continue this relationship, talk of God is not going to be part of it. Are we clear?"

"Crystal."

On the way home Corin tried to call Tori three times. She didn't pick up and he didn't leave a message.

Another relationship on the rocks. He was getting good at denting them. But he'd fix Tori and he once this chair thing settled down. The dust had to land sometime.

But he was afraid the particles would soon be stirred to their greatest height yet.

CHAPTER 43

Corin stood in the back of his store shelving a new shipment of lamps when the bell on the front door announced the arrival of the last person he ever excepted to spill a shadow across his oak floor.

"Hello?" a voice from the front called out.

A voice he'd heard forever.

"I like what you've done with the place."

Was it him? Had to be.

Corin jogged to the front, skidded to a stop at the end of the aisle, scanned the front of the store, and his pulse spiked. There. Right inside the front door. It was Dominique Shasta Roscoe.

His brother had hated the name Dom or Dominique from the moment he could talk. At eight years old he held up a can of his favorite drink at a family picnic—black cherry Shasta pop—and announced from that moment on his name was Shasta.

Corin stared at his brother for what seemed like ten minutes.

"Surprised to see me, bro?" Shasta tilted his head back and to the side.

Shasta's dark brown hair was shorter than he'd ever seen it. It was almost a buzz cut. And his face was thin. "Utterly." Surprise, fear, excitement all rushed through Corin's brain like a flash flood.

Shasta punched the throttle on his wheelchair with his chin and surged toward him, the electric wheelchair shuddering as he bumped over the uneven wood floor.

"I need to get that floor smoothed out."

"Why? Do you get a lot of incapacitated customers?"

Corin didn't know how to respond and said nothing.

Shasta stopped five feet away and stared at Corin. "I'm surprised I'm here too." His gaze moved slowly around the store. "How is business?"

"It's okay."

"I'm sorry."

"It'll come back."

Shasta nodded and the silence between them grew louder. Corin looked at his hands, then back to his brother. "I hope so."

Another segment of silence.

"Robin tells me you're dating a nice gal. Tori, is it?"

"Yeah." Corin rubbed his eyes with the tips of his thumbs. The conversation was straight out of *Insipid Talks for Any Occasion*. "We could probably make small talk for the next two hours, but I'm not really up for it."

"In other words, why am I here?"

"I think I know why you're here. But I have no clue what changed your mind."

"I'm here to go for a ride I'll never forget."

"But what changed your mind?"

"You did."

"Not when we were on the phone."

"No. After." Shasta wheeled his chair another foot closer to Corin. "What I had to face after we talked was the fact you'd been healed. Not someone else. Any other person I couldn't believe, but you, I do. And no, it wasn't a physical healing, but you've fought your claustrophobia most of your life. If it's gone, some type of miracle happened to you. If there's any chance of a miracle happening to me, I have to take it. For Robin. For Sawyer."

Shasta whirled and faced the front door as if to say that conversation was over.

"But not for you and me."

Shasta didn't turn back. When he spoke his voice was subdued. "No."

Corin pressed a knuckle into his chin. Shasta wasn't here to start building a bridge between them. He wasn't even willing to look at a set of plans. And there was nothing Corin could do to force his brother to put on a construction hat.

But if Shasta was healed . . .

Movement outside his front window drew his attention. Robin paced next to the elevator lift built into their red van, looking almost as thin as Shasta. Probably on a continual stress diet taking care of Sawyer and Shasta. She glanced everywhere except into the store.

It didn't surprise him.

She would do anything asked of her to help restore his relationship with Shasta, but if he knew his sister-in-law—and he did—she wouldn't pry into what kind of verbal volley was going on inside the store.

"The chair isn't here." Corin turned back to Shasta. "Do you think Robin would mind swapping vehicles with me for a few hours while we take yours to my house?"

"Nope."

When they reached Robin she grabbed Corin in a fierce hug and whispered, "I've prayed for this. I told you to never give up hope."

Corin hadn't almost given it up. He'd given up completely, but now it returned, full force, and was giving him a bigger rush than he'd ever had shattering the edges of his extreme-sports adventures.

It didn't matter that Shasta was still icing him out of any chance at restoring their friendship. Within forty minutes his brother would sit in the chair.

And Corin would believe in Shasta being healed.

On the ride out to Corin's, silence was in much greater abundance than conversation but he didn't mind. It was a chance to talk with God.

Look, God, I don't know how to pray and I don't care. I hope You don't care either. I have to assume You helped set up the circumstances to get Shasta to my store. So if that's true and You're part of this . . . just don't let me down, okay? Don't let him down.

Heal him, please? Restore us to the way we were before. I want him back.

A peace settled on Corin he'd never felt before.

He glanced at his brother. *His brother.* Riding alongside him in a car. How long since that had happened? The day of Shasta's accident, of course. One drive toward disaster, the next drive toward possible restoration.

But what if there was no restoration? What then? Corin tried to push the thought from his mind but it pounded back like the elastic cord on one of his bungee jumps.

C'mon, God, this has to work.

When they reached the house, Shasta's lift lowered him to the driveway. "I moved the chair from my basement to a hidden bunker I built back when I was making serious bank. It's a place for priceless artifacts I want kept absolutely safe. No one knows about it and I had to put it in a place where no one would find it. It's about fifty yards behind the house over rough terrain, which means I'll have to carry you."

"Fine," Shasta said, but he didn't look at Corin.

"Ready?"

Shasta nodded, his eyes dead. "Sure."

He hoisted Shasta out of his chair and almost dropped him a moment later from shock. So thin. More bones than flesh. He couldn't weigh more than 115 pounds. Didn't he eat?

"Am I doing this right?"

"It doesn't hurt. No feeling from the neck down, remember?"

"But still—"

"I'll survive. My physical therapists thrash me much harder than you will. I haven't turned completely into china yet, and you're much gentler than a bull."

When they reached the bunker Corin set Shasta next to an aspen tree next to the entrance and pushed the remote in his pocket. A section of the earth slid back to reveal a narrow set of stairs descending underground.

He tromped down the stairs, opened the bunker door, scrambled back up to Shasta, and picked him up. "It's going to be different this time." The words slipped out of Corin's mouth before he could stop them. He'd inadvertently let his hope spill out and splash all over Shasta.

He guessed hope was pressing in on his brother as well, but Shasta was probably resisting. Too much pain, too many times of trying when the healing didn't happen.

Corin carried Shasta down into the room and set him in a kitchen chair five feet from the chair.

Shasta gazed at the chair for a long time saying nothing. Finally he said, "So this is the miracle maker."

"I hope so." Corin eased over and touched the back of the chair. Nothing. "Are you ready?"

"Sure."

Corin lifted his brother and set him on the chair like he was placing a baby into his mother's arms for the first time.

"You'll need to hold me, keep me from falling over."

"Of course." Corin held his brother's shoulders and closed his eyes.

There was nothing to say, no instructions to give.

Ten minutes later Shasta said, "How do I know when it's long enough?"

"I don't know." Corin sighed. "Do you feel anything?"

"No."

Shasta's voice wasn't sad, wasn't hopeful, wasn't anything.

"Believe with me, Shasta. Think of the deepest thing you want."

Shasta's raspy breathing was the only noise in the room for the next three minutes.

"Anything?" Corin asked.

"Nothing." Shasta coughed. "What should be happening?"

"It's been different each time." *Please, God, heal him.*

Corin didn't know what he'd expected, but it wasn't this. Where was the peace and the lights and the warmth?

Ten minutes later Corin carried his brother out of the bunker at his request, across the lawn, and put him in Shasta's red van. They didn't speak on the way back to Corin's shop.

Before he and Robin drove away, Corin stood at the passenger side window trying to find the right words. "The healings have all come after sitting in the chair, not at the time the people sat."

"Okay."

"You'll call me if anything happens?"

"Of course." Shasta squinted up at him. "You'll be the first."

Would God come through? No idea.

But as the van pulled away Corin couldn't shake the feeling that was the last time he'd talk to his brother for another age.

CHAPTER 44

Corin was pouring over his sales figures in his office, trying to find even one statistic that offered hope when he heard the front door open softly. Problem. He glanced at his watch. Ten fifteen on a Thursday night? A little late for shopping. But maybe not too early for a little breaking and entering.

He stood and eased toward his office door. The sound of heavy shoes—boots by the sound of it—echoed toward him from two different spots on his showroom floor. There was more than one of whoever it was.

Corin slipped his cell phone out of his pants pocket and pulled up his text messages. Yes. A. C. was the last person he'd texted. *Please have your cell on, pal.*

Corin stabbed his thumbs at the letters. Faster. Have to get this out before they come back here. AT THE STORE. IN TROU—

His office door flew open and smashed against the inside wall as a man thick in the shoulders and neck with a glistening shaved head stepped into the door frame. A wide grin played on the man's face as he glanced around the office.

"Hello, Corin." The man extended his hand and beckoned with his fingers. "It's probably not a good idea to be texting anyone right now. We need to have a chat and I wouldn't want you to be distracted by someone texting you back in the middle of our conversation. Can I have your phone, please?"

Corin pressed down on his phone hoping his thumb was in the right spot to send A. C. the text, then slid his phone onto his desk and turned back toward the man.

"Thanks for stopping by Artifications, are you in the market for an antique?"

"Interestingly enough, we are. One particular piece we understand you might be able to help us with has caught our attention in a substantial way." The man ambled over to Corin's desk and fished out the cell phone from where it had slid under a stack of papers. He batted the phone to the center of the desk with a finger of his gloved hand and glanced at its display.

Corin's heart hammered.

"Let's hope"—the man peered closer at Corin's phone—"A. C. doesn't get the message before we leave, hmm? For his sake. And yours." He raised his elbow above the phone and brought it down hard. Then again. The man laughed. "I call that the iSmash. Almost as good as that *Will It Blend* guy on YouTube, don't you think?" He laughed again, then motioned Corin toward the door. "Shall we?"

Corin found two other men standing in the front area of his store. One was around five eleven and looked like he should work at a university from the 1950s. All he was missing was a tweed jacket. But his shoulders were broad and his boots looked steel toed.

The other was maybe six foot, his hair cut short in front with a ponytail in back, and a tattoo of a dagger on both sides of his neck.

"I understand you gentlemen are doing some late-night shopping." Corin forced his breathing to steady and wished he'd taken more of Tori's classes. His skills were at the level of would-get-himself-killed-if-he-tried-anything at best. And he suspected his guests knew more about street fighting than the average grizzly.

The man with the ponytail grinned. "Yes, we're interested in buying a chair. But the one we want doesn't seem to be on display tonight. However I have it on excellent authority you haven't sold it yet."

"And what chair would that be?"

"A powerful chair. A miraculous chair. One worth going to great lengths to possess."

"I'm not sure I know which piece you're referring to."

"I think you do." Ponytail Man tilted his head and closed his eyes. "I so wish you would be truthful with us."

"All the chairs I have for sale are on the floor. So if you don't see it, I don't have it."

The man sighed and pulled a photo out of his pocket. "It looks like this."

Corin glanced at the photo of his chair. He hoped his face didn't betray his question of how they got a picture of it. "I don't have anything like that."

Ponytail slipped the photo into his back pocket, eased over to Corin, and poked him in the chest. "Get me the chair. Now."

"It's gone. I sold it."

"I see." The man waved his hand at Baldy and Mr. 1950s. A minute and a half later Corin sat tied in a dining room chair from the thirties, thin brown twine cutting off the circulation in his wrists.

"We asked you to simply leave it in the barn, but you couldn't do that, could you? So let me ask again. May we have the chair, please?"

"I sold it."

Ponytail looked at Baldy, who backhanded Corin's jaw. His head snapped back and it felt like the car accident he'd been in two years earlier. Whiplash, lights, and exploding brain cells.

"Let me ask again, Corin." The man licked his lips. "Where is it?"

Corin let out a soft moan. "I don't have it." They could beat him all they wanted. He wouldn't give up the chair. Ever.

"Okay." Ponytail nodded and rubbed his temple. "Fine. But let me explain something to you. This isn't the movies. If you don't tell us, we don't give you a long speech or torture you, and we don't kill you. We all go find Tori and torture her and kill her in front of you very slowly."

Mr. 1950s wandered over to Corin, pulled a spartan knife out of his pocket, drew it along his jeans, and winked at Ponytail. "Then we quickly separate your muscles from your bones, without giving the cavalry time to come crashing through the door."

A moment later the cavalry crashed through the door.

CHAPTER 45

When A. C. got Corin's text he was three minutes from the store. Maybe two if traffic was light. He made it in one minute and forty-nine seconds.

Twenty seconds later he peered through the front window of Corin's store.

Three men stood in front of Corin, who was tied to a chair. One was an oversized gorilla, but the other two looked average height and weight.

He turned away from the window and punched in 911 on his cell phone.

"This is 911, what is your emergency?"

"The owner of Artifications is being held hostage inside his own store. The address is 16906 West Francis Street. Send a car; I need to get in there."

"Why do you think he's being held hostage?"

"He's tied to a chair!" A. C. bounced on one leg, staring at Corin. "You need to send a car *now*."

"What is your name, sir?"

"Look, don't be an idiot. I'm going inside to—"

"Sir, we need you to stay outside. And we need to know your name."

"A. C. Avena. Why do I have to stay outside?"

"You know why, sir. You don't know what you're dealing with here. They could have weapons."

A. C. pressed his fist into the side of his face. Yes, he'd thought of that. If there wasn't that possibility, he'd already be inside the store thrashing the men surrounding Corin. "How soon are you sending a car?"

"We've already dispatched a unit."

"How long!"

The phone hummed. *C'mon!*

"Police officers should arrive at the scene within seven minutes."

Great. Corin might not have five minutes. Maybe not even three.

"It's gotta be faster than that."

"They'll be there as soon as possible."

"Fine. But they better be breaking speed records to get here."

"Can you see what is happening inside the store and describe it for us?"

A. C. peered back through the window into the store. The man in the middle was talking to Corin, who glared back with seething eyes. A. C. almost laughed. Corin couldn't fight a Barbie doll even with all his kung fu training, but he didn't lack courage.

The man in the middle who looked like the professor from that ancient show *Gilligan's Island* said something to Corin . . . Corin responded . . . from the look on the man's face he didn't like it . . . the man nodded to the big bald guy. Baldy backhanded Corin, whose head snapped back like a spring.

"They just hit him." A. C. growled into his phone. "I'm going in."

"Sir, you need to—"

"Get that car here now!" He ended the call and took a deep breath.

As he strode around the building toward the back door, A. C. tensed his chest involuntarily. This would be an excellent workout. But before he started to roar, he had to assess the situation and make an educated guess if they had guns or not. If they did, he'd back off and try to figure out a way to keep them from inflicting any more damage on Corin. A distraction, something.

If they didn't, then it was rumble time. He flexed his biceps. Voluntarily this time. He stepped through the store's back door and strode toward the front.

After five steps his cell phone lit up to the sound of Journey's "Don't Stop Believin'."

Caller ID was *Unknown*. Probably 911. They'd tell him to stay outside and he'd tell them off and later regret it. A waste of time. He turned off the ringer and shoved his phone into his front pants pocket.

A shout from the front echoed through the store. "We have company! Go find them."

A. C. burst into the front of the store before any of them could move. Corin looked up at him through an eye already starting to swell.

"How are ya doing, Corin?"

"Wonderful. My new friends and I are discussing terms on a piece of furniture they're interested in acquiring."

The bald gorilla said, "My guess is we're gazing at the illustrious A. C. Am I right? Is that who you are?"

A. C.'s face morphed into granite. "I'm your worst nightmare."

"Excellent. Good to have you join us." A man with dagger tattoos on his neck and a ponytail clapped his hands. "Well done coming to the rescue of your bosom friend. What can we do for you?"

A. C. studied each guy. If they carried heat it wasn't obvious. So it was Las Vegas time. Time to gamble whether they had guns or not. If they didn't, he would make the next two or three minutes look like a UFC ultimate match, but if they did have guns . . .

But even if A. C. had seen bulges in the men's clothing, he wouldn't have stayed outside. Not when Corin was inside taking championship shots to the head. "I'd like you to leave if you don't mind."

"We do mind."

"In that case, if you don't get out of this store immediately, I'll escort you out. And not gently."

Ponytail wiggled his fingers, grinned, and opened his mouth wide to reveal a studded tongue. "Three of us. Two of you. And one of you"—the man motioned to Corin—"won't be of great assistance. We would make the floor shiny with you, big boy."

"I don't think so." A. C. smiled his sideways grin.

Baldy returned the smile and clenched and unclenched his fists. "So you want to make a little thunder, huh?"

"Definitely."

"These guys are serious, A. C." Corin strained against the ropes binding his hands. "Get out of here."

"Nah, I missed my workout yesterday so this will make up for it."

"A. C., don't."

"These guys? Piece of cake, piece of pie, and some tiramisu." He looked back at the three thugs. "Ready?"

They nodded and strode toward A. C., splitting apart like synchronized dancers when they were six feet away. Ponytail lunged at A. C. from his left, then pulled back while Baldy came at him from the right and spun silky smooth to deliver a roundhouse kick to A. C.'s side.

A. C. wasn't fooled by Ponytail's feint. He stuttered forward, feinted to the left as if to take on Ponytail, then spun and caught Baldy's leg in midkick with his iron-grip hands. He twisted the leg hard, then slammed the man to the ground, making sure his head was the major body part that cushioned his fall. If he wasn't out cold, he still wouldn't be moving quickly anytime soon. One down, two to go.

One of the others jumped him from behind—had to be Ponytail—threw his arm around A. C.'s neck, and squeezed. A. C. slammed his elbow into the man's ribs, loosing his grip around A. C.'s neck. Another blow to the man's rib cage and he dropped to the ground.

The professor came at him from straight ahead.

Feint right. Hand to the throat. Block. Parry. Strike.

This guy had skill.

A. C. took a hard blow to the jaw and staggered backward. In the next instant Ponytail slammed his fist into A. C.'s kidney from behind.

"Uhhh!"

"Want another?"

"Bring it," A. C. said as he spun and backed up, glancing between the professor and Ponytail.

Ponytail lunged forward first. The guy was quick, but A. C. sidestepped the attack and used Ponytail's momentum to toss him head first into an oak dresser. Ponytail lay on the ground and moaned. Out cold. Two down.

"A. C., look out!"

He spun around in time to see the flash of a shot rocketing out of a gun held by the professor.

The bullet struck him and it felt like a bee had stung him just below his rib cage. His hand went to his stomach, and a few seconds later blood seeped through his shirt onto his fingers. He tottered for a moment, then slumped to the floor.

"I told you I could take them." He coughed and blood spilled onto the floor. "But bullets always hold the trump card."

CORIN FELT HOT, then cold, then hot again. This couldn't be happening. He screamed and yanked on the cords holding his wrists so hard it felt like they had sliced off his hands.

Blood seeped through A. C.'s fingers and dripped onto the floor like a melting early spring snow. Little blood bubbles pinged out of his mouth as he took ragged breaths.

"Don't let him die!" Corin strained against the rope. "You have to get him to a doctor."

"Now why would I want to do that? I just shot him. I want him to die," Mr. 1950s said.

"No. Please. Not A. C."

"Why don't you get your precious little chair to save him?" The man smiled and glanced at Ponytail, who had just gained consciousness.

"If you'd simply given it to us in the first place, by the way, he wouldn't be in this conundrum. We would have been gone before he got here. But now, you're going to be saying good-bye very soon. And I'm guessing that will weigh on your soul, well, forever."

Corin screamed at them with every swear word he knew and again strained against the twine with all his strength. "I will kill you."

"No. You won't." Mr. 1950s lit a cigarette. "You'll give us the chair and we'll wave good-bye." He pulled a shiny penny from his pocket and massaged it between his thumb and forefinger. "Heads, I shoot A. C. again; tails, I shoot A. C. again." He smiled a thin, condescending smile. "Unless you want to tell me where the chair is."

"Who sent you?"

"That's not the response I was looking for."

Corin dropped his head and closed his eyes as the penny clattered to the floor and rang in his ears like a rock-concert cymbal. Idiot! What had he been thinking to text A. C.?

Mr. 1950s picked up the penny. "Ah, shucks. It's tails." He lifted his gun.

At the same moment Baldy's cell phone rang. He answered and seconds later shoved the phone in his pocket. "We're outta time; we gotta roll, now."

The three men sprinted out of the store without a glance at Corin.

He didn't think about why they left. His entire focus was on A. C. The floor in front of him grew darker—blood continuing to seep out of his wound and into the tiny cracks and crevasses of the oak hardwood floor A. C. lay on.

"A. C.!"

No response. No movement.

"Wake up!"

He had to get to his friend's cell phone. Where did A. C. stash it? Front right pocket? Always his front pocket.

Corin clumped his chair toward his friend in stuttered hops, each time he moved the twine cutting deep into his wrists. He ignored the pain. *Don't tip. Stay in control. Ten more feet. Move!*

When he reached A. C. he realized he couldn't get to his cell phone unless he lay on his side with his back to A. C. so he could try to reach it with his hands through the wood slats of his chair.

He would have to tip himself over. He rocked the chair once. Twice. And he fell.

No. He'd misjudged. He was too close to the footstool next to A. C.

Corin tucked his head to his chest but it wasn't enough. The crack of his skull against the footstool exploded in his head and he flopped onto the floor like a rotten pumpkin.

As the swirling blackness surrounded him one thought pinged through Corin's mind: *A. C. is going to die and it's my fault once again.*

AS CORIN STAGGERED up out of blackness the sound of sirens filled his world. And he was moving. Ambulance? Did that mean A. C. was okay?

His eyes fluttered open. Mistake. The light seemed to puncture his skull and turned up the throbbing in his brain exponentially. Was an elephant doing jumping jacks on his head?

"He's coming around."

The voiced sounded muffled and he couldn't tell if it was male or female.

"A. Zee okay?" Corin's head felt like it had been on the rinse and spin cycle for the past twenty-four hours. "My fend, izh zee okay?"

"Try not to talk. You're on your way to the hospital. You smacked your head in the wrong spot. You probably have a concussion. Another quarter inch over and there's a good chance you'd be riding in a different kind of car."

Corin opened his eyes a millimeter and waited a moment for his eyes to adjust. He tried to push up on his elbows and blackness rushed at him.

"Whoa, cowboy, you're not ready for that horse for a little

while longer." The man—it sounded like a man now—put his hand on Corin's shoulder and gently pressed him back down onto the gurney.

"I halve to know ehf hez okay."

"Your friend lost a lot of blood, but we stabilized him before we put him in the ambulance."

"Iz zhee?"

"I don't know. From what I saw I'm guessing he'll make it."

"Mhy fahlt, muine." Corin fumbled for his pocket. Had to get to his cell phone. Had to call A. C. to see if he was okay. "Godda scall himm."

"You have to stay still, sir."

"Havs to scall A. C.!" Corin opened and shut his eyes repeatedly, trying to get used to the lights in the ambulance blazing into his retinas.

"Relax. He's going make it."

"You're shure?"

"Positive."

A moment later he slipped back into the darkness.

CORIN WOKE TO the sound of the ESPN Sport Center theme song coming from a TV to his left. Where was he? He rubbed his eyes and the bridge of his nose with his thumb and forefinger and took a deep breath. In a hospital room, but why?

And why was his head pounding like he'd gone through four of Tori's demonstrations as the class punching bag?

A moment later the scene from the night before rushed into his mind.

A. C. He had to find out if A. C. was okay.

Corin glanced to his right and then left, scanning for a call button. There. On the railing of his bed. He pressed it once. A low pitched hmm filled his ears. Then again. *Ennnnnnh.*

"It might be a while."

Corin looked up. Through the curtain to his left Corin saw the outline of what looked like a man lying in the bed in front of the TV screen.

"What?"

"Let me put it this way. If the nurses around here were in the Olympics, they wouldn't be sprinters."

"Don't they come when you hit the button?"

"Always. But 'coming to assist' might mean within a few minutes to you. It might mean within a few days to them."

Corin glanced at the clock on the wall. Seven o'clock in the morning. "What day is it?"

"Saturday."

He glanced at the clock again. Unbelievable. He'd been out for over twenty-nine hours.

Corin studied the IV worming its way into his arm. "I have to get out of here."

"Hey there, what do you think you're doing?" A tall, slender man with a postsurgery Michael Jackson nose traipsed into the room.

"Getting this IV out of my arm."

The nurse eased Corin's hand away from his arm. "I can see you're trying to do that, but why don't you let us handle the removal when it's time?"

"What's your name?"

"Dondelar Myers."

"You're a nurse here?"

"Yes."

"I need to talk to someone who can tell me the condition of A. C. Avena."

"I've already checked on him—"

"And?"

"He's stable. More than stable. He's doing well."

"I gotta go see him."

"We'd like to watch you a little longer."

"I've been asleep off and on for twenty-nine hours even though someone kept waking me up every five minutes."

"Every few hours, to make sure your concussion was nothing more than that."

"I think I've maxed out on getting a good night's rest."

"You had a concussion. You needed the sleep. We gave you—"

"Not to be rude, but I really need to see my friend."

"Your friend went home. Signed himself out." The doctor sniffed. "There's no way we would have released him this early even with his wife being a nurse."

"But he'll be okay?"

Dondelar sucked in his lips and didn't answer.

Heat filled Corin. No. Not A. C. "What happened to him?"

"You should talk to him or his doctor."

"He's my best friend." Corin sat up in bed. "He saved my life on Thursday. Tell me, please."

"Are you sure you want to hear it from me?"

"Positive."

Dondelar shrugged. "Mentally he's fine, but the bullet grazed an important area of his spine. It looks like he's paralyzed from the waist down."

Heat scorched Corin's body and his knees went weak. Not possible. Not possible! It was a sick joke. "What?"

"I'm sorry."

Corin's pulse spiked and he swallowed hard. It couldn't be true. "I need to get out of here."

Dondelar looked his watch. "In two more hours I'm supposed to run you through a few tests to make sure you're okay, but I'm betting you'd like me to run them now and get you released ASAP, hmm?"

CHAPTER 46

An hour later Corin stared at A. C.'s doorbell, bathed in the soft glow of the porch light, wishing some of it would seep inside him. He needed light. Something to show him the way out of the downward spiral that had become his personal slide into futility.

He squeezed his quads, trying to find the right words to speak when he stepped inside. What could he say? "Sorry? It won't happen again? Try sitting in the chair one more time and maybe that will fix things?"

Corin felt like he was swimming in an ocean of guilt so vast it made the Pacific look like a kiddie swimming pool.

Finally he lifted his hand to A. C.'s doorbell and started to press his forefinger into the button. It felt like trying to move a solid steel wall. He pressed harder and heard the familiar ding of A. C.'s chimes inside.

The door opened a few moments later. "Hey, Cor, how are you?" A. C.'s wife, Dineen, stood in the doorway, a tired smile on her face.

"Feeling like a pretzel someone decided to double twist just for the fun of it."

"Don't let yourself go there; he's not mad at you." Dineen beckoned him inside and stepped back.

Corin raised his eyebrows.

"He isn't, trust me."

"He should be." Corin stepped into A. C.'s entryway.

"Why?"

"I've ruined his life. He's not going to walk again." Corin shook his head. "The irony of perpetuating the same horrific fate on my two best friends—"

"What did you do to him? Coming to rescue you was his choice, not yours."

"What did I do?" Corin stared at her. "Other than put him in a position where he'll be paralyzed from the waist down? Where his concrete company will go up in gray dust? Where he won't be able to play with his kids? Nothing other than that."

Dineen shook her head, took his hand, and pulled him into the living room. She sat on the flowered couch and motioned him toward the love seat next to it. "What did he write back when you texted him to ask if you could come over?"

"Nothing, just 'Yeah, come over.'" Corin glanced at the hallway leading to the back of A. C.'s house. "I figured this is when he confirms the bomb has exploded and destroyed our friendship and tells me to get out of his life." Corin glanced down the hallway again.

"Do you even know my husband? Even if he was paralyzed, he wouldn't abandon you. Ever. Your friendship means the universe to him."

Corin rubbed his neck under his chin. "Next to Shasta, A. C. is the person I love most in the world." Corin leaned forward, his knees on his elbows. "He is a better friend than I deserve."

"Not true." She smiled, a teasing look in her eyes.

A shot of adrenaline pulsed through Corin. What had she just said? That even if he was . . . "Are you telling me he's—?"

"Yes, Cor, I am." Dineen winked. "I thought that line might have skated right by you."

"Are you telling me he'll walk again? The nurse told me—"

"The nurse should've stayed quiet. The doctors say there's a 99 percent chance he'll walk again. I like those odds."

"Me too." Corin let out a breath with more force than he expected. "I like them a lot."

A monsoon of relief flooded through Corin. He'd assumed the worst. That at the very least A. C. wouldn't be able to walk again—maybe worse. But this? Back to normal? Corin needed news laced with hope. Any more bad would break him. And there wouldn't be enough horses and men to put him back together again.

Corin leaped to his feet. "I gotta go talk to him." He smiled at Dineen and slowly shook his head. "You don't know how glad I am to hear that."

She returned the smile but while the smile remained on her face, the happiness she'd shown earlier faded from her eyes. He'd known Dineen almost as long as he'd known A. C. Something was wrong. The story had another chapter Dineen wasn't telling him. Tears misted her eyes and she took a halting breath.

"What?" Corin sat back down.

She shook her head.

"Talk to me, Dineen."

She waved her hand through the air. "It's not that big a deal." Dineen blinked back her tears and tried to smile. "It's going to be fine; he's going to be fine. Really."

"What is it?"

"No, not from me. Go talk to him, Corin. It'll be good for you."

As he walked toward A. C.'s family room the air seemed to thicken. Every gray cloud had a silver lining, and every white cloud had one that's black—and he was breathing in the darkness.

Corin stood in the doorway leading to the family room. The UFC 52 championship bout between Randy Couture and Chuck Liddell played on the sixty-two-inch big screen A. C. bought three years ago and a framed eleven-by-sixteen photo of his daughter playing soccer hung over the built-in bookshelves that didn't have any books on them.

A. C.'s wouldn't be spending his time laid up reading the greatest novels from the past or present.

The back of his friend's thick head poked up above his lounge chair like a miniature mountain. Sitting up was a good sign, yes?

As he watched the two warriors battle on screen, Corin guessed what Dineen hadn't wanted to tell him. "Is it true?"

"Hey, Cor. What's going on?"

Corin eased around the couch and jammed his hands into his pockets.

"Is it true?" Corin motioned with his head toward the screen.

"That I can't take my shot at the title?" A. C. pointed at the screen, then offered a smile mixed with sadness. "Yeah, true. It's gone."

"No, don't say that." This couldn't be happening.

"It's a good thing, Cor." A. C. pulled himself up in his chair and immediately slumped back down to where he'd been—pain shooting across his face. "What kind of life would that have been? Traveling all the time, beating my body up so I couldn't move by the time I was fifty? Nah, I always wondered if I should do it even if the shoulder was good and now I have my answer."

"You cannot be telling me this." Corin cradled his temples between his palms and pressed hard.

"It's a good thing, bro." A. C. laughed. "Seriously. You know I wouldn't say it unless I meant it."

Corin paced from A. C.'s window looking out on his backyard to his blue couch and back to the window. "Next you're going to be describing what you're going to do since you can't do concrete work anymore."

"Yeah, that's quite the additional bonus surprise, huh?" A. C. ran his fingers through his thick sandy blond hair. "So Dineen told you, huh?"

"What?"Corin stopped pacing, turned to A. C., and blinked.

A. C. looked up, a puzzled look etched into his face.

"No." Corin slumped onto the couch. "She didn't tell me. I was being sarcastic."

"The doctors say I'm going to be fine. I'll be able to walk, run, do light construction, but putting the strain on my body that running a concrete company requires isn't going to be happening." A. C. winked. "Unless I do want to end up permanently in a wheelchair."

Corin's mind spun. How could he go from hope one moment to drowning in despair the next? He knew exactly how. It was all possible thanks to him, and thanks to the object that had turned his life and the lives around him into a 9.8 earthquake: the chair.

The chair that had introduced the most insidious lie possible. That there was a way out, a way to restoration with Shasta.

"What are you going to do?"

A. C. smiled. "I'll sell my company."

"And if you don't?"

"I will."

"And then what?" Corin was back on his feet, pacing again.

"You're going to wear out the carpet."

Corin ignored him.

"You think you've ruined my life, don't you?"

"The chair has brought me nothing but pain, and I've spread it out to my closest friend in a liberal dose."

"You did the opposite." A. C. waited till Corin stopped pacing and looked directly at him. "You set me free."

"What?"

"I have disability insurance. The policy is an excellent one. After three months are up, I'll get 85 percent of my salary for a year and a half. Can we live on 15 percent less income? Yes. And I'll have an abundance of time on my hands."

"And how does that translate into being set free?"

A. C. reached for a manila folder to his left and opened it. He snagged a small stack of 8 ½ x 11 pieces of paper and handed them to Corin. He gazed at the one on top. It looked like a CAD drawing of multiple buildings spread over a five- or six-acre piece of land.

"What are these?" Corin frowned and leafed through the papers underneath. There were other architectural drawings, photos of bunk beds, Web addresses for canoes, volleyball nets, pickle-ball court supplies, and food distributors. He held up the papers. "What *are* these?"

"How long have I been talking about building a camp for down-and-out teenage boys and being the director of the place?"

"Since before you were in the womb."

"Exactly."

"How does Dineen feel about the idea?"

"She's so pumped about it, it's unreal."

Corin walked over and slouched against A. C.'s pool table. "Answer me something honestly."

"What?"

"Is this really what you want?"

"I don't lie, Cor." A. C. squinted as if in shock Corin would question his integrity.

"I know." Corin folded his arms. "I just had to be sure."

"Cor?"

"Yeah?"

"You need to consider something."

"Okay."

"If there really is a God behind this chair, then maybe He knows what He's doing."

Corin walked over to A. C. "Can I squeeze your head?"

"Do it, baby."

He leaned down, hugged his friend's head, and gave the top of it a rough kiss. "Life isn't life without you in it, bud."

"Same."

Corin left A. C.'s house trying to believe good had come out of his friend being shot. But he couldn't. Sure, A. C. would have the time, but where would he get the money? Camps were risky business, attendance had dropped off, and in this economy the trees full of money had withered.

And would A. C. really be able live on 85 percent of his salary? He'd never been flowing in extra cash.

Just before he got home, Tesser's number lit up Corin's new cell phone, "Hello?"

"Excellent news, Corin." Tesser chuckled. "I've found authentic proof your chair was made by Christ. If we've had any doubts, they can now be laid to rest and won't be resurrected."

"I think I've believed for a while now."

"This will solidify your well-grounded faith."

"Tell me."

"Nay, nay, nay. This you must see in person. Can you come to my house at say nine tomorrow morning?"

"Sure." Corin turned into his driveway and shut off his Highlander. "Do you want to give me a preview of what you discovered?"

"No, I'm afraid that would spoil the surprise. And how I do ever so much want to see the look on your face when you see what I've found." The professor stifled a giggle.

Corin didn't bother to turn on any lights as he walked into his house. The only thing on his mind was sleep. But an hour later the land of zzz's still eluded him, because something in Tesser's tone sounded off and Corin's brain was determined to figure out what it was.

His conscious mind finally shut down around two in the morning, without coming up with a decent theory.

But knowing Tesser, whatever it was, it would probably stretch Corin's mind to Egypt and back. Hopefully without snapping his brain in two.

CHAPTER 47

Corin arrived at Tesser's home on Sunday morning two minutes before nine and reached for the doorbell, but before he could ring it, the door opened to reveal a grinning Tesser.

Strange. He'd never come to the door in all the years Corin had known him.

"You're here!" Tesser shuffled his feet forward and back in a little jig. "Finally. I've been up since four, squirming with anticipation."

"You've found something big."

"Very." Tesser motioned him into the foyer. "Come, come, let's get to my study."

Corin followed Tesser as he trotted down his dark hallway, muttering over his shoulder about how excited he was.

Tesser pushed through the halfway open door to his massive study and threw his arms wide, his gaze focused toward the middle of the room. "*Blicken!*"

The German word for "look." Corin stared at the back of his friend's head. He'd never heard Tesser speak German before. What was that about?

He stepped through the door to view Tesser's discovery. Immediately three emotions crashed into his mind simultaneously.

Disbelief.

Anger.

Fear.

Nicole sat in the middle of the vast study, in the duplicate of the chair, her hands tied with brown twine as were her ankles. The same type of twine he'd been tied with in his store three days earlier.

Her white hair was disheveled, her head cocked slightly to the side. Her countenance was worn, her skin pale.

Impossible.

Corin tried to speak but the shock of seeing his Nicole sitting in the center of Tesser's study bound against her will froze his speech, froze his mind, froze his words.

Tesser couldn't have done this.

Waves of heat surged through him as the sensation of vertigo made him flail for something to hang on to.

"What have you done?" Corin stumbled toward Tesser, who shuffled backward toward his oversized maple desk.

A moment later Corin spun toward Nicole and staggered her direction.

"No, I can't let you do that," Tesser said. "Help, please."

Immediately four men stepped out of the deep flickering shadows cast by the candles randomly placed throughout the room.

Their arms hung loose but looked ready to move like lightning if needed. He recognized two of them: Ponytail and Baldy. The other two were rail thin, but their craggy faces conveyed how efficient they'd be in a street fight.

This wasn't real. He was dreaming. He had to be.

Jefferies doing something like this would have been a bad dream come to life, but one he could have expected. This was a nightmare.

"I didn't want to do it this way." Tesser shuffled back and forth in front of his desk in his oversized slippers, fingers pressed into his forehead. "Really, Corin, I didn't." He glanced up, his face grim, then he slammed his hand down on top of the desk. "Why couldn't you have given me the chair when I asked you to store it here? Or left it in the barn? If you had we wouldn't be going through all this turmoil right now. A shame, it is."

"Let her go."

Tesser strolled over within a foot of Corin. "But all emotion aside, I am so very glad you came, because now we can end this subterfuge. I've been waiting for this moment since last night when I finally found Nicole and brought her here for a visit. And I have to assume she has been waiting as well." He motioned toward her with an ancient-looking pen. "Although I feel I've been a gracious host, I believe she would prefer not being here."

"Are you okay?" Corin said to Nicole.

"I'm fine." She blinked rapidly and breathed deep.

Corin glanced at Tesser's thugs. "Friends of yours?"

"Yes." Tesser glanced to his right then left. "Good friends. Loyal friends."

"Friends who throw rocks through windows and break into stores to steal what is not theirs."

"Yes, those kinds of friends." Tesser pulled on his sparse goatee.

Corin lunged for Tesser but Ponytail and Baldy grabbed him, flung him into a chair to his left, and began tying him to it.

As they did, Tesser frowned. "Yes, very, very regrettable about your friend. That wasn't supposed to happen. Not at all. Tsk, tsk. Truly."

"How could you do this do me?"

"You mean—why did I want the chair?"

Corin stared at him, no need to answer the question.

"At least three or four reasons, maybe even five. I haven't really thought about it."

"Think about it now." Corin yanked on the cords around his wrists.

"This is amusing since you're not exactly in a position to be making demands, but why not?"

Tesser paced in front of him, still pulling on the thin tuffs of hair hanging from his chin. "First, it's fun, don't you think? This is real-life Indiana Jones stuff." Tesser stopped pacing and turned to Corin. "Come, come, even though you're not having fun at the moment, you have to admit this has been one of our more fascinating adventures together. Yes?"

Tesser went on without waiting for an answer. "Second, I've been looking for this chair all my life. Most thought it a legend only." He shook his head. "My, did I start to get excited when I realized you might have the real thing.

"Third, I wanted to validate all the time I've spent trying to track the chair down. Fourth, I suppose it irked me that all these years Nicole was right under my proverbial nose and I didn't see it, so now I want to rub her face in it just a bit. And fifth, I want the power that surrounds the chair. I think anyone can understand that."

"You're an old man, Tesser. What good could the chair do you?"

"Yes, I'm old, it's true." He took off his glasses and rubbed his eyes. "But the chair is not for me. The chair is for those who have been given claim to the earth. Those who are destined to rule this world. I'm a historian. I've never thought in decades but centuries.

Look at the United States, Corin. Look at the world. It's falling apart.

"The Reich is needed. Hitler took it too far. His zeal overtook his wisdom. The killing of the Jews was an atrocity beyond imagination. But our destiny to rule the other races? That is true. It is good. It is right."

For the first time Corin heard the trace of a German accent that filled microscopic cracks in Tesser's voice. How had he missed that all these years?

Tesser's words from their first meeting almost two weeks ago floated through his mind: "*Think what kind of an army you could build with . . .*"

Corin stated the obvious. "You were raised in Germany."

"I always wondered why you never asked me about that."

"When did you move to this country?"

"Long ago." Tesser waved his pen in the air. "But my heritage has not been forgotten."

"I trusted you."

"You can still trust me. I am your friend, Corin, and I have no intent to hurt you in any manner." Tesser sighed. "As I tried to tell you out by the waterfall, I wish you weren't mixed up in this. And of course I tried with the rock through your window, and then with my friends who stopped by to pick up the chair and transfer it here, but in neither case would you listen. A shame." He motioned again to Nicole. "So I had to track down this elegant lady and—if I need to—I will use her as a most valuable currency in our negotiation for a certain piece of merchandise."

"Let her go," Corin repeated.

"Certainly. Of course, right away." Tesser smiled at Corin, an expectant look on his face.

"As soon as I tell you where the chair is."

"Precisely. So good to know we still understand each other in the, uh, midst of realizing my slight alteration of our friendship."

Tesser tapped his pen on his palm, weaved in between Ponytail and the bald thug from Corin's store, and stopped behind Nicole. "I have to say your building a decoy was an excellent diversion." He slid his pen into his pocket and patted the back of the chair with both hands. "I didn't see that coming although I should have. Congratulations on your skills—I didn't know of your woodworking talents. I'm impressed, really I am. It took me two full days before I realized you'd created a duplicate." Tesser tipped his cap. "You are an artist." He shook his head and smiled.

"How do I know you'll let her go if I tell you?"

"You don't, I'm afraid."

Nicole struggled to sit up straighter in her chair. "Don't let your emotions cause you to stray from the truth, Corin."

"What truth?"

"That we all die sooner or later. And delaying my death is not worth your telling him where the chair is."

"I can't lose you." He'd just found her. Losing her so soon would rip him apart. With Shasta solar systems beyond his reach, she was the only family he had.

"Yes," she smiled, "you can. If it is my time to go sooner rather than later it will be all right. I know it will."

Corin pulled on the cords cutting into his wrists and glared at Tesser. "Why didn't you tell me the truth from the beginning?"

"What do you mean?" Tesser smiled as if looking at a child. "I never lied. I simply didn't tell you everything I knew or what my ultimate motivations were for finding the chair."

"Holding back knowledge for personal gain that can hurt the other person is lying."

Tesser motioned to two of his men and they hoisted Corin to his feet.

"Since I never skirted over into the ethics department during my tenure at the university, I think we'd be wasting time on the semantics of truth telling." Tesser pulled down his glasses and looked at Corin over the top of them. "Tell me where the chair is."

"Never."

Tesser wagged his finger and the man on either side of Corin slugged him in the gut. Hard. It felt like two shot-put champions had dropped their shots into his stomach from thirty feet up. He doubled over and his stomach heaved, almost spilling his burger onto Tesser's cherry hardwood floor.

Tesser frowned. "A little too robust, gentlemen. Corin is my friend and we're trying to coerce, not kill the boy."

Tesser's thugs didn't respond but took a step back and stared at the professor.

"Now, Corin, I need you to tell me where the real chair is."

"No chance."

"Really?" Tesser glanced at the man on either side of Corin, then back at him. "You're sure?"

"Positive."

"Interesting." Tesser rubbed his forehead and paced in front of Corin, then looked at Nicole. "What do you think of that, Nicole? You must be proud of your protégée protecting your most prized possession."

Tesser waved his hand to the two men on either side of Corin. "Again."

This time the shots to his stomach felt like cannonballs.

"Corin?"

"No," Corin choked out.

Tesser shook his head. "I have no desire to hurt you permanently, Corin. I simply want the chair. You give it to me, I'm happy, you're happy, Nicole and you aren't dead, and we all skip off into the sunset whistling. Now tell me."

"No."

Tesser circled Corin, poking him as he eased around him counterclockwise. "Where is it?"

Silence.

Tesser poked him hard on his collarbone. "Games are over. Where is it, Corin?"

He glared at Tesser.

"Let's give this one more try." Tesser rubbed his hands together, then motioned to his thugs with a quick thwip of his finger. An instant later Corin's head was yanked back and the blade of a hunting knife was flashed in his face, then applied to his throat with enough pressure to make him cough. After a few seconds he felt a trickle of blood wind its way down his skin.

Tesser laughed. "Don't cough, Corin! It jiggles the blade. Then you start bleeding and make a mess out of that fine American Eagle shirt you have on. Donate your B positive at the blood bank, not here okay? Now tell me."

"No."

Corin tried to look at Nicole but the vise grip on his hair kept him from moving more than an eighth of an inch. He was yanked again.

The shuffle of Tesser's slippers moving toward him was mixed with a ringing in Corin's ears.

"Oh, let him move his head."

The grip on Corin's hair eased and his head flopped forward.

Corin looked at Nicole. Her back was straight, chin pushed forward, and even a hint of her enigmatic smile surfaced as she stared Tesser's direction. A moment later she turned and looked at Corin. It was easy to see what was in her eyes. Deep love. And peace.

As her eyes spoke of a joy that made no sense, Corin tried to soak it all in. It fanned the flame of his determination.

Corin coughed and pain ripped through his ribs like a knife. They were probably broken. "I'll never tell you."

Tesser glanced back and forth between Corin and Nicole three times before bending over Corin. "I think you believe that. I also think I will be able to persuade you to think differently."

Tesser let out a long sigh and ambled over to Nicole. "I hate this, I really do." He picked up a long serrated knife from the table next to her. He turned it over and seemed to study the blade. "Where is the chair?"

"Fine, I'll tell you."

"See that wasn't so hard." Tesser stepped away from Nicole.

"It's in my vault. In the store."

"Please, Corin." Tesser rolled his eyes. "We've been there, remember?"

"It's the locked room in my basement." Corin dropped his eyes. "In my house."

"Oh, dear Corin. We've been there too. Just the other day. Did I forget to tell you?" He stepped back to Nicole and placed the knife against her neck and drew it a quarter-inch to the right. A sliver of blood appeared and Nicole gasped.

"No!" Corin yanked on the cords constraining his wrists so hard it felt like he'd dislocated his shoulders. This couldn't be happening.

Tesser whirled toward him. "Come, come. Why all the drama. It's a shallow cut. It will take ages for Nicole to bleed to death with a nick like that. But you were lying to me and it's getting tiresome." The old professor turned back to Nicole, leaned down, and said to her in a mock whisper, "As soon as he tells me where the chair is, we'll get some antiseptic on that and bandage it up. The scar will hardly be noticeable."

He brought the knife back up to Nicole's throat.

A trickle of blood continued to snake down Nicole's neck and Corin tried to gauge how deep the cut was.

Tesser placed the blade against the other side of Nicole's throat and looked toward Corin. "Deeper this time, friend."

"Don't, Tesser. If you ever cared for me—don't."

"I do care for you; that's why I'm giving you one more chance. But this will be the last. Just tell me."

Corin's mind spun. He had to wake up! But it wasn't a dream. One of his oldest friends had gone insane. Think. There had to be something that would snap the old man out of his madness. But maybe giving in was the only way to stop it. "All right."

Tesser pulled the blade away from Nicole's neck and beckoned with his fingers. "Where?"

"Get away from her." Corin drilled his eyes into Tesser's.

"Fine." Tesser took a half step to the left. "Now speak."

"Give me your word you'll let her go."

"My word." Tesser gave a mock bow.

"In my warehouse twenty miles east of town. There's a basement full of old worthless antiques ready for restoration. In the far south corner buried under two feet of old blankets and a pile of worthless old lamps is a trapdoor. It's in there."

"Not so difficult, was that?"

"Now let her go." Corin stared at Tesser and willed him to back off. His breath came in short gasps.

"Have you spoken truth about the location of the chair?"

"All I want is Nicole. Take the chair."

Tesser pulled a cell phone out of his breast pocket and pressed a button. "It's in Corin's warehouse east of town, south corner basement, trapdoor." He ended the call and put the phone back in his pocket.

"Let her go," Corin growled.

Tesser paced back and forth in front of Nicole three times

before speaking again. "At this point we come to the most difficult part of our transaction." He stopped pacing and kicked at the floor with the toe of his slipper. "I don't like this part at all, but . . ." He glanced up, a sad, resolved look in his eyes. "I can't avoid it."

Tesser stepped around to the back of the chair, placed the blade against Nicole's neck again, and with a swift motion slit her throat. The thin line of blood that appeared grew in seconds to a stream that flowed down her neck, soaking her blouse with crimson.

"No!" Corin lurched forward in his chair almost tipping over. "Why? You got what you wanted!"

"Let's call it insurance. I'm absolutely positive you told me the truth about the location of the chair, but just in case you lied, I wanted to make sure you understand how serious I am about obtaining the truth. And how when I tell you I'll hunt down and kill everyone close to you if you *did* lie, you will believe me."

As Corin strained against the cords around his wrists he thought for a moment he would break them. Just as he would break Tesser's neck if he could reach the old man. Murderer. Manufactured from the same sick gene cesspool Hitler had been created in. Insane. Devoid of any shred of morality. A being whose evil had just shattered his world.

Tesser doffed his ratty baseball hat and bowed to Nicole. "Since I won't see you again, my lady, I bid you safe travels in the afterlife. And Corin, should I not see you again, which I won't unless you've lied to me, I bid you fair sailing as long as you continue to grace this earth with your presence."

The professor shuffled toward the door, then stopped and motioned to his thugs.

"My friends here will keep an eye on you until I can get to the warehouse—examine the chair—and make sure you weren't the ultimate sneaky fellow and made more than one duplicate."

Before Tesser reached the door to the hallway the windows surrounding the top of the room shattered and shards of glass pelted down onto the floor of the study in a wide circle.

"Don't move!"

A voice above and to Corin's left boomed down on them, its echo filling the room.

Tesser fell back and whirled like a merry-go-round toward the first voice, then the second, then toward the other six silhouettes hovering over them.

One of Tesser's thugs reached inside his coat. A bullet screeched past him and sent splinters into the air as it tore into the hardwood floor.

"Hands high!" The voice above them ripped through the air again.

Tesser and his thugs complied.

An instant later four men sprinted through the door into the study and leveled rifles at Tesser and his men.

After surrounding them the lead man shouted, "Clear!" to the men in the windows above, then glanced at Tesser and each of his men one at a time.

"Slowly. Like molasses in January. Guns out of coats and tossed to the center of the room. I would hate to see one of you maggots die." In perfect unison the men cocked their rifles.

Tesser sank to the floor, head in his hands. He sat and rocked back and forth, and in that instant his old professor went from ninety-two to four years old, a little boy caught doing something he shouldn't and feeling bad because he'd been found out, not because of what he'd done.

Thirty seconds later Tesser and his men were handcuffed and muscled out of the room.

"Help her," Corin shouted and jerked his head in Nicole's direction.

As one of the men sliced the twine that bound Corin to his chair, another cut Nicole loose and held a thick piece of gauze up to her throat.

The lead man of the rescue team pulled a cell phone from his vest and said, "We need an ambulance here now."

The moment Corin was free he lurched over to Nicole and took her hands in his. "An ambulance is coming; they'll get you to the hospital. You'll be okay."

"I won't," she rasped. "This is my time. The way it is supposed to be."

Corin rubbed her fingers and stared into her fading eyes. "No, I need you to live. To teach me, show me—"

"Listen, I only have moments left." Nicole coughed up blood. "Continue to protect the chair as you have done. Know that God is for you, who can be against you?"

"Don't leave."

"You were strong." Nicole gasped for air and her eyes closed. "You didn't tell him the true location of the chair."

Corin shook his head.

"Good, good. I knew you wouldn't." Her head settled to the side and the brightness in her blue eyes dimmed.

He blinked back tears. "Don't die."

She smiled. "I am going to the arms of the One who will never let me go, Corin." She pulled in another raspy breath. "Stay true to the path He has shown you." Her grasp on his fingers went limp.

"Stay with me, Nicole." Corin leaned in.

As her eyes fluttered open, she said, "Forgiveness. For both."

"Both who?"

"Remember, the chair is only a conduit for His healing power. Healing comes from inside you and from the Maker of the chair. Both. Give it to both." Nicole's head settled to the side, her eyes closed and she didn't open them again.

He kissed her on the head, then slumped to the floor. His body heaved as sobs of sorrow tore their way to the surface from the deepest part of him. Ages later as his tears slowed, Corin stared at Tesser's endless bookshelves and wished he could torch them all with superpowered heat vision, as if that could subdue the pain of the old man's brutal betrayal.

FOR ANOTHER AGE Corin sat at the base of the chair he had made, the chair Nicole had died in. The sorrow and anger faded and all he felt was emptiness.

"Excuse me."

He looked up through his tear-blurred eyes. The lead man of the rescue team stood over him, hands on his hips.

"I know this is a brutal moment for you, but I want to let you know I just called the police and they'll be here in five to ten minutes."

"You're not going to stay?"

"I'll be watching from a safe distance to make sure nothing happens between now and the time they arrive, but no, we're going to stay out of having to give the police any reports." The man winked. "Or an explanation of who we are."

"But they'll want me to give them a full explanation."

"Yeah, sorry."

Corin nodded, grasped the chair, and hauled himself to his feet.

"Who are you?"

"Friends." The man wiped his forehead with the back of his black gloved hand.

"But who sent you? How did you know we were here?"

"That will be explained to you."

"When?"

"Soon."

"By who?"

"The man who hired us."

"Who hired you?"

The man smiled. "Don't worry; he'll be in touch."

"Tonight?"

"Like I said, soon."

TWO HOURS LATER Corin drove away from Tesser's house feeling like his body had been shot full of a local anesthetic. His arms, legs, and especially his mind were numb.

Where did he go from here?

He drove to Woodmoor Lake and sat for three hours, not thinking, not crying, not fearing anything, just feeling the chill of the afternoon seep into his heart.

On his way home an image of the chair shot into his mind. What had Nicole said? The chair would bring joy and great sorrow. No kidding. But the scales were severely out of balance. Ninety-nine percent sorrow, one percent joy. A. C., his brother, Nicole . . . the good news was there wasn't anyone else he cared about that the chair could destroy.

As he pulled into his driveway he spotted Tori's car and her standing next to it. He puffed out a disgusted laugh. The laugh made his ribs ache. They weren't broken but they would be tender for a while.

Okay, not everyone had been devastated. But something told him the circle was about to be completed.

CHAPTER 48

Tori stood tapping her fingers on the roof of her car, a somber look on her face.

"Hey, I've been meaning to call you," Corin said as he got out of his car.

She nodded but said nothing.

Corin stared at her. She didn't move around her car toward him. She stood with her car between them, her face pale and she blinked as if she was in a storm cloud of dust.

"Are you all right, Tori?"

"I'm great, and you?"

She wasn't great, wasn't even good based on the look in her eyes. Something was wrong. Wonderful. Probably another weight to add to his backpack full of grief.

"How am I? Life has been better." Corin slammed his car door shut. "Nicole is gone."

"Gone?"

"Dead."

Tori circled around to the passenger side of her car and leaned against the door. "I figured she was the one they were talking about on the radio. When I heard Tesser was arrested I assumed the worst. I'm so sorry, Corin. You'd become close to her, hadn't you?"

Corin nodded and folded his arms.

She looked down on the frost-hardened ground. "I know my timing isn't great, but I need to talk to you about something."

A lump of granite instantly formed in Corin's stomach. *Here it comes.*

"What's going on?"

"It's what isn't going to be going on anymore."

"And what won't be going on anymore?"

"We're done." Tori wiped her nose. "I wanted to tell you to your face."

"Why?"

"I've seen it all my life. You're turning into a Jesus Freak."

Corin coughed out a bitter laugh. "You're wrong. After today I'm so done with the chair and anything and everything to do with God. Both have brought me nothing but pain. I'm going to get rid of the thing."

"When?"

"Soon."

"Call me when it's gone." Tori shoved her hands into her blue and black North Face jacket and shook her head. "No, that's not fair to you. Don't call me."

"I just told you—"

"No. It's not you, Corin. It's the whole thing. Too much of my past. Too much has been stirred up and thrown in my face."

"I told you, I'm done with the chair. It's over for me."

"And it's over for us."

CORIN SPENT THE rest of the day numbing his mind watching Tobey Maguire spin his way through Sam Raimi's three *Spider-Man* movies. If only it were as easy to heal his world as Spidey healed his. The flicks did little to dull the pain seeping into every crevice of his soul. Toward midnight as the credits rolled on the third movie, he told himself to look at the bright side.

His life couldn't get any worse.

It couldn't.

He staggered into his bedroom, flopped onto his bed, and closed his eyes.

Sure it could.

CHAPTER 49

Corin was only asleep for what seemed like seconds before his cell phone shattered his dreams. He glanced at his alarm clock. One a.m. He fumbled for his phone and squinted against the light coming from it and looked to see who was on the other end.

Adrenaline shot through him and in an instant he was awake. Shasta. Was it possible? Was he healed?

Corin rubbed his eyes and tried to remember how long it had been since his brother sat in the chair. Three days? With Brittan, A. C., and him the healing had come within twenty-four hours, so there'd been plenty of time for it to work.

Please.

"Shasta?"

He heard the faint strains of the soundtrack from *Gladiator* playing through the phone.

"Shasta, you there?"

"Yes, I'm here." His brother paused. "Are you well?"

"Yes, I'm fine."

"How does it feel, to be 'fine'?" Shasta's voice sounded like ice.

No.

Corin stumbled to his feet.

"How does it feel to have sensation in your toes, your feet, your legs, your fingers, your arms, your shoulders? Tell me, brother, what is it like to be fine? I'm dying to know."

"Don't do this, Shasta."

"I think it needs to be done. Because you had me. Really. Did you know that? I was convinced this was the time. Miracle city. When you told me that kid had been healed, I thought it was possible.

"When you told me A. C. had been healed, I called him. Did you know that? After talking to him I believed even more. Then the coup de grâce, telling me you'd been healed. In that moment I swallowed every worm on your hook."

Shasta's slow, labored breathing reverberated in Corin's mind like a windstorm.

"Congratulations on ripping open a hope I've been trying to bury for ten years. Well done."

"Shasta—"

"If you ever contact me again for anything, I will find a way to destroy you. No talking to Robin, no more presents for Sawyer, no e-mails, no Christmas cards, nothing."

"I didn't—"

"Do we understand each other?"

"Don't do this."

"You did it, not me."

"I thought—"

"No, you rarely have ever thought, just acted."

Corin dropped to his knees.

"Good-bye, Corin."

He let his cell phone slide out his hand and clatter to the floor.

Then his despair twisted and morphed into an anger that lifted him to his feet, a burning in his mind that formed into a crystal-clear vision of what needed to be done.

He strode to his garage, his whole body on fire, and flung open the closest hiding all his old sports gear. He dug through the pile, flinging hiking gear, basketballs, his tennis racquet, his golf clubs, not turning or caring when the sound of them smacking into his car filled the garage.

Where is it?

There.

His baseball bat. The perfect instrument for the song he was about to play. A bat he'd crafted himself in junior high school after seeing that old movie *The Natural* about a player who'd made his own bat when he was a kid. The bat lay at the bottom of the pile, its surface still gleaming from the finish he'd put on it twenty years ago.

He lifted it out of the pile and ran his hand over its smooth surface.

He'd picked the perfect piece of northern white ash to construct the bat. The perfect choice for slugging homers off John Vanos in high school.

He stepped back and swung the bat as hard as he could. The perfect tool to bestow on it what had been bestowed on him.

Something inside tried to rise in protest, but he ignored the message and whipped the bat through the air again, the familiar swoosh filling his garage.

He'd lost little if any of his bat speed.

This was it. Payback time.

CHAPTER 50

Corin strode over the frost-bitten lawn of his backyard, his breath filling the air with clouds of gray rage. Before he reached the bunker he pushed the remote and the earth slid back, the stairs dark in the night's shadows.

He staggered down the concrete steps, slid his key into the massive Master Lock padlock, and flung open the door, its momentum crashing the knob into the concrete wall of the bunker and echoing through the night like a gong.

Moonlight streamed into the room through the tiny skylight in the far corner of the room. One side of the chair was bathed in radiance; the other side cast a shadow that reached the wall. Light and dark. Yin and yang. Demon and angel.

He was about to be the former.

Corin's gaze moved from the chair to the moon framed by the skylight. Was the man in the moon smiling? Or laughing? At him, with him. It didn't matter.

Man in the moon. Man in the chair. Man of despair.

His stare returned to the chair as he strode into the room and stopped a foot in front of it, wishing he had Superman's heat vision to simply incinerate the chair instantly.

No, this way would be better.

"It's time to end this." Corin smacked the bat into his palm. "Are you ready? I certainly am."

Would God stop him? Freeze him in place, or make his muscles turn into syrup till someone arrived who would keep the chair from annihilation?

He angled around the right side of the chair on the balls of his feet as if he were a famished lion ready to pounce.

"You destroyed me. You destroyed everything and now I am going to return the favor."

Corin spun back and crossed in front of the chair back the way he'd come, the drumbeat of the bat smacking his palm in rhythm with his footsteps. The anger inside him surged like a strobe light going on and off, on and off, with each flash his rage growing brighter. He was going nova.

The bat felt as heavy as a sledgehammer and time slowed as he stopped pacing, lifted it straight over his head, and brought it down on the seat of the chair, his muscles straining to deliver all his strength.

Would the chair turn into something made of steel like the time he took a sliver from it? Would it protect itself? It wouldn't matter. He would find a way to destroy it.

The first blow crunched halfway through the seat, the second sent splinters spinning to the floor, the third—a full level baseball swing from his heels—tore the back of the chair apart and launched it into the air with a twisting spin till it crashed into the left wall.

Indestructible?

Hardly.

He tightened his grip on the bat as a voice in the back of his mind again asked, *Why are you doing this?*

He closed his eyes and squeezed tighter.

"Shut up."

Why?

"Shut up!"

Corin's eyes fluttered open, he screamed, then leaped toward the chair, bat high again in his hands, his grip so tight now his fingers ached.

Muscles taut, he rained another ten thousand blows onto the olive wood, each crunch of bat on chair fueling his rage.

"You took my life away!"

Another blow.

"Why couldn't you heal my brother?"

Another.

"Any hope of Shasta and me gone!"

Another.

Sweat seeped from his hands onto the handle of the bat.

"How does it feel!"

Two minutes later he slumped against the far wall gasping for air. The bat slid out of his damp hands and clattered to the floor as he braced himself with his palms and gazed at the pieces of the chair.

None was more than a foot and a half long and three inches thick. The inside of the wood was the same color as the outside, as if the years on the outside had seeped into the inside giving a uniform color to the whole chair.

It lay in a pile, not moving, not speaking out against what had just been done.

Corin shook his head and grunted out a laugh. What was he thinking? This wasn't a person. It wasn't a talisman—it was a plain, ordinary *chair*!

He expected his rage to subside as he stared at the wood, but the intensity of his anger grew.

"We're not done." He stumbled forward on his knees and reached out to grab the pieces of the chair. Smaller. The pieces needed to be reduced to splinters. The air felt thick, as if he were pushing his hands through Jell-O to reach the pieces. Harder. *C'mon grab them. There!* He snatched up a handful of pieces and dropped them a second later.

Hot. Burning hot. Corin rubbed his hands on his sweatpants and blew on his palms. He looked at his hands expecting to see blisters forming.

Nothing.

Hot? Impossible. It was just his imagination.

He grabbed the pieces again—now almost cool—and brought them down hard across his knee.

Pain streaked through his leg and he groaned. It was like slamming pieces of iron across his quad. "What the . . . ?"

He grabbed a piece the size of a letter opener and tried to snap it in two. Steel. Corin let go and it rattled onto the concrete floor. He kicked the shattered wood at his feet and staggered out of the room, swiping at the door with his heel to shut it. The door didn't close more than halfway and he glanced back for one more look at the remnants of the chair.

They lay, not moving, not glowing, just a pile of wood with no magic in them.

As he stepped back to his house all emotion left him and an overwhelming emptiness rushed in to fill the vacuum in his heart.

He shoved his back door open and slammed it shut behind him as the grandfather clock in the hallway chimed one thirty.

Corin trudged toward his living room, then glared at his reflection in the full-length mirror at the end of the hall. The look in his eyes surprised him. It wasn't relief, fear, or anger; it was sorrow.

Sorrow? Sure. Sorrow he hadn't destroyed the chair sooner. For a moment he embraced the thought. In the morning life would begin again. No, life had begun the moment he'd picked up the bat and took his first step toward the bunker.

What had Nicole said about the chair? Destined to be in his family for generations? Sure. Why not? He'd give one piece each to the hundreds of kids he wouldn't be having someday.

He glanced at his watch: 1:35. Tori wouldn't be up, but he didn't care. He wrenched his phone free of his pocket and dialed. Two rings. Four.

"Wondering what I'm doing? I'm wondering what you're doing, so leave me a message. I'll call you back and hopefully we'll both get what we're looking for."

"It's me. I'm wondering if you'd reconsider us. Just wanted you to know it's over. The chair is gone and I'm free."

He set the phone down and tried to believe the words he'd just spoken.

A few seconds later another emotion joined his pleasure. Horror. As if he stood on the edge of the beach as a tsunami was about to strike with nowhere to escape to.

Deep down he knew the chair was real. Knew the healing he'd experienced wasn't a mind game he'd played on himself. Same with A. C. Same with Brittan Gibson.

Instantly his living room filled with a brilliant light with so much power he gasped. Then an overwhelming peace swept him up and spilled over him like forty-foot waves.

A moment later the light vanished and the peace was gone.

Corin moaned and slumped to his knees in front of his couch as an image of the chair lying battered and broken filled his mind. He tried to wipe it away by picturing what the chair had done to

Nicole, but he couldn't hold the thought, and the image of the chair intensified. It lit up his vision, filling the air in front his eyes like he was staring at a movie screen.

Why have you done this?

The enormity of what he had done filled him.

What had Nicole said ages past?

"Do not let it go. Ever."

He'd failed her.

No.

Corin moaned and eased his head forward till his forehead rested on the carpet. He closed his eyes and pressed his head into the floor hard, then harder till it felt like his head would crack open. More pressure. More pain. More pressure.

When the throbbing in his skull wouldn't grow any stronger, he flopped onto his side, opened his eyes, and stared at the picture of Shasta and him skydiving that rested on the mantel he'd restored.

He knew what he had to do. There was only one solution. A glance out his front window told him the night was ideal. Clouds had moved in and covered the moon. Perfect. No light to help him see what would be rushing up at him.

He glanced at his watch. He could be standing on the edge of the cliff by 3 a.m.

CHAPTER 51

Corin's heart pounded as he strode to the garage, grabbed his parachuting gear, opened the trunk of his car, and flung it inside.

He backed out of his driveway, threw his Highlander into Drive, and mashed his foot to the floor. Two seconds later he broke the speed limit. In four he'd rocketed up to fifty miles per hour. Five minutes later he scorched through the first red light going ninety. A car horn screamed at him, but by the time it registered, he was already through the next stoplight, moving at over one hundred.

A few minutes later he slowed down. No point in getting killed here. He had to get to the jump in one piece.

An hour and fifteen minutes later he pulled into the parking lot at the trailhead. Two minutes after that he strode down the path leading to the edge of the cliff.

The stars and moon were shrouded by thick clouds and he stumbled on roots twice on his way to the edge. Trees that lined the path pressed in on him, but the fear they would have stirred two weeks ago had vanished.

The chair.

It had healed him.

Destroyed his relationship with Shasta.

Then Corin destroyed the chair.

Now he would complete the circle and join his brother and they would be friends once more.

An image flashed into his mind of Shasta and him sitting next to each other on the Blue Streak roller coaster in Cedar Point, Ohio. Ten and eight years old. They'd ridden it sixteen times that day. And came back the next day for more. It had been the birth of their adventures together.

Tonight Corin would usher in its death. His fast walk morphed into a slow jog as he clipped toward the launch point.

When he reached the edge of the cliff, a light wind buffeted his face. Perfect. Maybe the winds were stronger two hundred or five hundred feet down. Maybe they'd take him for a ride he'd never remember. All possibilities were good ones.

Corin stared at the darkness below. If his memory was still serving him accurately, he'd be able to float for five seconds, maybe seven, before pulling his chute. Without seeing the ground he couldn't be sure. But wasn't that the idea?

Once he was in the air he'd decide when to send his chute out behind him in a stream of salvation. Or maybe he wouldn't decide.

A deep breath. Then another.

Corin strode back five paces from the edge and turned. Both his legs bounced like mini jackhammers and his hands shook. He felt his palms. Dry. Cold. Same for this feet. Icy cold. The terror surging through him had probably pulled all the blood from his extremities.

A voice so deep inside it was only the hint of a whisper tried to speak. Corin shut it down and stared into the void in front of him.

He closed his eyes and slowed his breathing.

There was no question. He had to do this.

Do you? The voice inside grew louder.

"Yes."

Corin pulled his chute from his pack and slipped into his harness.

Pictures of Nicole and Shasta and Tesser and the chair swirled through his mind in a kaleidoscope of images.

Just before he lunged forward into his sprint toward the cliff, his cell phone pierced the night air.

How ironic. Was it God trying to save him?

It didn't matter. Because unless it was God on the phone, he wasn't backing down.

Might as well see who it was.

Corin yanked his phone out of his pocket. A. C. A good man, a good friend. Corin muted the ring and shoved the phone deep into his pocket. "Sorry, pal."

He stared into the blackness. Into the nothingness. Just like the lake.

He counted to three, then sprinted for the edge. Faster, something from behind pushing, digging deep into the dirt with the toes of his Nikes with each step. A moment later he was floating, not seeing anything, embracing the fear exploding in his stomach.

Start counting.

One.

Two.

The darkness surrounded him, pulling him down, wind pummeling his face.

Three.

Time to pull. The adrenaline in his stomach exploded.

Four.

Pull!

His mind screamed it again. But he didn't listen.

Five.

Pull the chute now!

Corin squeezed tighter on the chute.

An instant later the drowning flashed through his mind so vividly he was under the water again, struggling for air, tearing at his life jacket, his fingernails digging into his father's arm, then opening his mouth and sucking in a monstrous lungful of water, filling his ear canals, pressing into his mind, drawing him toward death.

In that moment clarity flashed like a lightning strike.

He'd been wrong for twenty-four years.

Drowning. He'd never been scared of it.

It had never been his fear.

It had always been the fear behind the fear.

He was scared of death.

Of dying.

Of the darkness he'd escaped smothering him forever.

Of the nothingness.

Corin's eyes fluttered open and stared into the black earth rushing up at him.

Was he too late?

"Ahhhhhh!" he shouted as he heaved his chute into the screaming air.

Release. Please . . .

His chute snapped open like the sound of a rifle's report.

Be my life jacket.

Too late, he was too late.

"I'm sorry, Shasta."

He glanced at the thicker darkness streaking toward him. The ground. Less than 150 feet. Too close. He was still moving far too fast. Milliseconds now.

He braced for impact.

As his legs slammed into the ground he tried to roll to lessen the impact, but the futility of the action filled his mind at the same time a freight train of pain ripped into his feet and legs and up his back.

An instant later a vise grip grabbed his lungs and squeezed.

He gasped and pulled in a teaspoon of air.

Not enough air.

Not even close!

He tried again, but it was like sucking air through a straw the size of a needle.

He had to breathe.

His head rolled from side the side, as he gasped again and again for air. Air that wouldn't come, that he couldn't reach, couldn't find. So close but ages away. And death was settling down on him like early winter snow.

Exactly the same feeling he'd had underwater.

He was about to die.

Corin rolled onto his back and screamed. Fire shot through his upper chest and right arm. "Uhhhhhhhhh."

Stay alive. He had to. What time had he jumped? Three a.m.? It wouldn't be light for another three and a half hours.

As he lay on the ground, feeling the moisture slowly seeping through his clothes into his skin, Corin thought back to Nicole's eyes just before she died and her last words:

"Forgiveness. For both."

Instantly he knew who she meant.

Killing or paralyzing himself would never bring restoration. Forgiveness was his only hope.

His last thought before blacking out was of Shasta.

I never asked you. Why did I never ask?

"Mr. Roscoe? Can you hear me?"

Corin moaned and squeezed his eyes tighter shut. It didn't do much good against the blinding light that shot through his eyelids and seemed to burn his corneas. What did it remind him of? Hadn't he just done this? Right—in the ambulance after A. C. had been shot.

"Bright . . . so bright." He tried to bring his arm up to shield his eyes but he couldn't move his arm.

"Nurse, do you mind . . . ?" The light in the room dimmed and Corin opened his eyes a slit.

"How do you feel?"

"Run over. Multiple times." Corin tried to move his legs, but the pain that shot down them was so intense blackness moved across his vision. "Run over by an aircraft carrier."

"Aircraft carriers float."

"This one was on wheels." He opened his eyes halfway.

"Having a sense of humor at this point is a good sign."

"I'm in a hospital."

"Yes."

Corin opened his eyes all the way and gazed at his surroundings. Off-white walls, off-white curtain half surrounding his bed, off-white coat covering an African American doctor with bright eyes.

"How bad am I?"

"Given what you almost did to yourself and the condition you should have wound up in, I'm required to tell you you're lucky to be alive."

"How lucky?"

"Extremely."

"How bad?"

"One leg sprained, the other badly broken, a sprained right arm, punctured lung—which is why you have a tube coming out of your side—and you almost ripped your right ear off." The doctor leaned in. "That's the bad news."

"What's the good?"

"You'll probably walk with a slight limp the rest of your life, but the rest will heal up fine. You'll be in some intense pain for the next few days, but—"

"Will I be going home tonight?"

"Like I said, I like the humor. Some people think it can cure everything from warts to cancer."

Corin stared at the doctor for a moment. "Do you believe in miracles? That people can be instantaneously healed by the power of God?"

"I think it's possible."

"Why? Have you seen one?"

"I believe there's a higher power. A being I would call God. I believe I'm not Him. Until I am, I'll leave room that He invades our world with His goodness and mercy. And that includes healing. Of the body." The doctor placed his fingers on Corin's good arm. "And sometimes, more important, of the soul." He touched Corin's chest over his heart.

"I need to see my brother."

"I think in a week or so you'll be able to."

Countdown. Six days to go.

CHAPTER 52

Six days later Corin sat at the lake—crutches lying on his right, pain pills in his left pocket—and prayed. For peace. For the meeting he would have with Shasta in a little less than an hour. For himself. For understanding. For forgiveness.

A few minutes later a cough floated toward him through the light fog that covered the lake and shoreline. He turned toward the sound.

"Good to see you alive, Corin." Mark Jefferies stood ten yards behind and to his left, hands jammed into his black leather jacket.

Corin blinked and couldn't stop a smile from forming. "It was you, right?"

"Yeah."

"You saved my life. In Tesser's house."

"True."

"And again when I jumped off that cliff."

"Yep." Mark gave a thin smile, slid onto the bench next to Corin, and leaned back, legs crossed, hands behind his head.

"I see you aren't limited to a few bodyguards for your protection."

"My friends know friends who know friends—nice to have them in cities and situations like the ones you found yourself in."

"Thank you."

Mark nodded. "The thing with Nicole? That was wrong. She was a wonderful woman. Who walked with God."

"You met her?"

"I did. Very recently." Mark scraped his feet on the concrete path. "She pumped my head full of wisdom. Wisdom . . . truth I needed."

"She was my grandmother."

"I suspected that."

"How?"

"From studying the legend. Sometimes the passing on of the chair skipped a generation. It's always been from woman to woman, but that was tradition, not an absolute mandate."

And now he'd ended the tradition, but there would be no chair to pass down to a daughter or a son. The thought filled him with an emptiness and a longing for forgiveness. But from whom he didn't know. Nicole? God?

Corin glanced at Mark. The man didn't make sense. So full of swagger and pride. Yet the pastor had saved him and seemed to want nothing in return.

"Why were you so obsessed with the chair?"

"I still am." Mark pressed the tips of his fingers and thumbs together. "It has always fascinated me. The possibility of its existence—the type of legend only seen in stories come to real life—the thought I might be the one to find it."

Jefferies said it with confidence, too much confidence.

"I want to know the real reason."

"The real reason?" Mark dropped his head back and chuckled. "You're perceptive." He leaned forward, blew on his hands, and set his arms on his legs. "Why not?" Jefferies said, more to himself it seemed than to Corin. "Because I needed it. I needed to sit in it and receive its power."

"The healing it could bring."

Mark nodded.

"In order to fight your demons."

"I've done things I'm not proud of. I still do things. I have thoughts I'm not proud of." Mark rubbed his face. "I need forgiveness. I need healing."

For the first time since he'd known the pastor, the macho tough-guy veneer melted off his face and Corin glimpsed the young kid underneath that wrestled with fame and power and who knew how many other demons.

"The healing isn't ultimately in the chair; it's in the One who—"

"What do you think you're doing? The student instructing the teacher?" Jefferies laughed. "But you're right. I was looking for an instant cure, the magic silver bullet that would wipe clean in an instant the parts of my soul that still remain hidden in the shadows." He made a gesture with his hand as if sweeping a table clean.

"Isn't this the kind of thing you can talk about to your board or other people in your church?"

"Not a chance."

"Why?"

"I'm an icon, the figurehead, the god they all scramble after. I can't show that weakness."

"Why can you tell me?"

"I trust you. We're eight hundred miles away from that life. And you're not a believer."

"I think that's changing."

"I hope it continues. Jesus is life." Mark smiled—a genuine smile without guile.

"Where will you look for the healing now?"

"In Him. Where it's always been."

"I destroyed the chair."

A wave of anger flashed over Mark's face, but it was gone in an instant. "That was foolish."

"I know."

"Why did you do it?"

"I lost control."

They sat in silence, the only sound their breathing in and out in the cool November air.

"Did you know about Tesser?"

Mark smiled. "Forever. I've kept one of my men watching him for years. I thought it was a waste. Obviously it wasn't." Mark smacked Corin's shoulder. Probably a deep expression of compassion for him. "I'm sorry he betrayed you. I'm sorry about Nicole."

"Me too."

"My prayer is what Tesser did doesn't stop you from trusting again."

Corin nodded.

Mark leaned forward, popped his legs with his fists, and stood. "Gotta roll. Let's stay in touch, Corin. You're a good man." Mark pointed at him, turned, and strode away.

A thought formed as he watched Mark walk into the fog and start to fade from sight. A way to thank Mark for saving his life.

"Hey, Mark."

The pastor turned.

"In about two weeks I might have something to show you. Might be worth a flight back up here."

"Sounds good. Call me." Mark spun away from him and disappeared into the gray.

Corin smiled at his audacious idea. God willing he would be able to do it.

But first he had to see Shasta.

AS CORIN DROVE to Shasta's house the next day, he wiped his hands on his pants every few miles and tried to keep his nerves in check and his foot on the gas. Fortunately the sprain in his leg was healing quickly and the pain from pressing the gas and the brake wasn't bad. He was much more worried about how his emotions would hold up when he stood in front of his brother. It felt like he was about to plunge into the lake with lead weights around his ankles.

He tried not to imagine how Shasta would react to his words.

But that wasn't his part in this play. His was only to speak and let his brother take ownership of however he chose to react.

CHAPTER 53

A deep sadness filled Robin's face as she opened the door and beckoned Corin to come in.

Corin leaned on his crutches, his left leg bouncing as his nerves continued to betray him. "Where is he?"

"In the movie room." She covered her mouth and dropped her head. "I'm not sure if he'll even acknowledge you're here. He's angry about you coming. He meant it when he said he never wanted to talk to you again."

"Shasta doesn't have to say anything. I'll say what I need to and then leave."

"You're right." Robin nodded and blinked. "Whatever happens, it's going to be okay."

Corin offered a weak smile. "Do you believe that?"

"Not really, but I'm trying to."

"Me too."

Robin took his hands and squeezed them.

Corin felt like he was floating, detached from his body as he hobbled toward his brother's media room. A numbness covered his mind—causing the emotions he carried into the house with him a few minutes earlier to vanish. He wasn't nervous any longer. He wasn't anything and couldn't decide if it was a blessing or a curse.

When he reached the movie room, Corin stood just inside the door and stared at the back of Shasta's head, silhouetted against the image of three men—two Native Americans, one white man—racing together through the forest.

As the scene ended the movie froze, the image of Daniel Day-Lewis staring out at him from the six-by-four-foot screen.

"Have you ever seen *The Last of the Mohicans?*" his brother called out.

The question was a barbed hook.

Nineteen years ago Shasta and he had seen it in the theater together. Had embraced it; made it the representation of their brotherhood and how they would always fight for each other the way Chingachgook, Uncas, and Hawkeye fought for one another. To ask if he'd seen it was another serrated blade across Corin's heart.

It didn't matter. Shasta could cut as much as he wanted. Corin's heart might bleed like a river, but never to death—and it would never stop his love for Shasta.

"I haven't seen it since the last time we watched it together."

The slow whir of Shasta's electric wheelchair was the only sound in the room. When it stopped, Shasta stared at him without anger, without regret, without emotion.

"Thanks for letting me come."

"Robin said it was imperative you saw me."

"It is."

"That you have something that has to be said in person."

Corin nodded and took half a step forward, then stopped. "Yes."

"I thought we'd agreed we wouldn't be seeing each other again."

"This is the last time I'll ever bother you, Shasta."

"Please don't call me that." Shasta jammed his chin into his wheelchair's chin controller and it spun to the right, his profile silhouetted against the movie screen. "It's Dom."

"When did you start—?"

"Try to explain to me why that's any of your business."

Corin rubbed his face and fought to remember the words he'd rehearsed countless times over the past two days that would provide an adequate introduction for what he'd come to say, but they'd disappeared. "It's not any of my business."

"What do you need?"

"I'm trying to put it into words." Corin pressed the knuckle of his forefinger into his upper teeth.

"When you figure it out, you let me know." He spun back to face the screen and the movie started again.

"I know what I want to say." Corin stepped forward till he stood four feet from the back of Shasta's head. "I need to ask you something."

"What's that?" The movie kept playing.

Corin glanced to his right then his left as if looking for a place to put down a set of weights he wasn't carrying. He pressed his lips together and blinked, trying to hold back the tears pressing to get out.

"Well?" Shasta said.

Corin slumped forward on his crutches and let the tears come. "I never asked you."

"Asked me what?"

"I told you I was sorry about the accident. I told you I wished it had never happened. How I wished with everything in me I could take that day back. I told you how sorry I was that I pushed you into going off the jump, but . . ." Corin's voice cracked. "I never asked for your forgiveness." He held his hands open, palms up.

The whir of Shasta's chair as he turned back to his left seemed like a thunderstorm in Corin's head.

"I never asked your forgiveness for stealing your life away from you." Sobs racked Corin's chest and his head fell forward. "Forgive me for trying to fix it, for trying to earn back your friendship, and for never once in all these years asking you to forgive me for what I did to you."

A slight move of Shasta's chin silenced the movie and the chair made a small rotation to the right.

"Forgive me."

The room was frozen in silence, Shasta's rhythmic breathing the only sound.

Corin steepled his hands and pressed them into his forehead. *Let my words go deep, tear off the ice around his heart, restore us. Shasta is—*

The whir of Shasta's chair made Corin whip his head up. He expected to know instantly from looking into his brother's eyes what he was thinking.

But once again all he saw was the back of Shasta's head.

"Good-bye, Corin."

The speakers roared back to life and *The Last of the Mohicans* filled the screen.

AS CORIN CLOMPED down his brother's front steps, Robin said, "I'm sorry."

Corin turned. "It's okay." He kept walking. It was.

No, the ice cave his brother lived in was just as thick. Part of Corin said he'd accomplished nothing, but a larger part said he'd spoken truth, that he'd set himself free even if his brother didn't want to join him, and that an invitation had been extended that couldn't be ignored forever.

As he drove away it struck him that somehow the water was no longer as deep and its color no longer as black.

And he believed the water would grow brighter.

CHAPTER 54

Corin trudged up his front porch steps wanting nothing but a pillow to bury his head in, and ten hours of unconscious thought, but one glance at his porch told him slumber wouldn't be an option for a while longer.

A black DVD case leaned against his front door. He balanced on his crutches and stooped to pick it up, the silver fluid script on the outside making him frown. Only one word was on it: Corin.

He didn't know the handwriting.

He glanced over his shoulder, opened his front door, and slumped through the opening into the dark. It still smelled like the garlic potatoes he'd had the night before. Corin set his crutches aside, flopped onto his couch, and flicked on the lamp next to it. Silence filled the room so completely his ears rang.

Nicole was gone, Tori was gone, Tesser was his enemy, and while Mark had saved his life and shown a surprising new side to his personality, Corin wasn't ready to be bungee-jumping partners.

A. C. would recover, but never be fully restored. And somehow he knew BASE jumping wouldn't have the same high-octane taste it used to.

Yet there was a type of hope he'd never known filling his mind—filling his heart. And a peace that didn't make sense, and made all the sense in the universe.

He knew where it came from.

Not from a chair.

Not from a religion.

Not from a set of rules.

But from a Person who loved him with a passion so vast the whole world couldn't contain it.

A Person he would follow the rest of his life.

He turned the DVD over in his hand, then over again. He opened the black plastic case, pulled the DVD out, pulled his computer onto his lap, slid it into the disc drive, and listened to the whir of the computer as the video booted up.

A few seconds later a shot of a small breakfast nook filled his screen, and then the sound of scuffling feet as a torso moved past the viewfinder. A second later the person came into view and sat at the oak chair at the end of the table.

It was Nicole.

"Hello, Corin." She smoothed her hair. "Let's have a little chat, shall we?" A sad smile played on her lips. "If you're watching this, my spirit is no longer on earth and my body is just a shell that used to hold my soul." She laughed. "Don't you think that's better than saying, 'I'm dead'?"

"Life ends for all, so don't cry over me. Yes, I might have lived a few more years, but it would be less than a blink in light of eternity. And who knows, we might be reunited someday. I believe we will.

"So what is your final conclusion? Do you believe the chair has the power to heal? I never did. But I have seen healings come through

the chair. Do understand what I'm saying? The chair in and of itself never had the power to heal. I know you think it did, but that power only comes from the One. Without Him the chair is wood, nothing more. And far more important to Him than that shaped piece of wood is the hearts of the people who sit in it.

"You asked me once what type of power was in the chair, but I didn't answer at the time." She leaned forward. "I believe the chair's greatest power is to bestow the restoration of relationships, for that is the greatest gift that can ever be given. The restoration of man's relationship to God and of our relationships with each other.

"My prayer is the chair will do this for you.

"Remember, all physical healing is temporary anyway.

"There is only one healing that lasts for eternity—the healing of our souls.

"I will see you again. Until then, live in His forgiveness, His mercy, His grace. Good-bye, Corin."

He slept that night without dreams and woke the next morning ready to do the impossible.

CHAPTER 55

At six o'clock on Saturday morning, before any hint of gray had touched the sky, Corin hobbled to his workshop dreaming he could do something that wasn't possible.

He opened the door, stood in the door frame, and took a deep breath.

A wave of anxiety washed over him.

Part of him wasn't even sure he should attempt it.

But it was a small part.

The larger part inside called out with a shout to pour himself into the idea with full-out abandon.

It didn't matter if he launched the idea and it exploded like one of the bottle rockets Shasta and he used to shoot off every Fourth of July. He had to try.

What was that old quote? Better to dare mighty things and go down in flames than attempt them not, and live forever in the shadow of regret. He smiled at himself. Wasn't even close. But that was the basic idea.

Corin eased over to his workbench. "I need skills beyond my ability, God." He settled onto his work stool and gazed at the shattered pieces of wood stacked on his workbench. The wood that had been a treasure so far beyond priceless he didn't have words to describe it. Wood that somehow had given Corin back his life and a life he never knew existed.

Restore the chair to the way it was before? Impossible. But with everything inside he would try.

He picked up a six-inch piece and ran his palm over its surface. No tingle ran up his arm, no warmth at the tip of his forefinger. It was all right. His desire was no longer to access the power in the chair; he'd met the chair's Maker. And found more power in Him than he could ever comprehend.

He carried the pieces to a small three-by-three platform he'd built and set them down like they were china, then taped four photos of the chair along the thick laminate post in the center of the room.

An assortment of glues stood at attention at the base of the table.

Here we go.

After three hours he took a short break, then poured another two hours into the restoration. Corin pulled back and studied the progress of his attempt.

Good start. The chair was coming into shape.

There was hope.

After another hour he flicked off the light in his workroom and ambled toward his kitchen. Time for something to eat and time to rest his eyes.

Before he reached his refrigerator his cell phone rang with a number he didn't recognize. He ignored it. Shortly it rang again with the same number. Corin flipped the switch to put his cell on mute and resumed construction of a bacon, tomato, Swiss cheese, sourdough bread, and avocado sandwich. Heated in the microwave, of course.

Out of the corner of his eye, he saw the phone light up for a third time.

Persistent.

He put down the piece of bread he was about to butter and answered.

"Corin Roscoe?"

"Yes." He didn't recognize the voice.

"Your presence is requested for dinner this evening at six o'clock."

"Who is this?"

"I'm afraid I have been instructed not to reveal that to you."

"For what?"

"Dinner."

"Today isn't good; I'm right in the middle of a project." Corin shifted the phone to his other ear. "Who is this?" he asked again.

"A friend of the person giving the invitation."

"What is the name of my host?"

"They asked me not to reveal it to you."

"In that case tell them they'll be dining alone."

The man on the other end of the phone paused. "I would counsel you against declining."

"Really? Is that a threat?"

"Far from it. The choice is entirely up to you as my friend would say, but my friend believes healing could come from this dinner."

Corin paused. Healing? Who would be calling him about healing? Intriguing. But not enough to stop working on the chair. "Maybe another time."

"I'm sorry you feel that way." The sadness in the voice seemed genuine. "My friend will be there waiting till nine. I hope you choose to come."

"Tell your friend next time he or she invites me to be a little less secretive."

"I will pass along your message."

"Anything else?"

"They did ask that I relay a sentiment to you should you decide not to come."

"What's that?"

"That no matter how long it takes, no matter how far, he will find you."

Was it him? Heat flooded Corin's body. It had to be.

"Tell the host I'll be there."

"He will be very pleased to hear that." Corin could almost feel the voice on the other end of the line smiling.

CORIN GLANCED AT his watch as he weaved in and out of traffic on the way to the address he'd been given. His phone's GPS showed it was in a residential district on the west side of town.

Twenty minutes to six. He would be early. He smiled, then gave into the urge to call Shasta. It had to be him.

"Hello?"

"You quoted Hawkeye."

"I thought it was a nice touch."

"Absolutely."

"I just thought it would be fun to shroud the invitation in a cloak of mystery."

He heard the smile in Shasta's voice. Corin's heart pounded faster than it ever had on any of their extreme adventures together.

"What happened? Are you . . . ?" The words stuck in Corin's throat.

"Yes, brother. I am healed." Shasta laughed. "Don't drive off the road on me."

Corin's body flooded with heat. "What? When did it—? Are you kidding me?" The words sputtered out of Corin like a torrent and a moment later he was laughing. "You're serious!"

"Completely."

A monsoon of belief and disbelief washed over Corin. "You're kidding. I mean . . . tell me!"

"I'll give you all the details when you get here. Are you on your way?"

Corin glanced at his watch. "I'll be there in ten minutes."

"Take your time and keep it under a hundred, okay?"

Seven minutes later Corin stood at the door of a house that was probably built in the late forties. Flower baskets hung along both sides of the covered porch and the light tan color on the siding looked freshly painted.

He rang the doorbell and waited. No answer. He rang again. A moment later the door opened revealing Robin.

"Welcome, Corin." Her smile lit up the porch.

"He . . . h-he's healed." Corin stuttered the words out.

Robin grinned. "Yes, I know." She motioned him in.

"Can I see him?"

"Of course."

She led him down a short hallway but stopped a few feet before reaching a doorway on the right.

"I'm going to let you see him for the first time by yourself." She hugged Corin. "Let me know if you need anything. I'll be in the kitchen. I'm sure you can find it if need be."

Corin tried to stop his hands from shaking. Finally he sucked in a deep breath, then limped into the room.

Shasta sat in his chair with the back of his head toward Corin, staring out the window in the small library.

"Shasta?"

As the electric wheelchair spun toward him, confusion filled Corin.

"You're here." A smile Corin hadn't seen in ten years radiated from his brother's face.

Corin blinked and gave tiny, involuntary shakes of his head. "What . . . ? I don't understand."

"Understand?"

"What are you still doing in the chair?" It didn't make sense. "I thought you were healed."

"I was healed, Corin."

He glanced at Shasta's wheelchair, then into his eyes. "Then why—?"

"Fully healed. Fully set free."

"When?"

"Two days ago."

"I don't get it. What are you saying? You're no longer paralyzed?"

"Exactly. I'm no longer paralyzed." A smile played on Shasta's face and he winked.

"Are you saying you could get up from that chair right now?"

Shasta pressed his chin into the wheelchair's control and eased toward Corin. "I've been living in chains since the moment I woke up in that hospital bed ten years ago. Hating myself for going down that slope. Hating you even more for pushing me into it. I blamed you. For a time I prayed for you to break your own neck."

Shasta inched the chair toward Corin till he was only two feet away. "I was a prisoner in an impenetrable cell I built using stones of regret and the concrete of bitterness. No one could get in and I couldn't get out. For the past ten years I haven't wanted to get out.

"Then you talked me into sitting in your chair and after it was over, I loathed you even more. Because for a moment I believed it would cure me. I even prayed while I sat there that it would restore my body and I could have my life back. And in that moment I felt something. A peace and a warmth I'd never felt. And I felt it not only in my head, but in my legs and my arms. I believed.

"But when nothing more happened, then and in the days after, I started building a thicker wall around my prison. After a week though I woke in the middle of the night to something or Someone standing in my room. Maybe I was dreaming. It doesn't matter. Somehow this person spoke. 'It's your choice to be healed or not.' That was it. He vanished and I woke the next morning with a pinprick of hope.

"I followed that hope and it led me to a tunnel that burrowed underneath the prison walls until I reached the outside and realized far more than missing our adventures together—what I've missed most deeply these past ten years is you." Shasta inched closer. "As I accepted that truth, I was healed of my bitterness and my self-pity."

Corin pulled a series of quick breaths. They'd been on parallel paths. "I think I know who the Someone is."

"I do too." Shasta smiled again and swiveled his head back and forth. "This life is short, Corin, but Robin tells me in the age to come, we will run forever with bodies that can never be broken."

Corin sank into a chair to the right of the doorway. "Shasta, I—"

"One more thing. Forgive me for the way I've treated you for the past ten years."

Corin gave a tiny shake of his head, then another. He hadn't expected this. Joy flooded him but it was tinged with sorrow. The chair had healed Shasta.

And it hadn't.

Tears pushed up from deep inside, but he shoved them back down. "I don't know what to say."

"Don't say anything. Just accept it."

Corin let his tears come.

Shasta spun his chair toward the window. "Light shines in darkness and the darkness can't fight against it. There is never enough darkness to overcome even the flame of the smallest match from hundreds of yards away."

Forgiveness. For both.

Restoration.

"Shasta?" For the first time in ten years, Corin took his brother's limp hands in his. "You've got my heart."

"And you have mine." Shasta's smile lit the room again. "I think God will be our most extreme adventure ever."

Corin nodded through his tears and his smile.

AS SHASTA LED him out of the room he said, "Did you notice the pictures on the walls as you came in?"

"No, I was a bit preoccupied."

"Take a look."

Corin gazed at the pictures in amazement. "You're kidding me. This is her house?"

"Yes."

Corin wandered in a daze down the long hallway as he followed Shasta. Pictures of Nicole dotted the walls on either side; from the time she was young till one that looked like it was taken last month.

"Why do you have the key to her house?"

Over dinner Shasta explained how yesterday he had received a packet in the mail that explained how Nicole had left everything she owned to Shasta and Corin.

"Being an attorney I suppose is what made her give me the information instead of you."

Corin spread his hands on the table and leaned his head back. "She knew how it would turn out."

"No, I don't think so. But I know what she hoped would happen." Shasta winked at Robin who pushed a worn leather book over to Corin.

"What's this?"

"Nicole's journal. She wanted you to have it."

He ran his fingers slowly over the smooth leather cover and smiled. A treasure to be savored.

"Also, I need you to sign something."

Robin slid a piece of paper in front of him.

"What?"

"I'm suggesting we sell Nicole's home and donate the money to a very worthwhile cause."

"Such as?"

"The purchase and remodeling of a certain downtown building that houses the world's finest store full of treasures from antiquity."

He'd never imagined his restoration with Shasta. To think his store could have a rebirth as well was almost too much to take in. Almost.

RESTORATION.

The word played through Corin's mind all the way home. Nicole had spoken of that as the chair's purpose. That the greatest healing came in the soul, not the body. They weren't merely words anymore.

Restoration.

Add an "s."

Restorations.

Might be a good new name for the store.

Before heading for bed he stopped by his workshop and sat in front of the chair for a long time. He'd finished the job. Corin stood and ran his fingers along the back of it. His fingers didn't tingle.

And he saw imperfections in every inch. The restoration was far from perfect, but it was enough. And as he soaked in the sight of the chair, joy welled up from within.

As he brushed his teeth that night he stared at the pills next to his sink. He kept brushing as he turned the bottle upside down over his toilet and poured them into the water.

As they sunk to the bottom of the bowl he realized exactly what he must do in the morning. It would be a worthy finish to this chapter of his life.

CHAPTER 56

Corin woke with a smile on Sunday morning, the vision of what he was about to do imprinted on his mind.

A cold breeze pushed through his open bedroom window and ruffled his hair as if confirming his plan. He put his hands behind his head and stared out the window at the dusty blue Colorado skies. It wouldn't be easy. But it was right.

He wouldn't leave till late afternoon. Sunset was the ideal time to do it. Fewer people if any would be there at dusk, and it was an action to take in solitude.

As he pulled out of his driveway and headed east on Highway 24, Corin glanced at the clock. He should reach the lake in less than three hours, which would leave him at least an hour of daylight. Plenty of time to do whatever he needed to do to get ready—even though he didn't know what that might be.

Maybe he needed to thank God for Shasta's return. Maybe grieve the loss of Nicole. Maybe work through the pain of Tesser's betrayal and contemplate the loss of his relationship with Tori. Maybe he needed to do nothing.

His cell rang.

Shasta. A smile grew on Corin's face, at first as thin as a strand of silk, then into a full-tooth grin. He didn't pick up; it felt too good simply seeing that number come up on his phone and watch it.

Restoration.

A few minutes later he called Shasta back.

"Are you on the road?" his brother asked.

"Yeah."

"Are you headed anywhere interesting?"

"Extremely. I'm going on an adventure."

"I thought you were going to dance less on the edge from here on out."

"I am." Corin slipped his sunglasses on against the sun pouring through his windshield. "Today's journey isn't about pushing physical extremes. It's about internal ones."

"Interesting. What are you going to do?"

When it was over he would definitely tell Shasta. Corin hoped it would be the final piece of his healing, and he wanted to explain it to his brother in detail. "I'd love to tell you all about it, but not until it's done."

"Then join us for Thanksgiving this Thursday."

"You're on."

"But before you agree, I need to let you know there'll be a special dish only for you on the table."

"What's that?"

"On the mountain the day of the accident? You said, and I quote 'If after we're done, if you don't agree it was the absolute right call to do this, I'll eat one of my gloves.' I told you I'd hold you to that."

Corin smiled. Shasta was joking about the day of the accident? Healing had indeed come.

"I'll bring my special knife and fork."

"Don't worry; it'll be slathered in my special gravy."

Something inside Corin snapped into place. He hadn't doubted he would be seeing Shasta often but to hear him ask about Thanksgiving, his voice full of passion, and joking with him for the first time in ten years stirred an emotion Corin hadn't felt since before the accident. One of belonging. The feeling of being connected once again to the one person he'd shared his entire life with, and had never stopped dumping his heart out to.

Mile marker five whizzed by on his right. Only 167 to go. "Bro?" Corin said.

"Yeah?"

Corin didn't know what to say. "I'm glad you're back in my life" would sound so lame.

"I, uh . . . about you and me, you know, what's happened . . ."

"What about it?"

"Well . . . I've waited a lot of years for this and . . ." Corin squeezed his steering wheel. "What I'm trying to say is . . ."

Shasta laughed softly. "You're really looking forward to Thanksgiving?"

"Right."

"I know exactly what you're saying. Me too."

The grin returned to Corin's face and spilled into laughter. Nicole was right. The greatest healing would never be physical, but a healing of the heart.

THE CLIFF DIDN'T tower over the lake as high as he remembered, but the trees were definitely taller. And still as silent as they'd been twenty-four years earlier when they'd watched him die.

Today they would be an audience again, this time to see him live. To see him cast fear aside. To see him crush it.

When he reached the base of the small cliff, he set his car keys and wallet behind a tree and covered them with a smattering of leaves.

He stared at the top of the cliff—thirty feet, maybe forty feet above him. It wasn't easy to get this far with the brace still on his left leg. It would be harder to climb the cliff. And painful. But he didn't care. He had to do this.

Had he made the right choice to come? Without question. But knowing that didn't keep his body from twitching—he wasn't sure if from fear or anticipation. Probably a tangled mixture of both. Corin wiped his hands on his khaki shorts, drew in a deep breath, and held it.

A wind rose from behind him as if cajoling him to climb. Seven minutes later he reached the top, the lake spread out in front of him like a giant piece of glass, light green color reflecting the trees and nearly cloudless skies.

The sun would drop behind the aspen trees at the far end of the lake in ten, maybe fifteen minutes. Enough time to pray. Enough time to ache inside for the loss of Nicole. Enough time to wrestle with his terror one more time.

But the fight wasn't necessary—his fear was feeble now, lapping at the edges of his emotions only as strong as the tiny waves that lapped at the edges of the lake. He'd already won, so he brushed the past aside, closed his eyes, and let the late afternoon sun massage his face with warmth and hope.

"Thank You. For freedom. For life. For restoration."

A few minutes later he opened his eyes and gazed at the darkening green water forty feet below.

Lake of death.

Lake of life.

It wasn't either.

The breeze created tiny ridges in the surface and a gold leaf from the aspen trees meandered across the water toward the base of the cliff underneath him.

A few minutes later he stripped off his shirt and took off his socks and shoes, and spread his arms to the sky.

He thought again of Nicole. Of Shasta. Of Tori. Of Tesser. Of the chair. And the One who created it.

Corin squinted through the branches at the sun as it seemed to speed its descent into the tops of the trees. A moment later the last of the diamonds flitting across the surface of the lake faded.

He closed his eyes and massaged the rock he stood on with his toes. Its coolness rose into his heart. Freedom was coming, almost here.

He opened his eyes. A few more moments and it would be time.

Corin stepped to the edge of the cliff and glanced once more at the water below, then back at the sun. The breeze rippled through his hair.

Minutes left.

The sun was now only a sliver of gold against the darkening sky.

Only seconds left.

He smiled.

A moment later the last vestige of light vanished into the branches.

Corin took a last look at the surface of the water, closed his eyes, and jumped.

Dear Reader,

In the fall of 2005, I had a falling out with one of my best friends and we stopped speaking. I had hurt him—he had hurt me—and we both walked away from our relationship.

But at the end of August 2008, God intervened.

I was over in eastern Washington on a writing retreat, and as I drove by my friend's vacation home, I heard God say, "Stop in and see Jeff."

I told God, "If it's really You telling me that, show me." I asked Him for a strange phone call or to hear from someone I hadn't heard from in a long time. That night at ten o'clock, I received a text from someone who had never texted me before.

When I stopped by Jeff's house at nine the next evening, I had no doubt he'd be there. After he opened the door, he stared at me for ten seconds, utter surprise on his face, then we wrapped each other up in a big grizzly bear hug.

The restoration of that relationship has been one of the greatest joys of the past three years. It gave me a renewed commitment to fight for my relationships because they are treasures, and they can be fragile.

All of us long to be restored. Physically. Emotionally. But I believe the restoration we long for most is the healing of broken relationships.

This is the main theme in *The Chair* and one I hope you will lift from the pages of this novel and live out daily.

May we choose to step into restoration in every moment,

James L. Rubart
www.jimrubart.com

DISCUSSION QUESTIONS

1. What character in *The Chair* can you relate to most? Why?

2. What themes did you see in the novel?

3. Nicole becomes a friend and mentor to Corin. Do you have someone like that in your life? If not, do you long for that type of person? Are you that type of person in someone else's life?

4. Corin unintentionally changes the rest of Shasta's life because of a tragic accident. While your circumstances might not be as dramatic, has someone done something that has significantly altered your life? Have you done something to alter someone else's life that you regret?

5. One of the themes in *The Chair* is restoration. What do you desire most to be restored and healed in your life? Something physical? A relationship? If it's a relationship, what relationship is it? Have you tried for restoration? If yes, what happened?

6. If you reached out and it didn't bring the restoration you'd hoped for, are you willing to try again? Why or why not?

7. Matthew 5:23–24 says, "Therefore, if you are offering your gift at the altar and there remember that your brother or sister has something against you, leave your gift there in front of the altar. First go and be reconciled to them; then come and offer your gift." We've all been wounded by others, but we've also done the wounding. Is there anyone you need to ask forgiveness from? Why is this so hard for us to do?

8. Do you have a story of a time you did go to someone and restoration of the relationship was the outcome?

9. Corin told Shasta he was sorry for what he had done, but had never asked for Shasta's forgiveness. Is there a difference in saying you're sorry and asking for forgiveness? If so, what is the difference?

10. If we choose to live a life of openness and vulnerability in our relationships, we will be hurt again. How do you reconcile this in your mind and heart? How can we still go forward, knowing we'll likely be wounded again at some point?

11. Jesus says we should forgive, "Seventy-seven times." Does this ever seem excessive to you? What do you do if someone continues to wound you?

12. Proverbs tells us to "guard our hearts above all else." How can we guard our hearts and at the same time live a life of acceptance and forgiveness toward those who wound us?

ACKNOWLEDGMENTS

I wrote my first novel, *Rooms* in six years; my second, *Book of Days* in two, and due to personal circumstances during spring and summer of 2010 needed to write *The Chair* in five months. When I turned in the manuscript to my editor I warned her it would be rough. Eighty-grit sandpaper rough.

After reading it she wrote back and said it was in better shape than I'd led her to believe, I'd done a fantastic job on the novel, and that her editorial letter would be my shortest yet.

I thought, "Where was I when *The Chair* was being written?"

Or put another way, what would I have done without my prayer team consistently warring for me in the heavens while *The Chair* was being written? Thank you, my friends, it definitely would have been eighty-grit without you.

Thanks also goes out to:

My wonderful team at B&H Fiction.

To the Great Ones for that white-hot brainstorming session in July of 2010 which put flesh on my skeleton idea and made it into a story.

To Darci Rubart and Susan May Warren for helping me find the soul of the story and shaping the final outline into a novel I hope will enter into the deep heart of my readers.

To my editor Julee Schwarzburg for once again being brilliant and a true pleasure to work with in every aspect.

And finally, to my wife Darci and my sons, Taylor and Micah. Being an author is my greatest dream come true, but it means nothing compared to you.